Zero Point

Wasique Mirza

ISBN 978-1-257-79192-7

To my parents – My guiding light
To Annina, Haqique, Rahique and Eliana – My inspiration

TABLE OF CONTENTS

x

ACKNOWLEDGEMENTS

I am grateful to so many of my friends, family and colleagues who encouraged me through this long process and enriched my ideas with their opinions and commentaries. I am especially grateful to Dave Reedy for spending countless hours helping me with painstaking editing of the original draft and Tom Burke for fine-tuning this manuscript before final submission. To Shirley and Dave Watkins for agreeing to be my test readers and giving me their unbiased opinion and encouragement, and to Misha Mirza for coming up with a host of brilliant ideas that led to her final version of the cover design. Finally, I could not have completed this book without the continuous support from my immediate family who had to endlessly endure my long stints on my laptop in the family room, which at times, infringed upon our quality time together.

PAKISTAN

TAJIKISTAN

CHINA

AFGHANISTAN

Peshawar •

Islamabad

Rawalpindi •

Kashmir

Miran Shah •

Jhelum •

Lahore •

Quetta

River

•

Indus

IRAN

INDIA

Gawadar

•

Jiwani

Karachi

•

Strait of Hurmuz

Arabian Sea

ARCHITECTS OF PAKISTAN

"The Story of Pakistan, its struggle and its achievement, is the very story of great human ideals, struggling to survive in the face of great odds and difficulties."

Mohammad Ali Jinnah – Father of the Nation

"Nations are born in the hearts of poets; they prosper and die in the hands of politicians."

Allama Muhammad Iqbal–The Thinker of Pakistan

Liaquat Bagh, Rawalpindi
Saturday, October 1st, 5:47 p.m.

In the deafening enthusiasm of the loyal crowd, the first gunshot went completely unnoticed. Even the victim ignored it. A minor sting was overshadowed by the surging adrenaline that pumped through his body. The crowd continued to chant loudly as a bright red streak of blood trickled down the neck of the victim from a shallow flesh wound.

Fireworks, amid loud chanting of political slogans and aimless gunshots fired by party enthusiasts, overshadowed the relatively subdued spit that emanated from the small, silencer-fitted pistol, held in a hand concealed under a traditional woolen *chaadar* or outer wrap. The perpetrator was a short man; timidly hunched forward, thus further diminishing his five foot six frame. He was a young man, about twenty-years old with a short beard that barely covered his chin. His apparent naiveté was in stark contrast to the fiery determination betrayed by his intense, bright eyes. Disappointment was evident on his half-concealed face as the bullet missed its intended mark in the middle of the victim's chest. Slowly, he slid the gun into a side pocket and weaved his way towards the exit.

The crowd was in frenzy as it waved the party flags in a brisk wind. It was the last big rally before elections, and the candidate on stage had won many a poor heart by promising food, shelter and clothing to all. These were the hollow promises, which had forever resonated with supporters and had seduced them for decades. In a country like Pakistan, elections did not come with ease. Governments were overthrown on a regular basis and the military took charge on most of those unfortunate occasions. Democracy, even on its best day, was a mere shell of the freedom and rule of the people that it promised. Things were different this time. It seemed that all roads led to a speedy and uneventful democratic recovery . . . until today.

Snipers were perched high on trees at the bank of the nearby seasonal stream known as *Nala Lai*. Security was, however, a mere formality. Despite all these precautions, entry points into *Liaquat Bagh Park* were limited only by the imagination of one seeking them. In all honesty, there was no possible way to effectively screen or search such a large crowd overflowing with raw adrenaline.

Malik Jahangir gazed at his adoring followers with a look of triumph, fighting off an eerie and restless feeling that suddenly came over him, a reminder of the mayhem that had followed Ex-Prime Minister Benazir Bhutto's assassination on this very venue, only three years ago. The haunting vision of the victim, covered with a bloodstained white sheet being transferred to an ambulance flashed through his mind. Beads of sweat appeared on his forehead. It had been a long and laborious campaign and he was suddenly glad that it was almost over. The life of a politician was never a safe bet in Pakistan, but he had an unwavering faith in his destiny. "Prime Minister Malik Jahangir," he reminded himself of the reward that awaited him barely a month away. He shook off the last few cobwebs of doubt that had crept into his mind and then raised his interlocked hands high in a gesture of triumph and solidarity, resulting in a rousing response from the crowd. . . everything was fine.

The second gunshot was louder and had caught a brief pause in the spirited rhetoric that promised the sun and the moon to the screaming crowd. Malik Jahangir looked up; his eyes were wide with horror and sheer disbelief as he scanned the top of the crowd for a split second . . . then fell backwards behind the dais.

CHAPTER 1

ISLAMABAD

Wednesday, August 31st, 10:00 a.m.

It was a glorious morning in Islamabad. The air was fragrant with the smell of fresh rain that had bathed the city overnight, adding a vivid shade of green to its tree-lined boulevards. Bright sunshine reflected from the pristine slabs of marble covering the geometric contours of Shah Faisal Mosque, one of the largest in the world, sitting majestically in the lap of Margalla Hills. A massive crescent plated with gold sitting at the summit of the pyramidal structure, shone brightly in the morning sun as a bold symbol of the religion that had given this city its name.

A black Toyota *Land Cruiser* with tinted windows entered sector E-7 and made a right turn onto a quiet street. Hillside Road, home to the elite of Islamabad, was lined with lush green trees guarding enormous homes hiding behind tall brick walls and reinforced barbed fences. Behind these fortified walls covered with bright pink bougainvillea, imported araucaria trees stood tall watching over the limited traffic that passed through this neighborhood. Security guards stood on high alert, seemingly staring at Margalla Hills forming the northern boundary of this capital city. Every inch of this neighborhood was in stark contrast to the struggling economy of an otherwise developing country. The ruling class seemed to love living in this contradiction.

The vehicle stopped before an enormous black wrought-iron gate guarding an expansive Spanish style villa with a sandy finish, tinted picture windows, and bright crimson shingles. A contingent of guards dressed in starched, slate gray uniforms and armed with loaded *Kalashnikovs* stood erect next to a wooden guardhouse. One of them hurriedly stepped forward flicking his half consumed cigarette in the bushes behind him and opening the gate with his left hand, his right hand staying raised in a half salute as the *Land Cruiser* passed by and entered the property. The concrete driveway lined with multihued chrysanthemums curved gently along a manicured lawn bordered by a vibrant assortment of rose bushes and entered a spacious portico, where a set of checkered black and white marble stairs led up to the massive front door. Naveed Khan a clean shaven man in his late thirties, dressed in a crisply starched white *shalwaar kameez* suit stepped out of vehicle and was briskly escorted through a spacious foyer to an elaborately decorated drawing room. He was a tall and well-built man with thick black hair and a broad forehead, a strong chin, and squinting eyes that always seemed to be focusing on something. A manservant handed him a glass of iced coca-cola, while he looked at photographs depicting his host with various heads of states and celebrities from all walks of life. Pictures were scattered throughout the room separated by paintings of rural Pakistan, and curios filled with fine china and crystal. He was admiring the thick silk carpet under his feet when a sharp voice startled him.

"*Salaamalakum! Ji Aayan Nuun, Khan Sahib*. I am so glad that you agreed to meet me at my humble dwelling." Raja Safdar Hussein had quietly walked right up to him and now stood beside him with open arms, and then he looked around the ornately furnished room, apparently amused by his own comment. "I have a feeling that we are going to become very good friends."

Raja Safdar was a short, portly man in his mid-fifties. A heavy and well-groomed mustache that rolled sharply up at the ends overshadowed the balding head. An unmistakably strong aura of ethnic superiority betraying his feudal roots was dulled only by a rimless pair of glasses sitting on a sharp nose with unusually flared nostrils giving him a somewhat hawkish, yet scholarly look. Raja Safdar was a third generation politician from a prominent southern Punjabi family. Ambitious and ruthless in pursuit of his goals, he had risen to unparalleled power in Pakistan's political elite, though not quite in the capacity that he may have imagined. A graduate of Yale and with a Bar-at-law from London's Lincoln Inn, his oratory prowess was unmatched. Even from a balcony in his palatial hometown *Haveli,* adorned by lavish gardens and marble arches, he could mesmerize his poverty stricken neighbors and devoted followers. They truly believed him to be the savior that would ensure a roof over their heads and food on their plates. They saw him as someone who understood them; who knew what it was like to be in their shoes, someone who truly cared.

They believed in him and the passionate words that came out of him, even if he had not been able to deliver yet, despite his multiple terms in the Parliament representing them and others like them around the country.

Over time, he had given up his quest for becoming the Prime Minister and shifted his focus towards the role of the King Maker. In the beginning, he missed the protocol, the motorcades and other fanfare that accompanied a title, but all that was eclipsed by the power he experienced in his new role. While his deep personal connections that stemmed from his large and politically relevant family, with roots in every major party, were the key to his legendary success, so were his years of careful maneuvering and making friends where needed and keeping them in mind when they needed him. Once he found himself in the middle of it all wielding the power to make or break political careers, he was never going back.

"I am not really sure why I am here," Naveed Khan, a somewhat perplexed guest asked of his host. "I need to be in Peshawar by the afternoon. I am sure that you know where I stand politically and that is not anywhere near where you are," he sounded impatient and a little irritated by this unexpected change in his plans this morning.

When he received the phone call that Raja Safdar wanted to see him as soon as possible, even if it was for a few minutes, his first reaction was to say no. As he pondered over it for a moment, his natural curiosity took over. With elections just a month away, he wanted to hear what the man had to say.

Naveed believed firmly in the fact that it was important to know one's friends and even more so in the case of one's adversaries. "He must be rounding up political allies to assure a strong coalition," he thought, and he decided to stop by on his way to Peshawar.

Naveed Khan and Raja Safdar could not be any more different. As opposed to the privileged upbringing, the Ivy League education and being groomed for a political dynasty, Naveed came from a humble background. His father was a schoolteacher in a village in the northern Punjab. After local schooling and a bachelor's degree from the prestigious and historical Government College in Lahore, he completed his MBA from Lahore University of Management Sciences. During his MBA, he ventured into student politics, gaining respect among political pundits for his incisive commentary on the local and national political scenes in his articles, and made regular guest appearances on private Pakistani news media networks. It was during that time that he was introduced to Sardar Shaukat Soomro, a well - respected and now retired politician. A former senator who had served as foreign and finance minister in previous governments, he immediately recognized the potential that this young and energetic man possessed and took him on as his protégé. The pupil soaked up the political wisdom of his mentor. With his charm, natural wit and the reputation of being home bred without any western affiliations or influences, he charted an unprecedented course through the political maze, on his way to his meteoric rise as a beacon of hope for a resurgent youth movement. Even though there were plenty of skeptics amongst seasoned politicians, his popularity among intellectuals and students was also a source of concern for them. Historically non-voters, youth between ages eighteen to thirty were becoming a new force in the electoral process, making him a bonafide dark horse.

"I think you have a very bright future," Safdar whispered in Naveed's ear as he wrapped his arm around his shoulder.

"*I* think that I have figured that one out myself," Naveed sounded edgy, sensing a hint of alcohol on his host's breath.

"You are very popular, especially among youngsters, but you know as well as I know that you can only win a handful of seats in the elections," he stepped back and rolled his moustache between his thumb and index finger. "That is why you need friends in the right places . . . friends like me."

"Oh, I see," Naveed rolled his eyes as he looked at his watch, "can we get to the point, I have long drive and you know how the roads can be at this time of the day."

Raja Safdar ignored the remark as he continued to groom the other side of his moustache, while leading his guest in a slow walk around the spacious drawing room. He finally stopped in front of a framed picture of himself in a bear hug with President and current Chief of the Army Staff General Hamid Ali, while the visiting United States Vice President stood by, with an amused look on his face, his right hand loosely wrapped around Raja Safdar's shoulder. The picture was taken recently since the Vice President had visited Pakistan only a month ago in order to ensure continuity of the democratic process.

"This is what I mean by friends in the right places," Safdar proclaimed with a wide grin that accentuated the upturned edges of his newly groomed moustache, giving it a Salvador Dali quality, as he pointed proudly at the photograph.

"And how does this concern me?" Naveed's patience was running out. If he was impressed by the chemistry evident in the photo, he did not show any outward sign of it.

"Don't you see?" Safdar pointed at the photograph. "This was a defining moment, a moment that could reshape the whole election . . . of course, provided that I play my cards right," his voice became loud, with a hint of a quiver.

"I know that there are some annoying obstacles. That *Khabees*, Malik Jahangir is running a very aggressive campaign, but I have a plan."

He lowered his voice to a bare whisper.

"And I will need your help."

CHAPTER 2

TAXILA

Wednesday August 31st, 1:00 p.m.

Naveed Khan was deep in thought, thinking about his conversation with Raja Safdar a few hours ago, and he couldn't help but admire his communication skills. Despite his utter contempt for the man and his politics based on unscrupulous compromises and ruthless exploitation, he was all ears, listening to his grandiose rhetoric about the new coalition that would rule the country.

"My friend," Raja Safdar had wrapped his arm around his shoulder, "I know how you feel about me. I read your articles . . . and listen to everything you say very carefully but ask yourself this question," he paused, weighing his next words carefully, "do you honestly think that Malik Jahangir will make a good Prime Minister?"

"I have my concerns," Naveed had replied rather nonchalantly.

"And . . . they *are*?" Safdar probed.

"Well, for starters, he uses his platform to promote self-reliance, shedding our dependence on the West. People love it, but then he turns around and talks to the Chinese. He is trading one form of slavery for another," Naveed said excitedly and then took a quick sip of coke from his glass.

"*Shabaash*, you *do* see the irony there; I knew I could count on you," a pleased Safdar slapped Naveed's back, almost making him choke on an ice cube.

"He's selling contracts to the Chinese and ex-Soviet companies, collecting upfront fees for guarantees of future deals. Most of these companies have been dropped by International Chamber of Commerce due to regulatory sanctions."

"I've heard rumors about such meetings but I don't think there is any concrete evidence."

"Maybe, but what does your heart say?"

"I am inclined to believe them."

"Aha, now we are talking," he thumped his back again even more firmly than before, but Naveed was better prepared this time. "Don't worry about the evidence. I just want the truth to be out there. I'll give you all the details and then you can make up your own mind about it."

"No strings attached?"

"None whatsoever. You may throw away the information if you choose to, but if you find it useful, then use it whichever way you want . . . that's all I am asking for"

"And that . . . is all you want . . . for me to be myself?"

"Yes, of course," Safdar smiled, waving his hand dismissively, "but enough about that, now tell me about your trip to Peshawar, is there a political *julsa,* or you have something else planned?"

The car hit a giant pothole right in the middle of the highway startling Naveed as he bumped his head on the ceiling.

"I need to get used to wearing seatbelts," he scolded himself. Seatbelt laws in Pakistan were only a few years old, suddenly requiring a dramatic shift in age-old habits that were hard to break.

This portion of the Grand Trunk road had been under construction for years and was still far from completion, remaining a tortuous mess of dust and loose rocks rolling around looking for a layer of tar to cover them. The dream seemed unlikely since the budget allotment for construction had already been spent . . . many times over.

Naveed had a successful, though unofficial, town hall style meeting with workers at the Heavy Industries at Taxila, explaining to them his view of an independent Pakistan that relied more on its own resources and ingenuity rather than foreign aid.

"Let them come to us and invest in *our* products, and not the other way around when we have to resort to the West in order to stay afloat," he had told the small but influential crowd amidst loud cheers.

It was after 5 p.m. when Naveed and his companions reached the northwestern city of Peshawar. Lengthening shadows were already merging together, announcing the arrival of another evening.

It was a weeknight and people were wrapping up their businesses. Vendors, actively gathering their goods: ranging from handmade leather and embroidered slippers, *khairri* style shoes, and elaborately carved copper vases to heaps of second hand clothes sent from all over the world for refugee aid programs. They were passing through the eastern end of *Qissa Khwani Bazaar,* the romantic 'Street of Story-tellers' that extends from west to east in the heart of the city of Peshawar. The *bazaar* is lined with its traditional teahouses or *kehwa khanas, Tikka Kabab, Chapli Kabab* and dry fruit shops along with modern storefronts displaying luxuries of the twenty-first century. Centuries ago, this *bazaar* was the center of a camping ground for trading caravans and military battalions where professional storytellers captivated their audiences of soldiers and merchants with ballads and tales of war and love.

It was almost dark when their car entered a neighborhood in the old part of Peshawar with narrow streets lined with ancient homes guarded by massive wooden doors and ornately carved wooden balconies. At first, he did not pay any attention to a loud noise that echoed piercingly from the walls of the narrow street, disregarding it as a stray gunshot, so common in this part of the country, where every citizen is proudly armed with a weapon and is not shy of firing it in the air as a show of power.

The second sound was louder and much closer. His car, though travelling very slowly through the brick lined street marred by countless potholes, swerved sharply to the right and before the driver could react, it skidded over a puddle of muddy water and then stopped abruptly, falling into a shallow draining ditch lining the street.

Naveed tried to get out but his attorney and right hand man, Taseer Rizvi, held up his hand, stopping him. Naveed was not sure why until he noticed that the other car in their group ahead of them had suffered a similar fate. Another loud sound, this time unmistakably a gunshot, shattered the windshield showering them with shrapnel of broken glass. The driver was hit, his face contorted in a painful expression as an enlarging bright patch of blood emerged on his left upper chest.

Naveed jumped out of his seat, ignoring Taseer Rizvi's warnings, and swung around the half open door, ignoring the splashes of stagnant mud that filled the drain; he opened the driver's door, pulling him out on the street. He was alive, but barely conscious. Blood gushing out of an open wound was now spraying its crimson mist over Naveed's previously immaculate white dress.

Another gunshot blew out the back window of his *Land Cruiser*. Taseer darted out of the vehicle and took cover behind it next to Naveed who had already controlled the bleeding with a rag torn out of the front of his shirt.

Suddenly, it was quiet. Distant sounds of fading footfalls running away from the scene was followed by a slight breeze passing through the wind tunnel created by the narrow alley taking away the smell of gun smoke, and replacing it with an appetizing aroma of freshly baked *naans* emanating from a hot *tandoor* nearby.

The deserted street suddenly filled with children and a few alarmed people, cautiously coming out of their hiding spots and starting to gather around the two vehicles. A Good Samaritan offered to take the driver to a nearby clinic in his truck. Naveed wanted to ride along but was held back by his companions to ensure his safety. It was getting dark and Naveed was growing more and more concerned about the safety of his party. Help arrived in the form of the local liaison that was provided to the entourage, as a courtesy by Raja Safdar before Naveed left Islamabad. The personable, middle-aged man was intimately familiar with the neighborhood and offered them shelter at a nearby house belonging to a friend of his, until an alternate vehicle could be arranged.

The rattled group was escorted briskly and under the protection of a contingent of guards that had magically appeared in response to a phone call by their liaison. They were local men, taller than average and unmistakably muscular under the loose traditional outer garb and complete with leather holsters and belts laden with weapons and bullets. Their fierce eyes were stern and locked at the intended destination, while the rest of their faces were partially covered by the loose extensions of their black turbans. They waved their *Kalashnikovs* as they made a tight ring around the group that scurried towards a large home, distinct from its neighbors by its newly renovated and more elaborately decorated façade. The massive doorway was secured by its original antique door, decorated with intricate floral carvings, massive cast iron knockers and brass inserts. The arched doorway was adorned with a mosaic of Uzbek style blue and white ceramic tiles transforming its intimidating dimensions into a warm refuge.

"Who lives here?" Naveed asked, now that he had composed himself after learning that his driver, though weak from losing a lot of blood, was still conscious and did not have any signs of injury to any vital organs.

"His name is Shabbir Jan," Sohrab khan, his liaison said. "He is a strong supporter of Raja *Sahib* and very influential in this part of Peshawar. He is delighted to have you stay at his house until we arrange some transport."

"Who do you think was behind this?" Naveed asked.

"Only *Allah* knows," Sohrab khan replied with a shrug as he banged the door with the butt of his *Kalashnikov*, ignoring the enormous knocker. "Our host enjoys a strong influence over this region; he will have a better idea."

The door opened immediately with a slight creak and a handsome face with a bright smile appeared.

"*Subhan Allah*, I cannot believe that *Allah* is being so generous to me. I am honored to serve you," he paused and gave a slight, barely perceptible nod to Sohrab Khan, then continued, addressing Naveed Khan. "I have already asked my men to bring two vehicles for your transport. Until then, you are our guests and you must stay for dinner."

CHAPTER 3

LAHORE

Saturday, October 1st, 1:34 p.m.

Jail Road traffic was at its usual craziness in the late afternoon. Loud vendors that flanked the front gate sold everything from fruits and vegetables to cheap Chinese toys and were constantly pushed back by exasperated guards to make way for official vehicles and ambulances entering the hospital. Noisy traffic—a mix of cars, trucks, buses, and loud motorcycles with their silencers removed manned by young men weaving in and out of traffic lanes, and, of course, the ubiquitous rickshaws sputtering their way through this maze—could be heard easily in the hospital hallways.

Dr. Kamran Haider was running late. His natural, usually infectious smile was replaced by a deep frown as he rushed to finish his work at Lahore's Services Hospital. He had to stop at his clinic to see two patients and then get to his hometown of Jhelum, 160 kilometers away, in time for his sister's wedding.

"My mother will kill me if I am not there to receive the guests," Kamran muttered under his breath as he fumbled with a file overflowing with loose papers.

"Do not worry, *daakter sahib*. Leave it and I'll make sure that the papers are delivered to Inspector General *sahib's* office," Majeed Khan, his steadfast secretary, shouted from his seat just outside his office.

"But I still need to put it in order and attach my report to it."

"I will take care of it. I know the order, and I'll attach the report as soon as I am done typing it," he said without raising his head from a vintage typewriter that he preferred over a computer. "You go on and enjoy the celebrations."

Kamran Haider, the perfectionist, was very uncomfortable about this whole situation, but he knew that he could trust Majeed. He had been a loyal aid during his three years at Services Hospital. Even if that was not the case, avoiding the risk of embarrassment at the hands of the inspector general was not worth exposing himself to his mother's wrath. Zarina Begum, his mother and the matriarch of the Haider family, was a strong-willed woman who had raised six children all alone after losing her husband to an act of random terrorism twenty-five years ago. Kamran, her oldest offspring, though a successful and well-accomplished surgeon, found himself as rattled by her as he did when he was ten.

Kamran was only nine when he lost his father—a hard-working civil servant who became a victim to a bomb planted on a train during the peak of the Afghan-Russian War. Such explosions were commonplace during the mid-1980s, a price paid by Pakistani citizens for a United States–backed war against the USSR. It was a war of convenience, a remote conflict, a hot war on a neutral turf, comfortably far off from the political Cold War being fought in the chambers of the Pentagon and Kremlin. Life went on despite news of another train, another bus, or another packed market blown into a million splinters. It always happened away from home, to someone else—until it didn't. Kamran ended up being the man of the family, taking care of his younger siblings. With his determination, and with the guidance and courage of his mother, he was able to beat the odds and not only guide his siblings on the right course, but also achieve his fellowship in general surgery and then a doctorate in jurisprudence. Despite his penchant for surgery, his true passion rested with the forensic aspect of the human body. With his personal tragedy as the driving force, he spent most of his youth studying explosives and firearms. As he mastered the mechanics and the explosive impact of various kinds and models of firearms, he transferred this knowledge to his study of the human body. His father wished for him to be a physician and that was partly the focus that shaped his aptitude, but his father's death was what triggered his passion. Trauma surgery was a marriage made in heaven, bringing the two seemingly divergent interests together. Services Hospital Trauma Center was his brainchild that had transformed from a two-room, three-bed corner of the Emergency Department to a sprawling thirty-bed, two-story complex next to it. He had collaborated with the police department to house a criminal and homicide desk, as well as a crime lab, in the trauma center. This provided immediate access to evidence as well as priority processing of all forensic samples. The trend seemed to have caught on as Kamran was asked by the inspector general to oversee the development of similar facilities in Rawalpindi, Karachi, Peshawar, Quetta, Faisalabad, and Multan. This project had been a cause for numerous and very frequent cross-country trips over the last three weeks. Dealing with seemingly endless meetings with government officials trying to cut through the red tape had left him mentally and physically exhausted.

***

Traffic on the Grand Trunk Road, to describe it kindly, was atrocious as usual. Even though the roads had improved dramatically in the last ten years, traffic had increased at an equal pace, while drivers' training standards had stayed in the nineteenth century. Passenger buses, overflowing with customers, continued to weave in and out of traffic, while oversized trucks operated by their often drugged-up and sleep-deprived drivers charged through the terrified group of motorists like Pamplona bulls. As the roads got bigger, so did the size and number of the vehicles. Eight-wheelers became eighteen-wheelers, and transport vans were replaced by behemoth buses, bursting at the seams on the packed highway.

Not exactly, what *Sher Shah Suri*, the ruler of India had in mind when he laid down the astounding Grand Trunk highway system connecting eastern and western India during his short reign five hundred years ago.

"Darn it," Kamran slammed his fists on the steering wheel.

"What is wrong with these people? Hey, watch where you're going," he yelled at a donkey cart leading a herd of cows across the road.

Weekend traffic was a mess. He could not drive ten miles before running into some kind of delay. He picked up his cell phone and called his brother.

"I am stuck in the worst traffic this side of *Ravi*. I'll try to get off GT road . . . maybe it won't be so bad through the city. I'll be there soon; just keep *ammi* busy so she doesn't care that I am late."

"Yes, yes, I know," he sighed as he hung up. "I'll owe him big time for this."

***

Marriage ceremonies in Pakistan are a colorful, loud, and elaborate events spanning several days, not counting the weeks of preparation along with song and dance gatherings that may begin as early as two months before the actual ceremony. Despite being mostly considered a woman's thing, men are always around, partly as spectators and partly as heavy lifters for all the manual work. These ceremonies are a seamless combination of Muslim traditions decorated with rituals originating in the Hindu customs, a natural consequence of their thirteen centuries of co-existence in South Asia.

Today was *rasm-e-henna,* the festival of Henna or *mehndi.* A ceremony filled with laughter, joy, and color . . . bright yellow to be precise. The groom's family brings henna platters heavily decorated with gold and silver ribbons and frills, and illuminated with candles. Today was not any different. Tariq, the groom, was a Captain in the Pakistan Army and the groom's party was led by a large group of energetic young officers dancing at the beat of the drum as they entered the bride's house. As man of the house, Kamran had the honor of receiving the guests, and he had made it home, albeit barely. This was the good news. The bad news was that his mother did notice his absence and the look in her eye upon seeing him gave a vivid glimpse of the wrath to come.

"You are so toast *Kami Bhai,*" his brother had made sure to remind him with a snicker.

"I know and I'll deal with it later, but now let's focus on the arrangements," he said, ignoring his brother's obvious pleasure.

Imran was three years younger and himself a Major in the Army, but their rivalry transcended the age difference or even the fact that now they were grown, successful men. Imran was now married with a two-year-old boy.

"I'll get back at him; one of these days," Kamran made a silent vow and went on with his chores.

The next twenty-four hours were a blur of rushing between home and the venues, last minute shopping and making sure that all visiting guests were settled in their respective accommodations. The bride's friends made sure that there was plenty of singing to the beat of *dholki.* Traditional wedding songs, passed on through generations, filled the air, keeping the festive mood high and frustrations low.

The marriage ceremony was at the Army Officers Club on Saturday afternoon and once the fun and games were over, it was dinner time followed by the solemn ceremony and tearful farewells as the bride was escorted to her new home by the groom, flanked by his family and friends.

Kamran was exhausted, both physically and emotionally, by the time they got home. His mother was visibly torn between joy and pain for the fact that her little girl was leaving her home to start a new life. After comforting her for a while, he attended to some loose ends including dispersion of payments to the caterers and other hired help; finally he had a moment of peace. He slumped on a couch in the living room, turned on the TV, and barely five minutes into a rerun, went into a deep sleep.

It was hardly thirty minutes before a strange sound and sensation woke him up. He was still in a fog, and it took him a few seconds before he realized that it was his cell phone ringing and vibrating on his lap.

CHAPTER 4

BLACK GOLD RANCH
OUTSIDE OF BEAUMONT, TEXAS

Friday, July 24th, 1:49 p.m.

Jack Donaldson was sitting in his office behind his massive mahogany desk. He had been deep in thought ever since his long conversation with his business manager an hour ago. The projections for next quarter's oil production had raised some serious concerns. He stared at a large panel on the wall that displayed a world map highlighting oil production and drilling sites, while his hand rolled Habanos cigar produced fine rings of smoke that ascended proudly, and then ducked out of the open window, overlooking the expanse of open land that surrounded the mansion.

Jack "Butch" Donaldson was a bear of man. He was tall, a hair above six foot three and solidly built; he had maintained his physical shape in his middle age with a meticulous workout ethic. Though balding at the top, he was able to hide it from common view with his signature ten-gallon hat emblazoned with the silhouette of a horseman lassoing an oil well, the insignia of his company. Son of a modest rancher, like so many of his friends, he saw football as his means to bigger and better things. After being the star of his high school team, he went on to play tight end for Texas A&M University. His future stars seemed to be perfectly lined up when the Kansas City Chiefs drafted him in the first round. That is when his life story made a sharp turn, and he never had the time to look back. Two weeks before he was scheduled to report to the rookie camp, he found out that his father's lung cancer had spread to his brain. The next two weeks turned out to be the most important of his life. As the clock ticked towards the reporting day, he had scrambled to assist his family in straightening the affairs of the ranch. The plan was to sell it to a neighboring landowner and have his parents and younger brother move into a smaller property near Kansas City where a state of the art hospital and treatments would be at a convenient distance. No one could imagine what came next. In order to prepare the land for sale, he was drilling a well to supply water to a relatively dry area of the ranch and needed to drill deeper than usual. The drill hit rock at three hundred feet. After losing two drill bits, he decided to give it one final try before changing the location, and out came a geyser of hot black oil. Football was pushed back as an afterthought and the next ten years transformed him into one of the most prolific oil producers in Texas and the major supplier of crude oil to refineries in the Beaumont and Port Arthur region of Texas. Over the years, Butch Donaldson focused on strengthening his connections in the influential oil industry. As his stature in the ultra-rich community of oil men and women grew, so did his influence, and with his immense amount of personal wealth to back him, he was able to pave his way to winning a seat in the US House of Representatives, and finally to the US Senate. A position the he had successfully kept for the last eleven years.

For the last two years, he had been exploring the possibility of a potential presidential bid, thus the stability and credibility of his business had become even more important. Recent conversations with Arthur Kimble, his business manager, directly affected this new venture.

Over the last ten years, oil production in Texas had gone down by forty percent with more and more companies exploring for more reserves in the Gulf of Mexico. Jack Donaldson, in anticipation for such a day, had gambled in the Pacific Northwest, acquiring large chunks of land in Alaska. This scheme, however, had backfired so far, because a strong environmental movement as well as strong opposition from the Democrats had halted any efforts to explore for natural resources in that region. Arthur Kimble had just informed him that the projected output from his ten most prolific wells would drop from twenty-five barrels to about thirteen barrels per day over the next quarter and that meant a net revenue loss of almost fifty percent or over a million dollars, not factoring in the decrease in output from other sites, as well as the effect this would have on his company's stock price when word got out. At the least, over one hundred and fifty million dollars was at stake if he did not come up with an announcement to bolster shareholder confidence.

The answer to his dilemma lay in South Asia. During the two Gulf Wars, he had been able to obtain multiple contracts in the United Arab Emirates regarding establishing oil refineries and their maintenance. The rebuilding process in Iraq had provided western conglomerates ample opportunity to solidify their presence in the region and share their piece of the pie. Butch Donaldson had not stopped there but had continued to use his contacts in the field of oil and gas exploration, and also in the political arenas to secure contracts, and continue drilling for exploration in the region. So far, news from the region was promising, yet without any concrete evidence of success. Revolving door democracies, constant political unrest, and unpredictability in identifying who is in charge made this process extremely labile. He needed an update from the region to make sure that his friends would stay in power long enough for him to finalize his deals.

"Cindy dear, can you find Hoffman for me? I think he is in Pakistan or Iran, or somewhere around there riding a camel these days," he said through the intercom taking another long puff from his dying cigar.

He was staring out the window at distant silhouettes of the Exxon Mobil Refinery when he realized that his cigar stub was burning his fingers. He threw it in the ashtray and took a fresh one out of the box. He was about to light it when the intercom beeped.

"Hoffman is on line one, Mr. Donaldson," his assistant Cynthia called in.

"Put it right through, Cindy," he replied, "and be a sweetheart and hold all calls and visitors while I'm on the phone. Even if it is the President or my mother, even Jesus Christ will have to wait this one out."

CHAPTER 5

BRONX, NEW YORK

Saturday, July 24th, 2:16 p.m.

Vincent Portelli was not a happy camper.

"I can't believe that I wasted my whole day on that loser," he muttered under his breath. He was staring at his half eaten calzone on a paper plate in front of him across the table. Bits of broccoli were picked out meticulously and now lay in a small heap on a napkin next to it. Obviously, Tony had overlooked his aversion to all things green, especially broccoli.

"Hey Vinny, do you need anything else? I am putting on a fresh pot of coffee . . . and my apologies for the broccoli in there, it's been crazy today," Tony Minnelli, the owner of Minnelli's Pizza, shouted from across the counter.

"Fo'get about it," Vincent waved his hand dismissively, "and coffee sounds really good," he replied, as he picked up the crust left over from his slice of pizza and dipped it in a small bowl of homemade marinara.

"I'll need something much stronger than coffee to get through this day," he thought to himself as he took a bite of the dipped crust.

Vincent had been on the trail of a small time crook in the Bronx. His job was to follow him discreetly to his contact.

"Why can't I just put some fear of God into him and get it out of him the old fashioned way?" he had pleaded, but his instructions were explicit.

"Be discreet. Do not make any move until you are told to," his contact had said firmly.

And that was nine hours ago. His target, obviously high on something, seemed to be as free as a bird and had decided to catch up on his errands. After picking up his laundry at a Grand Concourse cleaner, he had decided to go for a stroll in Franz Sigel Park, feeding the birds for almost an hour.

"What is this . . . he has some kind of fetish for these pigeons or something?" Vincent shook his head as he watched him from a safe distance. He was slumped on a park bench under a tree sipping on iced tea. Even in the shade, there was no refuge from the humid day. Temperatures were peaking at mid-nineties and sweat was pouring down his face.

As if this wasn't enough, he had spent the next hour and a half shopping for exotic spices in Jackson Heights. Driving into Queens was not so bad, but on the way back, his target had spent an hour on the Robert F. Kennedy Bridge, due to ever-present construction and toll line back up.

"What a friggin' moron," he sighed as the car inched its way towards the toll booth, "how smart do you have to be to get EZ-*Pass*? We could have been out of here in ten minutes."

Obviously, the man was hungry after all this activity and had decided to grab a sandwich from a deli across the street from Minnelli's, where Vincent now sat waiting for his next move.

Vincent was only five when his father, a bookie for a local underground gambling ring, was gunned down in a police shoot out during a raid. His mother did not deal with it well and during the next five years, she spent most of her remaining life at New York Hospital's psychiatric facility in White Plains, New York before jumping off the Cross Bronx Expressway Bridge onto North Bound Major Deegan during rush hour.

Vincent became an unofficial ward of his father's boss, now the head of one of the most powerful crime families in the Bronx, while living in an orphanage filled with children bearing stories that eerily resembled his own. The administrator of the orphanage, Father Nicholas, while making sure that the mistakes made by their parents were not repeated by these innocent children, could not escape the fact that his orphanage, as well his church's existence, depended heavily on the support of the same patrons that were responsible for creating most of the orphans in his care. Vincent spent his youth immersed in his two conflicting passions, books and guns. He spent countless hours learning about the world and its politics, trying to understand the injustice that surrounded him. Why was he in this situation, and not in a cozy living room surrounded by a loving family?

As an understanding of world history dawned on him, he felt more and more angry, realizing that he was just another victim to the rampant evil that ruled the world. Feeling helpless, he spent night after night, crying in his monastic room, pounding the walls with his bare fists until they bled. The release was therapeutic and made him feel better. As he grew older, the wall was replaced by a punching bag in a nearby gym. Even as a young boy, he amazed his friends with his prowess with a slingshot, knocking down crows, perched high up on the church's steeple without difficulty. As he grew older, he felt that he needed more out of his slingshot and started working as an errand boy at the local gun and rifle club, and became adept at handling any weapon that was allowed at that facility. Gradually, he made his ascent in the ranks to that of an instructor, training criminals and law enforcers alike, in their pursuit of mastering the art of handling, and firing a firearm. Legend has it that by the time he was eighteen; he could take down a fly one hundred and fifty yards away without using a telescope.

The word about his legendary marksmanship did not take long to reach his patrons, and on his eighteenth birthday, he received his first significant birthday present in twelve years, a .308 Winchester long-range rifle with a tactical 4.5-15x50 mm telescope. He stared, wide eyed at the shiny and sleek bluish metal body, while running his fingers over the barrel tenderly, as if caressing his lover. After all, guns were his first and foremost love. Human relationships had always felt shallow, temporary and far less fulfilling so when he was asked to use his skill and take out a mole within the organization, he had felt no hesitation in accepting an opportunity to test his gift on a real target. What he did not expect was the excitement generated by anticipation and the sheer rush of adrenaline that he had felt as he stared at his target through the telescope lens from a football field away. He had followed the spiral flight of the shining missile as if in slow motion, emerging from the little puff of white smoke, and at the end of its journey, effortlessly embedding itself into the forehead of his target sitting at a café having lunch. A drop of blood trickling down the face was the only blemish in an otherwise perfect afternoon setting of the sidewalk establishment.

Whether it was all the excitement or a glimpse of his victim's unfinished chicken Parmesan, but he had suddenly felt very hungry and had strolled down to the nearest bistro. This had become a ritual for him in the years to come. A nice Italian meal always complemented a successful mission.

Today was not one of those days. In fact, things had been slow for the past several months. A zealous homicide detective had been on his tail, and he had been forced to keep a low profile.

His day ended the way it started. His subject, after finishing his meal spent a few more aimless hours around the neighborhood, and then headed back to his apartment; Vincent spent the evening at the corner bar sipping on flat draft beer, wondering where his career was heading. That is when his cell phone rang and a familiar name flickered across the screen.

"Thank you, Jesus!" he said as he kissed the gold crucifix around his neck and pressed the talk button. "Hey boss! Where have you been hiding? Long time no see. I was wondering if those rattlers got you or something."

"How are you doing my friend? You should have taken me up on my offer to move west. Life is good here; you should reconsider."

"I know, I know Charlie, but you know how it is. I am comfortable here. I'll miss it too much if I move away. Bronx is in my blood. Besides, I like it when it snows."

Charlie laughed loudly, "you were always the stubborn one, committed, and that's why I love ya Vinny . . . and I need your help."

Vincent listened intently as Charlie explained the job to him. After he was done listening, he smiled broadly. This was exactly what he needed.

"You got yourself a deal Charlie; just tell me when and where."

"Where!" Charlie's response took him by surprise.

"Just stay low and don't go anywhere. I'll contact you with more details." Charlie chuckled, amused by Vincent's predictable response when he was told about the location, and then hung up.

CHAPTER 6

MURREE ROAD, RAWALPINDI

Saturday, October 1st, 5:56 p.m.

The ambulance raced through Murree Road towards Rawalpindi General Hospital. Traffic was crazy as usual. The ambulance weaved through a swarm of taxis, buses and motorcycles, while its blaring siren made the desperate efforts to get attention.

An Emergency Medical Tech desperately tried to locate the bullet wound as his partner hooked up the cardiac monitor. Heart rhythm was rapid but steady. The tech had located a bleeding entry point near the right shoulder and applied a pressure dressing on it. A large bore IV line was in place and saline solution was running wide open.

A bodyguard for the injured politician had joined them in the ambulance and was holding his head gently in his hands. He seemed shocked, shaking his head every now and then as if he blamed himself for this. After all, it was his job and the commitment of his employer, a multinational security firm, to keep an eye on the crowd and take action at the first sign of suspicion. As he ran his hand gently along the side of Malik Jahangir's face, he opened his eyes and gave a surprised look at the people around him.

"What happened? Where am I?" Malik Jahangir asked; his voice was weak, but clear and full of authority.

"You were shot, sir" the bodyguard said to him, "don't worry, and just try to relax. Everything will be all right."

Everyone in the ambulance seemed to have exhaled for the first time. Moods seem to have lifted suddenly, but the elation was short lived. One of the techs noted an ectopic beat on the heart monitor. He almost ignored it but it was followed by another and then another. Malik Jahangir seemed to be breathing heavier and his face appeared suddenly flushed.

"I don't feel right," he said. "I can't breathe!"

"Can't you go any faster?" the bodyguard, a tall muscular man in his thirties, yelled at the driver in a foreign accent.

"I'm trying, I'm trying," the frustrated driver replied curtly as he honked incessantly in a failed attempt to force a slow moving rickshaw out of his way. "I don't know why we have to go to General when CMH or Railway Hospital would be so much more convenient. Murree Road is impossible at this time of the day," the driver continued his rant, "get out my way, *harami*, he thinks the road belongs to his ancestors!" he added a few more expletives before driving onto the sidewalk in order to overtake the rickshaw and then stepped on the accelerator, screaming curses through his open window aimed at pedestrians trying to cross the road in front of the ambulance. Soon, a police motorcycle escort had joined them and had started to clear the road ahead of them.

The ambulance entered the hospital compound and headed towards the new Trauma Center. Two emergency physicians with their team and equipment stood ready to receive them at the ambulance bay.

Jahangir's breathing had become shallow as the monitor uttered a shrill alarm warning about an abnormal rhythm. His heart rhythm was now rapid and erratic; large irregular waves of varying intensity typical of *Ventricular Fibrillation*.

"He is in *V-Fib*," the tech shouted and started to apply the cardio-version pads on his chest.

The ambulance reached the bay and the doctor jumped in and immediately noticed the pads in place.

"What's the rhythm?" he asked.

"Still *V-Fib*," the Tech replied as he handed the paddles to the doctor. "It is charged."

"200?" the doctor asked.

"Yes sir."

"OK, all clear," the doctor, shouted as he applied them to the pads placed on Malik Jahangir's bare chest.

A sharp beep was followed by a loud thud as Jahangir's body arched upwards and then fell back to the gurney.

"Still in *V-Fib*," the tech said loudly.

"Charge to 300."

"All clear," warning was followed by another beep and a thud.

"Still *V-Fib!*"

"Charge to 360," the doctor's command was more subdued this time; a hint of frustration was unmistakable.

An endotracheal tube with an ambu-bag was in place; the second physician had injected a vial of epinephrine into the intravenous line as the tech started chest compressions.

"All clear," the doctor's voice betrayed his otherwise apparent calm as he delivered a shock of 360 joules. The body arched up once again and then fell back as the monitor's alarm turned into a long monotonous beep.

"It's a flat line," the second doctor declared in a somber voice.

"Atropine!" he ordered as the other doctor immediately injected another vial into the vein.

"What's the rhythm now?"

"Still asystole."

"Another epi!" the doctor shouted, now sweat pouring from his forehead, "and continue compressions."

Another five minutes passed.

Flat line . . .

Malik Jahangir seemed to be staring at something. His face contorted into a bewildered expression as if trying to figure it all out.

The doctor looked at his watch, took a long deep breath and removed his latex gloves.

"Stop CPR . . . time of death is 6:26 p.m."

CHAPTER 7

JHELUM

Saturday October 1st, 7:22 p.m.

Kamran sprang upright and fumbled to keep his cell phone on his ear.

"What! What did you say?" He was now fully awake.

"Malik Jahangir is dead. He was shot," Dr. Pervaiz Khalid, Chief of Trauma at RGH repeated from the other side.

"*Inna lillah-e- wa inna ilaihiraji'un*" (Verily we belong to Allah, and to Allah we return); he recited a verse from the Qur'an customary for such events.

"How . . . when!" Kamran was still in a state of shock, "I just met the guy two weeks ago," he shook his head in disbelief.

Pervaiz briefly stated the events. He was talking fast, stumbling over his own words. "This is not good . . . not good at all. I cannot do this alone. This is going to hit the fan . . . and really fast," he sounded very tense.

"I am really busy here, wedding and all. You know how it is. Do you really think that my mother will just let me walk out in the middle of things? There is so much for me to do here. I am sure you can handle it."

"No, I can't!" Pervaiz pleaded.

"Who else is there?" Kamran asked.

"Saleem Qazi . . . he is right here. He hasn't left me alone for a second."

"That's good; you'll have all the help from Qazi. You don't need me." Saleem Qazi was the Inspector General of Punjab Police.

"Kami, I am very uncomfortable around him. I know you like him and he is very good at what he does, but he scares me. He is like a drill master and I can't concentrate with him being all over me like this."

"Just relax. Just tell him that he can call me if he needs my input. I know how to handle him."

"That's the point, Kami. He doesn't want you here. I asked him but he told me not to involve you in this. I am calling you from the toilet. He doesn't know that I am calling you. You know me, Kamran. I am never comfortable with these things, in fact, anything outside the operation theatre. I don't know how to deal with the red tape; Qazi will eat me alive and . . . what about the media? You have to help me out; I need you," Pervaiz was desperate now.

Kamran took a deep breath and slid down on the comfortable sofa. He was tired and every muscle in his body ached. He did not want to get up but his mind was already way ahead of his body, trying to piece together information that could tie into the murder.

"Ok, give me a few minutes, I'll call you back."

"Leave me a message. I'll keep my phone on silent."

Kamran snapped his cell phone shut and sat up straight, holding his head in his hands.

Pervaiz was right. The whole situation was a mess, and Pervaiz was certainly not the man to handle it. Kamran and Pervaiz graduated from the same medical college and then completed their training together. While Pervaiz was a brilliant surgeon, one of the best he had seen, his legendary calm evaporated as soon as he left the operating room. The transformation was unbelievable; it was like Jekyll and Hyde, and the change turned him into a nervous, stammering wimp.

Pervaiz turned his phone to silent mode and came out of the bathroom, and then stopped abruptly in his tracks. Saleem Qazi was standing in the hallway, staring right at him with a dry smile on his face.

"You called him, didn't you?"

Kamran spent the next few minutes thinking about his next move. *Valima* ceremony was not until noon the next day. *"I'll be done way before then."* He just needed to make a good case to present to his mother. He could feel his level of excitement rising. This was exactly what he was trained to do. Then he thought about Pervaiz.

"He definitely needs me on this one," Kamran flipped his phone open to call.

He was about to dial back when the phone rang again. He looked at the Caller ID and sighed," I guess I have no choice now," he thought to himself as he pressed the talk button.

"Qazi *Sahib, Assalam-u-alaikum,* I think I know what this is about."

CHAPTER 8

RAWALPINDI GENERAL (BENAZIR BHUTTO) HOSPITAL

Saturday 9:32 p.m.

Rawalpindi General Hospital, located on Murree Road northeast of central Rawalpindi, is the principle teaching hospital affiliated with Rawalpindi Medial College. This major community hospital, renamed Benazir Bhutto Hospital after her assassination three years ago, had undergone major renovations in the recent years that included an expanded trauma center. Loyal followers of Bhutto had lined up to support these projects with generous donations and had transformed the facility that had provided her the last refuge in the medics' futile attempts to resuscitate her.

The hospital's main entrance was mobbed. Frenzied reporters and their camera crews pounced like a pack of hungry wolves at every vehicle entering or leaving the compound. Loyal supporters and political enthusiasts filled every inch of the road and sidewalks. Murree Road traffic was diverted to close the westbound lanes to accommodate the rapidly enlarging crowd. Angry mourners demanded blood for blood, raising inflammatory slogans, while the others stood silent in a vigil, intermittently sobbing, and at times wailing loudly at the loss of their leader.

Kamran parked his Honda *City* a few blocks short of the main entrance. There was no way that he was going to be able to drive through the main entrance; he decided to walk instead. Walking slowly and inconspicuously, he blended into the crowd and inched his way towards the gate. Military Police guarded the gate, which was closed and secured with a heavy chain.

"This is not good," he thought to himself. "By the time I identify myself and have the gate opened, the press will be on me like killer bees," especially since he had already spotted a few reporters that he knew would recognize him.

He decided to continue along the hospital boundary away from the crowd towards an area darker than the rest thanks to a broken street lamp and approached a part of the wall that was scalable. His days in the athletic team came in handy as he pulled himself up and swung across the wall into the hospital compound.

"That was easy," he thought, "looks like I've still got it."

The self-admiration, however, was short lived as he landed in a drainage ditch running along the boundary wall filled with stagnant mud. Barely holding on to a loose branch, he heaved himself away from the ditch towards a dry patch and landed on his knees. A sharp stabbing pain shot through him as loose pebbles jammed into his skin, but he was able to keep his balance. As he struggled to get up, he realized that streaks of mud, and not of a particularly acceptable odor, were splattered all over him.

"I guess the press won't be much interested in me now."

He scanned his clothes to realize that his trousers, in addition to being covered with mud were torn at the knees. He contemplated his plight for a moment, instinctively running his fingers through his hair, a habit that normally added to his boyish charm; however, under the current circumstances, it proved costly, as he had managed to smear the mud all over his forehead and hair.

"Great! Now I look like Shrek," he said to himself as he struggled through overgrown bushes towards the trauma center, making loud squishing sounds from his wet shoes.

Two heavily armed commandos belonging to the Special Services Group of Pakistan Army guarded the entrance to the trauma center. A few privileged camera crews, mostly belonging to the State Run Pakistan TV, were stationed outside the door. Sitting quietly, they were waiting for a cue to make a move. One of the cameramen noticed him walking towards them and started to roll the camera but his producer, after scanning the appearance of a disheveled stranger, motioned to him to cut; although, he seemed a bit perplexed by what he saw. He was not entirely sure, how on earth this seemingly ragged man was able to get through security. For Kamran, this was a blessing in disguise, and he began to not mind his general appearance, at least for now. The commandos were easier to handle as his recent endeavors with the police and related projects with the military had earned him a security clearance ID that helped him breeze through the door, again to the utter surprise of the intently watching media men.

Inspector General Saleem Qazi, a tall imposing man in his early sixties, was pacing impatiently up and down the hall outside Trauma Room One. He had just gotten off the phone with General Hamid, and the conversation was not pleasant. General Ali wanted answers but there were none.

He had given Saleem Qazi an hour to come up with at least a preliminary report that could be released to the media.

"Mr. Qazi," he had said in a calm yet authoritative tone, "by taking over as the President of this country, I have put my reputation and that of our military on the line. No one expected me to move swiftly and on schedule towards elections, but I have proven them wrong. The international community is watching us very closely. Our track record in terms of democracy has never been one to be proud of and I want to change that. I have received three phone calls from the US Secretary of State this week alone. Each one of them to make sure that we are on track to democracy and believe me, with all that is going on around the world we certainly don't want to disappoint them, do we?" His tone suddenly became cold, "I have CNN, Fox News and BBC, in addition to every damn reporter in Islamabad camped outside my driveway and I have to tell them something . . . and very soon; you have one hour." A loud thud followed as the receiver was unmistakably slammed down.

Qazi replayed the conversation in his mind repeatedly, and each time, he felt a chilling sensation travel down his spine.

"So . . . let's see how it ends," he thought, as he looked through a glass window at the man who held the future of this investigation, and the sight was not promising by any means.

Next to a procedure table holding the covered body of Malik Jahangir was a visibly panicked Pervaiz Khalid, hunched over a stack of photographs of the victim. Sweat poured down his face as he shook his head repeatedly, while clutching the stack with his both hands.

Qazi took a deep breath and then exhaled slowly; "This is going to be a long night," he whispered, shaking his head slowly, and then moving away from the window, he slumped down on a bench outside the trauma room.

CHAPTER 9

RGH TRAUMA CENTER

Saturday 9:40 p.m.

Saleem Qazi was in deep thought and staring at the large and generic black and white clock at the end of the hall when he felt a whiff of cold refreshing air coming from the now open front door. It was a welcome feeling in the damp and stale indoor air that he had been breathing. He inhaled hungrily and looked up towards the door. A strange sight awaited him. Instead of a meticulously dressed Kamran, there entered a ragged figure covered in foul smelling muck. A trail of muddy foot prints was left on the white tiled floor with every step he took, making a sloshing sound that echoed in the otherwise deserted hallway.

"What is this smell?" he said as he jumped up to greet his old friend surveying him from top to bottom. "I am not even going to ask," Qazi said to Kamran as he grinned, arching up his thick black moustache.

"Then don't!" Kamran snapped back. ". . . and I am glad to see you too, Qazi."

"OK, have it your way, now go and get cleaned up quickly so I can brief you. We have a lot to do."

Kamran noticed a hint of annoyance in Qazi's tone but decided to ignore it and headed for the lockers for a quick shower and a fresh pair of scrubs. When he came out, Saleem Qazi was standing outside waiting impatiently, taking short nervous puffs on a cigarette.

"Cigarette?" he offered Kamran, holding forward, a pack of Gold Leaf.

Kamran declined politely and walked briskly towards the trauma room. Qazi struggled to keep up with him while going over details of the shooting.

"I didn't want you involved in this," Qazi said, abruptly.

"What?"

"This could get very complicated, very messy . . . with lots of political repercussions. I don't have a good feeling about this. I care about you Kamran, and I don't want you to get caught in this and may be get hurt."

"I don't think that I have much choice, Qazi."

"You still do, Kamran. Go back . . . your family needs you right now. Everyone will understand; we can handle it here. There is no point jeopardizing *your* career too."

Kamran stared into the trauma room through the glass window.

Pervaiz was blankly starring at some imaginary object when he saw them approaching through a window and came running out giving Kamran a bear hug.

"You have no idea how glad I am to see you," he said, wiping the sweat off his forehead. "This whole thing makes absolutely no sense."

"We'll figure it out together," Kamran gently patted Pervaiz on the back and then turned around to face Saleem Qazi. "Do you understand now? I *need* to be here. I *don't* have a choice."

Over the next thirty minutes, Kamran poured over photographs of the crime scene and every inch of the victim's body, which had now turned to a grayish purple color. Kamran could see the two bullet wounds. The first one was a superficial graze across the right side of his neck just under and behind the ear lobe. It was hardly deep enough to cut through the skin and superficial fibers of the sternocleidomastoid, a muscle connecting the mastoid part of skull to the collarbone. A small streak of blood had trickled down along the muscle to just inside of the right shoulder. The second wound seemed more significant. The entry point was just below the outer edge of right collarbone and seemed to have had a clean path exiting in the back just inside of the shoulder joint. It was a clean wound with hardly any blood around the entry point. The exit wound, however, had a ring of dried blood around it. The rest of the body was clean, other than a slight burn mark on his left lower chest, showing the outline of a misplaced defibrillator paddle.

Pictures from the crime scene showed a stage left in shambles, with scattered furniture, and shattered decorative flower vases. A few feet behind the dais was a small pool of dried blood marking the spot where Malik Jahangir fell, after the second shot made him fall backwards on the stage.

"Were there any video recordings?" Kamran asked.

"We found two videos recorded by fans attending the *Julsa,* but I'm not sure if that could be helpful since none of them were recording the crowd," Saleem Qazi replied. "We have one over there," he pointed towards a wall mounted monitor, "one of my officers was sent to retrieve the other; we should have it by the morning."

"Morning!" Kamran looked up, surprised. "We need it now, Qazi. Have one of your men get on it as the highest priority. Even if it focuses on the stage, it can tell us a lot about the shooting, especially in regards to the victim. For now, we can look at the one we have."

"I've seen it. There is nothing there . . . you see him falling but nothing is very clear."

"Oh, well . . . any little thing may be helpful in this situation." Kamran replied, halfheartedly.

Qazi stared at the body, now covered with a white cotton sheet. "But you are right, Kamran . . . the other one might be more helpful . . . I'll have someone track it down and bring it over right now," he picked up his police issue wireless device and walked out of the trauma room.

The two of them were now alone, sitting on stainless steel stools next to the body.

"So, what do you think about all of this?" Pervaiz asked, nervously biting his nails, "I mean . . . does it make any sense to you."

"There is not much here," Kamran said, casually getting up and walking over to the body and then pulling back the sheet gently. "Right shoulder and chest wound is the only possible lethal injury."

"The only problem is that the bullet seemed to have traveled outside of any vital organs. It seems more like a generic gunshot injury to the shoulder," Pervaiz chimed in.

He had seen a lot of these over the years, as they are a common injury seen among the police due to bulletproof vests protecting the rest of their chest. He was much more relaxed now and seemed to have gathered some of his confidence back since Kamran had arrived.

"It could still have caught the lung and created a *tension pneumo*?" Kamran added. "The bullet traveled just below the *axillary neurovascular bundle*. It could also have transected the *subclavian* artery?"

"That's exactly what I had thought," Pervaiz added excitedly, "but I was reviewing the X-rays and then sent him for a CT of his chest. His lungs seemed to be fully inflated, ruling out a *pneumothorax*, or a massive air leak from a punctured lung," he elaborated when he saw a quizzical look on Saleem Qazi's face who had just walked back into the room. "Similarly, his *subclavian* artery, the major source of blood supply to the arm seems intact on the CAT scan. Besides, the amount of hemorrhage in case of a transected artery would have been massive. There was neither any evidence of it at the scene nor around the entry and exit wounds or any significant collection of blood inside the body."

Kamran pondered over this statement for a few seconds and walked towards the corner where Pervaiz had piled up CT films next to a view box. He did not need to see more than a few of them to conclude that Pervaiz was right. This did not add up. The only significant injury did not seem severe enough to be lethal.

"Of course, we need to confirm this through a formal post mortem," he said, turning around to face his colleagues.

In the heat of discussion, no one noticed a stranger walking in quietly.

"There *will* be no post mortem," his loud voice startled them.

CHAPTER 10

Saturday 9:35 p.m.

Sana Aziz was getting impatient. She had been stationed outside the hospital for more than an hour now, being the first journalist to arrive at the hospital, after tailing the ambulance through a chaotic Murree Road traffic. She was sure that by following her instinct, which had prompted her to get to her car when other ambitious reporters, still flocking the ambulance were making futile efforts to infiltrate the ring of security personnel in order to take a closer look. As soon as she realized that there was no way to get past the mayhem, she had planned her next move. If historical events were to be considered, Rawalpindi General Hospital was the obvious destination in case of an emergency, especially when considering the presence of its new trauma center, so she decided to act on that hunch. She was right, and after a prodigious display of improvised navigation and brilliantly executed reckless driving, she was able to plant herself at the main entrance, even before the ambulance made its last turn to reach it.

She was able to make a video and take some digital stills of the ambulance, zooming in on its panicked driver, even getting a momentary glance at its inside as the door opened to let out one of the emergency techs, who then ran in front of the ambulance to assist in opening the main gate. Inside the ambulance, the second tech was frantically squeezing an ambu-bag to deliver oxygen to the patient's lungs, while a second man in a security uniform sat at the head of the stretcher. The uniformed man, a solidly built male with intense eyes under thick eyebrows, locked eyes with her for a second, but then immediately turned back to focus on the frenzied, albeit methodical activity inside the vehicle. As the rusting gate opened with a loud squeak, she moved slowly, staying very close to the ambulance trying to enter the compound with it, but was harshly stopped by one of the MPs who had been a part of the motorcycle escort. As she backed off under his orders, the heavy gate closed with a loud clanking sound. A bulky chain was passed through its steel bars and fastened by a massive forged metal lock. Armed guards swiftly took their places in front of the gate after setting up an imposing barricade made out of red and white steel rods, and Sana knew that she had missed a great opportunity to score her career-defining story.

Sana was an instigative reporter for "The Capital Chronicle". A relatively newer addition to the crowded and competitive daily news market; it had forged a distinct niche for itself over a very short period of time. Its success was partly due to its stature as the first and only daily published from Islamabad, but mainly due to its maverick style of reporting that had not only won many hearts, but had also created a lot of hard feelings among the ruling elite, desperately trying to hold on to power. A scenario creating the perfect blend of intriguing controversy mixed with veritable journalism, which translated into a rapidly swelling circulation.

Sana was a perfect fit in this environment. She was an ambitious and bright journalist who relished the idea of boldly confronting, and then aggressively pursuing her assignments, going all out, following her sharp instincts. Fieldwork was her playground. Politicians and bureaucrats alike had started to notice her, and given any opportunity, tried to evade her. A young and beautiful reporter was always a welcome sight at official and political press conferences, and she had successfully used her charms, as well her femininity in a male dominated field to further solidify her position. The honeymoon, however, was over now, and the word had spread that she wasn't just a pretty face. Her brilliance was admired, but more often feared. Subtle flirtations, and at times blatant sexual innuendos, that were thrown her way regularly were hastily scaled back and replaced by clear and well thought answers to her pointed questions.

Thus, when at the unprecedented age of twenty-four, she was offered a promotion to an editorial position; she took it with a grain of salt. She was flattered by the confidence shown in her abilities; however, the conspiracy theorist in her saw this as a way to quarantine her away from those who did not appreciate her candidness. She declined the position and had continued on her quest for answers in the field.

The place was now getting very crowded. As the big guns arrived, so did their celebrity anchors and their ubiquitous entourages.

"*Lights, camera, action*" was the only way to describe it. Makeup crews worked on their subjects in preparation for a live relay. Broadcast vans were parked wherever they could; even the manicured front lawns of adjacent houses were not spared, leaving a muddy mess of deep tire tracks and trampled flowerbeds behind them. She saw a few chosen ones being given the permission to enter through the secure hospital gate, but that did not surprise her. It was common practice to give exclusive access to state run media and some select 'friends' of the government, but the material generated by them was mediocre at best and did not concern her. She did, however, wonder about the unusual delay, which, under most circumstances, meant only one thing: wheels of fabrication were churning and a near plausible alternative explanation was being manufactured. She looked at her watch, took a few sips of tea from her flask, and then went back to scanning her surroundings.

At first she did not think much of it, but the more she watched him, the more out of place he looked. The stranger that she had noticed did not have the halting, self-assured gait of an undercover officer, but at the same time, he was not wearing any stigmata of a journalist. No notebooks, no bag, no microphone or cameras. Instead, he looked uncomfortable, though exuding a somewhat restrained confidence. He seemed disappointed in what he saw as he looked around. In contrast to everyone else who was gravitating towards the gate, he seemed to back off from it. It was hard to see his face well in the dark, but at the same time, he looked vaguely familiar.

"I have seen this face somewhere," she thought but could not place it despite much effort. Feeling her frustration building, she abandoned the idea temporarily.

As he moved through the crowd, his upright, six foot one frame, among a crowd of average heights and slumped shoulders, was not too hard to follow. Dressed in casual, but well-fitting khaki slacks, a royal blue knit shirt and sneakers, he took long effortless strides towards the gate, while scanning his surroundings in a systematic fashion.

Once he got closer to the gate, he stopped and stood in one place for a minute or so, looking at the guards as if planning his next move. First, it seemed as if he was going to talk to the guard, but then he stopped and backtracked away from the gate towards the western most end of the growing crowd. For a moment, Sana struggled with what to do next. She did not want to lose her spot right next to the gate, but she felt that she needed to do something.

"God knows how long this is going to go on and then what? I am not getting any scoops with all these vultures around me any way." She turned around to look at the growing swarm of people around her and locked eyes with Nasir Chowdhary, the stalking reporter from the *Friday Times* who somehow managed to always be around her, no matter how hard she tried otherwise. His face lit up as soon as he saw her and nodded at her with a wide grin exposing his tobacco stained teeth. He waved excitedly while trying to make sure that his slicked back hair was as perfect as ever. Sana knew that he was going to come over, and there was no way she was going to survive spending the next several hours rubbing shoulders with him in close quarters. Her decision was made for her. As soon as Nasir bent down to gather his gear, she ducked and zigzagged her way through the crowd after her intriguing new target.

Behind her, the crowd had started to develop its own distinct personality, dividing into sections in complete contrast to each other. There were the mourners, huddled in a dark corner and away from the gate; men, standing in small groups exhibiting expressions ranging from shocked to profoundly morose, engaged in quiet conversations. Women, on the other hand, were much more vocal, sitting on the ground in tight circles wailing loudly. Every now and then, they stopped to scan their surroundings and then went back to beating their chests and crying out loud, making sure that *they* were louder than the group of women next to them.

Journalists were crouched down, right in front of the gate. Their microphones drawn, cameras aimed and note pads ready to record history as it took place; then there was a third group, taking full advantage of the situation, promoting their own agendas, standing right in front of the reporters with placards that varied in subject matter, from Malik Jahangir's praises to sharp criticism aimed directly at his party's policies, they targeted police and their ineffectiveness, denounced the military government, slammed the United States' foreign policies and everything in between. It was a live commercial break, selling ideas to the millions of viewers glued to TV screens for primetime entertainment.

As the stranger emerged from the crowd and walked away from it, he looked back as if he did not want to be followed. Appearing more comfortable, he started to walk much more confidently and seemed to know what he was doing. As she followed him along the hospital's boundary wall, she wondered if this was the right move;

what if he was just someone who lived around here and had stopped just to check out what was going on back there?

"I am going to give him another two minutes, and then I am heading back," she made a mental note.

Her subject was now looking for something on the boundary wall, getting closer to it with every step, and before she could process it, he jumped up and after resting his right hand at the top of the wall, swung his legs around and over it . . . then he was gone. Some angry mumbling followed a loud splash and then it was all quiet. Sana reached the wall quickly but realized that scaling it was not even close to being as easy as he had made it look. She looked at her stiletto heels and wished that she had put her vanity aside and worn more comfortable shoes. She did not want to lose him, especially since his jumping over the wall had validated her decision to follow him. Suddenly feeling panicked, she scrambled along the boundary wall, trying to find an opening, and soon found a wide crack in the wall where rains must have caused a part of the wall to sag forward, just wide enough for her to squeeze through. A drainage ditch running along the inside of the wall explained the splash she heard earlier, and the obvious consequence of it made her smile. A faint squishing sound coming from her subject's wet shoes was unmistakable and seemed to be heading towards the trauma building. She tightened the straps of her backpack and headed in that direction. Rawalpindi General Hospital, though relatively quiet at this time of the night, still had plenty of traffic going in and out of the hospital's main entrance. The Trauma Center, however, was on one end of the hospital complex and separated by a high fence to contain angry or plainly curious crowds that were often drawn during traumatic emergencies.

At the Trauma Center's main entrance, he did not seem to have any trouble with the guards. Sana saw the reporters from state run media dominating the scene flanking the entrance and stopped short of the main entrance. Still not sure of her next move, she decided to hide behind a parked van to wait.

CHAPTER 11

RGH TRAUMA CENTER

Saturday 6:12 p.m. – Three Hours Ago

The chaos at Trauma Center's main entrance settled down once the gurney containing Malik Jahangir's body was transferred inside, and to a trauma room by the trauma team. The two techs and the ambulance driver, all visibly shaken, were escorted into the building by two officers of the military police, and armed military guards took their positions outside the door in order to intercept any intruders. No one seemed to notice the security guard who had accompanied his employer in the ambulance and held his head in his hands during his last moments, climbing out from the back of the ambulance, calmly walking away from the trauma center towards a wooded area next to the boundary wall, and then disappearing into the lingering shadows of this early autumn evening.

Scaling the boundary wall was the last hurdle he hoped to encounter today. It was supposed to be easy, except for the fact that he grossly underestimated the architectural standards of government projects such as this, and a seemingly solid wall turned out to be less sturdy than he thought. His foot slipped on a patch of slick moss and his instinctive attempt to anchor himself by flinging his right arm over the wall failed as the poorly cemented bricks gave way under his muscular bulk and followed him all the way to the wet ground. His choice of curse words fitted this unexpected and dreadfully painful setback as he struggled to get up. He gathered himself and was able to complete a second, cautious attempt to climb over the six foot high boundary wall. He limped his way down the road, and to avoid attracting any undue attention quickly took off the bloodstained uniform shirt behind a dumpster, throwing it into a rotten heap of decaying fruit and vegetables from a nearby market. Using a large empty box as a shovel, he pushed some of the garbage on top of his belongings until they were buried under it. The overflowing receptacle had obviously not been emptied in days, if not weeks, reassuring him that no one was likely to find his clothes in the near future. Underneath the uniform, he was wearing a pair of Khakis and a full sleeved mock turtleneck. No one was around to witness this except for a few stray dogs that showed some degree of annoyance at this intrusion and growled reluctantly before scampering away from the dumpster to find a new resting spot.

Walking away from the hospital, he quickly fastened his gun into a holster around the lower leg and thought about the day that had passed. He was pleased with the success of his mission so far. As long as the parties involved did their part right to cover the tracks as planned, he would soon be on his way back home. The thought of home after two weeks of frenzied schedule, which included traveling around Pakistan, following a hectic campaign trail brought a smile to his face.

He flipped open his cell phone and dialed a number. A familiar but muffled voice answered.

"It is done," he said.

"I know!"

"What if someone raises questions? There are a lot of loose ends that can raise suspicions."

"Don't worry about it. Politics in a developing country is not so much different than ours. It's not very hard to manipulate the evidence. In some ways, it is much easier. Blame can be shifted in many different directions. As long as the trail ends away from us, it is not our concern who they find at the end. Now go catch up with the rest of the guys and then get some rest."

"I know, I am looking forward to a good night's sleep, but I just have this strange vibe about this."

"As I said before," the voice became a bit edgy, "your work is done. Don't worry about what does not concern you, go get some rest . . . get drunk, whatever works for you."

Walking seemed like a much better idea for now once the stale smell of rotting vegetables from the dumpster was behind him. He needed some fresh air to clear his mind. The cool breeze coming from the north was a welcome change from the confined interior of an ambulance. October nights in Rawalpindi though chilly are pleasantly tolerable; tonight was one of the mild ones. Walking up Murree Road, he tried to enjoy the sights and sounds of this busy artery. As he walked towards the city center, sidewalks started to get as busy as the road itself. Loud vehicles, randomly honking at every obstacle that interrupted the flow of traffic, or at least the concept of it, were flirting with the sidewalks, even bumping or driving on it at times. Seasoned pedestrians, totally oblivious of such transgressions, went on with their night out exhibiting a natural nonchalance. The Saturday night crowd was at its busiest. Women dressed in bright colored traditional dresses moved in and out of various shopping plazas, dragging along their noticeably bored husbands. Shops and showrooms lit with hundreds of bright fluorescent and neon lights displayed cascades of vibrant cloth, and mannequins wearing an array of fancy clothes ranging from the chic contemporary dresses, to those decorated with traditional patchwork of multicolored mosaics, to the expensive hand embroidered ones loaded with patterns of silver and gold threads sparkling in an already remarkable and brilliant ambience.

Most of the food shops were catering to the dinner crowd. Throngs of people, sitting on wooden furniture placed on the sidewalks, engaged in heated discussions about the current political affairs, dominated by today's shocking event. Neon signs highlighted various *Tikka-Kabab* joints displaying freshly skinned goats and chickens hanging from their awnings, ready to be selected by the connoisseurs that appraised them, and then would direct the chef sitting behind the counter to chop them up, before adding them to a mix of onions, tomatoes, hot peppers and a select blend of spices, before cooking it to mouthwatering perfection.

The aroma permeating the damp, cool air was intoxicating. He felt drawn towards it. His mind was in the mood but his stomach was feeling otherwise. A job had never kept him from enjoying a good meal but this time it was different. He could not get himself to feel comfortable. He tried to shake this feeling but to no avail. He kept thinking about the day, the vague assurances from his handlers and the undeniable fact that after all was said and done, he was in fact, utterly dispensable in the grand scheme of things. But this was not all that was bothering him. He could live with the former; he had for as long as he could remember, but there was a lingering undercurrent of discomfort that he could not put his finger on.

"As long as the trail ends away from us, it is not our concern who is at the other end of it," he recalled his earlier conversation.

"Who are we? Am I a part of them, or am I just the incidental casualty of war, the other end of the trail?" he asked himself.

"I can't leave myself at their mercy. I am a survivor and the only way to ensure it is to follow this thing till the end. I know that there are loose ends and I'll have to tie them myself."

A plan of action started to form in his mind. First thing to do was to get back to his team and explain his absence to his supervisor. Wandering the streets to clear his mind after an event that he solely blamed on his own miscalculation and lapse in sound judgment seemed like a good enough excuse. Nothing works better than a little self-recrimination in order to attract sympathy and divert further questions.

He felt a little better now and decided not to let his job get in the way of his palate. Still not quite in the mood for a full meal, he decided to get a drink, so he walked over to a small roadside kiosk with the picture of a teacup painted on the front and a steaming cauldron of tea placed over a blazing fire behind it. He asked for a cup of sweet-smelling *Kashmiri Pink Chai* loaded with sliced almonds and pistachio nuts. One sip of this heavenly delight lifted the heavy cloud that lingered on his mind. He hailed a taxi and got in.

"Pearl Continental Hotel," he gave his destination to the driver and took another long satisfying sip from his Styrofoam cup.

CHAPTER 12

RGH TRAUMA CENTER

Saturday 10:32 p.m.

"The family will never allow a post mortem. It is a disgrace. Haven't we suffered enough?"

Every one inside Trauma Room One was too shocked to respond immediately.

Malik Nisar Hussein, Minister of Interior for the caretaker government, and a cousin of Malik Jahangir, had arrived unannounced.

"Do we have *any* idea, what happened to my brother?" He said, as he briefly looked at the table bearing the body covered with a white cotton sheet; a pale hand with semi-flexed fingers in the form of a cup was visible, slipping out from under its covers as if begging for the same answer.

Malik Nisar quickly looked away, his breathing rapid as he wiped the sweat off his brow, while staring at some imaginary point as far away from the table as possible.

"What have we learned so far?" Malik Nisar raised his voice.

Kamran was the first one to get it together and reluctantly got up from the stool to face him, and then he briefed him about their findings and conclusions.

"So the gunshot killed him." he said emphatically, "I'll call the press conference right now, Haneef . . .," he turned toward his assistant, "bring in one journalist from each group with one camera man to the entrance. Keep it small, manageable. I want it to be quick . . . and to the point."

As Haneef turned around and walked away, a shocked Kamran quickly moved closer to the minister.

"Maybe we should delay the press conference."

"What!" Malik Nisar glared back.

"It is not as simple as it looks. The gunshots were not fatal. We don't think that we have a clear answer for what actually happ . . ."

"It doesn't matter!" Malik Nisar cut him off in mid-sentence, "he is gone, and that is the reality. Someone shot him and we've got the bastard."

"We did! . . . When, how?" Inspector General Qazi blurted out, caught totally off guard. "How come I was not informed?"

"I just got the call on my way over. SP Pindi . . . whatever his name is, called me. They were able to chase him down going north on GT road. A *Pashtun* must be one of those *Taliban* from the tribal belt."

"Did he say anything? Any leads to who was behind it?" Qazi asked, still stunned.

"No," Malik Nisar replied casually. "It appears that there was a gun battle. The bastard went to hell on the spot," his tone suddenly became harsh as he made a spitting gesture. "Good riddance. He deserved it!"

Leaving a shocked audience behind, he walked towards the door. The press was ready for him. Halfway towards the door, he stopped abruptly and turned around. "Good work gentlemen. As a member of the family, I owe you my sincerest appreciation. Our family . . . and the whole country have lost a true hero. He is a *Shaheed*, a true martyr for the cause of his people. I don't want this to be any more difficult for him or the people who love him. Let us not desecrate his legacy by dragging unproven facts into it. Please stand by me at the press conference while I deal with this very difficult situation," his stare became cold and distant as he added, "and let me do the talking . . . as far as you are concerned, this case is closed!"

The press conference went smoothly. Malik Nisar, a seasoned politician with decades of experience under his belt, remained as promised, on the point. With a heavy voice and tearful eyes, he gave a moving eulogy to 'Shaheed Malik Jahangir'. "A hero of the people, a champion to the cause of the downtrodden, and a beacon of hope that had been so cruelly and unfairly extinguished way before its time." He followed the emotional rhetoric with a confident statement regarding his, or to be precise, the official version of the events. Some softball questions lobbed by the state run media were answered briefly, while other, more penetrating ones, were skillfully deferred until more information was available.

As the media men were scampering back to their vehicles, talking into their cell phones in the process, Malik Nisar turned to the experts standing behind him. "You did very well, and in the future also, I'd appreciate it, if all questions asked of you are deferred to me, and any new information that you receive or stumble upon is immediately brought to my attention."

He waved at his chauffeur to pull his flagged department car up to the entrance.

As he was getting ready to get in, he looked back at Saleem Qazi and smiled. "It was good seeing you Saleem. I'll make sure General *Sahib* gets to know about your true professionalism in this matter."

The black Mercedes, purring gently while idle, roared under the chauffeur's foot and then drove away, disappearing into the dark night.

Sana was caught off guard by the sudden appearance of the press corps and stayed hidden during the press conference. She had a lot of questions and initially felt disappointed about not getting an opportunity to ask them, but she quickly realized that it was futile anyway. Malik Nisar had stayed tightlipped and very consistent about his answers. Her questions would not have served anything other than attracting attention to herself. Something, she felt she was better off without, at least for now. Instead, she continued to watch the proceedings from her secure location, thanks to her small Bushnell binoculars that had become a permanent part of her backpack.

She had recognized the Interior Minister immediately and then the Inspector General. A shy looking doctor in scrubs followed, and then stood there, staring at his feet throughout the press conference. She was surprised to see her subject from earlier in the evening follow the group and take his place on the right side of Malik Nisar. He had changed into scrubs and looked nice, rather dashingly handsome when she reevaluated him under the bright fluorescent tube lights illuminating the entrance.

"Of course he looked so familiar," she said to herself when the Minister introduced him. She had attended one of his earlier press conferences, introducing the concept of developing a comprehensive Trauma Center, and she was quite impressed by his passion, commitment, expertise, and of course, by his charm, but that was two years ago. Since then, they had crossed an occasional path during official events, but they had never officially met.

Today, he seemed a bit preoccupied and looked downwards throughout the proceedings, avoiding any direct eye contact with the reporters. His usually cool and confident demeanor was replaced by an aura of avoidance, as if he did not want to be there. Initially, she did not pay much attention to it, but realized that it wasn't just him. Even the usually robust Saleem Qazi did not seem quite himself and visibly flinched more than a few times during Malik Nisar's statement.

"Something is not right," she told herself as she shifted her weight from one foot to the other trying to get comfortable in her awkwardly crouched position. None of those standing behind Malik Nisar seemed too thrilled by what he was saying.

"Maybe it's just the whole situation. It can't be very comfortable for any one of them. How often does one finds oneself in the middle of a high profile assassination?"

The information presented to the press made sense and was consistent with the witnessed events of the day. No one exactly knew who may be behind it, but now that they had intercepted the runaway vehicle, she was confident that there must be some promising leads.

"They cannot afford to be complacent about this one. There will be a lot of international pressure to find out who is responsible for it. General Hamid must be like a caged tiger right now," Sana thought.

She was tired and just wanted to go home. Once the press had dispersed and the Mercedes passed by, she got up and gathered her gear to leave but got interrupted by the sounds coming from the main entrance. Kamran and Saleem Qazi were engaged in a heated argument. She could not hear what was being said, but it was nonetheless intriguing. The argument seemed to end when the Inspector General slammed his cigar on the ground, pointed towards his ranks and then wagged his finger at Kamran while he just stood there, as if in shock. As Qazi turned around and walked towards his car, Sana dropped her backpack on the ground and decided to stick around.

CHAPTER 13

RGH TRAUMA ROOM 1

Saturday 10: 55 p.m.

Kamran stormed back in to Trauma Room One and slammed the door shut behind him, narrowly missing an unsuspecting Pervaiz who was right behind him.

"Hey watch it, *yaar!*" he screamed, "I haven't done anything to you." Pervaiz walked up to Kamran, and put his hand on his shoulder. "I felt like plunking him too. Didn't I tell you to watch out for Qazi? I never trusted the guy."

Kamran did not answer and kept staring at the CT scan films, still clipped to a viewing box on the far wall. He looked around. Trauma Room One, the largest of the three such rooms with its white, ceramic tiled walls and bright fluorescent lights looked like a scene that originated in Stanley Kubrik's mind. A single trauma table was situated in the middle with a bright surgical light illuminating its one end bearing the remains of a once invincible, political giant. Someone had pulled back the sheet a bit and a pale gray face with partially opened eyes held a frozen gaze, still wondering about a future that was stolen so cruelly, so abruptly. The white cotton sheet that matched its sterile, unblemished surrounding was corrupted by a large, bright red bloodstain that was turning to a dark crimson as the minutes went by. It was surreal. Kamran took a deep breath and slumped down into a chair by the door, his head dropping into his lap.

"Let it go man . . . Kami . . . drop it! What can we do anyway?" Pervaiz continued.

Kamran lifted his head. His eyes were bloodshot. "I have nothing against Qazi. He is a good guy caught in the same quandary as we are. He has to think of his career, his future, and his family. In this unscrupulous political environment, careers, futures, and lives are lost regularly at the whims of those in power. It is Malik Nisar I have a problem with. Without an autopsy, we can never find out what happened. This is obstruction of justice; he can't make this decision on his own. Cant' we force him . . . legally I mean? There's got to be a way. It is a homicide for God's sake."

"That wouldn't work" Pervaiz interjected. "The assassination of Benazir Bhutto brought up the same question, and the police chief, and later the family was able to reject any hint of an autopsy, leaving of course, a lot of questions, accusations, and a truckload of conspiracy theories. One would think that they'd learned a lesson or two."

"That would have been nice." Kamran sighed, "but what do we do now?"

"Let me show you something," Pervaiz, said, as he walked to the table flipping away the sheet from Malik Jahangir's upper body. "What do you think of this?"

Kamran walked over. Pervaiz was pointing at the blood smear along the right side of the neck.

"The first bullet missed the carotid artery by a few millimeters. Under the circumstances, it would have been better if it had not, at least, we'd have known the cause of death," Kamran said bitterly.

"There are two very interesting things that I noticed while you were conducting your exam, but did not say anything in front of Qazi," Pervaiz sounded excited. He was relaxed, in his comfort zone now.

"First, while you were busy, I was able to take a quick look at the video taken at the scene. Take a look at this," he motioned Kamran towards the video camera sitting on a table in the corner, and then turned it on. A wall mounted flat monitor flickered, and then became alive with the typical sights and sounds of a political *julsa*. Malik Jahangir was speaking loudly and animatedly about his promises for a brighter future for the poor, to the frenzied delight of the massive crowd.

"Look at this. This is when the first shot hits him. He has his right arm raised and he is looking to the right. The shooter, obviously at his right, clips the right side of his neck."

"Makes sense," Kamran said nodding his head in approval.

"Aha . . . now this is where it gets interesting," Pervaiz said, now in an animated tone, his enthusiasm apparent from a sudden twinkle in his eyes. "The second shot hits him on the inside of the right shoulder. As he turned to address the left side of the crowd, he created a completely different angle of impact; get it?"

Kamran's eyes were glued to the screen and he continued to stare at it for a few more seconds, his mind racing, then he looked up, in a daze, "There was another shooter!"

"Exactly," Pervaiz agreed, nodding his head excitedly, "now look at this," He raced back to the head of the table bearing Malik Jahangir's body.

"On casual observation, nothing jumps off this run of the mill superficial graze; but if you look closely," he leaned closer to the body and Kamran followed suit, "see what I mean?" Pervaiz added.

Just above the graze, caused by the first bullet, there was a small, hardly noticeable speck of clotted blood, spreading towards the back of his neck. Both of them stared at it as the video continued to run in the background, sounds of chaos and screams following the second shot echoed sharply off the stark walls and filled the room.

Kamran examined it carefully. "Try this," Pervaiz handed him a magnifying lamp.

"This is strange," Kamran noted. "This has nothing to do with the bullet. It does not follow the splatter pattern and even if it did, it is in the wrong place. He was upright at the time. Any drops of blood would have followed gravity and traveled downwards." Then, something caught Kamran's eye. "Hey wait a second! Do you think this is a puncture wound?"

"It is too small to be a penetrating injury, unless . . .," he paused for a second, "unless . . . it is . . . from a needle stick?"

"You mean . . . a hypodermic needle? That's crazy! How could he get something like that?"

"I don't know," Pervaiz shook his head. "If it is . . . it has to be a very small gauge though, at least a twenty-seven G, most likely a twenty-nine . . . or even thirty. Any larger bore would have a left a bigger mark."

"I wonder how he got that, couldn't be before the rally?" Kamran added. "Can you swab the site; maybe we'll be able to get some residue?" The room was suddenly quiet as the video feed had ended abruptly. The person recording it must have panicked and turned it off. A haunting silence took over the room. Kamran felt a sudden chill, as if Malik Jahangir's spirit was there, looking over his shoulder, watching him. It rattled him for a moment, as the cold walls seemed to close in on him. He shook it off, wiping the sweat that had suddenly appeared on his brow, took a deep breath, and went back to work.

Pervaiz was already on it. Holding a sterile cotton swab wrapped at the end of a plastic straw, he made one smooth stroke as he rubbed it on the skin surface, and then placed it in a sterile specimen jar. He obtained another swab from the site after adding a few drops of sterile saline to the site and followed it with a few close up photos of the wounds as well as the puncture site. Trauma rooms were getting more high tech by the day as digital cameras, portable lab equipment with a powerful microscope and computer terminals with the latest analyzing software were always at hand, so that the trauma team, pathologists as well as forensic investigators, could work efficiently and in unison. This was the model that Kamran had been working on for the last two years. Today was, however, unusual as the regular teams were locked out allowing only a few chosen experts in, due to the security and political repercussions that accompanied this case. At present the two of them were the only people in the room.

They were hardly finished when three armed body guards entered the trauma room followed by Malik Jahangir's long time personal assistant who took one look at the body and turned quickly away, his face turning white as a ghost.

"We are here to take the body back to Malik *Sahib's* home. The funeral will be early tomorrow morning." He asked in a shaky voice, barely holding back his emotions. His eyes were visibly red from crying, tears still visible at the tips of his eyelashes, "do we need to sign anything?"

"Yes, yes, of course," Pervaiz was caught off guard. "We need to prepare the body for transport. If you wait a few minutes for us to finish and go to the reception desk, they'll be able to guide you regarding the necessary paperwork."

"Go ahead, take care of the paper work, I'll help these gentlemen with their work," Malik Nisar had followed the group into the room. "*Daakter Sahib*, I hope that I was not too blunt earlier, but you have to understand. It is a matter of family pride. He is a hero, and heroes are not dragged through a post mortem and the indecencies that it entails. I am just trying to make it easy for his family, as well as his loving supporters," he was addressing them but his eyes were constantly scanning the room.

Pervaiz, though panicked by the unexpected visit, was able to drop the camera quietly and discreetly out of his hand and into a trash receptacle at his feet; a pile of paper stuffed in the receptacle muffling the sound. Malik Nisar, a tall, imposing man who towered over an obviously shaken Pervaiz, swiftly moved forward and covered the body with the cotton sheet, noticeably avoiding any eye contact with it. While Malik Nisar was in the process of acquiring a fresh sheet from a cart next to the wall in order to replace the blood stained one, Kamran noted that the swab specimen and vials of blood drawn during resuscitation efforts were still lying on a tray next to the table, partially covered by surgical towels. He hastily moved in, standing in front of it, obstructing Malik Nisar's direct line of sight. He was reaching for them behind his back, one of the vials, in his hand when Malik Nisar suddenly turned around.

"I would sure appreciate, if you keep our conversation to yourself . . . you know how people are. They love to twist things around to benefit their causes," he was looking at Kamran curiously, his penetrating eyes focused on him, "are you well . . . *daakter sahib*? It looks like you are going to be sick."

"I'm fine. I am . . . really," Kamran fumbled with his words. His hand, still behind his back, dropped the vial back in the tray."

"Are you sure? You look pale. Maybe you need to sit down," he started to walk towards him.

Pervaiz, realizing the gravity of the situation, coughed softly, but loud enough to be heard. "Ahem . . . Malik *Sahib*, they are waiting for you at the reception. You need to sign release papers as a family member."

"Oh! I forgot about that," he turned around to face Pervaiz.

This was the moment Kamran was waiting for as he pushed the specimens to the edge of the tray and with a very casual stretching motion, picked them up and transferred them into his pocket.

CHAPTER 14

PEARL CONTINENTAL HOTEL, RAWALPINDI

Saturday 7:16 p.m.

"Pearl Continental Hotel, Sir," the taxi driver called the destination, looking at his passenger through the rear view mirror.

Vincent Portelli was half asleep as the taxi turned into the driveway, entering the hotel and then stopped at a steel barrier. A security guard looked in through the window and nodded at the guest, quickly scanning the inside of the taxi for anything that appeared out of the ordinary. Two others swept the undercarriage with mirrors mounted at the end of long telescoping poles, and then finished the inspection by looking into the trunk. This had been a normal practice in the 9/11 aftermath, as America's War on Terror had turned visiting foreigners and luxury hotels where they stayed, into an attractive target for terrorist activities. Guests of these establishments, especially the few western foreigners who were still willing to risk visiting Pakistan, did not mind this apparent inconvenience if it helped them sleep peacefully. This, however, was an illusion. While it served as a deterrent to the amateur hustler and created a feel-good practice for the guests, it still left plenty of obvious and easily penetrable holes for the professionals for whom it was primarily intended.

Vincent, being one of those professionals, chuckled every time he went through the charade, but not tonight. He could not stop thinking about the transparency of the whole plan. The fact that he was neither allowed to make any changes, nor to present any suggestions to his employer frustrated him, but he needed the money and a chance to get out of Bronx for a while. The chance to make a trip to this volatile part of the world was exciting, and full of challenges, something that he craved constantly.

He went straight to his room. At first, he felt like crashing. The softness of the bed and the fresh smell of clean sheets made his eyes heavy and he sat at the edge of the bed enjoying this feeling, but then, struggled to get up and forced himself to get into the shower. After taking a long hot shower, he was much better and, feeling the energy returning back into his limbs that felt like rubber only a few minutes ago. He changed into a fresh shirt and took the elevator down to the lobby. He knew where he would find the rest of his security team and he did, outside by the pool, enjoying the dinner buffet.

The evening had not been easy for them either. After the chaos had ended, the police and military personnel sidelined the security team. Lengthy questioning by police detectives in the presence of US Embassy personnel had followed in regards to their recent activities and schedule. Their security procedures and protocols were probed and their loyalty to their client questioned. Once released by police, they had to endure a web meeting with the security agency's head office in Washington, DC, and it was not a pleasant affair either.

Trojan Horse Security Solutions (THSS) was an internationally acclaimed security firm. Known for its all-out aggressive style and state of the art techno wizardry; over the years, it had won prominent clients on six continents. Its multi-tiered system had sections ranging from informal and basic deterrents to serious security details and electronic surveillance webs, complemented by aggressive mini militias. Its flagship contingent comprised of stiff lipped, black suit wearing, *Ray Ban* adorned replicas of the US Secret Service that gave private security to various traveling heads of states, politicians, as well as celebrities that enjoyed adding this extra air of legitimacy to their entourages. At the other end of this spectrum was the combat wing providing support in rather volatile parts of the world like the Middle East, India, Pakistan, Iraq and Afghanistan to an array of politicians, business executives, contractors, and anyone who could afford to pick up the overpriced tag for their personal peace of mind. Its least known section was a group of highly trained ex-marines, former CIA and Delta Force operatives looking for the monetary benefits of the private sector. They were unofficially engaged in anything from securing warlords in Africa to drug lords in Central America. They were hired by dictators to bolster their military strength, and at times, used by the

US government in covert operations, when direct US military presence posed a threat to innocent diplomatic fronts.

Vincent had gotten in touch with one of his colleagues and knew where to find the rest of them. He walked along the pool towards the outdoor barbeque patio. In the chilly autumn night, the warmth of two dozen or so open flames and earthen bread ovens made for a very welcome ambiance. Vincent picked up a plate and started loading it with a handful of chicken and beef *Kababs, Tandoori chicken tikka, Lahori* styled fried fish and some *basmati pulao rice*; he covered his food with a few pieces of flat *naan* bread, making a mental note of some other dishes to come back for. Despite his curiosity, and adventurous nature for trying out ethnic foods, he drew a line at trying the chopped and sautéed goat kidneys and testicles even though the spiced delicacy gave out a mouthwatering aroma. The rest of his team was huddled in a corner of the seating area, discussing the day over dessert. No one in particular was interested in his end of the story, nor did he show any eagerness to share it with them. THSS took its reputation seriously, and even though securing the perimeters of such a rally was not under their direct control and exclusively handled by the local police force, failure to protect a client was bad for publicity; its PR personnel were in full damage control mode. Everyone in this detail knew that whether fair or unfair, for appearances sake, at least one of them will have to be the scapegoat. Usually that meant a formal suspension or dismissal, and then a quiet transfer to a covert team. This would not be so bad, but as a rule, covert ops meant a move to rather remote parts of the world, usually in the middle of a guerilla struggle or a violent civil war, and that invariably translated into bad food, bad accommodations and a lot more risk to one's life, even though the salary was nearly doubled.

Vincent kept appearances as he enjoyed his meal, and then excused himself as it was getting late. He needed to get some sleep in order to clear his mind. The walk back to the room was refreshing, as he felt better alone, a feeling he had gotten used to over the course of his life. He took a few deep breaths, inhaling the crisp cool air around the deserted pool area before opening the lobby door. Hotel lobbies, as is usual for a luxury Pakistani Hotel, were geared towards providing visitors with a lavish taste of the culture without ever leaving its premises. Handicraft shops were loaded with embroidered wall hangings and throws, scattered among decorative vases and pots made of marble, brass and copper sitting on finely carved walnut furniture.

A carpet store next door overflowed with fine Pakistani, Persian, and Isfahani carpets. Vincent, while admiring the beauty of the craftsmanship, smiled over their exaggerated prices compared to traditional markets within the city. For tourists, this secure cultural experience bore hefty price tags and while they enjoyed shopping without worries of getting robbed or stumbling into a terrorist attack, these privileged vendors made a killing.

While buying a bag of mixed nuts at the small general store, he realized that he had not yet disposed of the syringe in his pocket and instinctively ran his hand over the concealed pocket on the side of his right thigh but did not feel anything.

"This does not make sense, it's got to be here," he muttered under his breath as he quickly ran his hands through the other pockets of his trousers and came out empty handed.

"Maybe I took it out in the room," the possibility came to his mind but he could not recall actually doing it. After quickly paying the clerk, he rushed to his room, but did not find anything. He sat down on the couch next to the window staring at the busy traffic on the Mall, trying to trace back his actions. If he had dropped it on the road or in the taxi, it may not have made much of a difference, but what if it was at the barbeque or worse, what if it was on the hospital property or around the dumpster where he took off his shirt. He was not wearing gloves and his fingerprints would be all over it. He put a jacket on and rushed out to the poolside. Dinner was winding down and only a few people were left, most were having tea. Two of his colleagues were still sitting there talking about football. Vincent casually walked up to them and scanned the surroundings but did not see anything unusual. Adding his two cents to the conversation, he made a few customary comments about the surging New York Giants and walked away.

He had made sure that the syringe was secure in his pocket. He had originally planned to dispose it off with the rest of the sharps in the ambulance, but sharps disposal was still not uniformly done in Pakistan and he could not locate a sealed container. Out of his element, in a different culture, certain things that he took for granted in the US, and were absent or deficient in this part of the world still took him by surprise, leaving a few unpredictable chinks in his armor. It was a fact that he was painfully aware of but could not come up with a magical solution to fix it. He had to improvise, and hence, had decided to discard the syringe later.

"Where could I have dropped it? It has to be by the dumpster unless . . .," he paused as he stared at his trouser pocket and noticed the muddy scruff marks on his knees. His eyes suddenly widened as he recalled his misstep while trying to scale the hospital wall.

"Jesus Christ!" he exclaimed as he punched his open palm with the other fist and walked towards the concierge desk to inquire about a rental car.

CHAPTER 15

RAWALPINDI GENERAL HOSPITAL

Saturday 11:25 p.m.

Kamran did not want any part of it and decided to leave once Malik Nisar and his men took over the trauma room. There was nothing left for him to do. Pervaiz had no choice but to stay and oversee the process of handing over the body. He walked over to the door with Kamran and as they said goodbye, he briefly squeezed his shoulder but did not say anything. He was still struggling to decipher the evidence they had collected and to understand the wisdom of doing anything about it. His heart was urging him to continue and analyze the fascinating findings, but his common sense warned him against it. He was aware of the power Malik Nisar wielded over the system as well as his close friendship, not only with General Ali, but also with key western players in the South Asian political scene. He had started to understand the path Saleem Qazi had chosen. Taking on the system, while jeopardizing his professional future and the safety of his family, was not the path he was ready to take.

"Oh Allah, couldn't you just challenge me with a ruptured aorta instead of this?" Pervaiz said to himself but rather loudly.

"What?" Kamran said as his own train of thought was interrupted by the comment.

"Oh, I was just talking to myself," Pervaiz said sheepishly. "Maybe I am going crazy. This is not my idea of fun, Kami, and you know that."

"I know", Kamran replied. "I am so sorry that you were dragged in the middle of this, and I fully understand your predicament, but don't worry about it. Just do not mention this to anyone. I'll do what I have to do."

"You don't have to do it either, Kami. These people are dangerous. If, in fact, there is a conspiracy behind it, they are not going to like you asking all these questions. It is a no win situation for either of us so don't do anything stupid. Go home and get some rest; you have a wedding to get back to. I'll see you tomorrow for the *valima* ceremony."

Kamran nodded, "You are right. I need to clear my mind, and maybe some time with my family will help me sort it out. Go home to your family and *Insha Allah,* I'll see you tomorrow. *Khuda Hafiz."*

"Khuda Hafiz."

Pervaiz walked back into the lobby while Kamran stood there for a second. He took a deep breath and walked out of the trauma center.

Sana was getting restless now. She had seen Malik Nisar and his goons enter the trauma center, but it had been quiet since then. She took out her BlackBerry and checked her messages. Her editor had left six messages, trying to find out if he needed to leave room on the front page, if she had something other than the generic official version being fed to the media. Subsequent calls had varied from annoyance about her lack of response to concerns about her well-being. She sent a brief text message back, promising to call as soon as she could and went back to her surveillance. When Kamran and Pervaiz appeared at the front door, she had just decided to kill some time and play solitaire on her phone. She immediately shut it off and sat up straight.

Kamran stepped out of the trauma center, deep in thought, not sure about what to do next. He was torn between his duty to his profession and the futility of this exercise in the current situation. Pervaiz was right. Whoever was behind it had made sure that the investigation was buried under political nonsense, right at its inception. Malik Nisar, though appearing suspicious for his actions over the past few hours, may just have been playing his part in safeguarding the family pride, while going on with his own version of justice. One could not trust the system in these situations, and for the politically powerful feudal lords, justice only meant revenge on their own terms, and anyone who interfered with this process, often found oneself as a thorn in each party's side, waiting to be plucked out and thrown by the wayside. He toyed with the specimen containers in his pockets, rolling his fingers around the smooth contours of the glass tubes and then started walking towards the main gate. His plan to walk away from the hospital and into the normalcy of his life got derailed rather quickly. The main gate, though considerably less crowded, still had a group of die-hard journalists waiting with their cameras ready for the body to be driven out. Some of them, with microphones seemed to be waiting for a quote from Malik Nisar, as well as the trauma surgeons on their way out. Kamran quickly backtracked on the driveway towards the boundary wall, painfully aware and duly prepared for the drainage ditch that ran along it.

A set of heavy footprints in plain sight, next to the main driveway was hard to miss. Kamran ignored them at first but got curious as he noticed more of them heading towards the wooded area. They had to be fresh since it had rained heavily earlier in the afternoon. His first guess was that it must be a military police guard using the woods to relieve himself, but when he compared them with military footprints along the entrance, the pattern was noticeably different, though made by similar grade heavy boots. This was significant since military personnel, especially those belonging to same regiment, wore the same brand of uniform shoes. These, not only had deeper treads as seen on combat boots, but also had an insignia in the middle suggesting a designer line, yet again, unusual for Pakistani Military or Police forces whose shoes were handmade by local craftsmen. The prints were distinct, deep and uniform, large in size, around a size 13 or 14, suggesting a large male weighing at least about two hundred pounds. He followed the footprints into the wooded area, using his pen light through a narrow path leading him to the boundary wall.

"Whoever it was made a one way trip to the boundary wall. This is where he must have climbed it to go out," he thought, while scanning the wall with his flashlight. The top of the wall had a few bricks missing, which were scattered on the inside of it. A distinct pattern in the soft ground included a handprint belonging to a left hand next to a deep circular mark, possibly made by a knee.

Kamran studied this for a while. "He is left handed and managed to knock off a few bricks trying to climb on the wall, falling backwards and then breaking his fall with his outstretched left hand and landing on his knee. Pretty good, Sherlock," he smiled and complimented himself on his powers of deduction. This self-admiration did not last long as the narrow beam of his light reflected off something shiny, right next to the print. He leaned forward to take a closer look and was surprised to see an object he was very familiar with.

Sana had stayed behind her cover when she saw Kamran leaving the Trauma Center. As he started towards the gate, she decided to go after him and if possible, get a quote. When he suddenly backtracked, she was just able to move into the shadows and watched him look around for something, walking between the main door and the woods looking closely at the ground. She moved quietly through the shadows keeping a safe distance until he reached the wall. Kamran was observing the wall and the ground next to it. His flashlight jumping in multiple directions until it focused on one spot on the ground. Kamran pulled out a pair of latex gloves out of his pocket and picked up an object off the ground. He then held it in his gloved hands while taking a closer look at it under the light. Sana sneaked right behind him but was not able to see what was in his hand, so despite her best judgment, decided to get closer. The loud cracking sound made by a twig snapping under her feet startled him; he jumped up to turn around and came face to face with an equally shocked Sana. They were only a few inches away from each other, frozen in the moment as they stared into each other's curious eyes. Kamran was the first to react and stepped back.

"Who are you? What are you doing here?"

Sana did not reply. She was staring at his gloved hands holding a syringe.

"What is this?" she was blunt and to the point.

"You still did not answer my question. Who *are* you and . . . why are you following *me*?"

"Oh, I am sorry," Sana stepped a little back, suddenly feeling embarrassed by her abrupt behavior. "My name is Sana Aziz, and I am an investigating reporter for the Capital Chronicle," she paused and observed Kamran, waiting for a response but he remained quiet, and all ears, waiting for her explanation so she continued, "I have been observing today's events . . . and I think that . . . I *believe* that, the official version of this story does not make any sense. I also think that you are on to something and considering the fact that ever since your arrival, you have been climbing walls and picking up evidence in the mud all alone . . ."she stopped momentarily as a mischievous twinkle appeared in her eyes, ". . . and since you have been obviously clumsy in your efforts, and seem to be ready to ruin another nice set of clothes . . . I think that you might be in need of some help."

Kamran stared back, suddenly at a loss for words. He was not sure what to make out of this situation. While annoyed by her intrusion, he was also shocked and rather impressed by the sheer chutzpah that she was exhibiting. He quickly gathered himself, "Why would you think I am onto something? Even if am, I don't think I need your help," Kamran blurted out. Suddenly feeling his earlobes getting hot and self-conscious about his earlier predicament, and the fact that she had witnessed it; he could not think of anything else to say.

Sana smiled, obviously entertained by his vulnerability. Her lips parting slightly, exposing a set of brilliant white teeth in the pale light of a street lamp, and Kamran, even in his panic mode, could not help but admire the infectious smile.

"I know that you are onto something because I have been watching you. Your body language during the press conference clearly showed your frustration, and I am sure that Inspector General Qazi and Dr. Pervaiz agree with you, because they didn't look very comfortable either. Also, how else can you explain your presence here, holding this syringe in your hands? Of course, it could be personal but you don't seem like the addict kind to me," Sana made a gesture towards the syringe, toying with him, and it worked.

"OK, you win, but I am not even sure what is going on and even if I did, I wouldn't have any idea if there was *anything* I could do about it. How do you suppose I can involve you in something like this?" he sounded frustrated, "and besides, I don't even know who you are. For all I know, you could be one of *them*."

"No! I am not one of *them!*" Sana replied with a faint smile, "and I am already involved. The fact is that I have been on this story for the last six months."

'Six months! What are you talking about?"

"Malik Jahangir had made some tough decisions in the last few months, decisions that raised a lot of eyebrows, and he made a lot of enemies in that process."

"Like who?"

"Too many; He had been swimming against the tide for some time now. Nothing public but if he had won, the changes in policies would have been dramatic," Sana ran a nervous hand across her forehead pushing a lose strand of hair back. "I have a lot of information. If you let me help you, I'll be willing to share it with you." Sana extended her hand to make a deal.

Kamran remained silent, pondering over it for a few seconds, hesitant to make such a promise while he wrestled with his own commitment. "My sister got married today, and the *valima* is tomorrow, right here, at PC. I don't want to make any decisions tonight. Give me your number and I'll call you tomorrow. Maybe we can sit down in relatively more comfortable surroundings," he looked around, taking in their current location, "and talk about it . . . off the record?"

"Off the record!" Sana replied enthusiastically and handed him her card. "You can trust me on that . . . and now . . . are you ready to climb . . . *Doctor*?"

"After you," Kamran said, as he helped to anchor her foot on a protruding brick, during her climb over the boundary wall. Once she was safely across, he followed with a quick jump and roll over the wall over to the other side.

"Very impressive, a lot smoother than the last effort," Sana commented on his effortless jump with admiration as they walked towards their respective cars. Kamran smiled and gave her a timid nod.

"So I'll hear from you tomorrow, doctor?"

"We'll find out tomorrow, won't we?" Kamran replied with a grin and gave her a quick and short salute as he sat in his car and turned the ignition.

"Oh, I know you will," Sana said softly, as she watched him drive away.

CHAPTER 16

RAWALPINDI GENERAL HOSPITAL

Saturday 10:50 p.m.

Vincent Portelli was happy to be able to find a rental car this late on a weekend. The reconditioned 2003 model Toyota Corolla, though clean and buffed, showed the signs of wear and tear with its worn fabric seats and small but visible cracks in the plastic dashboard, an inevitable consequence of exposure to strong summer suns. All the multinational firms like Hertz and Avis were sold out, and he had to settle for a local company owned by a friend of one of the night managers. The car ran smoothly, but every now and then when he hit a pothole or an unmarked speed bump, obstacles he could never seem to avoid on these roads, the resulting sounds made him feel a little uncomfortable. He recalled the agonizingly slow traffic on Murree Road, made even worse by the encroaching vendors, haphazardly parked cars and ever expanding display areas of the shops lining it, and wondered if there was some way to avoid it.

Every now and then some enthusiastic city official or a new City Mayor or *Nazim* would issue an ordinance to curb these encroachments, and for the next few weeks, officials were able to aggressively push them back using force, sanctions and warnings of legal action. *Chalaans* or tickets were issued in compounding numbers to vehicles parked in unauthorized zones and then for the next month or so, citizens got to enjoy a wider, more navigable Murree Road, while the traffic police benefited from escalating revenues. These revenues, however, were equally divided between those received by the department in the form of fine collections, and unofficial bribes collected by the police at the scene in order to ensure a lack of legal troubles for their patrons. Shoppers, though annoyed by their inability to park just anywhere, were happy to get to their destinations in time. Such honeymoons, however, did not last long as a few chosen ones, with political or administrative connections, managed to fall back to old habits without any major consequences. This led to a slow and illegal movement of neighboring stores towards the sidewalks, culminating in an avalanche of expanding shops, reappearing independent vendors and their mobile kiosks, and of course, a free for all parking lot that was never confined by such trifle obstacles as traffic lanes. To Vincent's dismay, today did not fall into those honeymoon periods.

A little homework, studying city maps came in handy, as vivid flashbacks of Murree Road traffic and driving on the wrong side of the road as far as he was concerned, came crashing into his mind. Old habits made him turn right upon exiting the hotel and right into oncoming traffic before realizing the left sided traffic pattern in Pakistan, left over from the ninety-year British rule at the turn of the nineteenth century.

Thanks to Rawal Road, a relatively new artery that connected the airport to the western part of Murree Road, he was able to bypass the congestion, emerging right next to Rawalpindi General Hospital.

Vincent drove by the hospital and saw the few remaining groups of reporters huddled together next to the gate. The rest of the crowd had thinned out. Curious onlookers had long gone back to their lives and only the diehard fans remained. He kept driving past them, until he turned left into a small street and parked the car in an empty plot, which had now turned into the favorite garbage pit for the neighborhood. This suited him fine as he drove behind a pile of refuse, partially concealing his car from plain view. It took him a few minutes to acclimatize himself to his location in relation to the hospital, and then he walked towards the general direction of the dumpster. It turned out that the streets were not numbered, or named, and intersected randomly without any rhyme or reason. This was in stark contrast to the almost ubiquitous grid pattern seen in the US cities, which, though convenient and efficient, was regarded as lacking character and a sign of mechanical urbanization in the New World by nineteenth century European critics. Vincent did not agree and cursed out loud, longing for the streets and avenues of New York, which he missed sorely. Finding the dumpster took longer than he expected as such dumpsters were scattered about on various streets, but after a few frustrating misses, luckily, he was able to spot the familiar sleeve of his uniform shirt partially pulled out of one of them by a stray dog that did not particularly appreciate this intrusion. The dog, growling loudly, underestimated the resolve of someone well accustomed to dealing with such tactics on the deserted back alleys of Bronx, turned into a whimpering retreat as Vincent hurled a large rock in its direction. His triumph against the stray dogs was, however, the only success he had as there was no sign of the syringe, in or around the dumpster, but then, after the first few cursory attempts, he stopped short of an effort that asked for a deeper dive into it. If the next stop in his search came up empty, he hoped that it was buried somewhere deep in the fermenting heap of organic waste that filled the overflowing dumpster.

Slowly, he walked towards the wall and braced himself to jump, but this time, well warned of its unstable structure. Standing right next to it, he reached up and carefully felt for any loose bricks to eliminate the element of surprise. Once assured that his chosen section of the wall was sturdy enough to withstand his weight, he reached up to anchor his hands, but instinctively pulled back. Something was not right, a faint rustle that seemed out of place. It was quiet, except for an occasional howl from a stray dog and the distant hums and honks of the evening traffic. There it was again, a soft footfall, and then a loud snap of a twig from the other side of the wall. Vincent jumped, but immediately controlled his movement, slowed his breathing and crouched down next to the wall, in its shadow. Then he heard voices, a man and a woman engaged in an awkward dialogue. For the first minute or so, he did not pay much attention to it. The exchange was mostly in Urdu and he could barely follow it, but as it progressed, as it is the case in most conversations between educated Pakistanis, English vocabulary started to dominate, especially where technical and scientific issues were concerned, making it easier for him to follow the content. He moved closer to the wall, his left ear, placed right next to it, listening, as he waited for the strangers to go away, but then suddenly, a mention of Malik Jahangir, the official story not making sense, and a mention of suspicious forensic evidence caught his attention; then came the word he hoped not to hear. The woman was asking the man about a syringe that he was holding in his hand. Vincent had to think fast. He reached down and pulled his concealed handgun from the ankle holster and then a small silencer from his pocket. Expertly fastening the silencer to his 9mm Glock 19 pistol, he inched along the wall searching for an opening in order to visualize his targets. The conversation on the other side did not last long. The couple, sounding much more cordial now and seemingly in unison, reached the wall and started climbing it. The young woman was the first to climb over, followed by a young solidly built man in scrubs. A group of teenagers appeared in the distance, busy in loud chatter and heading in their general direction. Vincent, still firmly holding the Glock in his hand and ready to pounce at a moment's notice, slid back into the shadows and watched his targets keenly, but did not make a move.

"Killing them here will only raise more questions. Besides, I have to make sure that all the evidence is in my possession before I eliminate them," he reasoned with the urge to finish it right now.

He wasn't worried about losing them. After listening to their conversation, he knew who she was and though he could not be sure of his identity, he knew exactly where to find him tomorrow, right there in his own hotel. He smiled at the irony as he listened to the parting exchanges between them, then walked back to his car to go back to the hotel, looking forward to a good night's sleep. After listening to their conversation, he was confident that they were not going to make any decisions tonight, which gave him plenty of time to plan his next move.

"Better catch up on some sleep Vinny." he said to himself as he made the right turn onto Rawal Road; this time on the correct side of traffic, heading towards his hotel. Once safely on his way, he relaxed, looked at the dark circles emerging under his eyes in the rearview mirror, and then flexed his knuckles, while slowly stretching his neck in a rotating motion that felt refreshing, ". . . tomorrow's gonna be a long day."

CHAPTER 17

PEARL CONTINENTAL HOTEL

Sunday, October 2nd, 9:30 a.m.

Kamran, still in twilight, rolled over in his bed, reflexively stretched his arms and then as he almost fell off the bed, woke up. He had a pounding headache, his heart suddenly racing, and ready to jump out of his chest. Last night's events ran through his mind like a heavy fog, a nightmare that was finally over, but not quite. Bright sunlight filtering through a pair of otherwise tightly pulled heavy curtains homed right into his still squinting eyes. As he tried to shield them with his left arm, he wondered why was it always impossible to keep hotel curtains together to keep the sun out. There was never enough overlap to achieve that. "How difficult can it be?" he said to himself as he casually turned to look at the clock, and this time he could not stop himself from falling off the edge of his bed.

"Nine thirty! How did this happen?" he exclaimed loudly as he got up in a hurry and half stumbled into the bathroom.

After leaving the hospital, he had called home to let them know them know of his whereabouts. Originally, the plan was for him to travel to Rawalpindi for the *valima* ceremony, the reception given by the bride and groom, usually the day after the wedding, along with his family the next morning. Now that he was already there, his mother, though still a bit upset about his decision to leave in the first place, convinced him to stay the night in Rawalpindi and join them the next day for the reception at the hotel, rather than traveling all the way back to Jhelum for a few hours.

"What kind of an idiot would do such a thing?" she had said, annoyed at his plan to drive back. "You looked tired and sickly yesterday. I want you to rest well. I want to see your fresh, well-rested and handsome face tomorrow. Lots of pretty girls will be there tomorrow, so look your best," she said firmly. "If you continue to work and look like this . . . I'll never be able to find you a wife," she closed with a sigh and her favorite punch line.

Checking into the same hotel was an obvious choice. He had planned to wake up early in the morning and go over the events of the previous day before getting busy with the day's activities, but of course, in his exhausted physical and mental state, he had successfully, albeit regrettably, turned the alarm off at the ridiculously early hour of seven.

A long hot shower cleared his mind. He stood under the steady stream of hot water and felt refreshingly energized, but as the cobwebs started to melt away, the nightmare from last night started to feel real again. As he came out of the shower, he instinctively turned on the TV. The news was on, showing the preparations for Malik Jahangir's funeral, later in the day. The services were pushed forward from the plans initially announced to give his fans, and more importantly, to give the major political figures, enough time to reach his small village outside the Southern Punjab city of Multan. President General Hamid Ali along with most of his cabinet had pledged to attend the funeral and that had led to further delays due to security concerns.

Kamran sat there, toying with the plastic bag holding the hypodermic syringe as he watched political pundits tout their own versions of what, why and how. All sorts of rumors and implausible speculations were unabashedly laid out since no one could convincingly state the facts without raising serious questions. Kamran was still not sure what his role in the whole issue was going to be. His only ally so far had been Pervaiz, but he understood the limitations of his commitment, and felt that as a friend, it was his duty not to involve him in this. He had a family to think about; Kamran did not have that excuse and felt a strong sense of duty, compelling him to go on and pursue this trail of evidence. The country was at a crossroads and whatever was to evolve out of this tragedy had the power to define its future. The fact that his actions today could pave the way to such a future did not make his decision any easier. He thought about the reporter from last night. Even in the fading moonlight, he could see that she was beautiful, in addition to being smart, and definitely a lot gutsier than he ever considered himself to be. Under any other circumstance, he would have jumped at the opportunity and called her without missing a beat, but this was different. He had to be responsible about any decision to involve other people in this mess. He was not even sure about his own commitment to it, and he was certainly not ready to trust anyone yet.

He surfed through the channels as he continued to think about his options until he reached the state run PTV (Pakistan Television) channel. A press conference presided by the Interior Minister, with Inspector General Qazi standing in the background, was providing the press corps with the latest information. The press conference was being broadcasted live from Multan airport where the two had just arrived for the funeral.

Malik Nisar looked much more relaxed and composed compared to their encounter the night before. He was wearing a black, traditional *shalwaar suit* with a charcoal grey vest and a black cap, decorated with local embroidery. Large gold rings were prominent on both hands which he used liberally as he talked with his usual swagger. He started with his statement:

"Assalam-u-alaikum. First of all I want to thank you for your cooperation and patience with changes in the funeral plan and also for being here, especially in this weather," he gestured towards darkening clouds looming on the horizon. "Please forgive me if I do not seem articulate enough as I am still trying to come to terms with this tragedy, and you are well aware of the personal loss that I am dealing with. I promise that very soon, we'll bring the perpetrators who are behind this to the justice that fits this heinous crime. We have some more information that I would like to share with you. After collecting all the information from the crime scene, the reports from the attending doctors, and reviewing the forensic evidence, we are certain that Malik Jahangir *Shaheed* was the victim of a bullet wound to his chest by a single gunman. We pursued the gunman, heading north towards Peshawar on GT road, and trapped him at a roadblock two miles north of Wah Cantonment. After an armed struggle, the gunman, identified as Shahbaz Khan, age 24, was shot multiple times and killed by the pursuing police force. An explosive device containing four pounds of C4 was found in the trunk of his car. We believe that he intended to blow it up, most likely along with himself, but due to a trigger jam, he could not complete the suicide mission. Some documents in the car have been traced to Sardar Jalaluddin Khan, who has been linked with funding the Taliban friendly militias in Waziristan Agency. We are still trying to trace the registration on the vehicle. I cannot elaborate any further about military or police actions planned for the tribal areas due to security issues, but we will inform you of any progress in this case. To conclude, I pray to *Allah Saain* that Malik *Sahib* finds him with His mercy and a place in heaven. I thank you once more and ask

you to join me for a moment of silence in our leader's memory," he lowered his eyes and prayed under his breath. After about thirty seconds, he raised his head and got up to leave.

"Malik *Sahib*, what is your response to the report that Malik Jahangir's recent meetings with the Chinese officials had made some people very nervous?" Atif Sherazi, senior correspondent for the daily *Dawn* asked.

Kamran sat up in his bed. "Excellent question!" he commended the reporter's direct approach.

Malik Nisar turned around, his soft smile now gone, "We do not want to tarnish a hero's legacy by needlessly stirring the pot . . . adding fuel to baseless theories. We have the leads to apprehend the culprits behind this. It is the anti-Pakistan forces, who did not wish him alive because he wanted to go after them. He had sworn to defeat those who are responsible for terrorist activities in Pakistan. He wanted to give security, power, and rights to the people of this country, and he died for them. So, I urge you to focus on what he stood for, and on the fact that we need to make sure that we continue the brilliant legacy that he has left behind. Overshadowing his sacrifice with these . . . " he paused; his face was contorted in a sneer, as he stared at the reporter, ". . . these irresponsible fantasies . . . they will only help the despicable people who are behind this," Malik Nisar abruptly got up pushing his chair back and walked away.

"Malik *Sahib* . . ."

"Inspector General Qazi . . ."

Multiple reporters tried to get their attention, but they were gone. Saleem Qazi did not say anything during the press conference and sat there like a robot, expressionless with his eyes locked at his hand in front of him.

"ARGHHH! How can they just go on lying about everything?" Kamran kicked the side of his bed in frustration and picked up his cell phone.

CHAPTER 18

MULTAN AIRPORT

Sunday 10:05 a.m.

Inspector General Saleem Qazi was deeply troubled. Throughout his career, he had been an honest and principled official. This quality had gotten him into frequent and at times open confrontations with political and bureaucratic officials. Even though he had reached the coveted position of Inspector General, he had been superseded on a number of occasions by his colleagues that played their social cards right and moved on to more lucrative positions in the Federal Government.

Though respected for his qualities by friends and foes alike, he often felt out of the loop. Still living in his small family home in Lahore, managing on his modest means, he could not compete with the sprawling properties, late model cars and a constant stream of money that was so easy to maintain in the police force. All he needed to do was to be just a little less scrupulous, and his life would be completely different. Opportunities were there but he had stayed strong, fending off the barrage of temptations that came his way over the years, but he was getting tired of fighting. For once, he wanted to stay out of a controversy and let people do as they please, and he had been very successful so far, at least for the last twelve hours, but that had seemed like an eternity and had not been easy. Listening to the so-called official version was becoming unbearable to the point of being nauseating. He could taste the bile every time Malik Nisar opened his mouth, but he had resolved to ignore it. Time and time again, he had seen the 'official versions' derail highly promising investigations, hiding the truth from everyone. He was determined to stand up and fight the system, but this was not the time. From humming his favorite tunes to imagining himself shooting targets at the police firing range, he had tried every distracting strategy but with every second that passed, he had become more and more impatient. Malik Nisar was going on and on about his love for his country and his slain cousin. His resolutions to get to the bottom of this were as hollow as his sincerity towards his voters, but that is where savvy political upbringing came in handy, as he scored more sympathy points with every syllable that left his tongue. Saleem Qazi changed his focus and now his newest fantasy involved using Malik Nisar as his target on the firing range.

Fur Elise in A minor filled the room, interrupting the chatter filled VIP lounge at Multan airport. "Thank God!" Saleem exclaimed; he was thrilled to be able to get away from it all as he walked towards a corner, letting everyone savor the genius of Beethoven for a few extra moments.

"Salem Qazi here."

"What on earth is wrong with you? Don't you have any integrity left?"

"Who is this . . . Kamran?"

"You know why I liked you, respected you? Even when you acted like a complete jerk and drove everyone around you crazy, you never compromised on your principles. You never gave a damn about what anyone thought as long as you got the job done the right way. I don't know what has happened to you. This is why you do what you do. This is what you stand for. This is your moment to shine!" Kamran paused, his voice quivering, "you need to show them what you are made of, and instead . . . you are out there wagging your tail behind the very same people that you swore to protect this country from," Kamran was out of breath now.

"Kamran, it's not as simple as you think," Saleem Qazi replied. His voice low, tentative but firm. "Do you really think it's easy for me? There are battles that you can win, and those you can't. There is so much good that you and I can do. I am not going to lose the opportunity I have by hitting my head against a wall. This case is closed, unanimously accepted by the blind eyes and deaf ears of this administration," he was keeping his voice down as a few curious eyes were still following him. "Kamran, listen to me and listen very carefully. There is a lot more to this than it seems. This may only be the tip of the iceberg. People behind it are dangerous . . . ruthless; their tentacles reach far and deep into our country's politics. Don't risk your career . . . your life over this."

"You don't have to say anymore. I get your message, and I am disappointed. I won't bother you again."

"Kamran, don't be rash, you don't understand . . . Kamran . . . Kamran?"

The line had gone dead.

"Damn it!" Saleem Qazi stared at his phone and then walked over to the glass window overlooking the tarmac. A lot of activity was going on. Security personnel were doing last minute checks before the air force plane carrying General Hamid Ali arrived. A red carpet was being rolled out where the aircraft was scheduled to stop.

He stood there for a few minutes, motionless. No one paid any attention to him as they got ready to head out and receive the President. Everyone wanted to be at the head of the line to shake his hand. Even though elections were just around the corner, and General Ali's reign was short lived, there was still a lot going on. Policies were being made, initiatives introduced and contracts granted on a regular basis. In short, a lot of money was to be made if only one made it to the right place at the right time.

He turned around and looked at the commotion that had erupted behind him with the announcement of General Hamid's plane's arrival. He could not help but smile at the sight of frantic bodies with eager faces, jammed against each other, trying to exit through a small opening, all at the same time. This was a scene that he had witnessed too frequently during his career, and despite its comical nature, it had always made him a little sad, seeing these so called leaders of the nation, losing all dignity in their blind and selfish pursuit of personal gains.

He shook his head as he took the phone out of his pocket and scrolled down the list of names in its directory, finally stopping at one. He stared at it for a minute as if not sure of his next move, then pressed the talk button.

CHAPTER 19

POTOMAC FALLS, VA
THE ISLAND COURSE, LOWES
ISLAND CLUB

Saturday October 1st, 10:04 a.m.

Mike Moxley held his finish after a smooth swing; his eager eyes tracking the high draw bringing it in from the right edge of the lush fairway.

The four some was at the eighth tee box on Tom Fazio's Island course. It was a beautiful morning in early fall, sunny and sixty degrees with only a light wind blowing from the Potomac; it was a perfect day to hit the links. Perfectly content with his drive, he was a very happy man in his mid-fifties. Tall, athletic and exhibiting a deep tan, he was wearing a black microfiber Nike shirt and khaki slacks. His thick black hair was covered with a USGA Cap from the US Open at Bethpage Black Course. He let his Cleveland Highbore XL drop gently through his grip and then triumphantly pointed to his ball three hundred plus yards down the right center of the fairway.

"Yeah baby, that's what I am talking about." With everyone else in the rough or worse, he had the perfect angle on this 502 yard par five. "This Nassau is mine."

"Don't be so cocky, Mike," said a short and balding man dressed in plaid knickers with a smirk. "There are still a lot of deep waters left for you to get into trouble, no pun intended." He eyed the lake that ran all along this hole and guarded the small green.

"Oh, don't you worry about me, Dougie; I've got the perfect angle, just focus on your own watery grave," replied Moxley, as he took long strides down the fairway towards his ball.

With a strong square face and thick black hair, only a touch of white in his temples hinted at his age. The headwind was getting stronger, calling for a conservative approach. An easy layup with seven iron, and then a small sand wedge had him eying an uphill eight footer for birdie that would give him the lead in the five dollar Nassau before the turn.

The cell phone vibrated right into his stroke. "Oh crap!" Mike shouted, as he pulled his putt just left of the hole and then threw his putter all the way across the green. "I hate cell phones!" If it was up to him, he would ban all communication devices from the course but then he would never be able to play. That was the irony that came with his job and he had to live with it. Reluctantly, he pulled out his cell phone and looked at the number, calming down a bit; he motioned his partners to continue; his one footer for par was conceded as he walked to the far side of the green.

He talked quietly and discreetly for a few minutes and appeared much more relaxed when he hung up. Enjoying the cool wind coming from the lake, he took a few deep breaths and then lit a cigar, giving it a few short puffs before inhaling deeply and dialing another number.

"It's me, we are in business," he sounded excited and listened to the response. "Don't worry about it. I have my best people on it. Everything is going according to plan."

The rest of his foursome was getting impatient and waved at him to hurry up.

"No sir, I am not planning to be there for another week. It'll be better to let it settle down a bit. I'll keep you posted."

He scratched his temple with his index finger, closing his cell phone with the other three as he walked back to the green still in deep thought.

"Sorry guys," he apologized for the delay and picked up his bag to walk towards the ninth tee, collecting his putter on the way.

CHAPTER 20

ZERO POINT

Sunday, October 2nd, 2:45 p.m.

Kamran was distracted, lost in his own thoughts, but he somehow managed to go through his social obligations of the day. The ceremony was beautiful, lavish and, as is the tradition, more sedate compared to the last few days of high intensity drama. The ambience was tranquil, and colors were shades of white and light greens compared to the reds, purples and yellows of the wedding and the days preceding it. His sister looked beautiful in her off-white *gharara* and a lime green blouse. A heavy *doputta* embroidered with strings of green silk and gold and complementing her makeup, covered, and weighed her head down just enough to keep the illusion of a demure bride intact. She looked radiant and that was all that mattered to him. Kamran was almost choked up with emotions as he looked at the happy couple from his seat, conveniently located in a secluded corner of the massive banquet hall.

He had spent the last few hours calling around to locate one of his friends from college, who ran a local private lab. Javed Cheema was an assistant professor of Pathology at Rawalpindi Medical College, and had recently started his own diagnostic laboratory across from District Headquarter Hospital, one of its teaching hospitals. Javed was surprised to hear from him after such a long time and Kamran had to apologize for being hurried, with a promise to catch up with him very soon without going into detail about the source of the three vials of clotted blood sitting in the mini bar of his hotel room. Javed Cheema sent a courier from the lab to collect the samples with the promise to get back to him as soon as he had run the basic panels. Detailed reports, including toxicology analysis would take longer.

After getting ready for the ceremony, he had gone down to the lobby to sit in a quiet corner of the Front Page Café. As he sipped on a soothing cup of *chai*, he planned his day, contemplating if he should call Pervaiz when his cell phone rang; it was Pervaiz.

"Hey, I am sorry to bug you; I know that you are busy today but I was up all night, tossing and turning. I had to call you."

"Oh it's ok, I am glad you did. This whole thing is driving me crazy too. You are the only one I can talk to. I tried to talk to Qazi but . . . ."

"I know. I saw the press conference. It was a disgrace."

"The worst part is that everyone is buying it. At least Benazir's supporters showed some emotions, well a little more than required . . . or a lot more," he referred to the series of violent demonstrations and wide spread destruction of property that followed her assassination. ". . . but what I am trying to say is that . . . I am not for destruction, in any shape or form but hey, a little skepticism wouldn't be so bad. What's wrong with questioning the facts, looking for some answers? Isn't there *anyone* out there who thinks like that?"

"I know the feeling," Pervaiz replied with a sigh, "when I couldn't sleep last night. I kept watching the tape."

"You mean you still have it! I figured that Malik Nisar seized all evidence before he left!" Kamran sounded surprised.

"Salem Qazi made me give all of it in . . . what a bummer? I had to comply . . . with all the *original* evidence . . . I guess it doesn't apply to a copy of the original. Does it?"

"You are incorrigible Pervaiz; I underestimated you, yet again. Where is it?" Kamran's face lit up.

"I have it at home. You know how I am into keeping a video library of my surgeries. I just downloaded this great program. You won't believe what you can do with a video on this thing. What a way to test it though? I saw something very interesting. It wasn't much at first but when I watched it again . . . and again, it just . . . jumped out at me.

"What did you see?" Kamran asked impatiently.

"At first, the scene looks like any other *julsa* but then, something did not seem right. There was this police officer with a walkie-talkie standing right behind the dais; it's hard to make out the exact rank. He seemed to be watching in the direction of the first shooter. He listened to his walkie-talkie and then scratched his right ear, just moments before the first shot. I didn't think much of it at first, but he repeats the same exact sequence looking in the other direction just before the second shot, and as everyone was running towards the stage, towards Malik Jahangir, he does the opposite . . . he turns around and walks off the stage. Interesting isn't it?"

"I've got to see it. If we can identify the police officer in the video, maybe he can lead us . . . or at least someone, to the killer. When can I come by?"

"Any time you can, but don't come to my house. I don't trust these guys. What if someone is watching us?"

"Don't be so paranoid. Nobody is doing that. I don't think we are that important yet," Kamran said with a chuckle.

"I would still prefer to keep my home out of it."

"That sounds reasonable. Where do you want to meet?"

"There is a small fast food place in F- 8 *Markaz* called Dainty's. I'll meet you there at four."

"I know the place, but aren't you coming to the *valima?*"

"I am sorry. I just can't focus right now, and I have this severe migraine. I'll take a little nap and that might help. I should be good to see you in the afternoon. My family will be at the *valima* though."

"Ok. I'll see you at Dainty's around four."

Sunday traffic on Murree Road could be unpredictable. Kamran was very aware of that phenomenon and decided to take airport road onto Islamabad Highway. Afternoon traffic was manageable except for a plethora of trucks, which roamed about freely in and out of traffic lanes like a herd of untamed cattle. It was annoying, but he knew that all truck traffic would get off the highway at the Faizabad interchange leaving a smooth ride into Islamabad.

The twin cities of Rawalpindi and Islamabad could not be any more different. It is like Neil Simon's Oscar Madison and Felix Unger, forced to subsist in an awkwardly close proximity. Rawalpindi is like any quintessential large city in a developing country. Sprawling sections of poorly planned residential areas interspersed with chaotic bazaars and customary slums. If it was not for the ever organized and relatively meticulous presence of the Military Headquarters, Rawalpindi might not even have escaped the ranks of generic medium sized cities, loved only by its loyal inhabitants. The expansion that was encouraged by this military presence not only gave it class, but also enhanced its cultural character.

Islamabad, however, the Jewel of Pakistan, stands out like a rousing contradiction in the shadows of the Margalla Hills. A grand idea emerging from the mind of Past-President, Field Marshal Ayub Khan, it is an optimistic glimpse of things to come. A city raised in the foothills of the Himalayas, built over millions of acres of fertile agricultural land; it is divided into alphanumeric sectors, grouped according to plot size and hence conveniently separating the haves from the have-nots. Its open thoroughfares lined with flame and paper mulberry trees, ample green belts, organized markets surrounded by grand plazas, and minimal if any hint of poverty, makes one forget the woes faced by the rest of Pakistan. Though Islamabad makes its majestic appearance as soon as one hits Islamabad highway past Faizabad, its true portal of entry resides at "Zero Point". A point where one sheds off the worries of economic and political instability, and leaves behind the hungry and the poor, to enter the dream one hopes will be the future for the rest of Pakistan.

Kamran Drove up to Zero Point and took a deep breath.

"This is it, the point of no return. Are you sure you want to keep going?" he asked himself. Traffic was slow at the intersection. He looked left and right and waited for the single lane traffic to pass through a construction zone. He could just call Pervaiz and have him destroy the tape. Just forget about it. It never happened. He felt his eyes getting heavy. Lack of sleep in the last two weeks started to catch up with him, and he had a strong urge to take the exit and take Kashmir Highway back to Rawalpindi. He gave it a moment; events of the last twenty hours ran through his mind. Staring straight ahead his eyes focused across Suhrawardy Avenue, at the top of the Agricultural Development Bank building, dominating the architecture of Zero Point. Fluttering in the light breeze of this pleasant autumn day with the majestic hills of Margalla in its backdrop was the green and white flag of Pakistan. To his right, perched high on a cliff to the right of Zero Point, guarding its capital city was the Pakistan Monument. A majestic structure built with red granite and marble, erected to tell the story of Pakistan and that of its proud citizens through breathtaking relief carvings and murals. Kamran had never missed an opportunity to visit it in the recent years, as he liked to sit there and enjoy the magnificent view, while surrounded by the stories that led to the birth of this country. He looked at the red monoliths, configured like a giant flower and took another deep breath. Traffic had started to crawl again. He looked ahead and his eyes darted back to the proudly waving flag. Kamran stared at it with reverence as the face of an old man flashed before his eyes. He could never forget that face. It belonged to the father of one of his patients. The victim of a motorcycle accident, the young man was not able to reach the trauma center fast enough.

After two hours of frantic efforts to save his life, he stood there, facing an aggrieved father, delivering the devastating news. He was a man of modest means but holding on to his dignity as much as he could; he had held Kamran by the shoulders with his shaking, arthritic hands, looking straight into his eyes. Seeing that Kamran was trying to fight the tears, he had said in a quivering voice,

"*Jeetay raho baita,* livelong, you did what you could; and remember, if it was not for you, he would not even have this chance. His time had come, this is *Allah's* will, but somewhere, sometime, someone else will be saved. Never stop trying just because the results are discouraging, or hope is lost. Keep your faith in *Allah* and success will follow you."

Traffic had started to flow again and so was the clarity of his conviction. He blinked quickly to clear the tears that had started to fog his vision and stepped on the accelerator, driving straight through the intersection on to Faisal Avenue.

CHAPTER 21

Sunday, October 2nd, 11:10 a.m.

Vincent had been busy. He had enjoyed a good night sleep; at least from his standards, and after a long hot shower, he was feeling fresh and ready to take any challenge. He flexed his muscles and stretched for a few minutes, then dropped down on the floor for a rapid-fire session of push-ups. Energy returned to his muscles as his chiseled biceps and torso twitched with vitality. He jumped back onto his feet and stood in front of the mirror, admiring his enviable form for a few seconds before slipping on his shirt, and then stepping out into the deserted hallway.

His first stop was the rental car desk to extend his rental agreement for a whole week. Still, no vehicles were available at other desks and despite its quirks, he had gotten used to the car he had used the night before. It was pleasant outside. The sun was bright and the breeze tame, a perfect day for a short stroll. He walked out of the hotel and casually entered the parking area, pretending to be a guest looking for his vehicle. It wasn't long before he was able to locate Kamran's Honda, parked in a corner, at the far end of the lot. He approached it nonchalantly, hidden from plain view, thanks to a large mulberry tree and stood right next to it. In a smooth motion, pretending to tie his shoelace, he bent down and placed a magnetic GPS locator on the undercarriage. After the successful mission, he walked back to the lobby, nodding politely at the doorman, traditionally dressed in a crimson long coat with gold embroidered patterns, and sporting an impressive and well-groomed moustache. After passing through the customary search at the door, he entered the Front Page Café. Once safely seated, he turned the GPS locator on, placed it on the empty chair next to him and picked up the breakfast menu.

He was pleased to see his day getting considerably easier when Kamran walked in and settled in the corner, two tables away from him. Instinctively, he moved one of the napkins from his table and covered the GPS locator. Now that all the pawns on his chessboard were in one place, he suddenly felt very hungry. Foreseeing a long day ahead of him, he ordered a Pakistani omelet with tomatoes, onions and hot peppers, an order of fried *paratha* bread, and a glass of sweetened *lassi*. Breakfast looked sumptuous and reminded him of some his favorite foods that he had not tasted in a while. He would have given anything to taste some of Roberto's veal parmesan. The thought of one of his favorite hangouts in the Bronx brought back sweet memories as he dove into the appetizing plate of breakfast in front of him.

Kamran was sipping on his *chai* when his phone rang. Vincent sat up straight and put his refreshing glass of *lassi* aside as soon as he heard the name Pervaiz. He could not make out the conversation completely but did hear the word video, and the fact that it contains some vital evidence pertaining to the assassination. He finished the rest of his breakfast in a hurry, downed the last of his yogurt drink in a big gulp and got up, just as Kamran was signing his check. Walking through the narrow passage between the two tables, he seemed to trip on the edge of a rug almost falling over only to be supported by a table. He managed to get back up quickly, and for a fleeting moment, using a surprised Kamran as support, hurried away after uttering a quick apology. Kamran did not feel Vincent's index finger, pressing briefly under the lapel of his suit jacket, placing a miniature microphone in the perfectly obscure location.

CHAPTER 22

Sunday October 2nd, 3:10 p.m.

V incent was relieved to be on the wide and organized Islamabad Highway. Despite being in Pakistan for the past two months, he had not been able to get used to driving on the 'wrong' side of the road.

"Damn British," he cursed as he almost made a left turn and drove into the oncoming traffic. *"Why did they have to be so different from the rest of the world?"*

And he was right. Like any other colonial power, the British wanted to leave their legacy behind them. Alexander the Great left a series of cities named Alexandria, populated with single mothers, and blue-eyed children with Macedonian blood in their veins. Romans left the concepts of a republic, democracy, architecture and of course, some splendid bathhouses. If it were not their penchant for human sacrifice and blood for the sake of personal pleasure, we wouldn't have *American Gladiators*, or Mixed Martial Arts and Ultimate Fighting Championships. The British wanted to be the civil ones, leaving a system of railways and roads that were to be driven under their standards. They also introduced an antiquated penal system, and of course, as a reminder of their now defunct barons, a feudal system that still haunts their ex-colonies. The funny thing is that all they wanted in return was the gold, the silver and the precious ancient artifacts for their museums, as commemorative mementos of another pack of rehabilitated savages.

Vincent drove through Zero Point into sector G-7 and continued down *Shahra-i-Faisal* towards F-8. The beautiful and colossal Faisal Mosque loomed in the foreground like a massive white Bedouin tent, erected in the shadows of the lush Margalla Hills. Unable to locate his turn into the sector in time, he drove all the way to the mosque and parked in its vast parking lot, admiring its unique architecture as he fumbled with the map.

After acclimatizing himself with the layout of sector F-8, he proceeded down Kohistan Road looking for street number 12. There was Street 10 and then 14 but no 12. Frustrated, wishing for his indispensable Magellan GPS to magically take him to his destination, he went around the whole sector in his futile attempt to find the elusive street. Finally, putting his ego aside, he asked for help and got a lesson in the peculiar geography of Islamabad's street layout from a bakery owner across the road from Street 10. Streets in Islamabad are not always where they are supposed to be. A product of some inexplicable whim, the streets suddenly abandon a perfectly reasonable grid system and branch out of earlier streets like kindling of a wild tree, making it impossible to predict their location if one does not anticipate branches this idiosyncrasy. So, Street 12 does not follow Street 11, rather it comes off it while the latter comes off an unnamed street that offshoots from Street 10. Vincent's brain was in a tizzy when he finally reached his destination and confirmed the house number. It was a relatively new Spanish style structure with earth colored Rockwall finish and dark orange shingles. Heavy shrubbery and an eight-foot wall customary for the neighborhood, bordered the front, secured by a black wrought iron gate. He parked his car across the narrow street and observed the neighborhood. Apart from a few kids playing cricket on the far side of the dead-end street, there was no one else visible. Adults of the street were either still at work, or were staying inside for an afternoon nap. He took his Glock out, fastened the silencer to its short barrel and carefully surveyed his surroundings once again; nothing had changed. A small side door next to the main gate was unlocked. He quickly crossed the road, and walked through the open gate, opening it just enough to minimize the slight squeak made by its rusting hinges.

Pervaiz had spent the whole morning in his study, watching the video on his computer. Most of the recording focused on the crowd. One could hear the loud and emotionally charged rhetoric of local political leaders energizing the crowd before the main attraction began, and they were as usual, highly successful in those efforts, proven by the crowd's fervent response.

"For too long, our country has been a victim of the politics of money, dominated by only a handful of privileged individuals. For too long, a few greedy families have exploited our people. For too long, the hardworking poor have been struggling to maintain a roof over their head and *roti* on their plates . . . ." A local ex-provincial assembly member, scion of a wealthy political family that had been in the circles of power for decades, was talking at the top of his voice and successfully heard over throngs of screaming fans, ". . . but not anymore! The time for the people has come. The time has come for the poor of this country, the down-trodden of this country to rise against this oppression and take back what is our right. We need a leader who is ready to lead us through this. Someone who understands . . . someone who cares . . . and that person . . .?" The politician, dressed in a raw silk *kurta* and donning oversized gold rings, who had not experienced a single moment of poverty in his life, asked the crowd, waving his hand; his gold Rolex wrist watch sparkling in the bright sunlight.

"Malik Jahangir," the crowd shouted back and erupted in a thunderous cheer, as Malik Jahangir appeared on the stage waving to the crowd. The crowd went wild, as he moved to the edge of the stage, while the police made desperate attempts to contain the crowd, unable to stop the torrent of supporters flocking the stage in an attempt to shake his hand.

"How can anyone protect these politicians in this kind of chaos? They must have a death wish," Pervaiz shook his head.

It took another five minutes or so before the applause died just enough for him to clear his throat and then motion them to settle down before he began his speech. "My dear countrymen, brothers and sisters, Malik Jahangir says his *salaam* to you," he started with his signature line and the ardent crowd erupted into another round of passionate applause.

Malik Jahangir was talking about his plan to eliminate poverty, ensure justice, and free Kashmir from India, et cetera. Pervaiz' attention, however, was focused on the police officer standing behind the podium. There was a private security detail surrounding the stage, and one of the guards was standing next to the officer in question. As Pervaiz watched closely, just before the shots, the security guard took a step towards his right moving from his position right behind the target towards a safer corner, obviously getting out of the line of fire. He zoomed in on the face; he appeared to be a foreigner, as were the other members of the security detail, but this one did not seem to be extremely focused with a stern look like the others. He had a strange, relaxed smile on his face as if he thrived on moments like this. Pervaiz played the scene back and forth a few times, then looked at his watch and jumped. It was getting late and he had to be at Dainty's by four.

The reflection he saw in the mirror was not the most flattering one. Remnants of a rough night, and an equally stressful morning, etched on a stubbly face with dark circles under the eyes made him cringe. He took a quick shower, shaved, and decided to get to Dainty's early in order to grab a bite as everyone in the family had gone to the *valima* reception.

It was sunny outside. Mild temperatures and a slight breeze from the north ricocheted off Margalla hills and added to the perfect ingredients of this autumn afternoon. As he walked out through his front door, a cool breeze gently caressed his face and instantly brushed off any lingering traces of fatigue. He looked at his front lawn and realized that some of his flowerbeds were getting dry. Fanatic as he was about keeping his flowerbeds in excellent condition, he could not let go and leave without attending to them. He pulled a hose from behind the bougainvillea bush and placed it in the flowerbed that flanked the rocky walkway connecting his front entrance with the driveway. As he was turning the faucet on, he heard the slight squeak made by the opening gate and turned around. The face appearing through the side gate looked very familiar.

"Where have I seen this face?" he asked himself the question but half-way through it, the answer flashed through his brain in the form of a clip from the film he had seen all through the morning . . . over and over again. The relaxed smile, the look of feeling pleasure from every step he took was unmistakable. The stranger did not say anything. Dressed in a casual outfit, a pair of khakis with a light tan jacket; he casually nodded to Pervaiz as if dropping in for a social call; his cold and ubiquitous smile broadened. Pervaiz, in shock and frozen in the moment, felt his heart skipping a beat as a chilling sensation going down the spine made him shiver. The stranger took a step towards him as his left hand emerged from under his half unzipped jacket. A flash of sunlight reflecting off the sleek black metal was the last thing Pervaiz saw before hearing a muffled thud. A piercing sensation of intense heat ripped through his chest and then everything went black.

CHAPTER 23

WESTRIDGE III, RAWALPINDI

Sunday 4:45 p.m.

The political atmosphere in Pakistan has always been dominated by its feudal system. During the ninety-year reign of the British, from the fall of the Mughal Empire in 1857 until the partition of United India into Pakistan and modern day India in 1947, these feudal lords ensured peace and obedience across the sub-continent. The British were exceptionally munificent to any of the colonial citizens who had shown loyalty to the crown, on many occasions acting at odds with the interests of their fellow countrymen and women. In return for their allegiance, they were awarded by the British Empire, a series of coveted titles like *Khan, Khan Bahadur* and *Sardar,* as well as large pieces of land. These titles gave them absolute power over their vast territories and the people who lived on them.

At the time of partition, the most notable of the leaders behind the struggle for independence came out of the Muslim minority areas because they realized the need for an independent country by experiencing the plight of the Muslim minority in India first-hand. These visionaries and architects of Pakistan, however, could not compete politically with the established, and better known feudal powers that existed in the Muslim majority areas of India that eventually became Pakistan, and failed to maintain their leadership role in the future of the country.

Suddenly, a young Pakistan was left to be run by British loyalists who not only were unable to identify with those who had experienced the worst aspects of being a minority, that is, losing everything, from their property to their jobs, endangering their lives and losing those of their dear ones when they migrated to Pakistan in search of independence, but they also could not understand what an independent existence really meant. Politics in Pakistan become all about the power of the political monarchies and the sheer business of amassing money, predictably passing its reigns from one political dynasty to the other in every election. As someone had once said, "Democracy in Pakistan is defined as a government *off* the people, *buy* the people, *far* the people." Recently, however, things were changing, especially in the urban constituencies, with a new wave of younger and more charismatic politicians of humble roots, who had defiantly stood up to face the old political powerhouses, and Naveed Khan was one of them.

Naveed Khan was still recovering from events of the day before. His success with the young and the educated of Pakistan had not come without a price. In his struggle to fight for a dramatic change in the political system that had dominated the country for decades, he had stepped on many toes. The guardians of a failed democratic system, wrapped in the shroud of feudal dominance had been weary of his transgressions. He understood that it was a dangerous game, but he did not see any other way to get his message across to the masses, overburdened by their struggles to make ends meet, mesmerized by the often hollow promises of a better future, and terrified by the prospect of losing their present by angering their benefactors. So far, the threats had been subdued, subliminal at best, but now, the hypothetical dangers of this game had evolved into a stark reality.

Naveed's meeting with Raja Safdar Hussein, barely a month ago, was also strange, as it brought two opposite poles in Pakistani politics together. On one end of the spectrum, it was the quintessential feudal lord luring the people with his hereditary mystique, while endlessly courting the powers that were responsible for their plight in the first place. On the other, it was the one politician who stood against everything that was wrong with this political monarchy. Raja Safdar had contacted Naveed off and on over the last month, and their conversations had been peculiarly civil. Frequently, the topic had been Malik Jahangir and his policies of centralizing the natural resources, and involving China to directly venture into oil and gas, as well as mineral exploration in the Southwest region. Naveed believed in total non-reliance, no matter how friendly the other country maybe; it was time for Pakistan to get out of policies that perpetuated its mounting debt. He was also weary of the blatant, West-leaning policies of politicians like Raja Safdar, however, as cautious as he had been; he had repeatedly used the information obtained during these conversations about Malik Jahangir's recent inclinations in his speeches around the country.

Initially, Naveed was ready to brush it off as a onetime meeting, but his trip to Peshawar changed everything and he decided to keep Safdar as an unlikely ally. He did not have to agree with his agenda, or to make appearances with him, but in this dog-eat-dog world of politics, having him in his corner did not seem like an ill-advised choice. The sniper attack on his convoy in Peshawar was a wake-up call for him. While he had vowed not to compromise on his principles because of fear, he had realized the harsh reality, that he could only achieve his goals if he lived to see that day. He was thankful to Raja Safdar and his resources during the incident. Though his driver had survived the wounds and was recovering well, his vehicle was never recovered. The episode had shaken him to the core, leading to many sleepless nights, until he resolved it in his mind that if he wanted to continue on the path he had chosen for himself, he must not let these events get to him.

The assassination had suddenly brought back suppressed memories of that fateful day. He had accompanied Raja Safdar to the funeral and had just returned home. As soon as he walked in, he kicked off his shoes and slumped on the sofa in front of the TV. Cricket was on. Pakistan was playing its traditional nemesis India, playing for the triangular cup played in Sharjah. Last five overs were on; Pakistan needed 46 runs with two wickets in hand. It was getting interesting as a towering six over mid-wicket brought the target to within 40 runs. He pushed his worries back and sat up straight cheering the national team.

"*Baba*, you're back!"

He turned at the sound of an excited voice.

It was his six-year-old daughter Amna. The sight of her made him forget about all that worried him as a broad smile brightened his tired face.

"Oh my little doll," he scooped her up, kissed her on both cheeks and sat her on his lap.

"*Kaun jeet raha hai?*" she pointed at the TV wondering who was winning.

"*Pakistan hee jeetay ga, dekh layna*, we are the best; let's watch and see what happens."

The doorbell rang just as he was celebrating Pakistan's one wicket win. He told Amna to go into the kitchen and opened the front door. Two tall men in white *shalwar* suites and grim expressions stood at the front porch.

"*Salaam alaikum Khan Sahib*, I am DSP Jamil Sheikh from Investigations section," the taller of the two, holding up his ID, spoke in refined Urdu with a hint of accent suggestive of his southern Punjabi origins. He was an imposing man in his late thirties, with broad shoulders, a thick neck with a crew-cut and a closely trimmed beard that was turning white at his chin. He had dark, keen eyes under a tanned and furrowed forehead. As he talked, he continued to shift his gaze constantly as if he was avoiding direct eye contact with him. "I am in plain clothes so as not to alarm anyone and I apologize for this intrusion, but I need you to accompany us to police headquarter. DIG *sahib* would like to talk to you."

"What is it about?" Naveed asked firmly, surprised by the visitors' demand as he scrutinized the ID to verify its validity. "If the DIG wants to see me, he is welcome to visit me at my home any time he wants."

"Sir, it is not that simple. Our orders are clear, and we have to get you to his office as soon as possible."

Naveed was perplexed by this situation. He could not think of any reason, which required his presence at the Deputy Inspector General's office. At first, he was going to demand that anyone needing to talk to him must come to him, but then the politician in him decided to think calmly. He did not need to create a scandal so close to the elections, and what if this was in regards to national security, requiring a camouflaged approach. Still, using such an unorthodox approach did not make much sense.

"OK, just give me a few minutes," he walked back in, quickly changed into a pair of black cotton trousers under a blue argyle cardigan and told his wife that he needed to go out for a while, promising that he would try his best to be back in time for dinner. He did not divulge any details so as not to alarm her. His schedule had been very hectic recently, and today was one of those rare nights that he happened to be home for a family meal. His personal guards were standing by the main gate. As they saw him emerge from the house, all dressed to go out, they started to get ready in order to accompany him but he waved at them to stay on guard.

"Khan *sahib*, take one of us with you. It is not safe; there is a lot of danger outside, especially today," one of them said politely and discreetly as he eyed the two strangers waiting by their vehicle.

"Everything is alright Jamal Khan," Naveed tapped his loyal bodyguard on the shoulder, "I am in safe hands with these good men," he looked in the direction of his two visitors and hopped into the unmarked Suzuki bearing official license plates that was parked in the driveway.

In the dimly lit office of the Deputy Inspector General (Investigations) of Police, DIG Tariq Khawaja sat behind his desk lost in deep thought. Tiny beads of sweat shining under the 100-watt overhead light slowly rolled down his slightly balding and deeply creased forehead. He looked tired; his eyes were devoid of the usual sparkle of ever-present energy that exuded from him. He had spent most of the past hour in this position poring over documents scattered about on his otherwise organized desk. It was an oversized wooden desk, covered with official green felt, standard issue for senior police officers at the headquarters. He had not even turned on the lamp sitting on the table, even when the shadows grew longer and sunlight faded outside the narrow window overlooking the courtyard.

The phone rang; its shrill bell echoed through the large room, startling him. He picked up on the first ring

"Tariq Khawaja speaking," he replied and then listened intently for a few seconds, then hung up, still in deep thought.

"Is he coming?" A calm, authoritative voice asked from a sofa tucked in a dark corner of the room. From his desk, Tariq Khawaja could only see a silhouette with a smoldering cigar engulfed in thick smoke.

"Yes . . . they should be here in about ten minutes?"

"Good, I am glad he did not resist. I don't want any unnecessary complications. Are you sure you can handle this?"

"I'll be fine . . . I know how to do this," Tariq Khawaja sounded irritated, annoyed by the patronizing tone of his visitor.

"Good," Malik Nisar took a long deep puff from his cigar, "I'll be in the room next door," then walked away, leaving a trail of thick white smoke behind him.

CHAPTER 24

DAINTY'S, F-8 MARKAZ

Sunday 4:40 p.m.

Kamran looked at his watch again. It was past four thirty, but Pervaiz was nowhere to be seen. His chicken corn soup was getting cold. He took a few spoonfuls and then sat back, sipping on his coke; he looked at the watch again; it was 4:44. He was getting worried now and tried his cell phone again but there was still no answer. Trying his home ended in the same result. He decided to leave and stop at Pervaiz' home on the way back but he did not have a good feeling about this.

F-8 *Markaz* is a series of shops in a randomly arranged rectangle situated in the middle of the sector. *Markaz*, or focal point, is the geographical center of every sector in Islamabad and depending on its location, varies from a small utility mall to a conglomeration of fancy restaurants and shops, with everything from old books and fancy boutiques to handcrafted walnut furniture on display. F-8 *Markaz*, in terms of size and variety, falls somewhere in the middle.

Entertaining the possibility of a miscommunication, Kamran walked out of Dainty's and walked up and down the street looking for Pervaiz' Suzuki but did not see it anywhere. He picked up a pack of mints from the kiosk next-door and started walking towards his car parked across the street.

He was bending down to get in the car when he felt the slight vibration of his phone in his pocket. He was surprised to see two missed calls. In his preoccupation with looking for Pervaiz' car, he had not been able to register an incoming call. Kamran scrolled through the incoming calls but did not recognize the number; however, he could see that there was a voicemail. He checked his voicemail and the message shocked him. It was from Pervaiz' wife Nadia and she sounded frantic.

"Kamran please call me as soon as you can, something has happened to Pervaiz."

Kamran did not like the sound of it. His mind was racing, *"What could have happened to Pervaiz?"* A thousand possibilities ran through his mind and then focused on the one that he dreaded the most, and had kept him up most of the night. It was the possibility of someone finding out what they were after; the mere thought of it sent a chill down his spine. His heart started to beat at a frantic pace as with numbing fingers, he started to dial a number. He did not have to wait too long after the first ring.

"What happened?"

"I don't know, I just don't know . . . !" Nadia was hysterical and could not complete the sentence.

"Nadia *bhabi* . . . please . . . please calm down, you have to tell me what happened."

"Someone shot him!"

"What!" Kamran slumped back against his car, "When . . . how . . . why?"

"I don't know," Nadia said sobbing, "one of our neighbors found him . . . he is in surgery right now . . . I don't know what to do . . . why is this happening?"

"Where are you right now . . . what hospital did they take him to?" Kamran's mind started to churn, trying to figure out how to get there as fast as he could. He could not take any chances. If those behind this had any suspicion that he might survive, they would go after him, wherever he was.

"He is at *Shifa* . . . I am almost there myself."

"Hang in there *bhabi,* I'll be there in 15 minutes."

Kamran had never driven this fast in his life. Fortunately, traffic on this Sunday evening was reasonable during his drive from F-8 to *Shifa* International Hospital. He drove right up to the main entrance but there was no place to park, so he drove his car onto the greenbelt median dividing the two-way main road like many others in the same predicament, and ran towards the emergency entrance. It did not take him long to locate Nadia sitting on a bench resting her head on an adjacent stone pillar. Her face appeared pale as if all the blood had been sucked out of it. Smeared makeup on her cheeks showed traces of countless tears that she had shed. She looked up at him when she heard his approaching footsteps but continued to stare right through him. Her eyes were dry now, as if there were no more tears left to be shed. Her lips quivered briefly but words froze before making any sound. Tears appeared again at the brink of her eyelids as the dams broke and flooded her eyes again. Kamran slowly walked to her, and sat down beside her on the bench; she didn't say anything, and neither did he. She buried her head in his embrace. He gently held her head between his two hands, kissed her on the forehead and then held her close to him as she continued to cry softly.

"Did you hear anything?" Kamran asked, finally gathering his emotions.

"No, he is still in surgery, Kami *Bhai* . . . is he . . . is he going to be okay?"

"He'll be fine. I will make sure nothing happens to him. I'll go and find out what is going on."

Vincent was not happy, a branch of bougainvillea was in his line of sight and he could not get an open head shot. He went for the next best thing and aimed at his heart, and he did not miss. He quietly ran towards Pervaiz, lying still on the marble floor with a dark red circle growing slowly around his left breast pocket. There was no sign of activity. Vincent walked around his victim towards the open main door and pulled him back through it into the hallway. He walked by a small table placed in the hallway and threw it down on the floor. Next he entered the office and turned the writing table upside down. He opened the drawers and threw papers all over the floor, making it look like the aftermath of a burglary. He quickly ran up the stairs towards the master bedroom, opened the closets and stuffed his pocket with anything valuable that he could see. It only took him a few minutes to accomplish that and then he was back, standing by the door looking at his victim. While in the office he had not seen any sign of the videotape; he quickly ran through Pervaiz' pockets and there it was, right in his breast pocket. The mini DV was covered with blood and severely damaged, as the bullet seemed to have hit it on its way into the chest wall. He took a plastic bag out, placed the mini DV in it, and put it in his pocket. He could barely see any movement in the chest as the circle of blood around his victim grew rapidly. Satisfied with what he saw, he took out his pistol and aimed at Pervaiz' head to finish the job. He was about to pull the trigger when he heard some sounds coming from the house next door and stopped, making sure that he was fully concealed behind the half ajar front door. Sounds of children playing next door were getting closer to the wall; he quickly took his gloves off and walked out through the kitchen door. Standing in the shadow of a narrow alley between the house and its boundary wall, he put on a baseball cap and pulled the visor down to partially conceal his face, then made sure that he looked presentable before walking calmly through the open side gate.

Only a few moments had gone by when a tennis ball flew into the yard from the house next door, courtesy of an afternoon game of backyard cricket. A young boy who was given the task of retrieving it followed. He must have been the batsman who hit it over the wall. After climbing over the boundary wall, he went straight for the ball. He was about to turn around and head back when he saw the open door and what appeared to be a foot partially visible through it. He cautiously walked towards the open door, "Uncle Pervaiz, is that you?" There was no answer so he kept going, peaked in through the door . . . and screamed.

The ambulance did not take too long to come and before long it was on its way towards the emergency room. The bullet had miraculously missed the heart; however, it had nicked the thoracic aorta causing a small leak and had lodged itself in the liver. The bleeding was perfuse, requiring urgent transfusions, while the thoracic as well as a general surgeon simultaneously began their race against time.

Kamran walked into the operation theater, escorted by a surgical registrar who, after learning his identity, did not hesitate for a second in providing him with a gown and mask before leading him into the surgical suite. Kamran wanted to help in any shape or form that was possible, but he was too nervous. He felt his hands shaking as his rapidly beating heart seemed to jump out of his chest at any moment. A leading team of surgeons was already on the case; there was nothing more he could do in there. Nadia needed him more, at least until her family arrived. He turned around and walked back to the lobby. As he updated Nadia and then walked her towards the waiting room, he did not notice a tall man with sunglasses sitting by the main door, observing his every move.

CHAPTER 25

Sunday 5:32 p.m.

Naveed Khans at alone, in a small anteroom waiting for his meeting with the DIG. Every moment that passed left him more and more angry. He did not deserve to be treated like this. He had met DIG Khawaja before and he seemed like a smart and reasonable man, but this unusual situation was making him very uncomfortable. The characterless room was sparse, besides a small worktable and three wooden chairs. Walls were standard governmental whitewash and bare other than a generic police calendar, and a large black and white clock that seemed too slow as far as Naveed was concerned. An old ceiling fan squeaked as it slowly rotated giving the stale air in the room a little bit of relief. He had been there for a mere twenty minutes that somehow felt like hours. He got up and started pacing back and forth and finally decided to call his personal assistant to inform him of this unplanned meeting. He was about to take the cell phone out of his pocket when the inside door opened and a stern faced Tariq Khawaja, dressed in his uniform, entered the room.

"I am sorry to inconvenience you Khan *Sahib*," he said politely. His eyes lowered, hands loosely locked in front of him, "but this is extremely important and there is no easier way to address this."

"I am not sure that I understand. What is this all about?" a perplexed Naveed replied.

"Please follow me to my office so we can talk in a more private setting," said, DIG Khawaja as he turned around and walked out the door.

The DIG's office was lit much brighter than it was an hour ago. Naveed looked around. It was in stark contrast to the naked surroundings that he had endured waiting for this meeting. The décor, though simple, demonstrated the good taste of its occupant. Walls were the standard whitewash but adorned with watercolor paintings of rural Pakistan, depicting cattle and stacks of wheat during harvest. The far wall, however, was painted a light yellow and in stark contrast to the paintings, was decorated with three black-and-white Ansel Adams photographs in black and gold frames. A medium-sized blue and maroon Afghan rug sat in the middle of the room in front of his desk. The narrow, west facing window overlooking the courtyard was letting the orange glow of the setting sun, adding even more character to the spacious room.

DIG Tariq Khawaja walked around the bulky desk and sat down in his plush leather back chair as he motioned Naveed to take a seat on one of the woven wooden chairs across it. It was getting dark outside; very soon, a streetlight illuminated a part of the courtyard, playing a game of light and shadows with a giant pipal tree fluttering gently in the light breeze. Tariq Khawaja shifted uneasily in his chair, cleared his throat twice, taking his time while he came up with the right words, aware of the fierce stare of an increasingly impatient Naveed.

"Khan *Sahib,*" he finally spoke; his manner was cautious, his speech halted, unsure. "The reason for this inconvenience is a very delicate matter. You may be fully aware of it, although I hope that such is not the case."

"I am not following you, and to tell you the truth, if you don't come to the point right now, I'm getting up and walking out!"

"Okay Khan *Sahib*, I'll come right to the point. During our investigation of yesterday's assassination, we have been able to trace the car that was used by the alleged assassin."

"That's very good . . . congratulations . . . finally, the police have been able to find something useful," sarcasm exuded from every syllable in Naveed's curt response, ". . . but, what does that have to do with me?"

"The car's registration traces it back to you Khan *Sahib*. One of the guns found in the car is also registered to you."

"This is ridiculous, what are you trying to say?"

DIG toyed with his next few words very carefully before responding slowly. "In the light of available evidence . . . I have no choice but to detain you under suspicion . . . for the murder of Malik Jahangir," Tariq Khawaja uttered the words while staring at the top of his table. He could not bear to look into the eyes of a person he had come to admire greatly over the last few years.

Naveed did not say anything. It appeared as if all the blood was drained from his face. His eyes did not show any hint of a reaction, their bright sparkle lost in a dull cloud that now lingered in their depths. He could not believe what he was hearing. He could see DIG Khawaja trying to say something to him, but he could not hear anything. It was an eerie silence heralding the arrival of a fierce tempest.

"It's happening!" he mumbled in a barely audible whisper.

"What?" Tariq Khawaja did not understand.

"I was warned. I didn't think they had the guts to pull it off. It's really happening."

"What are you talking about?"

"I have nothing to do with this," Naveed sounded better, his voice stronger, more confident.

"That isn't for me to decide. My job is to collect and study the evidence. The rest is up to our judicial system."

"That's reassuring!" For the first time, a slight smile appeared on Naveed Khan's tired face. "Exactly what are you referring to . . . collection of evidence, or its interpretation?"

Tariq Khawaja suddenly felt relaxed, recognizing the sarcasm. He was enjoying this surprisingly candid moment.

"To be honest, I'm not too thrilled about either one of those."

"I can see your concern Khan *Sahib,* but I must reassure you that I will do everything in my power to make sure that all the evidence is true, and is not tempered with."

"Where am I staying tonight?" Naveed asked.

"Right here, until we have an official arraignment in the morning."

"Can I call my wife?"

"Go ahead," Tariq Khawaja said softly as he pushed the telephone towards him.

Through a slightly open side door, Malik Nisar heard the whole conversation. He was satisfied with the way it was handled. Tariq Khawaja was a seasoned police officer and he did not expect any less from him. This situation needed a delicate approach, although if it was him in DIG's shoes, he wouldn't have been so sensitive to the feelings of his cousin's alleged killer. He looked at his watch. It was six thirty.

"Wait till the press gets a hold of this." he thought. The exact timing of disclosing this to the media was a tricky question. Holding it under wraps till the morning was a reasonable thing to do. He thought about it for a few moments and then smiled, as he pulled out his cell phone and quickly punched in a text message to the editor of the state run daily, *Pakistan Times*.

"Naveed Khan arrested. Evidence suggests involvement in MJ murder. Source anonymous. Details to follow. Wait for cue."

CHAPTER 26

One week ago

Senator Jack Donaldson stood at the head of the table beside a large pull down screen, waiting for the board of directors to respond. Dressed in a form fitting, charcoal grey pinstriped suit, and a dark maroon and black checkered tie, his large frame towered above the low set table, silhouetted against the warm glow of Texas sun behind him. A map of South Asia marked with the location of current oil fields and future exploratory targets, served as background on the power point presentation.

Chief Geologist Larry Jordan had just finished his elaborate presentation, outlining the South Asian Strategy for Intervention (SASI) plan. He had outlined possible areas of interest for future exploration and drilling based on preliminary geological surveys. The board of directors who were also the principal investors had been very patient during the lengthy presentation packed with technical jargon, and they were now engaged in a quiet discussion around the massive rectangular conference table.

Butch Donaldson was pacing back and forth impatiently, trying to read their faces as they leafed through informational binders in front of them, making up their minds about one of the most important decisions in his business career; not only his company's future, but also his potential presidential bid depended heavily on its success.

Oil production in the local fields had diminished steadily over the last decade. While the industry had continued to be a profitable venture, it had gradually moved from the echelons of a rapidly growing empire to a closely-knit gentlemen's club. Investors had found sexier alternatives to the now politically incorrect oil industry by investing in the tech companies, and recently even more appropriately, in alternative fuel sources. AmeriGulf had endured dwindling share prices during the last two quarters, and it needed a unanimous nod here to boost its market standings.

Over the last few years, due to increasing demands on his public and political life, Senator Donaldson had stayed in the background of his office and company affairs, leaving all but the most vital decisions to a team of trusted associates. Recently, however, he had been forced to take an active interest in the daily decision-making process and had traveled regularly between Houston and Washington, maintaining a delicate balancing act. This meeting was extremely important to him, as he stood in the boardroom of a company that he had built. It had been his vision that had helped it grow from a few peripheral oil fields in eastern Texas to its current status as a multinational conglomerate, spanning over four continents.

Outside the tall glass windows of the boardroom, the view seemed serene. The traffic at the intersection of Walker and Louisiana from fourteen stories above the streets appeared to be in slow motion. Across the street, the glass windows of Shell Plaza reflected the afternoon sun from its rounded façade like bolts of energy beams, a surreal reminder of recent efforts by the Shell Corporation to take over AmeriGulf.

Butch Donaldson turned around to face the board of directors. It appeared that they were ready to vote. He bent at the waist, resting his outstretched hands at the edge of the conference table.

"So, gentlemen, the time to embrace the future is now. I think that Larry has enlightened us with an excellent presentation about opportunities that we have before us. The future of AmeriGulf, the hopes and dreams of our shareholders depend on it. These opportunities hold the power to transform this company into an international phenomenon beyond our wildest imagination. It also holds the key to play a central role in the geopolitical structure of South Asia." Butch Donaldson finished his statement and let go of the table. His grip holding the table's edge had tightened during his statement, his knuckles turning white under its pressure.

"How accurate are these reports?" Ben Lewis, a short man with thick bifocals who owned a cargo shipping company on the Gulf Coast asked in his distinctive squeaky voice. His accent giving away his humble, country roots in western Texas.

"Ben, I'm surprised you're even asking the question. You're well aware of the expertise and immaculate credentials of the team of experts that created this report. Some of the top geologists, statisticians and chemical engineers have analyzed the terrain, subsoil composition and core samples for the last ten months before marking targets for further exploration."

He turned around to address the entire room; his imposing silhouette, outlined by sunlight coming from the large window further enhanced his mythical dimensions. He walked to the table, pulled back his chair and sat down at its edge so that his upper body leaned into and rested on the table in front of him.

"Gentlemen, the Southwestern region of Pakistan, also known as the Baluchistan province has been the largest source of natural assets in the Indo-Pak subcontinent. Pakistan has an estimated 25.1 trillion cubic feet of proven gas reserves, of which 19 trillion are located in Baluchistan. Various multinational oil and gas contractors are already eyeing extensive exploration in Baluchistan; and this interest in the natural resources doesn't end with oil and gas. Baluchistan has one of the largest reserves of copper and gold in the world, and bids for those contracts are only just beginning," he picked up the folder sitting in front of him and opened it. "Please open your copies to page twelve and look at the bold text in second paragraph."

According to the *Oil and Gas Journal* (OGJ-Environmental News Service, October 2006), Pakistan has proven oil reserves of 300 million barrels most of which are located in Baluchistan, but there are other estimates that place these oil reserves at over 6 trillion barrels, which include possible oilfields both on and off the coastal region.

He paused briefly, and took a quick sip from a glass of water in front of him. When he looked up, his expression had changed: his countenance solemn, his eyes intensely focused. Within a few seconds, he had transformed from a nervous pitchman to the shrewd entrepreneur he was known and feared for. The board members took notice instantly. Donaldson continued:

"This is a golden opportunity. Uncharted waters, saturated with treasures that have eluded us for decades due to ongoing power struggle between 'Baluchi Nationalists' and Islamabad, but finally, we have laid down the infrastructure needed to ensure our success."

"All of this sounds very exciting Butch, but Exxon and BP have been trying hard for years to establish their base in that region, and even with their immense influence on local economy and politics, they

have not been able to strengthen their presence in Baluchistan."
Jonathan McDaniel spoke up from the back of the room.

Jonathan, the youngest of the board members and arguably the
most handsome with his flowing blond hair, sharp looks and lean
athletic built, was the owner of one of the fastest growing luxury
construction companies in the Southwest. "I have been trying to land a
development project on Gawadar port for the past six months but it's
not easy to get it passed through Pakistani bureaucracy. You cannot
achieve it without a wide open cash flow, something, as it seems, I
have a lot less than a few other billionaire developers, most of them
Chinese!" he sneered in disgust, "And I absolutely refuse to bribe their
bureaucrats. Each one of them in return, wants a furnished villa in
Scottsdale."

"But that's where our project becomes exciting," Butch replied
with a smile and an understanding nod, as he got up and walked
around the conference table tapping the backs of his colleagues, going
all around until he was standing right behind Jonathan and put both his
hands on his shoulders.

"Over the last few months, I've been able to make a few good
friends in that part of the world. I have assurances from some of the
most powerful players that finalizing our project is only a matter of
time."

"But what about the upcoming elections? How do you know that
the new government will honor these commitments?" McDaniel asked.

Butch Donaldson smiled and rolled his eyes. "It seems my friend,
that you haven't been paying much attention to politics in that part of
the world. Governments change, titles change, even parties may come
and go, but the reins of power always remain in the hands of a chosen
few, and we have always made sure that not only their grip on power
remains strong, but that they are also extremely well taken care of.
These evergreen politicians visit the United States frequently and are
showered with our most generous hospitality. Their wives go on the
most lavish shopping sprees from Rodeo Drive to Fifth Avenue, and it
is no coincidence that their children end up in the best US universities.
My friend, their cooperation is the last thing you have to worry about."

Decision of the board was unanimous, as well as favorable.

CHAPTER 27

SHIFA INTERNATIONAL HOSPITAL ISLAMABAD

Sunday 7:18 p.m.

Shifa International was teeming with purposeful activity. Inside its light green stucco exterior was a labyrinth of long and narrow hallways paved with concrete chips flooring, clinics, waiting rooms, and inpatient floors. The level of cleanliness achieved on the property was strikingly above the average Pakistani standard. Doctors, nurses, orderlies and medical students crisscrossed each other at high speeds, acknowledging each other with a polite nod at best. Loud sounds of patients and family members chattering in adjacent waiting rooms echoed from their stark walls. Started as a joint effort by overseas Pakistani physicians, mostly those moving back home from the United States, *Shifa* had emerged as one of the leading and technologically advanced institutions in Pakistan,

Kamran stood by the glass door, looking at the activity inside the intensive care unit room eight. Pervaiz had just been brought in from the operation theater. A team of nurses was rearranging and reattaching a multitude of tubes and wires hanging from his body. He had survived the long and complicated procedure that included repairing his liver and descending aorta, as well as closure of the defect in his diaphragm. A chest tube had been placed to keep his right lung from collapsing. He had lost a lot of blood prior to the procedure requiring multiple units in blood transfusion, and there was no way to tell if there was any permanent brain damage due to a lack of oxygen supply.

Within a few minutes of arrival, the staff had put everything in its place like a perfectly timed, well-oiled machine. Sights and sounds of medical technology filled the brightly lit but sterile room lined with light green ceramic tiles. The electronic beeping sounds of the cardiac monitors broke the silence every few seconds or so, almost perfectly synchronized with the monotonous hum and intermittent swoosh of the ventilator that was keeping Pervaiz alive. Nadia entered the small room, sat down on a chair next to him and held his hand, resting her head on the edge of the bed.

He watched them fondly for a few minutes, his mind racing back to a similar autumn afternoon fifteen years ago when he was first introduced to a shy, bespectacled transfer student from Nishter Medical College, Multan, and they had formed an instant bond. The remaining four years of Medical College and then four more of post-graduate training raced through his mind like a runaway train. Carefree years of practically living on the streets of Lahore, late night meals in *Gawal Mundi,* shopping sprees at 'Liberty Market' and aimless motorcycle rides on Canal Bank Road, culminating in occasional, but intriguing meanderings in front of Kinnaird College for Women brought a smile to his face. He looked at Nadia's grief stricken face through the glass partition and felt his heart sinking. It was he, who had introduced him to her, a friend of his sister at a wedding during their medical officer days. Tears started to fog his vision as he turned around to leave. He stopped briefly at the door to say a quick prayer and then walked away. There was not much he could do here; he had some important decisions to make.

CHAPTER 28

Sunday 7:30 p.m.

Vincent Portelli felt very tired. He was not satisfied with the way things went. He was really good at what he did and it wasn't like him to leave so many loose ends. He was still trying to adjust to his new surroundings, but despite his best efforts, he had not been able to feel totally comfortable in his current assignment. Something was wrong, something was bothering him from the moment that he landed in Pakistan, but he could not put his finger on it. He was ninety percent sure that the doctor's wound was fatal, but it was the ten percent part that was making him cringe. He would have finished the job if it weren't for those pesky little kids; he would have shot him in the head and then he would not be in this predicament. It was getting dark, and he realized that he had not had anything to eat since his early brunch at the hotel. He saw the sign for a small restaurant called The Red Onion and decided to take a quick bite before planning his next move.

He ordered a cheeseburger, fries and a coke. He had an uneasy feeling about this whole debacle. He had no idea how much Kamran knew, but he was sure that he posed a significant risk. He had noticed an unnerving sense of commitment and determination in him that made him believe that he was not going to let this be until he got some answers. This was a big problem in itself, enough of a reason for Vincent to get rid of him.

The burger looked exceptionally good. He could not be sure whether it was the food or just the plain fact that his stomach was in knots from hunger pangs, but he did not care. Assassination targets could wait, his appetite couldn't. The first spurt of ketchup out of the bottle was explosive, splattering the bright red condiment all over a bed of fries and the side of coleslaw. Vincent examined the mess, amused by its analogy to the thoughts going through his mind. It was an intriguing omen; he shrugged his shoulders and smiled as he bit into his scrumptious burger, *"I hope it is not as messy in real life."*

Finding Kamran was not a problem. He had confirmed that Kamran was not planning to check out until the next morning, and even so, he did not want to rush his plan. Vincent gently and habitually tapped on the GPS receiver in his pocket to ensure it was there. As long as he was within ten miles of his target, he did not need to worry. He was much more concerned about the condition his earlier target was in. Just the fact that the doctors had gotten an opportunity to save him was worrisome. He did not want to add another victim to the list of high profile doctors associated with Malik Jahangir's assassination.

He needed to wait but that could mean tailing Kamran and being very patient, and then there was the matter of the woman with him last night. Who was she? He did not have a clear answer, but he was convinced that if he stayed close to Kamran, he would lead him to her. His Glock needed a break. This one had to look like an accident, and that meant finding out everything about him. His schedules and routine, his passions, his weaknesses, and of course, about any skeletons that could rattle his closet, and he knew just the person who could help him with that. As soon as he finished his meal, he took out his phone and dialed a number that might as well have been etched on his brain.

Kamran needed fresh air. It was dark already, and he had been aimlessly driving through Islamabad for the last half hour, finally ending up at Aabpara Market, a famous late night hangout. Holding a styrofoam cup of hot coffee, he sat down on one of the stairs, leading up to the raised sidewalk and row of shops. Nightlife was busy, mostly with groups of youngsters hanging out having tea, coffee or sodas. Sitting on the stairs, sidewalk benches as well as on the hoods of parked cars, they were a lively bunch, carefree and noisy, just the kind of distraction that he needed.

The warm cup in his hands and hot coffee sliding down his throat felt refreshing and cleared his mind. The temptation to call up just anyone and pour out his feeling had died down, and he was thinking more rationally. His family was safe in Jhelum, and they did not expect him back until the next day or so. He did not want to worry his mother with news about Pervaiz until he knew more.

A gypsy woman with her young daughter was walking around, asking people for money, telling them her sob story. In a crowd of young men and women devoid of worries and more importantly, spare cash, he stood out like the perfect target and before long, the sad piercing and well trained eyes of the beggar girl, hardly seven or eight were squarely fixed on him. The mother, showing full confidence in her protégé's charms, had backed off and watched from a safe distance.

"*Allah, fazal karay ga,*" she started with the standard blessing. "He'll give you a pretty bride, and a nice baby boy," she targeted him according to his age, noticing that he was alone on a Sunday evening. "We have been hungry all day. I have six little brothers and sisters, and my father is crippled, *duss beece rupey daydo na*, just ten or twenty rupees," she gave her demands. Kamran tried to ignore her, but the mother seemed to have noticed his distress and jumped in, double teaming him towards surrender, "May your mother live long and healthy," she came from a different angle.

The cup of coffee was empty; he got up to leave while the little girl tugged on his shirt, gently but with no obvious intention to let go. Exasperated, he dug into his pocket and pulled out a ten-rupee note to the delight of his pursuers. As the little girl, victorious grin and all, ran back to her mother, clutching onto the banknote, he noticed a piece of paper that had fallen out of his pocket. Instinctively he bent down to retrieve it and realized that it was a business card:

The Capital Chronicle

Sana Aziz
Investigative Reporter

Off: 051-9745555 Mobile: 0395-5550055

Kamran stared at the card for a few minutes after he walked back to his car, toying with his cell phone, trying to figure out what to do:

"She is the only one I can talk to, and maybe the only one who can understand."

The encounter with the gypsy beggar girl, as annoying as it had been, reinforced his belief that political games, bureaucratic corruption, and resulting economic disparity was eroding this country at its roots. Children like her belonged in schools . . . in the comfort of their homes . . . not on the streets as potential income sources for their struggling families. It all started to become very clear as if a dense fog had lifted from his tired mind. He had made up his mind. He raised the business card in the dim light coming from the shops to look at the phone number and started dialing.

CHAPTER 29

Sunday 8:04 p.m.

Sana had been restless all day. After handing in her story about yesterday's events, perfectly blunted to leave certain specific details out, she had spent most of her day watching television coverage of the funeral, while going over stacks of newspaper clippings that she had collected over time, and tracking down the missing ones on her laptop.

Her neck felt stiff. She picked up her head and rotated it in a circular motion to ease the muscles in the back of her neck and realized that she hadn't even turned the lights on. Her apartment was small but had a cozy feeling to it. Furniture though spartan was tasteful and combined with the Afghani carpet under it had a strong ethnic feel to it. Cream-colored walls were covered with pictures of her and her family interspersed with framed clippings of her most notable journalistic achievements. She turned on a table lamp, filling the room with a rainbow of colors emanating from its stained camel skin lampshade. It was getting chilly; she covered herself with a shawl and picked up one of the several throw cushions decorated with Sindhi embroidery scattered around and set it behind her back for support. It was time to get back to work.

Over the last few weeks, Sana had closely followed some main contenders in the upcoming elections. What went on in the political back alleys of this country was not much of a mystery but beyond the back biting, corruption and the ubiquitous palace intrigue was the urban legend, prized by the ever active conspiracy theorists; the belief that governments changed when someone wanted them changed, and more than likely, that someone represented a foreign hand. Working to validate or invalidate this theory, Sana had started to closely monitor the activities and contacts, as well as detailed itineraries of all potential Prime Ministerial candidates as soon as the elections were announced.

In the beginning, the main purpose of this exercise was to write an exposé, addressing these conspiracy theories in order to shed some light on what really went on behind closed doors so close to the elections; however, as time went on Sana had started to see some interesting patterns of mutual cooperation between opponents, who would otherwise be bitter enemies in public. Her plan was to keep working on the story, following it through the whole process and then publishing it as a series of articles. Malik Jahangir's assassination changed everything, and now she was sitting there going through her notes trying to make sense of it all.

Malik Jahangir was not a run-of-the-mill politician caught in mundane compromises, as was the norm in Pakistani politics. He was somewhat of a maverick. Even though it seemed that his background, his upbringing, the traditional ways of political dynasties showed with every controversial decision he made, one could not but credit him for thinking outside the box. This trait not only opened windows of opportunity for nontraditional markets, but had also led to a growing set of enemies determined to derail his plans. One of the most noticeable aspects of his plans dealt with enhancing political cooperation with China and the Central Asian Republics. Two months ago, he had a highly publicized meeting with the visiting Chinese Minister for Trade and Technology. Details of the meeting, held behind closed doors, had not become public, but political pundits had, it seemed, made up their minds about what went on and what was discussed based on their own hunches and interpretation of various unauthorized leaks. The most prevalent theory revolved around Malik Jahangir's increasing stress on domestic production and self-reliance. On several occasions, he had denounced Pakistan's dependence on Western resources, stating that the only way to break these chains was to develop our own technology with the help of our friendly neighbors like China, Iran and Kazakhstan.

This declaration had not resonated well with traditionalists who had been comfortable with the way things had been. A strong Euro-American influence on Pakistani economy was a convenient and time-tested arrangement, at least in terms of the steady stream of economic benefits that flowed in their direction.

Following his meeting with the Chinese Cabinet Member, Malik Jahangir had traveled to Kazakhstan, meeting with the CEO of Kazakh National Oil and Gas Inc (KNOG), one of the largest regional suppliers of crude oil. KNOG had been closed to foreign investors for years, keeping its Soviet way of doing business, but recently, it had realized the advantages of foreign partnerships, especially due to the recently labile crude oil prices. KNOG had been heavily courted by the Indian government over the last year or so in an effort to make a deal before Pakistan could. Over the past two decades, India had invested deeply in diplomatic relations with strategically placed Afghanistan in order to strengthen inroads into Central Asian resources, thus cutting off any such efforts by Pakistan. Sources were stating that Malik Jahangir's meeting focused on building a pipeline and trade route to bring crude oil and other raw material along the western Iran-Afghan border to planned refineries along the southern coast of Pakistan. Pipeline was to pass through Uzbekistan, Turkmenistan and Eastern Iran, while by passing the less cooperative and politically unstable Afghanistan in the process. Tashkent and Ashgabat were offered heavy subsidies to bolster their own industrial ambitions, and finally utilizing Gawadar Deep Sea Port in Southern Pakistan as the regional hub of these activities. Financial arrangements with Iran were still in discussion.

"These two meetings alone were enough to get him killed, I suppose," Sana said rather loudly, "Now let's see how others responded to that?"

She started to cross reference above dates to itineraries and schedules of the other candidates. Most of them were related to mundane activities of a generic politician involving public meetings, rallies and media interviews, but nothing specific to her interest. In a press conference, the day after Malik Jahangir's meeting with the Chinese Minister, Malik Nisar was asked about it and he had responded very calmly:

"We all have our personal visions, all of which may not be entirely practical but there is no harm in pursuing them. Malik Jahangir has been exploring some options that may not be entirely compatible with *my* vision of the future, but I know that in his heart, he wants the best for this country. Also, I must say that a lot of stories that are out there tell only part of the truth, and you should not believe everything that you hear. Beyond that, there is nothing more I can comment on."

"Savvy answer," Sana thought to herself as she scrolled down the web page until she saw a small blip at the very bottom. *"This doesn't make sense,"* she continued to read.

Unholy Liaisons

*"**Lahore, Sept. 13** – In a rare display of mutual cooperation and solidarity, Interior Minister Malik Nisar and opposition leader Raja Safdar Hussein, met briefly after a dinner arranged by the National Cancer Research Foundation. They engaged in a private discussion for about thirty minutes and then posed for a friendly photograph. They did not elaborate on the topic of their discussion, but upon questioning an aide, it was learned that the dialogue revolved around ways to ensure transparent and fair elections. In the last few years of intense debate and merciless bashing of each other's political agenda, this is the first time that these two leaders have publicly spoken to each other. Knowing their history and unabashed contempt for each other, this unscheduled meeting appears to represent a lot more than its official explanation and thus raises a lot of questions . . . ."*

Sana was surprised to see this. As a journalist who had been reporting on such activities on a regular basis, the fact that she had missed it all together when it first came out bothered her even more. She decided to make these, apparently opposite poles of the political spectrum, her primary subjects. As she looked through the schedules, she found out that Malik Nisar left Pakistan the very next day to attend a regional congress of interior ministers in Dubai.

Raja Safdar Hussein, on other hand, was in Islamabad, attending a series of meetings culminating in the final, but most intriguing meeting of the day with a delegation representing the multi-national petroleum giant AmeriGulf. The meeting itself was not that unusual as such meetings between politicians and their economic alliances took place on a regular basis, but what made this interesting was that this particular meeting took place at the US cultural attaché's official residence.

Two weeks later, Malik Jahangir presided over a consortium representing local and Central Asian interests in oil and gas exploration, reiterating his strong interest to continue in this direction. The same evening Malik Jahangir was paid an unscheduled visit by a military attaché from the US Embassy. Incidentally, Malik Nisar happened to be in Washington, DC on the same very day.

The timing and circumstances of these meetings were too predictable to be just a coincidence. Sana created a timeline chart and started filling in these seemingly random events. The more she wrote, the more sense her suspicions made. She could have gone on and on with her research when her raw adrenaline-rush was interrupted by her phone. It was the paper.

"Hello?"

"Sana!" The familiar and warm voice of her Chief Editor came through.

"Agha *Sahib*? I didn't expect a call from you at this hour!" Sana replied, surprised to hear his voice.

Agha Kamal was an affable grandfather of a figure with every conceivable journalistic award under his belt. In his mid-sixties, he had kept a rigorous regimen of exercise, bicycling through the streets of Islamabad and was in excellent shape despite his balding head, a grey but neatly trimmed goatee and worsening vision requiring thick horn rimmed glasses. An idealist to begin with, tough lessons of his early youth had forced him to accept the importance of calculated albeit conscientious compromises in order to achieve the greater good. In his capacity as a journalist, and later in his career as a member of the editorial staff, he had tried to stay loyal to those ideals of reporting the truth, but he had been repeatedly interrupted by every possible cliché in the book: red tape, progressive diplomacy, preemptive political strategy, national security . . . you name it. Frustrated by his inability to tell the whole truth amid threats of retaliation, fears of a professional suicide and the ever present incompetent and even worse, wimpy bosses, he had decided to retire in order to write his memoirs. That did not last long, as his unsuccessful attempt to resist being a journalist failed miserably, and he resurfaced as the Chief Editor of the *Capital Chronicle*, his brainchild, meant to resuscitate the dying flame called factual journalism.

From the first moment when Sana walked into his office, he had noticed something special about her. In addition to being brilliant at what she did, she had the chutzpah to face the truth, and then go after it with the zeal and determination of the kind he had not seen in years. In short, she reminded him of himself, thirty odd years ago, and he swore that he would protect her from the hyenas of the industry that in the past, he was not able to fend off. His mentorship meant a lot to her and she had lived up to his expectations, proving that he was right in choosing her to help him make the Chronicle what it was today.

"Is everything okay?"

"How is the story going?"

"Good . . . good, but I've not really been working on it," Sana lied, not wanting to acknowledge that she was working on it instead of doing something else. Agha Kamal did not see her total devotion to work as healthy and he always pushed her to go out and socialize more.

"Don't lie to me, Sana . . ." Agha Kamal chuckled. "You are sitting with your laptop working on it right now, aren't you?"

'How do you know that, Agha *sahib?*" Sana was caught off guard.

"Because I know you too well . . . because that is what I would be doing."

"Okay, okay, you caught me . . . ," she laughed, ". . . now what's on your mind?"

Agha Kamal, cleared his throat, "I know that you have been working on your election story, and I can picture you tying it in with the assassination, but I just want you to be careful . . . it is not safe," Agha Kamal said, haltingly, as if trying to find the right words.

"What do you mean, not safe; is there something you want to tell me?"

"I have heard that the two doctors who attended to Malik Jahangir were not pleased by the way the investigation was being conducted, and were raising questions."

"What kind of questions?"

"That . . . something did not fit; there are holes in the official story. Obviously, someone took notice and . . ."

"And what . . . ?" Sana stood up straight; she had a bad feeling about it.

"One of them was shot . . . about four hours ago. They are calling it . . ."

She felt a sinking feeling in the pit of her stomach as she braced herself to keep herself from falling; she tried to say something but words seem to get stuck in her suddenly parched throat.

". . . an armed robbery," Agha Kamal completed his sentence.

"Is he . . . okay?" Sana finally gathered enough strength to ask.

"Last I heard he was still in the operation theater. He'd lost a lot of blood. I hope he pulls through."

"That is horrible, I can't believe it," she paused, 'I just saw him, last night . . . ,'" she stopped herself from saying too much. ". . . I mean last night . . . at the hospital," her heart suddenly felt like a ton as she thought about her impromptu meeting last night.

"I can't believe it either," Agha Kamal, replied, "I can't stop thinking about his family. His children are still so young."

"Children . . . ? He doesn't have any . . . chil . . . oh," Sana suddenly felt a sense of relief but then immediately felt terribly guilty about it. "Did you hear anything about . . . Dr. Kamran . . . is *he* okay?" Sana tried to sound nonchalant about it but her emotions filtered through.

Agha Kamal was a very perceptive man who had come to know Sana very well. "Why don't you call him and ask yourself? Dr. Pervaiz is a very close friend of his . . . I'm sure he could use someone to talk to," he replied, smiling at this great social opportunity for her. "Let me know if you hear anything, I'll keep you posted too."

As she hung up, she saw her reflection in the mirror and caught herself blushing.

CHAPTER 30

Monday 1:00 a.m.

Captain Hasaam was alone on deck. The rest of the crew was sent downstairs to take a short break before work began. Hasaam had tried to relax in his cabin but could not get comfortable. He walked up to the deserted deck. It had started to drizzle when he decided to return to the bridge. It was 1:00 a.m.; they were getting close to their destination as he stood there, staring at the dark expanse of Arabian Sea through the window peppered with raindrops, wondering what new surprises awaited them under its immense depths. He returned to his charts and verified their position, slowed down the speed to three knots and the strident grunts of the engines died down to a loud hum. The waters were calm with a light westward breeze, adding to the wind chill. He took a deep breath, taking in the damp and cold air through a partially open window to sharpen his senses before blowing the whistle to alert his crew.

Oil exploration ship *'Marhaba'* had taken an uncharted detour from its journey through Strait of Hormuz to Port Salalah in Oman, and now drifted just off the coast of Baluchistan. Hasaam looked at his watch, he had about five hours in which to finish his survey, pack up and get back on its charted route, before the coast guards changed shift at 0600 hours.

His task was daunting. Usually it took this long just to stabilize the streamer and then get the guns in place. Firing them and then collecting data was a whole different project. It was the middle of the night; MMAD (Marine Mammal Acoustic Detection) software was quiet and he did not have to worry about any whales.

Controls were on auto now. He ran back to the loading area. Instead of the usual number of forty to fifty, he was functioning on a skeletal crew of twenty-two men. None of them, however, was fully aware of their exact plan or location. For them, it was another opportunity to make some extra cash through a last minute, one night project.

Hasaam looked at his watch; a sudden shift in the winds earlier had slowed him down, pushing them behind schedule. The streamer had been rolled out already, and only a layer of it was left, rolled around the giant reel. It was a six-kilometer long fiber optic cable and was fitted with hundreds of ultra-sensitive hydrophones. Once trailing behind the ship in a straight line, it could record sound waves, reflected from the ocean floor to reveal a two-dimensional view of the ocean sub-strata through a seismic, gravity and magnetic survey. The results were then uploaded to a computer program that reconstructed it into3-D images. Hasaam made sure that the hydrophone connections were functional, and motioned the foreman to start deploying the guns. To ensure being efficient, he was content using only fifteen guns for this survey.

By 2:20 a.m., all the required equipment was in place and it was time to gather the first reading. The guns fired in perfect synchrony, sending bolts of compressed air towards the ocean floor. Loud enough to travel to the floor and back, and subsequently able to be registered by the hydrophones; their only evidence on the surface was a few inconspicuous bubbles. Hasaam looked at his watch again and smiled, running his hand through his thick and black hair . . . he was right on schedule.

This activity continued in a tight grid pattern for the next three hours, covering every meter of the marked ocean floor. He walked back to the control deck, made sure that all readings were in place, and confirmed his position. The wind had died down and the cloud cover was blowing away, exposing a bright quarter moon. He walked up to a portside window facing north, picked up his flashlight and flicked it on and off four times at equal intervals.

CHAPTER 31

Monday 4:30 a.m.

Mark Zeigler was pacing back and forth impatiently. He should have heard from them by now. Mark was a nervous guy, even under the calmest of circumstances, and this was certainly not one of them. He was an unassuming guy; short and scrawny with thick old-fashioned glasses that constantly needed to be pushed up his hooked nose in order to prevent them from falling. He was wearing faded jeans and sneakers under a red and gray MIT sweatshirt. A Boston Red Sox baseball hat covered his curly black hair. Strictly going by first impressions, if it wasn't for his prodigious expertise in petro-geology, his prospects in any job interview appear destined to be doomed from the moment he entered the room.

Fortunately for him, however, his interview continued beyond first impressions, and now he was the main reason behind every successful exploratory project undertaken by AmeriGulf Inc. In the past two years, Butch Donaldson had made it very clear to Arthur Kimble that no project was to be given green light unless endorsed by his favorite geologist.

It was just after four thirty now, and Mark was at the verge of a nervous breakdown. As was his habit, he was gnawing rapidly on his fingernails, while repeatedly looking at his satellite phone to make sure that it was turned on.

At this hour, the Arabian Sea was pitch dark in the cloudy night; howling wind over sandy dunes, and waves crashing into the rocky cliffs were completing this haunting ambience. The wind chill had dropped a few more degrees, chilling him to the bone, and it was time to get another cup of hot coffee from his van parked just off the beach. He could feel his heart beating out of his chest, and he was not entirely sure if it was his nerves or the caffeine, that surely by now, had taken over the blood stream.

Sipping on his now full, though stale cup of coffee, he looked towards the open sea and saw a momentary flash, though feeble but unmistakably made by an artificial light. Hoping for a miracle he squinted his eyes, looking towards the open sea through a growing fog, "Please, please . . . please God, let it be them!"

And then there it was; another flash of light followed by two more and he took a deep sigh of relief. His laptop had suddenly come to life with an endless stream of data running across the screen. Mark stared at it for a few minutes and then smiled.

"I was so right about this. This is already looking good."

Marhaba was a moderate sized oil exploration ship, mostly stationed in the Indian Ocean and around the UAE. Its main purpose was to study the ever-changing ocean floor, and locating new or expanding oil reservoirs. It was owned along with a fleet of other explorers, oil tankers and cargo ships by Moeez-al-Khairi, a shipping magnet based in Abu-Dhabi. He was also a major shareholder in AmeriGulf Inc.

Oil exploration permits were hard to obtain, especially when exact timing was critical. Under normal circumstances, obtaining one from the Pakistan Government would have been a breeze, especially for someone with deep pockets and the right connections. However, due to the uncertainty of the current political situation, and a potential new government on the horizon, it was unwise to apply for one right now. Political regimes were known to go after any deals made by their political rivals, and as a way of asserting themselves as more competent and hard on corruption, in a swift knee-jerk reaction, they dismantled almost every project and deal that was initiated by the previous regime. That could mean wasting billions of rupees already spent towards that particular venture and starting fresh with a new set of pet projects that too often were left incomplete, since governments rarely completed their mandated terms.

This was not any different from the time of ancient Emperors and Pharaohs when all signs, symbols and lingering legacies of the conquered were brutally desecrated and subsequently deleted; hieroglyphs were covered with thick layers of plaster and mighty obelisks turned to dust, thus rewriting history after each conquest. Rules were, however, different for the privileged and the well-connected, as projects and deals reappeared under different contexts, that is, if itchy bank accounts were scratched in a timely and discreet manner.

It was risky nonetheless, and hence AmeriGulf was making sure that it had some solid ground to stand on.

The coast guard cutter on duty was conveniently patrolling around the opposite end of its assigned territory, leaving plenty of time and opportunity for *Marhaba* to complete its 'detour'. It was not a cheap project, but money was not a factor in its success or failure.

A small blip appeared on the radar, about twenty miles to the west of *Marhaba's* current location, and all action halted. Coast guards were in the opposite direction and could not be showing up this far west of their location.

"Silent drill, hold all activity!" Hasaam cautioned the crew as he slowed the ship down to a complete halt. "Most likely it is a fishing boat dropping its nets, but we do not want to attract any unnecessary attention."

In reality, he was not at all sure who it could be. The worst-case scenario was also the scariest one. He could not help but think about the fact that they were merely miles from the Iranian coastal boundary and any prospecting in this region could have serious political repercussions, especially if potential reservoirs extended into Iranian territory.

The blip on the radar was getting closer by the second . . . and suddenly, there were two of them. Hasaam frantically looked at his GPS locator and consulted his map to make sure that they had not drifted off course into Iranian waters, but was relieved to verify his current location. The blips were too small to be cargo ships, but too big to be fishing boats, more so in the general vicinity of standard coast guard cutters.

The crewmembers on *Marhaba's* loading deck were relaxing. Divided into distinct groups according to their native language, mostly Arabic, Urdu and Hindi or Bengali, they chatted quietly while a fourth group huddled in a less windy corner smoking cigarettes, brought together by their common need for tobacco, irrespective of their background and language barriers.

One of the boats seem to have turned around heading towards the west, but the other one was now coming straight towards them.

"Code Red . . . Code Red!" Hasaam yelled towards the crew and with clock-like precision, all evidence of any active geological mapping disappeared from plain sight within ten minutes. Reels were dropped into the sea attached only to an out of sight safety hook under the dock.

Although it was unmistakably a coastguard ship, under the foggy condition, it was practically impossible to see whether it was of Pakistani or Iranian origin, and the later possibility was certainly not a pleasant one.

Hasaam could feel his heart beating rapidly and rather loudly, as he felt sweat dripping down his brow despite the cold night. He checked his charts once more and was comforted again by the fact that he was not off course.

The coast guard cutter was now right beside them, and a bright searchlight illuminated the decks of *Marhaba.*

"Announce yourself," a stern voice in thick Farsi laden English came through the loud speaker.

"This is *Marhaba.* Our electronic system went down due to lightning and knocked off our navigation grid; we are a little off course."

"What is your destination?"

"Port of Salalah, Oman."

"Amazing . . . do you realize how far off course you are?"

"Yes sir, but we have already contacted the Pakistani Coast Guard and they are aware of our position. You can confirm this with Captain Sohail at their HQ."

"I'll do that; you are in their territory anyway, but be careful, you are very close to Iranian waters," he replied in a much softer voice as the searchlight continued to inspect every inch of *Marhaba* in a systematic manner. "Do you need any help?"

"No sir, thank you, our system should be up and running within fifteen or twenty minutes and we should be on our way."

"Good . . . keep your frequencies open . . . just in case you need anything."

"We will, and thank you for your assistance."

The Coast Guard moved away, turning off the searchlight, and Hasaam finally exhaled.

CHAPTER 32

Monday October 3rd, 8:15 a.m.

Sana looked at herself in the mirror once more and liked what she saw. Despite all the excitement and the rush of raw adrenaline, surprisingly, she had slept very well, and felt thoroughly refreshed. She was wearing a teal colored cotton *shalwaar kamiz* with a high neckline, decorated with Sindhi embroidery. A matching hair band pulled her shoulder length black hair back though loosely, highlighting her natural curls. She quickly glanced at her face again to inspect her makeup, something she did not use much of, and which mostly consisted of a light foundation and lipstick, then she turned around halfway to look at her dress, which though modest was hugging her curves just enough to make an admiring eye wonder.

She thought about Kamran and despite her focus on the professional task at hand, she could not help but smile, and was surprised to detect in her a certain eagerness to see him. His call the night before, though welcome, nevertheless took her by surprise. He was tentative, seemingly unsure of the nature of outcome resting on his call.

"*Assalam-u-alaikum* . . . can I talk to Sana . . . Aziz?" he sounded coy, his voice low, halting and missing its usual self-assuredness.

"This is Sana, Who is this?" she asked although, she had instantly known who it was thanks to the marvel of caller ID.

"This is Dr. Kamran . . . we ran into each other last night at . . ."

" . . . at the hospital, when I interrupted your stroll in the woods," she smiled, completing the sentence, "I remember it very well."

"I need to see you," he went straight to the point with urgency in his voice.

"Right now . . . ?" she was surprised by the suddenness of this development and was caught totally off guard. She felt her temples getting hot, her heart beating faster.

"If possible, yes . . . certainly," he replied with a hint of eagerness in his voice and then paused, "well maybe later, but soon . . . I apologize; I didn't even consider the fact that you may have other plans."

"Oh, no, no other plans, none at all," she blurted and then caught herself, "I mean, it is late now, how about early tomorrow morning?"

Kamran had paused for a second, thinking more clearly now. He needed the time to get his thoughts together. As impatient as he was, he was not ready for the meeting himself. The realization relaxed him. "That will be fine. How about Marriot's Nadia Coffee Shop, say at ten tomorrow morning."

She thought about it for a second, "Okay, I'll see you then."

"Allah Hafiz."

"Allah Hafiz."

She was ready, as she had been for the past one hour. It was still early, but she wanted to be prepared and get there before he did to get comfortable with the surroundings. She liked to have that edge, and it was a routine that had paid off well for her in the past. She looked at the stack of papers still on the coffee table once more and picked up some of the summary pages that she had prepared last night.

A few puffs of Givenchy's *Amarige* completed the job and she was off.

CHAPTER 33

PEARL CONTINENTAL HOTEL RAWALPINDI

Monday 8:15 a.m.

Kamran had not slept very well. Before getting ready for bed, he called the hospital and inquired about Pervaiz' status. He was still unconscious and on ventilator support, though doctors had been able to control the bleeding. He tried to call his house to check on Nadia and the kids, but there was no response. He made a mental note of making the call first thing in the morning.

As usual, with the meteoric increase in the number of networks and channels, there was more and more duplication of programming and, as the cliché goes, there was nothing good on TV. He spent about an hour or so, aimlessly surfing channels before settling on Geo News, the popular Pakistani news channel, based in Dubai. There was a report about the aftermath of Malik Jahangir's assassination that had swept the nation, especially in southern Punjab. Loyal supporters had gone on a rampage, protesting and accusing the government of a cover up, leaving behind charred remains of burnt cars and buses, ransacked shops and plundered department stores. Visible through the thick clouds of smoke spewing from stacks of burning tires, were scattered shoes left by the hurriedly dispersing rioters, laying around major intersections of Lahore and Karachi, sprinkled amongst the still-smoldering shells of tear gas unleashed by the police.

Military regiments and police battalions in full riot gear patrolled the deserted streets and stood guard at all sensitive government buildings and installations. Dozens had died; hundreds were injured as the monetary toll of property damages reached a multitude of millions. As expected, General Hamid Ali had enforced a state of emergency and imposed section 144, barring any public gathering of four or more people, and a strict curfew after ten p.m.

Kamran was frustrated and extremely disheartened by the destructive events of the day. He wasn't sure if the next few days were going to be any better. These were ominous signs, graphic reminders of the system's inability to sustain itself.

Physical demands of the day, and their toll on his fatigued body was catching up to him, his eyes grew heavy, and soon he was fast asleep.

The fast-paced and terrifying events that made up his eerily vivid nightmare revolved around a heart-pounding run through the woods trying to evade unseen monsters that loomed and struck from every unexpected perch in the dark forest. He wasn't alone, but was not sure about the identity of his companion. He could see the light through an opening, made by the high arched canopy of trees. A shrill, piercing sound coming from that direction seemed to pull him towards safety, but his feet seem to be stuck. The soft ground under his feet seem to suck him in as he tried in vain, wildly clawing into his surroundings to grasp any branch or similar object that could hold his grip. He woke up to the same shrill piercing sound, now sounding much more familiar as the ringing of his cell phone. He had broken out into a sweat, huddled in a corner of his king-size bed, painfully aware of every pounding beat of his racing heart. He struggled to get to his cell phone, trying to free his feet, stuck in the cotton sheet twisted around his legs, knocking down a few objects from his bedside table in the process, before finally reaching and picking up his phone.

"Hello," he said in a hoarse and barely audible voice.

"Kamran *bhai,* this is Nadia. Did I wake you up?"

"No, no. I was just waking up. Is everything all right?" Kamran was suddenly very alert. "Is Pervaiz okay?"

"He's fine," Nadia said in a shaky voice, " . . . as good as he could be, I guess. The doctor said he is stable, but this is not why I called you," she paused.

"What is it Nadia?"

"Kami *Bhai*, I don't know what to do. In the beginning, I believed what the police told me, that it was just a robbery, now I'm not so sure."

"Why do you say that?" Kamran was suddenly wide-awake.

"I'm not sure what to make of it, but I think Pervaiz was watching a video of the *Julsa* and the assassination, just before . . .

before . . . ," she paused to gather herself,. . . before he . . . he . . . was shot; he had transferred it to the hard drive."

"Is there an original?" asked Kamran.

"He had it in his pocket. It got destroyed. At least that's what the doctor thinks. The cassette is missing, but they found its fragments in his pocket. The doctor said that bullet hit it first, deflecting just enough to miss his heart. It saved his life . . . ironic isn't it?" she could not go on. Kamran could hear her voice change as she struggled to fight back her tears.

He gave her a few moments to settle down. A few silent moments passed. Breathing on the other side seemed to have become more regular and less shallow.

"Can you email it to me?" Kamran asked.

"I will try; you know how I am with this computer stuff. This has always been his department," she sounded a bit relaxed now. "I'll do it right now and then I have to get back to the hospital. Let me know if you find something on it."

"I will. Keep me posted on his condition; call me anytime."

"Thank you for all your support, Kami *bhai.* I couldn't go through this without you. Keep him in your prayers," her voice started to crack again.

"He'll pull through. He is one tough *rajput,* and believe me, I've learned it the hard way. When he wakes up, tell him that he owes me some money."

There was a brief chuckle at the other end. "I'll make sure to tell him that," she said, and then the line went dead.

Kamran was staring at a still frame of the video, periodically looking around to see if he was still alone in the business center as he zoomed in on the bodyguard. The face looked very familiar, but he couldn't place him. He struggled with it for a few minutes, trying to remember, but in vain. It was almost nine.

"Oh, God, I'll be late!" he got up in a hurry, hitting the print button. The print out was not very clear, but good enough to identify the features. Running towards the door, he turned around briefly to make sure he had picked up all his belongings and realized that he had left the browser open. He rushed back and closed it, letting go a sigh of relief before running out the door again.

Vincent looked at himself in the mirror. He had slept better during the night; however, that was only a relative term. Anything that resembled even a short spurt of a sleep cycle was better than what was his routine. His plans were set, and he did not need any interference, but he needed to report to his contact before he went to bed.

"Just keep them silent," the authoritative voice of his contact had said in heavily accented English. "I'll do what I can do to make running a bit more difficult for them. Maybe they can be a source of just the right kind of diversion you and I need. Now get some sleep."

He examined the darkening circles around his eyes, but they seemed a little less prominent, thanks to a tan courtesy of a still intense October sun. He hadn't shaved in three days and the patchy growth of hair on his face seemed to have organized into what could be called a closely trimmed beard. He had thought about shaving it, but the more he looked at it, the more he liked it. The deep tan and beard had transformed his rugged Italian features into a face perfectly capable of blending into the crowd in any Pakistani city.

He was wearing a traditional light blue *shalwaar* suit with a grey woolen short coat, a combination seen so frequently on the streets of Rawalpindi and Islamabad, and made even more popular by its preference by the political elite.

He was pleased with the look. He was often told how soft his eyes were. How he exuded a warm glow from them so he had learned to squint his eyes, and he had developed a deep frown on his brow to intensify a look that matched his job description. He would have forgotten this softer side of his nature altogether if it weren't for an occasional fleeting moment when his guard was lowered; a force field flickering to show a vulnerable side. He had learned to recognize it, and was able to switch on his defenses in an instant, hardly noticeable to anyone, but a few chosen ones who were close enough to have gained his confidence; a rare group indeed.

A thin, though jagged scar along his right jaw line remained hairless and conspicuously without a tan, an eerie reminder of a childhood lost. The piercing sting of a fingernail digging through his skin felt hauntingly fresh and painfully real. Instinctively, he grabbed his right wrist, still sore on cold damp days; it once bore an ugly bruise for days, a reminder of Father Joseph's strong grip to keep him from running.

He was only ten, and it was Father Nicholas who had been his savior, proving that his stories about championship boxing days in the Bronx, and a legendary left hook were not just fairy tales told to eager-eyed orphans. Father Joseph was discreetly transferred to a different parish and Vincent had learned never to trust anyone but himself.

It was time to go. Kamran's car was still in the parking lot and his GPS locator was silent, but he did not want to take any chances. He inspected his appearance once more, nodding approvingly while unconsciously running his fingers over the scar. Turning around, he stopped and tapped on his left leg with his index finger, making sure that his holster and belt were securely in place before leaving the room

CHAPTER 34

MARRIOTT HOTEL, ISLAMABAD
NADIA COFFEE SHOP

Monday 9:50 a.m.

Kamran was very pleased with his driving time and the ability to weave in and out of the morning traffic. Deep down, however, he was thankful for relatively light traffic this morning, unlike the usual mad rush. He hated being late for any occasion, and this particular one had a special significance to it. He needed to start fresh with Sana, and develop a relationship of trust. Being late for their first meeting hardly said that. He was suddenly very excited about the meeting. His pathologist friend had just called with the preliminary report. Residue around the puncture wound on Malik Jahangir's neck matched the contents of the syringe.

"Interesting specimen, Kamran," Javed Cheema appeared surprised, "Highly unusual strength; where did it come from? . . . okay, okay . . . don't tell me if you don't want to . . . ," he backed off, recognizing the delay in getting an answer.

"Concentrated solution of what?"

"Oh, nothing unusual, just a solution of potassium chloride, however, this one is strong enough to kill an elephant if injected intravenously."

"Thank you, Javed, I owe you one. Let me know if you find out something else," he hung up. Things made a lot more sense now.

As he turned onto Agha Khan Road, driving towards the Marriott, the triumphant smile on his face transformed into a whimpering sigh. He was faced with an elaborate series of checkpoints reinforced with steel barricades, and manned by military details in full combat gear. It had been a while since he had been to Marriott and had forgotten about the aftermath of the deadly bombing back in 2007, killing fifty-three people, and ripping through the façade of this upscale Capitol establishment. The hotel, though completely renovated and esthetically resurrected, had completely lost its innocent appeal thanks to bland white and thick, reinforced concrete walls lined with stacks of sand bags, and narrow entry points secured with steel gates and metal detectors.

Finding a parking spot was not easy and that, too, at an uncomfortable distance from the hotel, but the walk itself was uneventful. Rather refreshing in the crisp morning air. Going through checkpoints was easy thanks to his credentials, however, thoroughly annoying. As he walked in through the small gate, collected his metallic belongings at the far side of the metal detectors, and prepared to be frisked by an intimidating security guard, he remembered his father's infectious smile and could not help, but to reflect on the heavy price Pakistanis had paid for being in the middle of someone else's wars.

He walked in through the newly constructed lobby of Islamabad Marriott. The hotel was reconstructed at record pace after the suicide bombing by militants in retaliation to Pakistan's involvement in the war on terror. After heatedly debating its future, the decision was made to reconstruct it, and better than before as a symbol of the resolve of Pakistani people in their fight against terrorism.

As he entered the coffee shop, he looked around for an empty table, and he was surprised to see her, sitting at a corner table by the window, watching him intently. He felt a little self-conscious, smiled and nodded before walking towards her.

A few awkward moments followed, as neither of them was sure about how to start the conversation. He pulled the chair across from her and sat down.

"I hope that . . . I am not bothering you. I don't want to drag you into something you don't want to get involved in," he said coyly.

"No, not at all, I want to help," Sana said. "Besides, I really want to get to the bottom of it. I'm glad that you called . . . and just in case you are hungry, I've already ordered tea and some sandwiches if you don't mind."

"Oh no . . . not at all, I am all in for a cup of tea."

Both of them were silent for a few seconds.

"Do you . . . ?"

"I've been . . . ," they started simultaneously and then abruptly stopped.

"Sorry, go ahead."

"No, you go first," Sana conceded.

"Thanks."

"You are welcome."

"Do you think there is a deeper conspiracy behind the assassination?"

"Do I *think*? . . . I am sure of it," Sana replied. "I have been following this story for a while and believe me," she lowered her voice to a bare whisper, "there are so many people who benefit from this that I am not even sure where to start."

"What about Malik Nisar?" Kamran offered a name.

"That's a good one," Sana nodded and started to tell him details about the meetings, their timings and their potential significance.

She was excited, talking fast, consulting her notes every once in a while, but mostly recalling facts from her memory. Kamran just sat there, watching her intently, looking into the hazel eyes sparkling with excitement, her hands, delicate, with shapely long fingers endlessly moving to back her words, as she knitted one captivating conspiracy theory after another to explain the recent events. When she was done, Kamran was not sure if he was more impressed by the brilliance of her deductions, or just by her. As he stared at her moving, perfectly sculpted lips, he seemed to lose track of the words coming out from them.

"So, what do you think?" She caught him off guard.

"What . . . what do I think about what?" he fumbled with words, but quickly recaptured his composure.

"Oh . . . I can't believe it!" he replied. "I would never have thought along those lines, but I do know that there is more to the story than what the media has released so far."

He went on about Pervaiz' injury, the video and then briefly went over events at the hospital. Sana was all ears, taking notes and feverishly jotting them down in shorthand.

A waiter walked in with tea and a plate of egg and cheese sandwiches, and both of them stopped talking. The waiter greeted them with a polite nod and salaam and then went on, meticulously placing delicate china teacups, milk, sugar, and a matching teapot that he then covered with an ornately embroidered tea-cozy. Kamran suddenly felt hungry, realizing that he did not have any dinner the night before, and he smiled at the sight of an appetizing plate of sandwiches. He leaned back on his chair to give the waiter room to set it up, casually looking around the room, and that is when he saw him.

Sitting in an isolated corner of the coffee shop, partially hiding behind a newspaper was a face that seemed very familiar. Their eyes met for a single second before the man lowered his head, raising the newspaper just enough to impede his line of sight.

Kamran had seen this face before.

"Where have I seen this face . . . when?" he thought, then looked up and was surprised to see an empty table; he was gone.

That is when flashbacks started to flood his brain . . . coffee shop at PC, waiting room at *Shifa* . . . the video.

"The video . . . that's it! He is the bodyguard in the video," Kamran said, thinking out loudly, and then caught himself as he noticed Sana eyeing him quizzically.

"Why is he here? Is he following me?" the question lingered on in his mind for a few seconds before the answer came crashing through. His pulse quickened, his pupils dilating with fear, as suddenly the floodgates let go a barrage of adrenaline into his blood stream.

"Are you okay? You are scaring me," Sana inquired.

"We need to go, it's not safe here," he said as he got up to leave.

"What's wrong?"

"We need to leave . . . *right now!*" he said firmly, "I'll explain everything once we are safe."

Sana looked at him again and saw the resolve in his eyes, and did not say more. She quickly left some money on the table to cover the bill, grabbed her things and followed Kamran who was already halfway towards the door.

CHAPTER 35

AGA KHAN ROAD, SHALIMAR 5, ISLAMABAD

Sunday 10:56 a.m.

Vincent wanted to keep his options simple. On the way out, he made a little detour to make sure that his targets remain in his view. Sana's car was easy to locate in the small parking lot. Worn treads of the beat up Suzuki Alto were no match for a Swiss Army knife and flattened at the mere glance of its sharp point.

Comfortable with his options, he sat in his car listening to the conversation between Kamran and Sana. Despite his high tech listening device, the reception was poor. He had taken a crash course in Urdu before this mission and had brushed up on it further since his arrival, but even under the best of circumstances, he could understand only parts of a conversation. He could not even make out half of what went on between the two of them, but he picked up some vital parts, thanks to a lot of references in English; he knew what to do next.

"They know too much and it's time for them to pay for it," he slammed his hands on the steering wheel.

"Kamran . . . Kamran, wait for me," she called, struggling to catch up with him.

He slowed down, waiting for her as he walked through the lobby heading to the main entrance.

"What is it, is someone following us?"

"Yes," Kamran replied briefly as he looked through the glass, trying to locate his pursuer who was nowhere to be seen. "I don't know how he found us but we need to be somewhere safe."

Sana thought about it for a second and then came up with an idea. "Let's drive in opposite directions. We'll take side roads and small streets to lose him, and then meet at 'Rose and Jasmine Garden.' Do you know where the star and crescent sculpture is?"

"Yes."

"There is a back road next to it that leads to the stadium. I'll meet you there in an hour."

"Okay, but be careful and take your time. Make sure you are not followed."

Sana nodded in approval and quickly exited through a side door towards her car in a lot next to the hotel. Kamran waited about thirty seconds before carefully looking around, and then hurried down hotel's driveway towards the secured gate. The notion of involving security crossed his mind briefly as he walked out of the narrow gate, sensing a curiously scrutinizing stare of an armed guard, and instinctively slowed down his exit, but then as quickly as it came, he discarded the thought. Without any hard evidence, he did not see himself coming up with a very convincing argument, so he decided to take his chances as he walked away, gradually picking up his pace as he neared the spot where he was parked on the street, across from the hotel.

It was cloudy and a little chilly this morning. A brisk cool breeze rustled through the flame trees, taking the yellow autumn stricken leaves on a free ride, as they wandered aimlessly before resting peacefully on everything that gravity offered, the street and its adjacent manicured lawns, as well as on idle windshields of cars parked around them.

Kamran used his hand to wipe a handful that had found his car, realizing from the wet feeling that it had rained quite a lot, albeit briefly. As he unlocked his car and settled in, he took a deep breath; taking in the fragrance of freshly rained on earth as he planned his course of action, and then turned the ignition on. The cold engine of his car sputtered briefly before giving in to his foot's extra pressure on the accelerator, and then roared to life.

At first, he disregarded it as his imagination, brought on by a sudden influx of heavy traffic on the adjacent Aga Khan road, but then he heard it again. Someone was calling his name and it seemed louder and nearer this time. He turned around towards the general direction of the sound and saw Sana running towards his car; her face contorted in an expression of sheer panic, her eyes open wide. He tried to get out and help but she did not give him a chance as she opened the passenger side door and hopped in, breathless, sweat pouring down her face.

"Let's go . . . *now!"*

Kamran did not say anything as he nodded to acknowledge her instruction, looked over his right shoulder, found a quick opening in the traffic and drove away.

Vincent was very pleased with the result. He had managed to corner them in one vehicle. He had lost the element of surprise, as he was sure that Kamran had recognized him back at the coffee shop. He also knew that two flat tires were a clear sign for his targets to recognize this as a set up, but that did not bother him at all. In fact, it was exhilarating. He had placed himself right in the middle of his favorite sport of cat and mouse.

The little red blip on his GPS locator had started to move. It was time to get back to work.

"Let the games begin," he said with a broad smile as he merged into the traffic.

CHAPTER 36

Sunday 11:30 a.m.

The drive from the Marriott Hotel to the garden was uneventful. Kamran had taken every possible precaution. After reaching Constitution Avenue, he had circled around the roundabout in front of the Parliament building and Presidency several times to make sure that he was not being followed. To ensure added security, he decided to enter the heavily guarded Diplomatic Enclave, courtesy of his security credentials. He drove about aimlessly through deserted streets lining the massive and heavily guarded enclosures of the palatial foreign embassies, before taking Kashmir highway towards Rose and Jasmine Gardens. All these precautionary moves were certainly therapeutic, as they felt assured about the fact that no one was following them.

Sana told him about the tires on her car. Kamran was not surprised, as he told her about what he saw in the video, the facts about their mysterious pursuer, and the fact that he believed the same person was responsible for the attack on Pervaiz.

"So, what do we do now?" she asked. "Should we go to the police?"

"It's not so simple. I have seen how useless the police are in this matter. Whoever holds the strings of this show is controlling from the top, and by that I mean the political top. Even IG Qazi seemed helpless, and I know the guy. Nothing could stop him from going after the truth . . . until now . . . , the police will be of no use. I am sure that Malik Nisar has his goons in every department. We'll have to figure this out all by ourselves. At least until we have some concrete evidence . . . or we can find someone we can trust."

They were parked on a dirt service road leading into a thickly wooded part of the garden. Air was thick with moisture, as it had started to rain lightly. Kamran left the engine running and turned the heater on. Sana was still in shock and trembling slightly. She had been mostly quiet, nodding every now and then, trying to absorb all the information. She was staring straight ahead where a small opening between the trees showed a glimpse of one of the flower gardens that gave this garden its name 'Rose and Jasmine Gardens', home of many varieties of jasmine and around two hundred and fifty different kinds of roses. In the spring, when they were in full bloom, and their heavenly fragrance filled the air, she would come here at least three times a week to walk, sometimes run through the rose and jasmine bushes, and frequently stopping by to admire the traditional chrysanthemum exhibitions that adorned its lawn, despite a recent wave of cutting down of trees, and construction projects that had marred the gardens' natural beauty. Nonetheless, its charm for her was endless, a passion for flowers, especially roses that she had inherited from her father. Knowing it as one of the most romantic destinations she had known, she dreamt of getting married on its grounds someday. Running and hiding from a ruthless assassin was not at all, on her list of potential uses for it.

Vincent patiently watched as Kamran went around in circles at the roundabout in front of the parliament building, before heading down Constitution Avenue. It amused him while he watched this from a vantage point on a service road in front of a row of shops. He saw the vehicle passing through security at the diplomatic enclave, and he decided to wait. He could have used his credentials to pass through the heavily armed security guards of the exclusive community, but he did not want to raise any flags. His patience paid off and after randomly driving through streets for a few minutes, his targets exited the enclave towards Kashmir Highway. He kept a safe distance between two cars, watching them as they entered Rose and Jasmine Gardens. At this hour of the morning there wasn't much traffic around, and he continued to drive slowly behind them as they drove deeper into the expansive park and then finally turned left. He increased his speed as he was not sure about roads in this part of the park, and he was relieved to reach a three-way junction. The moving dot on his GPS locator was slowing down. He decided to park his car on a dirt patch off the road as he saw his target making a sharp left turn into the trees. A few seconds later, the dot came to a halt.

Things could not have gone his way any more than this. His two targets were together, in the middle of a forest with no one to hear them scream and beg for mercy. It started to rain; *"even better,"* he thought while softly caressing the metallic curves of his handgun, *"This is going to be fun."*

CHAPTER 37

Monday 11:55 a.m.

Mark Zeigler had been analyzing raw data from *Marhaba* for the last eight plus hours. He was not expecting a first rate prospecting report in the middle of the night, but he was hoping for a decent topographic picture nonetheless. Unexpected interruption from the Iranian friends had left him frustrated. He took pride in himself for being the perfectionist that he was, and that is the way he liked his data, crisp and precise.

Donaldson had used his defense contacts to obtain satellite imagery and altimeter gravity data from GEOSAT in locating offshore sedimentary basins. Mark combined the data with his seismic survey data to bring up a composite of the ocean floor. He was especially interested in a small area of focus that had shown hydrocarbon deposits during limited studies with small fishing boats over the last few months, and there it was. Mark felt his heart racing as he stared at sheet after sheet of green and red images pouring out of his laser printer. He was in his room at a small but clean hotel in the town of Jiwani. It was no Waldorf, but it did give him some privacy, albeit mixed with ubiquitous sounds of a busy market as a backdrop.

Jiwani was a peculiar mix of old and new. An old style city of twenty-five thousand, with its obvious tribal roots influenced by neighboring Iran, as well as remnants of Omani rule over nearby Gawadar until fifty years ago. Touted as a vital part of the future transportation of goods in and out of Gawadar's deep sea port, it had responded well to the change with massive construction projects around a historic and very compact city center, making it a strange mix of new versus old, mud brick versus glass and steel and traditional restraint versus contemporary chutzpah.

Mark was looking at an area still unexplored by the multinational giants who had been actively exploring around Gawadar. Due to its uncomfortable proximity with Iran and potential controversy surrounding drilling rights, further exploration in the area had been pushed as an afterthought even though prospecting reports were highly optimistic. Potential deposits were scattered around the area, and any misdirected slant drilling could reach Iranian territory, resulting in a diplomatic nightmare reminiscent of the Iraq-Kuwait conflict of 1990. It was a complication where potential spoils were heavily outweighed by the obvious risks. This cautious approach had kept all the major players in a virtual standby mode.

But there it was, in a deep ravine just beyond the relatively shallow basin. Hard volcanic rock, which was making the shelf, could be a *guyot*, definitely an area to avoid but beyond that, topography changed dramatically, highlighted by a vast floor made of porous rock with definite signs of carbon emissions.

"Eureka!" He said under his breath, throwing a tame but definite fist pump into the celebration, before falling back into an uncomfortable, modestly cushioned armchair and picked up his cell phone.

Michael Moxley fumbled with the paraphernalia that cluttered his nightstand. Buried somewhere, underneath a stack of files, amongst his pager, wristwatch, and a bottle of Tylenol was his vibrating, department issued BlackBerry. After knocking most of those items off the nightstand, he finally located it, and in the process of retrieving it, instinctively looked at the illuminated digits of his alarm clock.

"Two a.m.! Great, it better be good," he quietly sat up and looked at the phone. The incoming call was from a familiar number. He got up and tiptoed towards the bathroom, turning slightly to look at his wife who seemed to be sound asleep, undisturbed by this interruption, and then closed the door behind him.

"Do you realize what time it is in this half of the world?" Mike said in a hushed but obviously annoyed voice.

"I am sorry . . . I hope I didn't disturb anything with the missus over there," Mark chuckled on the other end, "No such luck in this part of the world. Unless of course I have a death wish; in that case, I see some mighty juicy, though covered up prospects out there in the street," Mark sighed deeply.

Mike relaxed a bit as remnants of a deep sleep started to lift from his brain, "so what's the news? Did you find it?"

"Of course I did. They don't call me the 'sniffer' for nothing. I could smell that sweet aroma of carbon emissions from miles away."

"Yes, you certainly can, and that is obviously a great talent, but frankly, I don't give a damn about that sniffing flair of yours. You know, and I know that the real reason I love you is that twisted little brain of yours."

"I do have one of those don't I," Mark was obviously enjoying the compliment.

"So what have we got?" Michael Moxley said, getting back to business.

"Mike you are not going to believe this," he sounded excited. "You see, that is why I'm such a genius. The prospecting report suggested possibility of only a moderate sized reservoir in that region. They did see some flattening, but the initial speculation was that it is just a *guyot* and believe you me, no one wants to put a straw in a lava field, you know?" Mark was talking faster now, his childlike excitement palpable in every syllable. "So, anyway when I looked at the site for the first time, the report did not match the hydrocarbon foot print that I saw. It was too big, but was difficult to differentiate it from the thermal emission from a *guyot*. 2-D seismic data does not show much, but 3-D reconstruction made it even more interesting, and thanks to your GEOSAT, the final image made up for all the missing links. It's beautiful, Mike. I'm not joking, but if this data was a woman, I'd marry her right now. Oh hell! It's so perfect, I'll do it anyway."

Mike was trying hard to concentrate on the jargon but it was getting harder and harder. "And what does all this . . . ?"

Mark continued, ignoring him, "We found this large plate of porous rock, a possible reservoir but it wasn't until I generated the 4-D data using imagery from GEOSAT that I saw it, and you have no idea what a thing of beauty it is," he paused briefly to breathe, giving Mike a slight opening to jump in,

"So that means . . . ," but Mark completely ignored him.

"There is nothing but structural traps, and all the way to the Iranian boundary, which of course can get tricky, but the point is, it matches the original carbon foot print, and that baby is ginormous. You have no . . ."

Mike had to intercede. "Mark . . . Mark, Slow down and could you please repeat that in English."

"Oh, I am sorry, got a little carried away," Mark said apologetically. "What I mean to say is that we are looking at a huge reservoir, bigger than anyone of us could have imagined. My conservative estimate, we are talking forty to fifty billion barrels, most likely more."

"And . . . ?" Mike asked.

"Don't you see . . . this could be the largest single reservoir of crude oil discovered in decades, third largest in the world behind *Ghawar oil field* in Saudi Arabia and *Burgan* in Kuwait?"

"Are you sure?" Michael Moxley felt his heart skip a beat.

"Well, we can't confirm this until we actually start drilling, but as far as strength of data and my geological sixth sense go, we have hit the jackpot!"

"Good, I have to report this ASAP, and I'm gonna quote you on it. Okay?"

"Be my guest," Mark said, ". . . and Mike."

"Yes Mark?"

"Ask for a raise for me will ya."

"I'll try but in case you don't realize, if you are right, we won't need a raise. We could just retire and move to the Hamptons."

Sounds like a good deal. Now let me call the other side, or maybe I'll wait till the morning. Is that okay?"

"That's okay. Just give me a couple of hours in the morning to work some details."

"Don't worry about it. These political types are never available before ten anyway." Mark replied with a muffled laugh before hanging up.

Mike stood there for a minute or so, looking at himself in the mirror: thinking of the possibilities, trying to fathom the true magnitude of this news. Should he call to deliver the news now? It was too early. He decided to wait till morning, and came back to bed. His wife noticed his return, still half asleep; she turned towards him, and rested her head on his chest. He caressed the back of her neck gently for a few moments, as she squirmed in his embrace and then went back to sleep.

He tossed and turned unable to sleep and then turned his head to look at the alarm clock. It was 4:15. He was still awake, his mind racing, planning the days that lay ahead. His interest in the whole deal was mostly peripheral. Drilling oil wells did not interest him and thus, he had not paid much attention to it, other than what was required as a part of his job. Now, things had changed. Even he, with his limited knowledge of geology, could appreciate the magnitude of this discovery and the possibilities, both financial and political, were going through his mind at a maddening pace. He did not foresee much sleep in the near future.

CHAPTER 38

ROSE AND JASMINE GARDENS ISLAMABAD

Monday 11:40 a.m.

Vincent slowly advanced his car down the road, steady rain muffling its sound as he cruised to a stop. The sharply angled road kept him from coming in direct view while he partially blocked its entrance and thus, the escape route. He lowered his window, and the cool crisp fresh air hit his face. Vincent took a few deep breaths, and then lit a cigarette, inhaling deeply, blowing circles of white smoke that rose nimbly, fading slightly, and then ducked down to rush out the partially open window. A quick dose of nicotine jump-started his system, and he flexed the muscles of his forearms, clenching and unclenching his fists. He could feel his heart racing a beat or two faster than his usual rhythm. He took another deep breath, taking in the cool moist air. As a calm seem to spread through him, his heart seem to come to a complete, yet momentary stop, and then started back, down to a slow and steady rhythm like a war drum, signaling the start of an offensive; he was ready.

The unpaved service road led to a glorified cul-de-sac barely wide enough to park one vehicle, usually belonging to the gardening staff. A small walk way zigzagged through overgrown bushes and led to a rose garden on the far side of the woods. Vincent quietly walked through the trees, careful not to make too much noise on loose autumn foliage strewn all over the ground, even though heavy rain had taken care of it already, turning the crisp mat of drying leaves into a soggy and soft mess. He could see the back of their heads through the rear window, facing each other, while their hands, engaged in animated movements suggesting a heated discussion. He ducked down as he reached the car, and while he crouched beside it, gently toggled the handle. It was unlocked. He took a deep breath, looked at his watch, and then pulled out his gun from its secure holster, making sure that it was loaded and unlocked. Once satisfied, he pulled on the handle and in one brisk motion, opened the door. Before they could react, Vincent jumped into the back seat, his Glock pointing directly at Kamran's head.

Deep in thought, Kamran barely noticed the door opening, until Sana's loud scream caught his attention.

"Who are you?" Kamran asked, startled by the sudden intrusion, his eyes wide open, staring at the gun pointing right at him. "Oh, it's you . . . ," Kamran's speech faded to a bare whisper as the identity of the intruder dawned upon him.

Vincent smiled but did not say anything. He just let it all filter in: the pleasure of watching the fear on their faces, sweat on the brows, and their dilated pupils; he always got a kick out of it.

"Why have you been following us?" Kamran asked again, his tone firm, his voice more in control. "Who sent you?"

"It's a long story doc, believe me, you don't wanna know," Vincent replied with a grin. He was enjoying the warmer interior of the car and was not necessarily in any mood to rush things along. "The two of you have been a pain in my neck for the last two days. Why don't you just mind your own business, and leave the important stuff for the big boys."

"What are you talking about?" Sana finally composed herself enough to enter the conversation.

"All I'm saying is that you have no idea what you are dealing with. You're like flies circling the dessert and sooner than later, you'll get swatted. Didn't you learn *nothin'* from your doctor friend?"

Kamran suddenly sat up straight, his eyes glaring, "If anything happens to Pervaiz, I'll . . . I'll . . . ," Kamran could not find any words strong enough to express his emotions.

"You'll do what?" Vincent's tone changed dramatically. "What will you do *Doctor Haider*? Are you going to hurt me? Oh . . . oh, I am so scared," He pretended to lean back as if protecting himself and then burst into a robust and unrestrained laugh that echoed loudly in the confined space, "as far as I know, dead men don't hurt no one . . . are you ready to die . . . *doc?*" Vincent moved his gun forward, now barely a couple of inches from Kamran's forehead.

Kamran felt a shiver travel down his spine. He needed to buy some time. He had to stall him until he could think of a way out. His mind was racing, trying out various scenarios, but nothing made sense; beads of sweat appeared on his forehead, and he could feel them transforming from a warm sensation, and then cooling instantly in the chilly ambiance, before tracking their way down towards his eyes, bringing a salty sting along with them. He desperately wanted to rub them, to ease the discomfort, but he could not bring himself to make any sudden moves. It was by far, not the best of ideas, with a loaded gun pointing directly at him.

Sana was quiet again, almost as if she had zoned out. She was looking straight out through the windshield, her gaze fixed at the trees beyond, her hands tightly held between her knees, white knuckles only partially visible above them.

"Why did you go after Pervaiz? He didn't even want to be a part of it," Kamran finally spoke.

"He knew too much. It's as simple as that. Just like you two. I can't take any chances," Vincent replied coldly.

"Why are you doing this? Why did you kill Malik Jahangir?" Kamran asked. He figured that keeping the conversation going might be his best bet.

"Ah . . . so you did figure that one out. The reasons behind it are a little more complicated than that."

"It's about the oil exploration isn't it?" Sana spoke for the first time.

Vincent looked at her amusingly, "I have to admit that it might have played a role, but what do I care. I just do my job, and then call my bank. What they do with the spoils is none of my business."

"Is it Malik Nisar who put you up to it?" Kamran asked

"That name . . . let me see . . . nope, doesn't ring a bell, give me some more," he was obviously having a lot of fun. "You know, I haven't been in your country for that long, but I have learned a lot about it. I love the food. Definitely a lot better than the Pakistani and Indian food I am used to eating in New York. People are nice, simple folks, a bit gullible, but definitely nice. They'll believe anything in a shiny wrapper presented with a little hoopla. This is not a surprise though. We have plenty of those back in the United States. Half of them still believe that Saddam Hussein masterminded Nine Eleven. Politicians keep feeding it to them through manipulative talk show hosts and they just sit there like wide eyed kindergarteners, waiting for the next big threat to be announced."

"I am fully aware of your politics, and the political IQ of your geopolitically challenged countrymen, but this still does not answer my question. Why are you here? Why are we a target?" Kamran had eased into a dialogue that seemed to be his only option, to delay the seemingly inevitable.

"Because you fit the picture; you are the villain. We like our villains. We need them," Vincent ignored him. He was getting animated; his voice excited, his words pressured.

"We love Hitler . . . funny isn't it? We still hate him as a villain, don't get me wrong, but we love him as an investment. We make movies about him, write about him, and open museums about him. Seventy years in, he is still one of our most profitable cash crops. The evil Japanese Empire that was evil enough to unleash nukes on them. Killed quarter of a million civilians but hey . . . *they* were the bad guys! Those despicable Reds, they were next; they were everywhere, within us, destroying our roots. McCarthy literally plucked them out, one by one, whether they fit the picture or not. Nukes were aimed, angry statements exchanged, and then a Hot and a Cold War later, it was over. Look at Cuba; we are still not over them, but Castro doesn't scare us too much. What do we do now, no enemies?" he flailed his hands around as if trying to get attention. "But the public needs to be scared. If they are not, they notice things they are not supposed to notice. Know what I mean? So they threw the worse of the global warming in the mix. What's a better enemy than the wrath of our own mother earth in response to our own behavior?"

"How can you say that? Global warming is real! It is not a political hoax?" Sana spoke suddenly in an angry tone.

"See, that's exactly what I meant. You were silent, even when your life was on the line, but look at those juices flowing at the mention of *the environment,*" Vincent smiled, his white teeth flashing in the solitary ray of sunlight escaping the thicket. "I like angry women; I am finding your rage very arousing," He winked at her, making her cringe. "Don't you ever think that when there are two opposing viewpoints, the truth lies somewhere in the middle? Environment is in danger, but isn't it always in danger? Global warming is real, but the political agendas stretch the truth so far that reality is lost somewhere in the fanfare," Vincent relaxed, and leaned back in his seat. "But you've got to hand it to them. It did work. We became our own worst enemies. Too busy blaming ourselves to notice anything else that went on, giving the kingpins a free ride. It was okay to drive gas-guzzlers, and build worldwide factories without emission codes, but we did it with a sense of responsibility, clutching onto our ever-growing sense of guilt. But that was not enough. The previous administration tried to pursue its own version of fear, and added an Axis of Evil . . . and a war on terror in the mix. This one is perfect, and even better than the commies. Enemies of our freedom, enemies of our lifestyle, they want to annihilate us, well maybe not, but it is scary enough, so we took the money from our children's piggy banks, our social security, healthcare, education, and fought a war against enemies that may have nothing to do with terrorism," His voice started to quiver, his glassy gaze, focused somewhere in the distance.

"And look what that act of aggression did to you. You destroyed your economy, and your credibility in the whole world. Yet you continue your war, and your fancy drone attacks without any regard for innocent human lives," Kamran said with a look of intense hatred on his face.

"Do you really think of these wars as a wild goose chase? . . . Well not exactly for those who will reap the profits of this war economy. It's all about money for those who benefit, and they are happy . . . really happy," Vincent took a deep breath and stopped. He wiped his forehead with the back of his right hand, now covered with glistening beads of sweat.

"You seem to have a good understanding of world politics, the deep impact of social injustice and international interference . . . then . . . why are you doing this?" Sana seemed surprised at the insight and passion exuding from her potential executioner.

Vincent sat up straight and smiled. "It sure feels good to get it off my chest . . . but, my ideals have nothing to do with what I do. I see, I hear, and I learn from my surroundings. That is my passion, but when it comes to my job, I focus on the task at hand, and deal with it efficiently and quickly . . . that's why I'm one of the best . . . and still alive. Besides, it pays well, and for this one, I'm promised a lot more than usual, so for the sake of staying on top, I think we have talked enough. Let's just kiss and say goodbye. I'm not one to prolong the pain; my MO is quick and simple," his voice, gradually reverting to its cold, controlled character.

Kamran had run out of ideas. A golden opportunity had been lost. During Vincent's, speech, he had seen a ray of hope, and noticed a sliver of humanity through a tiny chink in his armor, and now that opportunity was lost. Vincent's stare had turned into steel, his lips taut. He seemed to be going into a state of intense internalization. Rapid and shallow breathing that Kamran had noticed earlier had become regular, his grip on the gun steady, and now pointing to a spot right between his eyes.

"This is not good!" The blur of frost on the windows was spreading to engulf everything around him. His own breathing was now becoming rapid and shallow. He noticed a tremor developing in his hands, and he tried to hide it by clutching them tightly together. He tried to see what Sana was doing, but found her eyes to be in a daze, frozen, and unable to move away from the Glock aimed at him.

"Who did this to you?" Sana suddenly spoke, she sounded almost monotonous.

"What?" Vincent said, obviously surprised by the intrusion.

"Someone must have abused you as a child, for you to be so cold, so inhuman . . . for you to turn into such a . . . *monster?*"

It was obvious that Vincent was not happy with this question and appeared visibly disturbed. Kamran noticed a slight shake in his hands, made even more evident by the sway of the round hollow barrel that had become the center of his universe for the last minute or so.

"It's none of your business. *You!* . . . ," he pointed the gun at Sana, ". . . you scheming journalists impose your opinions on people, play with their emotions and capitalize on exclusives. It doesn't matter if you destroy lives by targeting their souls, and ruin careers for the sake of cheap tabloid sensationalism."

A bold headline on the front page of '*The Daily News*' above a picture of his slain father, lying awkwardly in a pool of his own blood, surrounded by a curious crowd, flashed through his eyes. "MOBBED" the caption had read. The photograph won an award, a haunting testament that exposed the underworld of New York. Vincent was young, but could never forget the grisly image as it stared at him from a newsstand display case.

His lips started to quiver. "You think that you are better than me? I do the same, but more directly. I do not hide behind words. We are more similar than you give yourself credit for; both of us do it for profit, and never look back. We are the same, and now I'm glad that you can die with this burden on your heart."

His voice was a little shaky. The steely resolve in his eyes had faltered momentarily, and Kamran recognized it as possibly the last opportunity to make a move. The next few seconds were purely instinctive and a sequence of highly effective blurs as he jumped up from his seat, swinging his left arm in a backward motion, striking Vincent squarely in the left temple with the back of his open palm.

Vincent was caught totally off guard; he fell backwards, his finger squeezing the trigger in the process.

The bullet shot out of the Glock grazing Kamran in the shoulder and then shattered the windshield on its way out. As if on cue, Sana responded to this development and her hands, hidden between her knees appeared with a small bottle of her perfume, catching Vincent during recoil, with a direct blast in the face.

Kamran and Sana, themselves caught off guard by this turn of events, looked at each other. As their eyes met briefly, the future course of action seemed to synchronize between them instantaneously, and as if joined by a clairvoyant connection, they opened the doors simultaneously, and rolled out.

"Run!" Kamran shouted and Sana complied without hesitation, as soon as she could determine the direction Kamran was heading, and then disappeared into the wooded area behind him.

Vincent felt a sharp stinging pain. Events were blurred as he was recovering from the unexpected blow to his head.

"Son of a bitch is stronger than he looks," he uttered loudly as he clutched the left side of this head. He could feel a sharp linear area of pain, as well as a steady trickle of blood originating from it. The first gunshot was purely instinctive, but he planned his second one better, aiming at Kamran's left eye as it fixated its gaze at him for a moment after the impact.

Still in a backward motion, resulting from the blow to his head, Vincent's quick thinking, and instinctive reactions that have become second nature, took over his actions. Time slowed down to a crawl as he visualized the trajectory of his next shot, calculated the perfect angle for a quick and effective result, followed by a subtle shift of his hand to the left, and aiming at the right temple of his second victim. He was halfway through the process when he noticed Sana turning around in an awkward but rapid manner, bringing her right hand in position from the passenger seat, twisting her wrist internally and activating the spray while it was still in an upside down position.

As he tried to deal with the intense pain in his eyes, he dropped his Glock on the floor. He heard the doors open. "Run," was the last thing he heard as running footsteps faded into the distance before it was quiet again. Steady rain continued to play its symphony on the roof of the car, now considerably louder through open doors.

CHAPTER 39

HALL ROAD, LAHORE

Monday 10:20 a.m.

Naveed Khan was on the phone talking to his attorney Taseer Rizvi. This was his second phone call. His first was to his wife, but he avoided letting her know about his exact whereabouts. He made up an excuse about emergent party meeting that may go on all night. His wife was used to such unexpected changes in plans, especially so close to elections, and though disappointed, did not ask any questions.

The second call was a little hard to get to. DIG Tariq Khawaja was not very keen on him talking to his attorney, who was known for his sharp wit, and brought an impressive rolodex along that was essentially a who's who list of movers and shakers in politics, as well as, in the national and international media. He had been an activist for human rights and liberalization of legal system for years, a quality that had drawn him closer to Naveed, and together they have become a formidable team.

Taseer Rizvi had been an unquenchable radical all his life. From student union activities and peaceful agitation to human rights activism, he was at the forefront of every movement that promoted democracy and challenged military rule. Sitting in his modest office on Hall Road in Lahore, he was going through a proposal by a labor union that he was representing. The view outside the narrow window highlighted by an appreciably old and chipped wooden frame was the usual myriad of motorized vehicles, from motorcycles to small trucks, navigating through the increasingly congested swarm of pedestrians and bicycles. A thick layer of smog and dust gave a hazy look to the view of street lined with hundreds of electronic stores that had been synonymous with the mention of Hall road for decades.

The phone had been ringing incessantly all morning. Calls ranged from simple follow-ups on various cases, to pleas from major human rights NGOs, who wanted him on board to assist in their newest venture. Some wanted his advice and legal expertise, others were just as happy to have his name show up on their letterhead. It was not different from any other day, until his intercom chimed in the middle of such a phone call.

"Sir . . . ,"his secretary's annoyingly shrill voice pierced his ears.

"I've got to do something about her voice," Taseer made a mental note about her new assistant.

"Mr. Naveed Khan is on the line, he says it is extremely urgent."

"Okay, just give me a minute," he realized that the person on other side of his current phone call was still talking, oblivious to the interruption. Taseer smiled, as this was so typical of these calls by his zealous clients. This one was going on about a legal action against the Lord Mayor of Lahore for authorizing cutting down some older trees in order to promote reforestation of a green belt in the Model Town area of Lahore. The trees being discussed were home to a rare brown ant that according to this client was rapidly becoming extinct. This action though developmental, and geared towards beautification, apparently had severe environmental consequences . . . he went on and on.

"Rizvi *Sahib*, we do not realize that unless we have a plan to transplant those colonies to . . . ."

"I'll have to get back to you, Mr. Lodhi," Taseer had no choice but to interrupt him in mid-sentence.

"I need to address something urgent. I truly apologize, but I'll have my secretary arrange a follow-up interview." Without waiting for a reply, he transferred the call to his secretary.

The nature of the call from Naveed Khan was totally unexpected, shocking to say the least. The conversation was short and to the point, and lasted only two minutes, which was all the time that Naveed was allowed for it.

The ripple effect of it, however, continued long after as Taseer sat there, staring at the busy Hall road below. Its loud nature, ubiquitous sounds of its passionate vendors and equally energized customers, along with the strident rickshaws were now only a steady random hum in the background. A universally recognizable, black-and-white portrait of Ché Guevara was staring at him from behind his desk.

The next few hours were spent frantically devising a strategy to contact as many allies before news of Naveed's arrest hit the media outlets, hungry for a sensational sequel to the now old news of Malik Jahangir's assassination.

The first call went to the editor of the daily '*The News*,' a good friend of his who could be trusted to keep this under wraps for now. Two influential members of cabinet who owed him favors were next, and only after promises of utmost secrecy. The next call was placed to the Inspector General of Punjab Police Saleem Qazi. Taseer realized that a huge step, such as Naveed Khan's arrest, could not have been achieved without making sure that various political elements were okay with it, as a backlash to the news was inevitable. Saleem Qazi, however, had always been above the fray of political hegemony and could be trusted to uphold the law while resisting external pressures. He was a little confused by the IG's silence about recent events, especially because the official conclusion of its preliminary investigation made no sense at all, but at the same time, he could understand Qazi's reluctance to create public controversy unless his claims were substantiated by veritable facts.

Saleem Qazi was not in his office and his assistant was unsure of his current whereabouts. In this day and age of electronic leashes, anyone was only a cell phone call away, so the explanation given by the IG office was rather odd, but he had no choice but to leave an urgent message and then wait.

CHAPTER 40

Monday 7:30 a.m.

Michael Moxley flashed his badge at the security, and then in a regimental fashion emptied the contents of his pockets into a small gray bin, took out his laptop out of its case, placed it into a larger tray, sliding it through the scanner before walking through metal detectors. He masterfully managed to balance an oversized coffee mug through this process, as he had done every day for the past several years, and took a long sip from it as he gathered his belonging at the other end. Regular coffees did not hold the caffeine punch to his liking, and he relied heavily on the freshly ground kick of a strong Hawaiian Kona blend, a generous stash of which was always readily available to him, thanks to a friend in Waikiki.

The main atrium was bustling with activity despite the early hour. He stopped right in the middle of the expansive lobby, to make sure that his BlackBerry, wallet and other paraphernalia were in their place. While taking another, fulfilling sip of coffee, he glanced at the large granite CIA seal spread sixteen feet in diameter around him, he smiled. The image of the bald eagle, perched on top of a compass star, filled his heart with satisfaction. As a little kid, he had heard stories of valor and sacrifice by early CIA men and women told by his father, who worked at the Office of Strategic Services, a precursor of the Agency, and then he served as a senior analyst under DCI Allen Dulles in the early days of the Central Intelligence Agency. His untimely death in the field heightened Mike's interest in pursuing his dream of becoming a field agent in the Agency. To this day, no matter how bad a day he was having, a glimpse of this seal brought his mind back into perspective.

He took the elevator to the fourth floor atrium connecting the Old Headquarter Building (OHB) to the New (NHB) and sat on a granite bench under the suspended replica of an A-12 Blackbird plane to enjoy his coffee, until his boss arrived rather than waiting in his office.

Patrick O'Neal, director of The Office of Near Eastern and South Asian Analysis (NESA) was a small man, hardly five foot seven and easily overlooked in the swarm of oversized agents, if it was not for his exuberant personality and the erratic, albeit a feline agility, with which he navigated the crowd. Unfortunately, his office mirrored his chaotic personality and was the sole reason why Michael Moxley had decided to wait for him here.

O'Neal was surprised to see Mike and quickly grabbed him by the waist to steer him towards a quieter corner.

"Did you hear anything?"

Mike cleared his throat and nodded, "You are going to like this . . .," and replayed his conversation with Mark Zeigler.

O'Neal was quiet, and composed as he listened intently without even raising an eyebrow until the conversation reached the projected crude oil output.

"Fifty billion barrels!" his excitement echoed through the spacious four story atrium; he quickly lowered his vice as soon as he noticed heads turning in their direction.

They were standing in a corner overlooking the Old Headquarter Building. Morning shifts were now coming in, and the lobby was filling up with business suits, meticulously fitted on taut and erect bodies, and for some others, rather awkwardly worn and hanging over hunched shoulders, depending on the department and job description, separating geeks from the jocks.

"Are you sure it wasn't five billion? Even that is pretty good," he was talking in a bare whisper.

"No, I am positive. Actually, he said this was a conservative estimate; he expects more."

"Holy Mother of God, does Butch know about it yet?" he asked, his usually red face flushed with excitement as he pushed his rimless glasses higher on his nose, and then nervously ran a hand through his thick, reddish brown hair.

"Not yet, but he will . . . soon. We have about two hours."

"Hmm, I have to get hold of the other guys," he looked at his watch. "It is 1800 in Pakistan right now. They should be reporting shortly. I need you to get hold of Jamshed Khan in Kabul and get an update. I'll need maps, and satellite images, GEOSAT and others of the coastline, and have Zeigler send his maps and data too. I'll meet you in conference room two at 0900."

Mike nodded, pulled out his BlackBerry, and dialed a number, as he watched Patrick O'Neal bump into an oncoming agent, before hastily apologizing and then disappearing around a corner.

CHAPTER 41

Monday 11:58 a.m.

Kamran and Sana scrambled towards the south entrance of Jinnah Stadium. Cold and drenched to the bone, they stood there, shivering in front of the deserted arena. Sana was leaning against the wall, her heart racing wildly, while Kamran stood there, bent at the waist holding his knees, trying to catch his breath.

They had run through the wooded area that separated Rose and Jasmine Gardens from the Sports complex, and the journey had not been easy. As they ran away from the car, the direction was not a priority, and they stayed with the path they took and followed it without stopping. A navigable opening in the wooded area soon disappeared into the thickening forest. Overcast skies and increasing rain was making the visibility worse, as they scrabbled and swatted their way through the thick and prickly underbrush. Stumbling into a stream that ran through the garden was an added insult as they now stood there: covered with mud, and scraped and bruised, looking at the large steel lock staring at them from a formidable wrought iron gate.

Vincent's unfamiliarity with the area was advantageous to them, but they knew that it would not take him long to make his way there. Sana had her cell phone with her but reception was worse than patchy, and every attempt ended up in a dropped call. Unable to take refuge in the locked arena, they walked briskly along the parameter of the stadium's eastern wall away from the direct line of sight, in case their pursuer followed them there. The sports complex was deserted, especially these days as no events were scheduled.

Liaquat Gymnasium, a ten thousand seat arena sat just to the north of the stadium. Usually a much popular venue for concerts and award shows, however, at present, just like the former, it was devoid of any obvious activity.

Kamran looked at Sana who was huddled under an arch, trying to keep herself warm. He walked over to her, gently touching her shoulder. They had hardly spoken a word since their initial escape. She looked up at him with a strained smile as Kamran wrapped his jacket around her.

"Are you okay?"

"Thank you," she sat up straight and shivered as she put the jacket on, and closed it tightly around her. "I'm alright, and you?"

"I am hanging in there," he replied, while rubbing his hands together to keep them warm.

"What are we going to do now?"

"I don't know. We have to figure out a way to get out of here. He can't be too far. Let's try that cell phone . . . ."

Rain had suddenly intensified. Heavy raindrops on the metal canopy covering the arch played their music in unison with the howling winds coming from the Margallas.

Screeching tires of a speeding car in the distance interrupted the steady melody, stopping Kamran in mid-sentence. A deep frown appeared on his forehead as his face, in the shadow of the arch, turned to a darker shade of gray.

He did not need to say anything as Sana was already scrolling through her phone book.

Agha Kamal sat in his office overlooking Jinnah Avenue in the heart of the Blue Area business district. It was a modest looking building overlooking the fancier skyscrapers on the opposite side of the busy commercial artery, running through the heart of Islamabad. *The Capital Chronicle* maintained its editorial office on the third floor.

Traffic was flowing relatively smoothly on Jinnah Avenue below, and he could see the thick cloud cover that extended well beyond Margalla Hills. Drops of rain streaked down the surface of a plate glass picture window. Staring curiously at the patterns created by the errant raindrops, he continued with his editorial . . .

As I watch the droplets of rain rolling down the glass window of my office, separating me from the streets of our capital below, they seem to be taking the shape of tiny tear drops as if being shed at yet another near fatal blow to democracy in our country . . .

"Agha *sahib*, did you see this?" his assistant stormed into his office without knocking, and dropped the latest edition of '*The Pakistan Times*' on his desk. The banner headline, in bold lettering dominated the page:

Naveed Khan Arrested
Linked to Jahangir's murder

Agha Kamal jumped out of his seat. He could not believe his eyes.

"What is this?" he looked at his assistant. "Where did this come from? Why didn't we know about this . . . ?"

"There is more, sir," his assistant interrupted him, pointing gingerly, at a secondary headline under it:

Prominent doctor, journalist possible co-conspirators
Sought by authorities, whereabouts unknown

Rawalpindi – Anonymous sources in the government have reported that prominent surgeon Dr. Kamran Haider, and Sana Aziz, a journalist for *The Capital Chronicle*, are being sought for questioning as alleged co-conspirators in the Malik Jahangir murder case. Their whereabouts are currently unknown. Dr. Kamran has been in the news recently . . .

Agha Kamal slumped back in his chair and grabbed his head in his hands. It took a minute or so for him to gather his senses before he raised his head again.

"Call them," he pointed at the newspaper. "I want to talk to the chief editor right now. And where *is* Sana? Have you heard from her today? Why isn't she here? Does *anybody* know?" he glared at his assistant, who could only muster enough energy to faintly shake his head, trying to avoid any direct eye contact with his chief editor.

Agha Kamal tried Sana's home number, and then her cell phone but there was no answer. He left a message for her to call back as soon as she could.

"I have him on the line one sir," his assistant spoke through the intercom.

"Okay," he replied as he pushed the blinking button on his phone.

"Agha *Sahib*," what a pleasant surprise, I was just about to call you," the high pitched and annoyingly loud voice of Kaleem Niazi pierced his ears.

Kaleem Niazi was Editor in Chief of the state run *Pakistan Times*. His rapid ascent to this post was not any surprise as his family connections in recent political regime were well known, and his strong inclinations, and biased spins did not leave him with many admirers in the journalist community.

"I am sure you were," Agha Kamal replied curtly. "Was that before or after you decided to throw me and my most admired journalist under the bus?"

"Oh, *mutty pao*, Agha *ji*, forget about it. You know how it is. News is news."

"*No,* I don't know how it is, Kaleem. Why don't *you* tell me?" Agha Kamal was seething. "What is your *government* source?"

"You know better than that Agha *ji*. That is confidential. It is not a simple matter. National security is at risk. I can only say that my source is so credible, that even you would trust it."

Once the call ended, he tried to call Sana again, and when he failed to reach her, he spent his morning trying different contacts in order to get to the bottom of this story.

It was just after noon when his phone rang. He picked it up immediately as Sana's name popped up on the screen.

"Hello . . . Sana? Where are you, are you alright?" constant static and driving rain in the background made the conversation hard to decipher. Sana was talking fast, and he listened intently.

"Sana. Did you see the newspaper?"

"No . . . what newspaper? Didn't you hear me say I am trying to save my life running from this guy?"

"What guy? Who is this guy?"

Sana did not seem to be in the mood to explain right now, "Just get us out of here," she pleaded.

"*Us!* What do you mean by *us*? Who is with you? Are you with the doctor? My God, they are looking for both of you, do you have any idea what kind of . . . ."

"Sir, we don't have time for this right now," Sana was desperate.

"Alright . . . just stay out of sight. I'm leaving right now," he walked over to the window. "Traffic seems reasonable enough. Give me about twenty minutes."

Relieved by the fact that they had finally made contact with someone who can get them out of here, they focused on finding a better hiding spot. They did not hear any vehicles coming in their direction; it was time to move. Kamran peered over to make sure it was safe, and then both of them dashed across the road towards the pool complex. The small road leading to a service entrance was inconspicuous and relatively hidden from plain view. They slid under an alcove for a side entrance and waited.

CHAPTER 42

Monday 11:00 a.m.

Naveed Khan looked exhausted. A copy of the newspaper lay open in front of him, with the massive headline glaring at him; it seemed to have drained the last few ounces of energy out of him.

"I am not sure how this got out," DIG Tariq Khawaja said apologetically. "We had been trying very hard to keep it under wraps. I don't know how it could have leaked out." He raised his head and gave a quick and fiery glance towards the adjacent room where Malik Nisar had been sitting.

Naveed did not say anything and kept staring at the newspaper.

"Are you familiar with someone by the name of Sarmad Jan?" Tariq Khawaja asked.

Naveed shook his head," No, it doesn't ring a bell."

DIG Khawaja sifted through a file in front of him, then turned it around towards Naveed and pointed at a photograph. It was a middle-aged male dressed in white *shalwaar* suit and a black and white turban. He had a long flowing black beard without a moustache. A pair of thick-rimmed glasses gave his otherwise stern look a milder touch.

"Ring any bells?" he pointed at the photograph.

Kamran looked at it intently and then shook his head again. "Face is familiar but I can't say that I know him. Do you have any idea how many people I see on a regular basis, especially during campaign trips?"

"If I say that not only do you know him, but you had an intimate supper at his house, how will you respond?"

"I'll say that you are bluffing. Stop playing games and tell me what you really have against me. I've already told you about the incidence in Peshawar, and my car getting stolen. You've always known that because I reported it immediately. You've even seen the FIR," Naveed was losing patience.

"Sarmad Jan has been under surveillance for arms trafficking and mercenary work; he was arrested yesterday," Tariq Khawaja said calmly.

"He has stated under oath that not only did you spent an evening at his house last month, but you also asked him to help you with long range rifles and to recruit someone willing to pursue a potentially suicide mission. He says that he declined your offer since you did not match his demands."

"That's a lie. I never made any such offer to him, or anyone else," Naveed was furious.

"We also have two witnesses who not only saw you at his home, but also state that you spent about fifteen minutes alone with him. Enough for . . . say . . . a proposition."

Naveed just stared back with a look of bewilderment. He could not believe what he was hearing. He leaned forward to take another look at the dossier.

"I can't compete with this. Whoever planned this obviously did his homework. I have no idea what to do," he threw his hands up in the air and then slumped back in the bare metal chair.

"Do you want to say something else"? DIG Khawaja asked gently. He still felt very uncomfortable interrogating Naveed in this way.

Naveed looked like a ghost. Beads of sweat had appeared on his forehead. His tightly clenched knuckles had turned white. He cleared his throat to speak but the words barely came out as a whisper. "I remember him now," he paused for a second as if trying to gather his thoughts. "His beard looks much longer in this photo, and he wasn't wearing glasses when I met him," Naveed paused as he tried to think about that fateful day one month ago. "After the ambush on my group, we left the cars behind and were not sure how to get back. One of our contacts suggested that we spend the evening at the home of one of his friends until things settled down and a ride can be arranged. We spent about two hours at this house, having dinner before someone picked us up. The house belonged to this guy; however, he was referred, as far as I can remember, as Shabbir."

"That is his name, Sarmad Shabbir Jan."

"I see," Naveed said flatly, nodding his head while staring right through his interrogator.

DIG Tariq Khawaja got up, his hands held tightly behind his back as he paced back and forth in the small room. Finally, he stopped in a corner, toying with a loose piece of peeling whitewash on the far wall, as he contemplated his next words.

'What is your relationship with Dr. Kamran Haider?"

"Who?" Naveed blurted.

Tariq Khawaja picked up a copy of the newspaper and dropped it in front of Naveed who flinched again, still shocked by the stark headline. "This was a surprise for me too," he pointed at the mini headline.

"What was *his* role in this?"

"I don't know what you are talking about."

"Do you know him?" Tariq asked again, this time in a firmer tone.

"I have . . . met him a few times. Last time in May or June . . . I think. We worked on a proposal to fund public hospitals, but that's the last time I saw him."

"You also met him in Peshawar once. Two of you had gotten together with Sardar Jalaluddin Khan. What was that meeting about?"

Naveed was getting restless. "As I said, we worked to increase public funding for hospitals. Our meeting with Sardar Jalaluddin was for the same reason. He wanted us to help him in planning and funding new hospitals in North Waziristan and Kurram Agencies . . . ."

"But . . ." Tariq Khawaja interrupted, "wasn't it you who introduced Kamran to him?"

"Yes, I had met him a few times as a part of my campaign. When he showed interest in the hospital, I thought Dr. Kamran might be the best one to involve, so I set up the meeting with Jalaluddin."

Tariq smiled, "And now he is being considered as the mastermind behind Malik Jahingir's assassination."

"What do you mean?" Naveed asked.

"Well, Malik Jahingir was your principle rival in the elections. Is it just me, or is it really peculiar that your top contact in the Tribal Area allegedly had your main rival killed. I think of it as a very convenient arrangement."

Naveed did not say anything.

"So, where is Kamran now?"

"I don't know."

"We'll see to that," Tariq Khawaja said staring right in his eyes, and then picking up the dossier from the table, he left the room.

CHAPTER 43

ISLAMABAD SPORT COMPLEX

Monday 12:30 p.m.

Tires rolling on a wet road make an unmistakable sound. In this case, that sound meant survival. Agha Kamal's twenty-minute estimate was right on. As the gentle hum of the engine, and splashing sounds made by wet tires got closer, Kamran jumped out of his hiding place and waved towards the incoming car. He was excited, not only about getting out of here, but also about meeting someone he could trust and, of course, he was eagerly looking forward to a hot cup of tea.

The temperature was dropping, and the cold air mixing with rain had covered the heavily wooded area in a blanket of thickening fog. The incoming car's headlights blinked, acknowledging his presence. It was hard to tell the make and model of the car due to increasingly poor visibility. To his surprise, the car did not slow down as it approached nearer, and as it got within a hundred feet, started to gain speed. Something was not right. As the powerful engine roared, announcing a suddenly increased pressure on accelerator, Kamran finally was able to look through the windshield. His eyes locked on the driver behind the wheel. A pair of intense, squinting eyes looked right back at him.

"Run," he screamed at the top of his voice as he dragged Sana out of the alcove towards the woods.

The wooded area behind the pool complex was not much of a refuge, as a thin row of young eucalyptus trees led to a wide open practice facility. Fragile trees were no match for the raging car, as it ploughed through an opening in the tree line towards its intended targets.

Kamran was not pleased with what he saw in front of him. The practice grounds were not exactly what he had in mind in terms of a camouflage. On the run, they were easy prey for their pursuer. As Sana pulled him forward, he stopped and turned around, picking up a large piece of wood in the process. Sana tried to protest, but he stopped her with a wave of his left hand.

"No matter what happens, keep running . . ."

"But . . ." Sana interrupted, "this is too dangerous, don't be stupid."

"We have no choice. Keep running till you get to the Gym. Agha Kamal should be getting there any minute. I'll be right behind you. *Now go.*"

Sana hesitated for a moment and then ran.

Vincent saw Sana running away as his car emerged from the trees. He leaned towards the passenger seat to pick up his gun but was interrupted by a shattering sound followed by a shower of broken glass on his face. A thick and dried tree branch emerged out of nowhere, and lodged itself among jagged remnants of the windshield. Instinctively, he closed his eyes and swerved towards his left smashing right into a tree. Vincent saw a bright spark before the airbag deployed, followed by a sharp pungent smell, and a stinging sensation in the middle of his chest. The long continuous echo of the car's horn was the last sound he heard before blacking out.

Agha Kamal sat across from Kamran and Sana on a low woven *charpai* with painted, red black and yellow spindle legs, at a truck stop near *Bari Imam*. Half an hour ago, he had picked them up in front of Liaquat gymnasium as they ran away from their pursuer across the practice track. The loud piercing sound of a car horn had caught his attention before he noticed two people frantically running towards him. There was no sign of any one following them. A car drove past him. A young couple, probably looking for a quiet corner to 'hang out', were probably too focused on the prospect of a good time, to find this situation unusual.

A stunned silence prevailed inside Agha Kamal's comfortable and warm Mercedes. He did not want to risk being spotted in the city, as he expected the authorities to be on alert for the two of them. Looking for an inconspicuous spot to talk, he continued to drive on Murree Road, and then turned north towards Quaid-i-Azam University. Bypassing Islamabad's thoroughfares, he turned left at the university towards the shrine complex of *Bari Imam* and stopped at a relatively quiet roadside restaurant inhabited only by a few trucks at this time of the year. Devoted followers of the Sufi Saint Shah Abdul Latif Kazmi were too focused on the salvation waiting for them at the shrine and hardly paid any attention to the unusual trio of a well-dressed man in his new Mercedes, accompanied by a wet and disheveled couple.

Bari Imam is a busy place year round, attracting over a million visitors paying their tribute to the seventeenth century Sufi scholar. The busiest time of the year is in May, at the time of his *Urs* or death anniversary, when tens of thousands of devotees descend on this small town to take part in the festivities, attending lectures, and spiritual and musical get-togethers, or just to have a chance to kiss the green cloth that covers his grave. Colder, rainy days in fall and winter like this day were relatively quiet and gave them an opportunity to talk in private.

Rain had let up a bit, but left over droplets still dripped from the straw roof that sheltered them. Small breaks in the cloud cover were letting scattered rays of sun to shine through. Cups of hot, strong tea fit for truckers, warmed their hands; soft music from a *harmonium* soothed them, while men clad in traditional green of shrine's caretakers sang a *qawaali,* making the few sitting around them shake their heads in a trance like rhythm.

Agha Kamal had his eyes closed, as he played his fingers on the side of his cup, matching the melody that surrounded them.

"Have you gone completely mad?" he suddenly spoke up raising his head; his voice loud, his eyes glaring as he looked straight into Sana's eyes, "Do you have *any* idea what kind of trouble you are in?"

"I don't think we had much of a choice," Kamran interjected.

Agha Kamal did not say anything for a while as he contemplated what to say next. "Fine, maybe I am being too harsh; I would have done the same thing . . . I guess, but what do you intend to do about this?" he flung the folded newspaper at them. The news headline and his picture were hard to miss, as it landed in Kamran's lap.

"What is this?" Kamran said in disbelief, as he quickly read the first few lines, and then he passed the newspaper to Sana. He did not need to read anymore. His face looked pale, as all the blood had been drained from it, "How can they do this? What gives them the right to play with human lives like this?

His face started to flush as his voice quivered, his lips pursed and his breathing became rapid. "They didn't even leave Pervaiz out. *Beghairat loug,* bastards, couldn't they have even a little regard for what his family is already going through?" he held his head in his hands and fell backwards on the tightly woven *charpai* he was sitting on.

Sana did not say anything as she sat there, motionless. Her eyes glued to the newspaper story.

A flash of lightening near the mountains followed a distant sound of thunder. Cloud cover had thickened as heavy rain started to fall again.

CHAPTER 44

Monday 2 p.m.

Sardar Jalaluddin Khan sat on a low couch. His left leg folded under him, while his right foot dangled off its heavily carved edge. A boom box sitting on a corner table filled the room with the enchanting music of Nusrat Fateh Ali khan.

Allah hoo . . . Allah hoo . . . Allah hoo, the folk singer's crisp and powerful voice resonated around the room as Jalaludin Khan shook his head in tune to the melody. His right hand was moving in a gentle up and down motion, diving down, and then soaring up, as a high note echoed from the walls. He was in the vast receiving chamber of his palatial *Haveli*, meticulously adorned with swords and antique guns.

"Sardar ji, Ijazat hai?" A young manservant standing at the door asked for permission to enter.

The feudal lord seemed annoyed at this intrusion and took a deep puff from a long and elaborately decorated pipe of his *hookah* before giving him permission to enter. The man servant took his shoes off at the threshold, and then half-bent at his waist with eyes fixed at the floor just a few paces in front of him, he took fast, shuffling steps towards his master, kissed a ring on his outstretched right hand and then touched his both eyes with it before shuffling backwards to sit down on a designated spot just to the right of his masters dangling foot.

"Sardar ji", he leaned forward to get as close as he could, without undermining his master's place in this room. "The man from Lahore is here."

"So where is he?" he looked annoyed, "Go bring him in."

"Sardar ji . . . he is not alone," he whispered. "There is a *maime saab* with him."

Sardar Jalaludin smiled; his eyes were suddenly bright with excitement. "*Shaabaashi, Zaman buchay*, good boy, go bring them in . . . no wait . . . take them to the drawing room and offer them *chai pani,* ask the *bibi* if she would like some coca-cola.

Zaman got up and walked backwards, making sure not to turn his back towards his master until he was well past the threshold.

Jalaluddin leaned back on his chair, listening to the suddenly louder beat of *tabla,* complementing the sound of the *harmonium.*

Cell phone in his hand, he dialed a number and uttered a brief statement.

"They are here, get the vehicles ready."

The *Haveli's* elaborate drawing room was in stark contrast to the receiving chamber. While the later was a traditional room with low settees, and adorned with embroidered throws, and colorful floor pillows that lined the walls on a floor covered with thick Afghani rugs; the former was a private and compact room, decorated mostly in the western style. Leather upholstered furniture in neutral tones sat on a bright colored Isfahani carpet next to a curio brimming with Waterford crystals. Off white walls were decorated with replicas of impressionist paintings; a replica of Monet's Water Lilies set on the far wall, welcomed the guest as they entered the room.

Jane Lockhart, though dressed in a closely fitted dark blue business suit, was covered in a generous white wrap, customary to traveling women in this conservative region. She was not too thrilled about being sent to this small town in the foothills of the Hindukush Mountains, brimming with raw testosterone. Despite the fact that women were second-class citizens, and without many rights in this tribal region, powerful men secretly admired accomplished women. While locally, basic rights such as schooling and voting were scarce to native women, Jane was there, on the contrary, just to use her feminine charm, along with strong diplomatic and negotiating skills in her dealings with Sardar Jalaludin, who had a well-known penchant for 'white' women.

The man accompanying her was familiar to the locals, as he was a regular to these parts of the country. Young, clean-shaven and dressed in jeans, he wore a broad smile on his face and exuded the youthful aura of a college student. His collegial appearance, however, belied the tormented and ruthlessly detached soul hiding inside. Junaid Ahmad, a onetime popular, albeit controversial, student leader at the University of Punjab, was widely known for his total disregard for authority when it came to the execution of his plans, whether it involved a student body strike or stretching the law to fulfill his own social goals. Using his influence on the student body to bolster political gatherings, he had made a lot of friends in the political underground, a loosely organized mafia that transcended political ideologies and other mundane concerns, such as party affiliations. While on ground level, political foes resorted to mudslinging, generic criticism and other rhetorical and at times physical attacks; their goons, after all was said and done, congregated underground to make sure that the power base was equally distributed between their bosses. No matter who occupied the big office, there was always an unwritten law that ensured even distribution of massive amounts of public wealth between a handful of political elite who were always within an earshot of democratic strongholds, and privy to all the whispers that echoed from its walls.

Junaid was a powerbroker who maintained such delicate relationships. He never exhibited any qualms about doing the dirty work as long as it served the purpose, and in most cases, that purpose made him and his clients very rich.

"Welcome, welcome to my humble abode," Sardar Jalaluddin walked in through a side door, his outstretched hand holding Junaid by the waist, "How is my favorite *Lahori. . . . ,*" he stopped in mid-sentence, noticing that Junaid's accompanying "*maime Sahiba*" was much prettier than he had expected. "I am Sardar Jalaluddin," he said as he withdrew his hand from Junaid's waist and walked straight towards Jane almost pushing Junaid aside in the process, "and I am honored to have you in my home, madam. I hope that you had a comfortable trip," he said to her in deeply accented yet clear English, as he, after quickly surveying her from head to toe, stared directly into her blue eyes, rendered a shade deeper thanks to her contact lenses.

"Thank you very much, your men made sure that I was comfortable," Jane replied with a restrained smile, recoiling a little under his intense scrutiny, and relieved to see him stop just short of physically engulfing her in his massive arms.

"Please sit down," he offered them a seat before settling down on his own special winged chair decorated with the skin of a mountain lion.

"Great job in Pindi, Junaid; I am very impressed."

"We could not have done it without your help, Khan *Sahib*". Junaid said with his signature smile, "you have always been very kind."

Jane watched this exchange with amusement as the two of them continued their superficial pleasantries as if they were two long lost friends, while in reality, neither one of them would have entertained a second thought about destroying the other if their negotiations went sour.

"So . . . ," Jalaludin started, "what gifts have our mutual friends sent to me this time," he continued while winking at Jane at the same time, making her suddenly feel very uncomfortable.

"For starters, enjoy this," Junaid picked up a heavy briefcase and handed it to his host.

Jalaluddin eagerly eyed the case, and then opened it only slightly, seemingly pleased with what he saw. *"Subhaan Allah* – what a beautiful sight," he took another quick look into the stuffed briefcase, and breathed deeply, enjoying the blissful smell of brand new hundred dollar bills.

"I am happy with the way things are going except . . . ," Sardar Jalaluddin stopped, his expression darkening a bit, "what are you doing about Saleem Qazi? My name was not supposed to be out there, and I am not very happy about that."

"I know, I know," Junaid said apologetically. "Your connection was only because of your address on a slip of paper found in the car. It was only a reference to your meeting with Naveed Khan. A statement to clarify this will be in tomorrow's papers. As far as Qazi is concerned, you need not worry about him; I can take care of him," Junaid lowered his voice; his boyish smile was nowhere to be seen.

"Fine . . . just make sure this does not happen again." Warning was direct, stern and strictly business.

"Now let's drop all this unpleasant business and pay some attention to our lovely guest," Jalaluddin said, raising his palms in Jane's direction and backing it up with a big smile.

"So, my dear . . . ?"

"Jane . . . Jane Lockhart."

"Ah, Jane . . . ," Jalaluddin seemingly savored the sound of her name for a few seconds.

"So, Miss Jane, tell me something about you that I don't already know."

"Mr. Khan, we need not waste precious time on such petty things, let me give you what I came to deliver," she handed him a plain sealed envelope.

Sardar Jalaluddin smiled and conceded, taking the envelope from her outstretched hand, and opening it to remove a neatly folded hand written note on fine, unmarked stationary. He looked at it and smiled. The handwriting was very familiar and brought back memories of a different time, long ago.

Dear Jalal,

It's been a while since I had the pleasure of enjoying your fine company and even finer hospitality.

These are trying days that we are dealing with and you have been a loyal friend. It's time to proceed with the next phase of our plans.

My emissary will give you the details and a link to required finances. God bless.

Your friend,

Pat

CHAPTER 45

Monday 4:00 p.m.

Agha Kamal was not thrilled with the idea at all. As confident as he was in the power of his words, he was not cut out for this kind of covert operation, but Sana had a way of twisting his arm and rendering him helpless.

They were driving towards the hotel; Kamran had an Afghani cap and sunglasses on, while Sana was almost entirely covered in a large white wrap. Agha Kamal presented his credentials to the security guard who after checking the undercarriage and trunk, looked suspiciously at the shy looking couple holding hands in the back seat.

"They are guests of our newspaper, just arriving from Kabul," he told the guard who was still staring through the window. The woman with only her eyes showing moved back, uncomfortable with the direct stare. Her companion, not happy with the situation, gave an intense and disagreeing look back, causing the guard to back off.

"Okay, sir, go ahead. He waved his hand at a guard manning the gate who released the rope holding a weighted iron bar. Agha Kamal finally exhaled as he drove through the open gate.

This, however, was the easy part. After passing through the metal detectors, they walked towards the management offices and knocked at a door. A brass plate on the door read, Assistant Manager of Housekeeping. Javed Karim was an old acquaintance of Agha Kamal who had been instrumental at times in providing him with inside scoops pertaining to high profile guests staying at the hotel. Exclusively, it was limited to information focused on their activities and contacts; it did not involve breaking and entering, but that was exactly what was on Kamran's mind this time.

Javed Karim shifted uneasily in his swivel chair and then wiped his brow nervously with a handkerchief. He was a hefty man who was used to heavy sweating, but it was pouring out profusely now. He did not seem very comfortable with the plan, and the fact that two of the three people sitting in front of him were wanted by the police was not very reassuring.

He quietly listened to their brief explanation, an account that was a seamless blend of need to know facts and some creative fiction.

"Javed, I don't want to put you in a difficult position, but this is the only way to clear their names," Agha Kamal pleaded.

"I know Agha *sahib*," he responded, "but try to be in my shoes. If any one finds out, I'd be ruined. I believe you one hundred percent, and I never believed anything in the papers. I have known Sana *bibi* long enough to figure that out . . . but this is not easy."

"I understand your viewpoint Javed. If I was in your shoes, I'd react the same way," Agha Kamal said, standing up. Kamran and Sana gave each other a panicked look as they started to follow, "but before I leave, can I talk to you alone for a minute?"

A few minutes later, he came out of the office alone, holding a key in his hand.

"Let's go. We don't have a lot of time."

Sana was caught off guard.

"How . . . how did you do it? How did you get him to change his mind?"

"He is a big fan of yours. I just made sure that he understood how much his helping us means to you," he said with a playful smile. "He will have security call him as soon as our guy returns to the hotel. I don't think we have more than fifteen or twenty minutes."

Vincent was staying in room 3018. They took the elevator to the third floor. Javed had sent someone from housekeeping, making sure he was not in.

"I can't be a part of it any more than I already have. I'll wait for you in the lobby," Agha Kamal walked towards the elevator, "Just be careful."

Kamran stood by the door for a few seconds, weighing the pros and cons of his next move, then slowly pushed the key card into its slot. After a second's delay, the indicator-light on the lock turned green and with a gruff swoosh, it unlatched. Kamran looked at Sana who in return nodded with approval.

The door opened with a slight creak, hardly perceptible yet it seemed excruciatingly loud under these circumstances as they tip toed into the dark room.

The room was a standard deluxe, recently cleaned and neatly tucked, nothing out of the ordinary. An open duffle bag lay in a corner with a pair of jeans folded and placed on top of it. A few loose papers and the morning's newspaper lay on the desk. On the nightstand, there was a worn-out leather bound copy of the Bible. Sana picked it up. Inside of the front cover an inscription read:

For Vincent
May this be a guiding light in the journey of your life
Affectionately,
Father Francis

The book appeared extensively read and analyzed. Pages were creased by multiple dog-ears, and verses were underlined with handwritten notes in the margins.

A plain silver crucifix on a gold chain marked a page. She opened the page and read the deeply underlined verse:

"If we confess our sins, He is faithful and just to forgive us our sins and to cleanse us from all unrighteousness." (1 John 1:9)

Aimless doodling around it suggested that he had spent a long time reading this part of the Bible. The words, confession and forgiveness written in cursive, as well as in block lettering were repeatedly added along the margins.

Kamran was standing by the writing desk when he noticed a few crumpled pieces of paper in the trash next to it; he picked them up.

Two were receipts, one from the dry cleaners, and the other one from a shoe store for a pair of sneakers.

The third paper, a page from hotel's writing tablet, had handwritten notes that appeared to be a combination of random words and numbers:

Liaquat Park . . .
A drawing of a gun with a 'bang' flag was sketched in a corner.
Islamabad . . . 32 2
242 . . . 68 . . . 00 . . .

Scattered numbers were written randomly with aimless scribbles in between.

call Mike . . . Langley? Butch?

In a corner, next to a jumble of idly drawn concentric circles and intersecting lines were words that sent a chill down his spine:

Kamran . . . 4023 Honda City white
Jhelum
Sana Aziz capital chronicle
68-B, Shaheen . . . G94 IBD

Kamran stared at his name, as well as Sana's name and address; his eyes open wide with horror.

Obviously, the paper was jotted down during a conversation with someone who was giving him the information. Other names were meaningless at present but could be of importance as events unfolded. The numbers were random and did not make much sense. Kamran looked at them again.

"It could be a house number. The bottom one may be an amount," Sana said from over his shoulder. She had walked up to him, and leaning over his shoulder, was looking at the paper in his hands. Kamran turned around, his face, barely inches from hers. He could smell her perfume, and for a moment, he lost his train of thought.

"Ah . . . I'm . . . I'm not sure, there is no currency sign, but could be. Other numbers could mean anything. They could even be coordinates'" he quickly gathered himself.

Kamran neatly folded the paper and put it in his pocket, still running the numbers through his mind, but he finally gave up, sensing a growing frustration.

Sana was looking at the nametag on the duffel bag:

Vincent Portelli
Hawkeye@bluedragon.com

There was no address or phone number, just the email address. She quickly jotted down the e-mail address in her notebook next to the verse from Bible.

The rest of the room was clean. She walked into the bathroom. Toothbrush, paste, aftershave and deodorant were lying scattered around next to the sink, along with a bottle of capsules labeled as temazepam, a prescription tranquillizer she recalled from her father's medicine cabinet.

She noticed something red along the edge of the sink. She looked closely; it seemed like a drop of dried blood. She carefully wiped it with a tissue and after folding it into a small ball, stuffed it into her purse and walked back into the room where Kamran was sitting at the edge of the bed deep in thought. She sat down next to him, watching him fidgeting with his fingers and staring in space. A few minutes passed, but he continued to randomly move his hands while still in deep thought. She reached forward, held his hand and squeezed it gently.

"It will be alright."

"I sure hope so, I sure do," he replied, squeezing her hand back with his other hand. It was delicate and soft, and its warm touch helped him relax.

"What do you think these numbers mean?" He was holding the paper in his hand.

"I don't know. It certainly links him to Liaquat Bagh; the rest could be related to his contacts. Isn't Langley the site of CIA Headquarters?" she asked, her face flushed a bit, and she withdrew her hand slowly.

"I know, but that is a common misconception," he replied with a playful smile. "Actually, the CIA headquarter is in Mclean, Virginia. Langley is an incorporated community, within Mclean, however, I am sure that by Langley he means the same, and that could be very interesting, but I am not surprised if someone from the CIA is part of this; I want to find out who is helping him *here*, in Pakistan."

"Smarty pants . . . but I *am* impressed," she gave him a sheepish nudge with her elbow. "It has to be Malik Nisar. I am telling you, the guy has a definite creepy side to him."

"I agree with the creepy side, but I am not entirely sure about the other part, we are definitely missing something."

"Any way," Sana changed the subject, "what do you think about this verse from the Bible?"

"Looks like one of his favorites. He certainly seems intrigued by the thoughts of sin and forgiveness."

"Maybe it's his way of dealing with his inner struggle about what he does for a living. I noticed a very distinct conflict in him during our encounter," Sana used her background as a Psychology major to analyze the subject.

They were quiet for a few seconds trying to piece together all this information.

"We should leave," Sana said, realizing that they had been there too long.

"I know," Kamran, replied, sill staring at the paper in his hands.

Sound of footsteps outside the door made him jump.

"He can't be back; Javed Karim said he will give us a warning," Kamran whispered, visibly rattled as he grabbed Sana's hand and pulled her towards the wall away from the door.

The footsteps had stopped just outside the door. The sound of someone fumbling through pockets came from just outside in the hallway, and then a familiar but ominous swoosh led to the clicking sound, announcing an unlocked door.

They stood still, flat against the wall, holding hands, hearts racing.

Kamran held a trash can tightly in his right hand, ready to attack as the door unlatched, and then slowly opened towards them.

CHAPTER 46

ROSE AND JASMINE GARDEN ISLAMABAD

Monday 2:50 p.m.

Vincent Portelli was no stranger to pain. From being the scrawny kid at the playground in a tough neighborhood, to a barely lightweight boxer in sparring, he has had his share of hits: blinding pain from misdirected punches and their throbbing reminders in the days to come.

This was different. In past, he had been able to visualize a potential attack, and in the process, he had learned to anticipate and move with it just so slightly in order to dampen its impact. With his agility and reflexes, quicker than most, not only was he able to avoid many punches, but was also able to control their severity, as well as the extent of bruising that showed up the next day.

This, however, was different . . . and entirely unexpected. His mind, focused on his potential prey getting away in front of him, was so busy relishing the spoils that he completely overlooked the fact that his prey had turned into the hunter.

He had no idea how long it had been, maybe five minutes, if his recall of previous events and time was accurate.

His forehead, now swollen with a painful bump, throbbed with a pounding headache. A faint but ominous white cloud of smoke was rising from the smashed front end of his car.

"I'm such an idiot!" he said, while struggling to push the air bag away from his face.

"What was so hard about avoiding a . . . tree!" He screamed, as he struggled to squeeze through the half-ajar door and rolled onto the ground, writhing with a sharp stinging pain in the middle of his chest where the airbag had hit him. Out of the corner of his eyes, he could see two people getting into a car. Through his still watery eyes, he could not clearly identify them, but was convinced that the two were his targets, getting away.

It took another few minutes for him to get his senses before he gathered his belongings from the car, packing them in a small backpack as he looked around. No sign of life was in sight, which was a good thing, but equally bad was the answer to the question, how to get back, as it was clearly impossible to expect a taxi in this wilderness.

He thought about calling his contact, but his ego stopped short in the process.

"I'm a survivor, and I'll survive on my own. I'm not ready to declare my failure to anyone . . . not yet." And that is when it occurred to him. Kamran's car might still be in the woods, as obviously someone else had picked them up, and then had driven in the opposite direction.

Walking around the stadium was not easy. With every step taken, he was introduced to a new bump and a new bruise as he staggered, still wobbly and lightheaded towards the woods retracing his earlier drive.

Kamran's car was in the same place as expected, its engine still running as Vincent covered the last few steps in a hurry and scrambled in through a partly opened door. It was warm, a relief from the damp cold air outside as he slumped into the driver's seat, trying to catch his breath. A fragrant air still dominated the inside, though an unpleasant reminder of the perfume spray that had blinded him, ruining his plans. He pondered over his next course of action, as he was not familiar with this part of the city. His GPS guide was damaged and he had to make his way out of these gardens on his own. He closed his eyes, resting his head back for a few minutes and felt the fog lifting from his brain; his breathing became more regular as he took a deep breath, before putting the car in reverse gear to get it onto the main road. Remembering his last drive, he turned right at the next turn and was soon relieved to see the signs for Zero Point and Kashmir highway.

Driving was not easy as cold air coming in through the bullet hole in the car's windshield kept the inside temperature low and thus repeatedly fogging the window. He could barely see as he struggled to wipe the inside of the windshield constantly in order to maintain visibility. Massive construction projects had dominated the roads in Islamabad. Generally considered as a good idea, the unfinished project had been marred by the whims of changing rulers, corrupt or simply aimless contractors and bureaucratic red tape.

Construction of overhead bridges and underpasses aimed at decreasing congestion and preparing the roads to accommodate rapidly increasing traffic volumes had led to endless detours. In order to streamline traffic, drivers were not allowed to turn at signals, and instead made to use U-turns down the road. If this was not enough, the dirt created by all this construction had mixed with unregulated traffic emissions and the damp and heavy winter air to create thick smog that constantly dominated the air.

The makeshift entrance to Islamabad Highway at Zero Point was hard to see through the foggy windshield, as he missed the exit and kept driving straight on Kashmir highway. Frustrated at his quandary of not being on a familiar road, he made the first left turn into sector G-9. Having no idea where he was, he decided to rely on his sense of direction as he turned into a street following a sign to Rawalpindi.

Something did not look right. The landscape had changed dramatically as he screeched to a halt realizing the blurred outline of a tiny figure suddenly appearing in front of his car. It was a child, comfortably running around in the middle of the road. The child, about six, did not seem to be surprised at all at the sudden appearance of his car as he walked around towards the driver side window, and knocked. Vincent could see two big bright and inquisitive eyes on the dirty face with a runny nose, trying to peek through the driver's side window, his tiny nose and lips pressed against its cold exterior, smudging it with a mix of spit, mucus and mud. Vincent rolled down the window and looked into the brown eyes shining with unbridled excitement as a tiny hand came through the window and spread in front of him expectantly.

"Hai..lo," he whispered in his tiny voice, spotting his foreign looks.

Vincent could figure out the fact that the child was asking for money, something commonly seen in the poor neighborhoods of Pakistan, a gesture that he had repeatedly encountered during rallies in rural Pakistan, but this was entirely unexpected, and the last thing he imagined in the prosperous Capital city. He had a chance to visit numerous cities of this country during the last few weeks, but had mostly stayed in crowded bazaars and upscale-neighborhoods. His encounter with the common folks, and the politically passionate poor was mostly limited to a safe distance behind the podium; the last place he expected to see a neighborhood like this was in the middle of a sector in Islamabad.

Still a bit shocked by what he saw, he opened the door and walked out, hoping to find somebody who could speak English, and show him the way. It was a narrow street lined by small brick walled quarters. Some had doors, weathered wooden or rusty tin, while others were only covered with makeshift curtains made from pieces of thick white cotton or coarsely woven *bori* sheets made from jute for privacy. Straw sheds could be seen everywhere for added room and shelter from the elements. The street was only partly paved, muddy due to recent rain with potholes filled with stagnant water; a pungent smell of nearby garbage dumps filled the air. He'd never seen anything like this. It was as if he had been miraculously transported to an alien dimension.

The arrival of a car, and a stranger, was news that did not take very long to spread through the compact neighborhood. Children, not very different from the first one he saw, emerged from all over and gathered around him, looking at him expectantly with bewildered eyes, trying to figure out his features and speech that differed from their usual encounters with outsiders.

He got out of the car but did not feel good. He was feeling lightheaded again and tried to ask one of the children if anyone could speak any English, but all he got in return was a few chuckles and a twist of hands, telling him that he wasn't getting anywhere. His headache was getting worse, as he stumbled on to a nearby wall to brace himself: his vision was getting blurred, his legs ready to buckle under his suddenly dead weight. From the corner of his eye, he saw an elderly man, slowly walking towards him, holding a cane. Rushing rainwater in a nearby stream and barking dogs dominated the background as throngs of children dressed in soiled, at times tattered clothes, gathered around his car and started to converge towards him. He felt suffocated, and he tried to breathe hard, but that made him even dizzier. He tried to clutch at the nearest wall but a loose brick gave way to his touch and fell from the top, making him lose his balance; through his rapidly blurring vision, a hazy convergence of eager faces was the last thing that he remembered before losing consciousness.

CHAPTER 47

Monday 2:30 p.m.

Sardar Jalaluddin Khan sipped on a steaming cup of tea facing his two guests, who now looked at him expectantly for his decision. "Would anyone like more biscuits? I had them flown in especially from this excellent bakery in Islamabad, just for you," he pushed the untouched plate of biscuits towards Jane.

"Thanks," she said, and took one, then delicately nibbled on it.

"See, they are good aren't they? And don't worry about anything. Everything is in control," he said smiling. "I'll take care of everything, as long as you work on getting my name out of the newspapers."

"What about the weapons . . . ?" Junaid Ahmed asked, hesitantly, unsure about the degree of trust he was willing to put in his host.

"I told you, don't worry about it. Weapons are one thing we know about. You have to trust me on that."

"What is one to do in order to make sure . . . that none of this is linked to us?" Jane Lockhart asked.

Jalaluddin seemed a little annoyed, and tried to paste a forced smile on his face, "We never use American weapons, and you know that. My supplier from India gets the latest Israeli weapons, still modeled on the Russian stuff that we had captured during the war. Believe me; you have no reason to worry."

"What about this supplier . . . in India. What if the Indian government suspects his hand in all this?"

"Suspect . . . ? I'd be surprised if they didn't."

"What . . . ?"

Jalaluddin smiled, "You see, every government in this region, or . . . oh well . . . any government *anywhere* in the world, thrives on weapon sales. The Indian government does not care where they go, as long as they are not used against them. Actually to tell you the truth, they probably don't mind them being used in Pakistan at all."

"What do you mean? They just look the other way?" Junaid asked, a little surprised at his answer.

"A little instability . . . this side of the border is not necessarily bad for them . . . you know."

"So they are okay with this, and of course . . .our politicians are okay with this as it distracts people from the real issues. What a twisted world we live in . . .and I love it! Junaid was all smiles.

"Very interesting indeed," Jane joined in. "I had studied all this during my briefing but . . .the reality is so much more fascinating."

"I know, I know but . . .we are still concerned about all the attention we are getting; I think we need a little distraction," Junaid said in a worried voice.

"I know exactly what you mean," Jalaluddin replied. "I have a few guys in place. I know exactly what to do; just make sure you do your part and feed the newspapers," he said as he got up and started walking toward the door.

"What are you planning to do?"

"Don't worry about it. Leave it up to me. Whatever it is, it'll be big enough to serve your purpose, and that should be your only concern. Now if you'll excuse me, I have to be somewhere soon, but as my guests, you're welcome to stay as long as you wish. My servants will be at your service," he stopped just outside the doorway and locked eyes with Jane, a big grin appearing on his face, "and please . . .do not hesitate to ask for *anything* that you need."

Walking out into the narrow hallway, Jalaluddin pulled out his cell phone and dialed. Someone answered, immediately.

"It's a go for the Pindi Project. Do you have everything in place?"

He listened for a moment; a furious expression appeared on his face, obvious, even in the darkened corner of the empty hallway. "Yes . . . I couldn't be surer. That sleeper cell has been dormant for a long time. Seventy virgin *Hoors* cannot hold their religious devotion forever. There is only so much time before their sentiments fizzle, and our investment is wasted. The timing is just right. We need the diversion right now," he whispered into the phone and then listened intently to the other side.

"Faizabad bus terminal would be perfect and the afternoon rush will add to the drama. Do we have everything ready?"

His face was stern, his manner serious, deeply focused, and all business.

"Activate one of the websites. Send out some emails just before. Use a different group this time, something less known. It's time to add another sinister, *fundo*-religious group in the discussion to throw everyone off.

He stopped for a moment to revisit his plan, nodding absently to details coming from the other side, and then spoke quietly, "Pick two more targets, any two will do and spread them out, you know what I mean."

The response from the other side made him smile. "I know. Just make sure we have plenty of witnesses. Start the suicide bomber rumor immediately. People are vulnerable in a time like this. They'll believe anything," he paused for a moment. "One more thing, if any one of them does not make it; make sure to send a check to the survivors. It is far easier to recruit these crazy zealots if they know that their families will be secure."

CHAPTER 48

SATELLITE TOWN, RAWALPINDI

Monday 2:55 p.m.

In a small basement storage room, a solitary figure sat in a dimly lit corner. The room was mostly bare except for a calligraphic poster of a Quranic verse and a cheaply framed picture of the *Kaaba* on the unfinished plaster wall. A rusty, metallic door represented the only access to this eight by ten foot cell; a small ventilation slit, secured with a wrought iron grille formed its only direct contact to the outside world.

A musty odor dominated the stale air. Faint rays of the afternoon sun filtered through the ventilator, highlighting the dancing particles of dust pushed into the basement by cars speeding on the road outside, which were marred by unsightly potholes filled with a mixture of mud and sewage. A naked low powered light bulb dangled from the ceiling over a woven *charpai* bed covered with a thick brown blanket.

The only inhabitant of this dismal lodging, a young man in his early twenties, remained motionless. His head was down, his lips fluttering, making soft clucking sounds as he recited verses from the scripture; his bright eyes were locked in on the glowing screen of a cell phone held tightly in his visibly shaking hands.

"It is time," was all that the text message said, but he did not need more. He knew exactly what it meant. His lips moved faster, his chanting becoming louder as his trembling hands, pulled out a picture of his family. It was taken a year ago as they celebrated his Master's degree in physics. Clean-shaven then, he stood tall in his new suit and a rented graduation gown with a big smile on his face. But, that was an eternity ago, in a different life. It was before he had met his new mentor, a local Imam who had instilled in him a new love for *Allah* and eternal life and contempt for the worldly ways of the people around him. "A misguided herd of religious masqueraders," he called them, "they have lost their way by becoming slaves to the infidels from the West. They are the hypocrites and they need to be punished for that."

It was before he had accepted his new life, certainly before . . .his father, the guiding light in his life had become a collateral casualty in the war on terror when he visited his family in the tribal belt for a wedding. A drone attack had missed its intended target by a hair, yet again.

He raised his head. His tears were dry now. A peaceful resolve dominated his countenance, as he stood up, kissed and then gently placed the photograph in his breast pocket, and walked towards a darker corner of the room. His hands were not shaking anymore as he bent down to pick up a heavy duffle bag and walked up the stairs towards the room's solitary exit.

"The end justifies the mean," he reminded himself. He trusted his leader and it was not his place to question his decisions. *"I am a mere vessel in the grand scheme of things, a soldier of Allah."* There were a lot of questions, concerns, trepidations that frequently crossed his mind. "Is this the only way? Does *Allah* truly want us to wage this war that will kill so many . . .some guilty and a lot more innocent? Who is the benefactor, who so generously funded their operations?" He had raised these questions many times and had been satisfied by the eloquent answers he received from his teacher. "Allah works in mysterious ways, my son. Sometimes, we need to close our eyes and ears, and just focus on the paradise that awaits us. Too many questions are a distraction from the disgraced *Shaitaan*. Do not fall for them, or you too will lose your way," his teacher had advised softly after explaining their mission to him.

"I apologize for my transgression my leader," he had replied, with tears in his eyes while kissing the silver ring on his teacher's outstretched hand, "I was weak for a moment; it will never happen again."

The thought of his teacher's words reassured him. He was ready for the ultimate test of his faith.

"Allah-u-Akbar," he said firmly, as he stood at the front door of the modest home, and then briskly walked towards his motorcycle parked on the sidewalk.

CHAPTER 49

KUTCHIE ABADI, ISLAMABAD

Monday 4:00 p.m.

Islamabad is a city of contradictions. Not only is it in stark contrast with the rest of the country because of its cleanliness, unique planning and contemporary design but also within itself, where different sectors cater to different social classes by zoning according to plot sizes. As in any other major city of the world, it has its share, though modest by comparison, of poor neighborhoods, but unlike the other cities, they are hidden behind perfectly camouflaged perimeters formed by green belts and at times tastefully erected walls.

These are the *kutchie Abadi* neighborhoods, or literally 'raw settlements', interspersed among the upscale neighborhoods without any outward signs of their existence. Residents in these settlements belong to the labor class that is responsible for the basic upkeep of their affluent neighborhoods. A large number of them belong to the Christian minority and are home to the cleaning crews that are responsible for keeping Islamabad in a spic and span condition. Unfortunately, in a predominantly Muslim country, these Christian minorities remain on the outside of the target areas favored by religious and most other charity organizations.

Recently, various new initiatives by conscientious citizens involved with locally stationed diplomats have started programs that have brought their plight into the public eye, giving these people new opportunities that include adult education but still, the disparity seen in a *Kutchie Abadi,* can be a shocking experience for the unsuspecting eye.

Vincent opened his eyes and saw the old white bearded man he saw earlier looking at him through soft eyes full of compassion. He seemed generally pleased to see him awake and quickly got up from the woven stool next to him.

"Angreji bolta hai?" a woman said from behind him, commenting on his mumblings in English while unconscious, asking her husband if the stranger spoke English. Vincent turned around and saw the smiling face of an older woman holding a plastic glass in her hands. He tried to smile, but even the slightest effort sent a sharp piercing pain through his head. She held her hand out to offer him the glass.

"*Paani* . . . vaater?" she said hesitatingly but in a soothing, affectionate voice.

"Who . . . you . . . are?" the old man asked, in broken English.

"My name is Vincent . . . Portelli, where am I . . . how long was I . . .?"

"Maybe . . .ten minute," his host replied, holding his hands up, all ten fingers extended.

Vincent was sitting up now.

"You look . . . white . . . weak . . . you hurt?"

"I am fine," Vincent held the glass of water in his hand and poured it down his throat in one gulp. He felt parched and the cold glass of water made him feel much better.

"Need . . . more . . . rest," the old man insisted, as he tried to gently push him back onto the wooden platform bed lined with a thin quilt filled with cotton. It was soft and very inviting, but Vincent was already trying to stand up.

"I have to go, but thank you very much for helping me," he said slowly as looked around. The house was simple: two rooms attached to a small earthen verandah and courtyard with an outside latrine. Two woven beds and some scattered straw stools made up for all the visible furniture. A small outdoor kitchen covered with a straw roof was emanating the scrumptious aroma of supper on the stove and made him aware of the fact that he had not eaten anything since a cup of coffee in the morning. He quickly dismissed the thought and saw several members of the family: a young girl covered in a large *chaadar* peeking through a partly open door, several young children staring at him from a distance with intense curiosity. As soon as they noticed his attention, they scurried into different parts of their small but neat home.

Despite repeated pleas from his hosts, inviting him to stay for supper, he mustered up enough energy to get up, thanking them for their help and walked towards the front door. As he walked towards his car, throngs of local residents followed him curiously, watching this banged up foreigner, a rare sight in these parts of Islamabad. Various expatriates living in Pakistan and diplomats, especially their wives, had been seen more frequently in the recent years working with NGOs aimed at improving the living conditions in these neighborhoods, but those people came in late model chauffeured cars and were dressed up, commensurate with their stature in society. This particular foreigner, however, did not fit the picture.

Vincent got into the car and tried to start the engine. But as before, it sputtered a few times and then shut down again. He slammed his hand on the steering wheel, frustrated, not sure of his next move as he noticed three blinking green lights on a small console just under the steering wheel, and just like that, he got the answer to his predicament.

Petrol prices in Pakistan had been rising for years, out of proportion to the income of its citizens. In order to supplement this pricey dilemma, the people of Pakistan had improvised and embraced a novel solution, converting their vehicles to run on natural gas instead of petroleum. Most of the older cars in this country now ran on compressed natural gas or CNG. Petrol is used only in emergencies or during times of natural gas shortage. Unfortunately, an advantage in price comes with a compromise on speed and acceleration and thus somewhere during the chase through streets of Islamabad, Kamran had converted his car from CNG to petrol in order to achieve better acceleration. Vincent flicked the small switch next to the flashing green light, pumped the accelerator a few times and turned the ignition key. When the engine started with a roar, a small group of children still left watching the spectacle clapped and whistled with joy as Vincent backed the car out of the street, waved at his new friends and drove away.

Driving away from the *Kutchie abadi*, Vincent could not help but think about the simple, deprived people who had shown so much love to him. He was amazed at the existence of such a neighborhood in the middle of a city known for its meticulous upkeep, manicured vistas and upscale affluence. This contrast seemed to represent everything that Pakistan was, and Islamabad wasn't. His lips curled in a smile as he thought about the curious eyes of those mud covered children prancing around, utterly oblivious to the realities of life that surrounded them, reminding him so much of himself, in a long lost childhood.

Once he was on the main street, it was not difficult for him to navigate towards Rawalpindi. He got on to Agha Shahi Avenue, the newly constructed thruway aimed at taking the burden off Islamabad Highway. Traffic was light, and he was able to make up for some lost time. He was lucky to have found a gas station attendant who could speak English and had given him explicit directions to get to Murree Road. At the end of Agha Shahi Avenue, he turned left towards Faizabad to get to Murree Road and was welcomed by the swarm of disorganized traffic and congestion, a hallmark of Rawalpindi, and certainly a welcome sight for him in the current circumstances.

Slowly and patiently, he inched forward in slow moving traffic towards his destination. He needed to hurry, in order to catch up with his targets, but somehow, did not feel any sense of urgency or frustration. Instead, he felt calm, at peace with himself. After idling at a traffic light, as he moved slowly with the traffic he was still thinking about the enormous gap that existed between the haves and the have-nots of this country, when a loud explosion filled the air. The earth shook around him with such intensity that for a moment he lost control of his car. His ears felt as if they were going to burst and then he could not hear anything.

It was a few minutes before he regained his senses. His headache had returned and this time with a vengeance. Every inch of his body throbbed like a sore. The blast wave had shattered his windshield, pinning him back into his seat. Tiny fragments of broken windshield were all over him, scratching him in all the exposed areas. Fortunately, his eyes were spared as he carefully brushed the glass off his body. His vision, blurred in the beginning, was getting better and he was able to focus better. The ringing in his ears had subsided though every sound was still muffled and everything around him appeared to move in slow motion. With much effort, he dragged himself out of the seat and then out of the car holding on tightly to keep his balance.

The scene before his eyes was uncanny. Staggering forward from behind the car door, he encountered a blast of hot air mixed with a swirl of dirt and debris. Pieces of paper flew around in circles matching the echoing screams that filled the air, with emotions ranging from excruciating pain to sheer horror.

It seemed as if the world had stopped around him. Vehicles, both private and public, cars, vans, pickup trucks and local transit buses were stopped as if forced by a magical hand in mid motion, scattered around at odd angles. People around him were trying to gather themselves. Some were nursing their wounds, but nothing grave being at the periphery of the blast zone, while others just stood there, trying to absorb the horror that confronted them.

Vincent looked back at his car; it was not in any condition to drive. He decided to walk but the path was strewn with debris, which got denser as he moved towards Murree Road. The cries and screams emanating from a frantic crowd were getting close. He could see the twisted remains of the bus at the center of the explosion. Its decorative, aluminum studded sides were interrupted by gaping holes from the heavy shrapnel; its roof was blown up into a million tiny pieces, all in turn becoming lethal missiles made up of wood and metal, had lodged themselves into objects, inanimate and otherwise, near and far.

Clothes flew about aimlessly in the breeze, intrigued by the sudden warmth in this cool autumn afternoon, a woman's underwear, thrown about in the open, a sight otherwise unseen and hard to imagine, in this conservative society. A mud strewn object thrown randomly in the midst of a heap of tattered suitcases, travel bags and shoes turned out to be a severed limb charred at the end to which was attached a body, only a few minutes ago.

Vincent, shaking with a sudden chill that went through his body, moved forward, unable to keep his focus away from a child marred by blood stained clothes, crying over the still body of her mother. He lunged forward, away from it all, trying to hold the crucifix around his neck before realizing that he had left it in the room. He turned away towards a quiet corner behind a half blown shelter, fell to his knees and threw up.

Shaken to the core, he gathered all the strength he could find to walk away, trying not to look anywhere but straight at the short span of road in front of his feet. Noises around him were now a cacophony of screams and loud shouts mixed with instructions from rescue workers. Sirens of police vehicles, ambulances and fire brigades got louder every second. He waved to a passing taxi. The driver, reluctant to leave the scene at first, could not pass up the several thousand rupees thrown at his lap, and agreed to take him and drove away.

The drive back to the hotel was a blur. Vincent remained in a daze, unable to focus. Events of the morning felt like a remote and hazy memory as he entered the hotel, stumbling, barely able to concentrate. He could not hurry enough to get back to his room, take along bath and then go to sleep.

While fumbling through his pocket to find the key, he heard sound of people talking. It appeared to be coming from his room. The door was locked. He tried to listen but could not make out the words. Instincts took over and he took his Glock out of the holster, keeping it at his side, out of sight from any casual observers in the presently deserted hallway. He crouched down halfway; shifting his weight onto the balls of his toes, ready to propel him forward. The Glock in his right hand, he rapidly engaged the key card . . . in and out in one smooth flick of his wrist and then in one swift motion, opened the door with a rapid forceful thrust.

CHAPTER 50

CIA, NEW HEADQUARTER BUILDING MCLEAN VIRGINIA

Tuesday 8:24 a.m.

G abriella Gomez sipped on her coffee, as she half reclined on her chair, wiggling it left and right, her head thrown back. The sensation was soothing, especially with her eyes closed. It gave her a feeling of freedom as if she was on a sailboat like the good old days when she spent time on her grandfather's boat off the coast of Mayagüez in Puerto Rico. Her eyes were half closed, blocking out the brightness of her multi-screen console. Memories of her childhood brought back a sensation of total freedom and made her smile. She took a quick peek at the digital display of international time zones and closed her eyes again; a little over half an hour, and then she would be home free.

Her shift as an analyst at the South Asian Desk's communication room was almost over. Considering the ongoing instability in that part of the world, and the fact that her shift actually covered most of the day in Pakistan, her night was pretty uneventful. A few news reports needed to be summarized including a report from the Embassy in Islamabad, updated the new developments, and aftermaths of recent events. She had her paper work ready and waited for eight thirty, when her relief would show up, hopefully on time. A quick briefing and after that, she just needed to walk over to her director's office, leave the reports in his inbox and walk out. She was off the next day and looked forward to doing absolutely nothing.

"Oh what now?" she exclaimed annoyingly at the sound of an incoming message.

She took another long sip from her cup, and without changing her position, with a sweep of her left hand, picked up the paper just spewed out by the noisy printer.

"Holy crap!" she stood up straight as soon as she saw the first word, underlined and printed in bold red:

Urgent

Massive Explosion, Rawalpindi at 1629 local time. At least 150 dead including five missionary workers, three US citizens - Standby for details.

She slumped back into her chair and closed her eyes for a few seconds. She needed to relax, and erase any thoughts of a leisurely time that were going through her mind, and then she was ready. She needed details before she could file a report so she turned to the secure line and connected to her liaison in Islamabad.

Patrick O'Neal's red face turned crimson as he slammed the paper down on his desk. He was in his office early, preparing for a meeting with Senator Harding, chairman of the Defense Appropriations Committee later in the morning. The last thing he needed was bad news, and unfortunately for Gabriella, she was the one holding it. She would have been very happy just faxing the report to his office, and then leaving the dirty work to his relief, but he was in his office earlier than usual, and she did not have a choice but to face his music. She could swear for a moment that she saw froth coming out of his mouth, and fully aware of the dire and time tested consequences of interfering, stood still, her hands locked in front of her, her eyes looking straight and down at his desk.

"Jesus Christ! Who did this?"

"We are not sure sir, there was a blip about some previously unknown organization called *Paasdaran-e Jihad,* or faithful of Jihad, but I could not locate any more details about them."

"Idiots . . . you are all a bunch of idiots!" the froth was unmistakable now as he took his reading glasses off and stood up, walking around the desk towards her, "Did you talk to Jane?"

"No sir," Gabriella kept her eyes down.

"And you dared to come in here . . . without even talking to her," walking over to her, he looked up and waved his index finger inches from her. She could smell a hint of cognac on his breath

Gabriella remained calm. She was used to this. "I tried, but she had been out of her office since this morning. Her cell phone is out of range. I have paged her; she should be calling back any minute."

"Okay, fine, you can go now," he stepped back, and dismissed her with a flicking motion of his hand, giving her barely enough room to squeeze between him and the table.

"And patch her to me as soon as she calls."

"Yes sir," Gabriella replied and walked out of the office.

O'Neal walked over to the window, looking down towards the west parking lot and stared at the woods beyond. He was holding the paper that was just handed to him. He looked at it again and then crushed it in his fist, squeezing it so hard that it made the veins on the back of his hands pop up, and then he threw it across the room towards the door.

Patrick had been overseeing covert operations in South Asia for more than three decades, and had seen it all. He was recruited as a young graduate out of Georgetown: thanks to a legendary photographic memory, and his major in political science and advanced calculus; he was tagged, and then scooped up by a CIA recruiting team, always on the lookout for prospects on campus.

He showed a great prowess for international conflict analysis and joined Gust Lascaris 'Gus' Avrakotos on the Afghan desk. It was1977, and dark clouds were threatening on the northern borders. Marxist opposition of PDPA (Peoples Democratic Party of Afghanistan) seriously threatened Afghani President Daud's Government. Unrest in the Panjsher valley by religious parties that opposed the struggling government was supported by Prime Minister Zulfikar Ali Bhutto's government in Pakistan, actively engaged in an effort to suppress the emerging issue of the separatist movement for an independent Pashtunistan in the North West Frontier Province, a movement that was allegedly supported by the Daud government. In August 1977, Chief of the Army Staff, General Zia-ul-Haq overthrew Bhutto's government in a military coup amid accusations of corruption and massive rigging in the general elections, and the whole situation became even more complicated.

In July 1979, the CIA launched its support for the rebels fighting against the Communist government of Nur Mohammad Taraki, and contrary to popular belief, six months before the soviet invasion of Afghanistan. After the assassination of Taraki, they found a friend in the new President Hafizullah Amin. President Carter's advisor

Zbigniew Brzezinski, in a 1998 interview with *Le Nouvel Observateur,* recalled: *"We didn't push the Russians to intervene, but we knowingly increased the probability that they would. That secret operation was an excellent idea. It had the effect of drawing the Soviets into the Afghan trap. The day that the Soviets officially crossed the border, I wrote to President Carter. We now have the opportunity of giving the Soviet Union its Vietnam War."*

On July 3, 1979, US President Carter signed an authorization to fund anticommunist guerillas in Afghanistan, and thus started the massive arming of Afghan *Mujahedeen* as a part of the CIA operation known as "Operation Cyclone."

Patrick joined Gus Avrakotos and was thrown into the midst of the largest covert operation in the history of Central Intelligence Agency.

All through the Soviet-Afghan war, learning the intricacies of this brutal, yet delicately balanced conflict, gathering data to support Congressman Charlie Wilson in securing unprecedented appropriations, he had made a lot of friends in that region. Sardar Jalaluddin Khan was one of them. As a young tribal scion, Jalaluddin was willing to do anything in order to keep his wealth and power base intact, and that stemmed directly from the expansive poppy fields under his control. He was given a free reign to export heroin from his region, as long as he kept some key Pakistani politicians and Generals in the loop, and ran his trade in a way that facilitated the money made to be recycled into arms supplies for the *Mujahedeen.* By the mid-eighties, more than eighty percent of the world's finest heroin was supplied by people like him, while the authorities looked the other way.

Patrick picked up a secure line and dialed the number. A familiar voice answered on the second ring,

"JK . . . this is Pat."

"Of course you are. How can I forget the voice of my old friend? What made you think of me so early in the morning; it must be early morning up there in Washington, yes?"

"Yes Jalal, it is. It's too damn early to be pissed off, but guess what? I am!"

"Why my friend . . .is there something wrong . . .they didn't pass you over for promotion again, did they?" Jalaluddin acted surprised, "Do you want me to talk to the Vice President about it?"

"Yes, there *is* something wrong," O'Neil ignored the remark, "and you damn well know what this is all about. It is about the explosion in Rawalpindi. *Please* . . . tell me that you have nothing to do with it."

"What would I gain from something like that? You get all the reports. I am sure that by now you know exactly who did that. You probably even know what he had for breakfast, or even, what color underwear he was wearing," Jalaluddin said with a loud guttural laugh.

"You mean to say that for a change, it really *is* done by one of those religious fanatics?"

"Who else; you know that Patrick, it has all the finger prints of Al-Qaeda? Isn't this what the state department will say in its press release?" Jalal toyed with Patrick.

"God damn it Jalal, you can't just go on making decisions like this on your own. DCI will be hitting my head off the tee this afternoon, unless I give him at least a semi-plausible explanation. Your Al-Qaeda bit works for CNN; it doesn't work on my boss."

"I know, I know. I was just joking. There will be references on a website. I'll send you a link; you can add it to your report . . . and don't worry about the head count, it's only the usual collateral damage."

Patrick was not known for his sense of humor, and he did not appreciate Jalaluddin making light of this situation. His manner became more serious as he sat up straight in his chair, and then leaned forward to barely inches from his speakerphone.

"Look, JK, I am being very clear, and our close relationship set aside, things are different now. We are not in the eighties anymore. Anything developing in your region directly impacts our interests. You have to let me know before any such measure is taken, and especially . . . especially if there is even the slightest chance that American lives are in jeopardy. I hope that I am being *crystal* clear."

"Yes you are," Jalal responded, somewhat taken aback by the sudden change in the tone of their conversation.

"I am glad that we have this clear. Now, is there something that I still do not know?"

"Well . . . actually . . .," Jalal paused, trying to choose his words carefully. "There may be two more targets . . . I don't know all the details, but . . ."

" . . . Jesus . . . JK! Please call me back as soon as you find out!" He hung up the phone, sliding down in his chair, locking his fingers behind his head and squeezing it hard in the process. Suddenly, very aware of a throbbing headache, he opened his desk drawer to look for aspirin.

His intercom rang.

"DCI is on line one sir," his secretary's voice chimed in.

"Jesus . . .couldn't wait to humiliate me, couldn't he!" he sat up straight, took a deep breath and picked up the phone.

The conversation with the DCI was, as expected, short, to the point and full of the usual verbal insults that he had gotten used to since the arrival of this young, energetic boss who had vowed to reform CIA for good. A sentiment he did not appreciate, or agree with; however, along with a number of his veteran colleagues, he had learned to deal with the change.

"I'll take care of it, sir, and report to you before noon today," he said politely, holding back his emotions as he hung up.

He was not happy with the current situation. Things were not the same since the new Director of Central Intelligence had arrived. Covert operations were monitored very closely to avoid any diplomatic fiascos. Early missteps during the war on terror had left the United States more vulnerable to terrorist attacks, as well as International criticism in regards to its foreign policy and tactics. A change in management style of the Agency was in line with the new administration's efforts to reclaim some of the old glory, and solidify the stature and role of the United States, as the leader of the free world. Sardar Jalaluddin Khan had been a good ally during the Soviet-Afghan War and had continued to be an invaluable asset, but things had changed. Their relationship with Pakistan was more delicate now. Pakistan's Inter-Services Intelligence (ISI) and India's Research and Analysis Wing (RAW) were escalating their own agendas in order to gain supremacy in the region. Pakistani and Afghan versions of the Taliban, and various regional religious organizations sympathetic to their cause, were gaining strength in the North Western Frontier Province, while Pakistan's political future was dwarfed by the large and ever changing cloud of uncertainty that loomed over its democratic institutions. In this situation, considering that special interest groups of varying backgrounds were actively involved, and a massive amount money was flowing, and increasingly so at an alarming rate, many other options were available, so Jalaluddin had become more of a liability.

It took him a few moments before Patrick regained his composure. He wiped the glistening sweat off his brow before getting up and walking to the window. The parking lot was almost full now. A tour bus had just arrived discharging an excited group of tourists; they huddled together trying to organize their photography paraphernalia while waiting for their assigned guide to arrive. An earlier group, already roaming the grounds had gathered around the ever-intriguing 'Kryptos'. Some were taking pictures of the S-shaped sculpture by Jim Sanborn, whereas others were feverishly copying or photographing its cryptic text with hopes of cracking the well-known code. A look of disgust appeared on Patrick's face; it was another testament to his disapproval of the new and more public image of the Agency.

Deep in thought, he walked to the coffee maker and poured himself another cup before returning to his chair and dialing another number.

Michael Moxley picked up on the first ring.

"Mike, do you have any operatives in Waziristan Agency . . . on JK specifically . . . right now?"

Moxley's response pleased him.

"Reliable?"

"Very," Moxley replied

"Good. I want him to go ahead and clean up. I can't afford to put it off any longer . . . and also, your guy in Pakistan, what's his name?"

"Vincent?"

" . . . Ah yes, Vincent . . . he knows too much. Once he's finished the job . . . deal with him too."

CHAPTER 51

Monday 4:01 p.m.

Kamran asked Sana to move away from the opening door. His hands, tight around the edge of the trashcan, throbbed with a dull ache, his knuckles white from the tight grip. He heard something metallic hit the door. Expecting a gun, his grip tightened even more as he stepped towards the door, not leaving even a moment to chance.

Sana was not sure what the plan was. She felt her heart race so fast she feared it would jump out of her chest. Beads of sweat appeared on her forehead, and then one of them slid into her right eye. The salty bead started to burn her eye but rubbing it made it even worse, blinding her momentarily as she struggled to keep her line of vision intact through the half open left eye.

The door opened swinging hard towards Sana. Kamran jumped up from his semi crouching position and bolted towards the door. A loud scream . . . a feminine scream, almost stopped him in midair, his gyrating arm flexing violently to break the impact of his swing as the trash can hit the wall just short of the door with a loud thud.

A terrified woman in housekeeping uniform jumped back, almost toppling over her cart, cursing loudly in the process.

Kamran looked at Sana who gave him a sheepish smile, a sigh of relief followed as she walked out of her corner and then rapidly moved towards the terrified women to help her get up.

"I am okay," she raised her left arm to signal, refusing her help as she pivoted on her right arm and sprung her body back up. She was a short, dark woman in her fifties and she seemed very agile. In one fluid motion, she bounced back to an erect posture, pulled her loosened salt and pepper hair back under her *doputta,* gave them a fierce look and walked towards the next door, still mumbling under her breath while pulling her cart in tow.

Still recovering from the scare they just had, they locked the door and walked briskly towards the lobby. Agha Kamal was waiting for them in the coffee shop.

Sana was relieved to be safe and back in the open. Standing in the middle of the spacious lobby, as soon as she saw her boss, she waved at him excitedly. Her arm rose for the gesture but did not finish the movement as Kamran grabbed her wrist and pulled her hand down and towards him. Startled, she tried to protest, pulling it back in the process. Kamran gripped it even harder, almost hurting her, using his other hand and brought his index finger to his lips. She understood the caution to be quiet, but still somewhat confused she tried to look up and towards the lobby, but Kamran, in one sweeping motion, slid his hand around her waist pulling her close to him and walked towards the picture window of a carpet shop. To an onlooker, from behind them, they looked like a young couple nestled in each other's arms full of love, looking at things to buy for their new home. Fortunately, no one could see them from the front where the alarmed look on Sana's face would have raised some serious questions.

Momentarily alarmed, but trusting Kamran's judgment, she felt comforted by his closeness and for a fleeting second began to savor the firm, yet gentle grasp of his arm around her waist while resting her head comfortably on his chest. The feeling lasted only a moment as she spotted Vincent in the reflection off the shop's window walking into the lobby. They walked slowly, holding hands, and then moved behind a large plant next to a thick marble pillar. Vincent looked disheveled, obviously hurt. His eyes had a blank stare that did not seem to be interested in anything around him, his face grimacing with a painful expression that seemed to transcend any physical pain that he was having.

Vincent walked slowly to the elevator and pressed the call button, nervously shifting his weight from one leg to the other as he waited for the next elevator, visibly relieved when it arrived, and then vanished from their view. Sana, still staring at the now closed elevator door did not move for several seconds, comfortable in her safe zone.

"Ahem," Kamran coughed gently to remind her that she was still holding him, squeezing his hand a little too tightly. Embarrassed, she blushed and released his hand, stepping away slowly, "Agha *Sahib* must be waiting for us . . . ," she said, not sure about what to do next, ". . . we should go."

"Sure . . . yes . . . yes," Kamran said hurriedly, "he must be worried," as he started walking towards the coffee shop.

Agha Kamal was finished with his cup of *chai* when he saw them coming and did not wait for them to come in. He seemed tense when he met them in the lobby. Deep furrows on his forehead, a ubiquitous part of his well-known countenance, were deeper than usual. He waved his hand towards the door asking them to follow him. The valet had already brought the car upfront. No one said anything along the way, and both of them, somewhat nervous about his serious demeanor, did not dare to be the one to break the silence as Agha Kamal put his car in gear and drove out of the hotel premises. ·

Vincent stormed into the room propelled by his own weight. Two terrified housekeepers ran out the door leaving the cart behind at the sight of him holding a gun now pointed straight at their faces. His head still spinning, he wondered if he had a concussion, but then decided that he did not care if he did. He walked into the room, pushed the cart out into the hall and threw himself on the bed. He thought about taking his shoes off first but decided that he was too tired and exhausted, mentally and physically, to even raise his head off the pillow once he got to it. He was too tired to notice the oddly placed trash can by the door, scraps of loose papers next to his bed, or the fact that his bible laid open on his bed instead of the table. He especially did not notice a golden ballpoint pen next to his bible bearing the inscription "Capital Chronicle" on it.

CHAPTER 52

Monday 4:30 p.m.

Naveed Khan was surrounded by his family. His wife sat next to him and was quietly reading the Qur'an, her eyes red from crying, her tears dried along wavy lines on her cheeks left by running mascara. His daughter, who was just glad to see her father, now slept peacefully in his lap while clutching her favorite doll. Naveed's brother and sister had come in from Lahore and now sat quietly. His sister, Ayesha, consoled his wife while his brother sat there watching the news on privately run GEO News channel that was showing an endless loop of banner headlines that mentioned the rising evidence incriminating him in the murder of Malik Jahangir. Finally, he gave up, raising his hands in the air.

"What is wrong with these people? Why don't they stop with these lies? Who is paying for all this?" he said, agitated by the continuing rhetoric.

"Let me get my hands on them, I'll kill them!" His face was turning red.

Malik Nisar was on TV talking to his supporters at a small rally about the legacy his cousin had left behind.

"My brother, my friend . . . ," he choked up a bit, " . . . blood of the hard working poor was running in his veins, what made him special was his love for the people who loved him back, because he was one of them. He showed them the future, and we are not going to let him down. We will not let his enemies detract us from his mission. We will finish what he started, and we will not stop for anything less. Our enemies are everywhere; some of them have been apprehended, and we all know who they are, and we swear on the grave of our *shaheed* leader, we will not let him down. Thank you and *Pakistan paindabad.*"

"*Haraamy,* Bastard," Nadeem Khan, Naveed's elder brother threw an air punch at the TV, "Who does he think he is trying to fool? Anyone can see through this charade."

Taseer Rizvi entered the room and smiled at the emotionally charged Nadeem, and then nodded a *Salaam* at Naveed's wife Salma, as he walked through the living room into the adjacent study. Naveed carefully lifted his daughter who squirmed at the movement and opened her eyes before going right back to sleep in her mother's lap.

"How can they do this to me?" Naveed said, pacing back and forth in the small room.

They were alone in the study. Taseer Rizvi stood by the window holding a pipe, taking small puffs intermittently.

"They have no proof, no credible witnesses. Even the motive they state is sketchy at best."

"I know," Taseer spoke up after exhaling a long and lingering trail of smoke that raced towards the partly opened window and then broke up, mixing with fresh air and disappeared. "The evidence is all circumstantial. They don't have anything on you, but we'll need to be very careful. Malik Nisar has been in this business for a long time. He has a lot of friends, and on both sides of the law."

He looked out the window at the gathering crowd of press corps that had begun to set up their equipment just outside of the main gate.

"We need to talk to someone . . . someone on the inside," Naveed chewed over the answer for a moment, "What about Qazi? You two are close . . . aren't you?"

"I know," Taseer replied uneasily, "I was thinking about him too, but. . . ."

"Then what are we waiting for?" Naveed interrupted him in mid-sentence. "He's got to know more about all this. He may know where it all started. Who gave the order to arrest?"

"That's the problem," a somber Taseer replied, "It was Qazi who gave the order."

CHAPTER 53

Monday 5:30 p.m.

The Police Department in Pakistan suffers from a lot of maladies, none of them more restricting than a lack of adequate resources. In a country where border security is the top priority and overshadows law and order security within the country, flow of federal funding finds the military as its principle recipient. While it ensures peace and psychologically comforts people that their borders are secure and any military transgression from their nemesis India will be thwarted instantaneously, it does not provide the same sense of security about their immediate neighborhoods.

Inadequate funding, and inferior, and at times, archaic training methods have left the police force as an ill-equipped, financially frustrated, and politically exploited department that has perpetually struggled to maintain a position of respect in the eyes of the people.

Inspector General Saleem Qazi was packing his bags to leave for Islamabad. It had been a hectic day. Dealing with the mundane routines of daily administration was taking over his growing itch to go back to Rawalpindi. He had just heard of the car bomb that hit Faizabad, but his bags were on his bed waiting to get packed long before the news arrived.

He had not had much rest over the last thirty-six hours. Maintaining focus on his day-to-day activities, while keeping in touch with the investigation in Rawalpindi, had not been easy. He had always been a workaholic and a tough boss, but he had also realized very early in his job as a boss in the Punjab Police that things never got done unless he took a personal interest, and incessantly hounded his subordinates to pull at the frequent strands of slack in their work ethic. He had tried very hard to maintain a level of excellence in the Punjab Police, keeping corruption and the rampant cases of bribery in check, but he had found himself frustrated. Looking at his own financial struggles, he could understand the moral dilemmas faced by his lesser-paid colleagues on a regular basis.

His phone vibrated, it was Kamran. He picked it up immediately, trying to balance his bag on his shoulder as he walked out of the house.

"Hello . . . Kamran . . . is that you?" he said as soon as he pressed the call button. "For God's sake where are you? We have been looking all over for you."

"I noticed that," Kamran replied curtly, "I am sure you have your best hounds looking all over for me."

"No Kamran, it is not like that . . . ," Qazi tried to explain.

"Do you really think I am involved in this? Don't you remember that it was *you* who had me called in for this investigation in the first place?"

"Kamran, listen to me. It is not as simple as this. There are things that I have no control over," Qazi replied," I have to be at the airport, just tell me where you are and I'll send you an escort as soon as I get to Islamabad. You need to come in Kamran. I cannot help you if you keep running."

Kaman was tempted and wanted to tell him, but he felt Sana staring at him; he looked at her and saw her shaking her head.

"I'll call you later," he said quickly and then hung up.

Qazi took a deep breath and shook his head, then flipped the phone closed and walked out the door.

"What!" He almost jumped out of his seat.

Qazi had gone through the security and boarded the plane. His phone vibrated again. Thinking it was Kamran he answered immediately. It was DIG operations.

"What do you mean there were two more?"

"There were two more explosions," DIG replied

"God have mercy. Where?"

"The first one was at Tolinton Market, right around the evening rush; we are estimating around a hundred and twenty."

"Oh God!. . . and the second?" Qazi was shaking.

The plane had started to taxi.

"It was a bus stop in Gujranwala. A car slammed into a bus, but luckily it was empty. The driver was the only casualty. About a dozen injured but none too seriously."

"*Shukr Alhamd-u-lillah,* thank you Allah," Qazi said. "I need to get off this plane. I can't leave now," he was sweating profusely.

"It's OK sir. I have the situation in control and my team is on it. Besides, your meeting with the President is very important."

"Please turn your phone off, we are ready to take off," a polite admonishment from the flight attendant interrupted him. He ignored her.

"Are you sure you don't need me?"

"Sir. . .we are fine . . . don't worry about it."

The plane was on the runway; its engines now roaring.

"Sir, you have to shut off your phone," the flight attended shouted firmly from her jump seat.

He glared back at her, "I'll call you as soon as I get there," he said quickly and then turned his phone off.

The plane had gained speed, the fuselage rumbled and growled with a final thrust of its twin Pratt and Whitney engines, and then it was airborne.

CHAPTER 54

Monday 9:26 a.m.

The New Hampshire Presidential Primary was still more than three months away, but Butch Donaldson was not taking any chances. Preliminary polls showed him trailing just behind the front-runner in the Republican race, but recently Governor Oliver Jones Jr. of Ohio had dealt with his own difficulties with rumors of an extra-marital affair. Even in the national picture, economic turmoil and a mounting national debt had shifted the winds in Butch Donaldson's favor. The country was looking for a change in direction, and he was right there, ready to take the helm.

This was his third stop in the critical primary state in the last two months, and he had a feeling that Independents were finally warming up to him.

A large crowd, the largest by far during his rallies, had come out to listen to him, despite the chilly October morning, and he was ready to enchant them with his Southern charm.

He looked at his watch; it was 9:26. He raised his hand with four out-stretched fingers towards his security chief standing by the backstage door and mouthed . . . "four minutes." In return, he received a thumbs-up signal telling him that everything was all set. He looked over his notes one more time before handing them over to an assistant and started walking towards the stage entrance.

"Senator . . . Senator!" he heard the loud voice of his chief of staff, followed by quick footsteps coming towards him, "There is a telephone call for you."

Butch Donaldson stopped and then turned around, his eyes fiery with rage. There was nothing he despised more than being late for an engagement, and his chief of staff, more than anyone else, knew it well. The fact that he had even thought about taking the call did not sound good.

"C'mon Jessie, I'm sure this can wait. Unless the President of the United States is dead and they are offering me his job on a silver platter, I don't think I'm interested."

"Well, POTUS is safe and sound Butch, but I still think you should take this," He quickly walked over to him talking quietly as he held his shoulder and walked him towards a quiet corner, "It's Charlie."

"Charlie . . . what the hell is this all about?" Butch took the phone and said annoyingly. "I thought everything was going okay at your end. I heard the best news of my life yesterday, what can be more important?"

"I know Butch," Charlie replied, "I know, oil and all . . . great news but I have a problem with Vinny. I think he has become a liability."

"So deal with it. You have people there. Have someone take care of him or something. Why are you bothering me with this?" Butch said, lowering his voice to a bare whisper.

"It's not so simple, Butch. There were some problems. Apparently, there are people sniffing clues over there, and they seem to have a lead on Vinny. I just got a very disturbing call from him. He is the toughest rascal I have ever met; I can bet my life on him, but something has gotten to him. He sounded scared. If he is caught, or something happens to him, either way it can lead to us."

"Damn it, Charlie!" Donaldson wiped his brow and sat down on a stool, "What do we do now?"

"I'll take care of it. I just wanted to give you a heads up. Jessie knows exactly what to do if any rumors start to fly. He has the entire contingency plan ready. I am leaving for Pakistan right now. One of my contacts is already on it. I'll keep you posted," Charlie hung up.

He gave the phone back but sat there in deep thought, a deep frown developing across his forehead as he steadied his nerves for a minute, then he looked at the watch . . . 9:33.

"Good heavens!" he got up quickly, took a long deep breath, wiped his brow with his handkerchief and looked up. In an amazing transformation, all the worry had vanished from his face. He smiled as he walked towards the stage, *"It's show time."*

The crowd roared as he walked on the stage. Waving to his adoring fans until the applause died down, he looked at them over the teleprompter.

"My fellow Americans, thank y'all, for coming up here so early in the morning. I am heartened by your support despite the cold weather and the lingering threat of rain," he pointed towards dark clouds gathering on the eastern skies, "but your love is all I need to feel warm today."

" . . . But, it is all worth it when one thinks about the direction the country is heading into. The American Dream has been taken away from us. The economy is in shambles, healthcare is practically non-existent, despite their tall tales of so called band-aid reform, and global terrorism is reaching the confines of our neighborhoods, threatening the comfort of our homes. And what are we doing about it? We are sitting at Pennsylvania Avenue having a Cuban cigar, trying to be friends with those who threaten our freedom."

The crowd was warmed up and buzzed with excitement.

Butch Donaldson knew this moment too well. This was what he thrived on. It was his moment to shine. The crowd was his, and he went for the kill.

" . . . It is time for us to take action and vote those liberals out of the White House. It's time to throw away their expensive policies and their large governments. Let's stop those cozy walks with terrorists on the beach. It's time to stop twittering with Hugo Chavez, and delete Ahmadinejad and Kim Jong Il from our Facebook profile," The crowd broke into a loud laughter.

He waited for them to settle down, "We are the greatest nation in the world. I say that we need to forget about the world. I say we need to forget about their problems. It is time to close our borders, fortify our strengths and stop interfering with affairs of those that do not concern us. Countries like Pakistan and Afghanistan need to be left alone to solve their own problems, on their own bankrolls, and if anyone acts against us, we can take care of it. Our brave soldiers know exactly how to defend our great traditions."

The crowd erupted into a loud applause as he pointed to a group of Marines in uniform propped up on the stage behind him.

"God bless the great state of New Hampshire, and God Bless America."

The crowd was still cheering when he reached backstage and snatched his overcoat from an aid.

"It's a wrap, gentlemen; now let's get the hell out of this God forsaken tundra."

CHAPTER 55

GRAND TRUNK ROAD, RAWAT

Monday 6:12 p.m.

Agha Kamal pulled into a gas station just outside Rawat. They were about fifteen miles south of Rawalpindi. After refueling the car, he drove it into a parking area next to a small restaurant. Evening traffic was heavy; two passenger vans were parked at the restaurant with their passengers, who were busy stretching their legs during a half hour respite from the cramped seating that awaited them for the next few hours. The parking area, an extension of the gas station was a popular rest stop for travelers: it consisted of a small restaurant, an outdoor barbecue shop, a kiosk selling snacks and a well-stocked convenience store built next to a small but neat mosque.

Agha Kamal was busy with a phone call. He seemed distressed, listening intently while pacing back and forth, taking nervous puffs from his cigar. At the end of his conversation, after patiently being on the receiving end, he became increasingly animated. His ubiquitous cigar, now a half charred stub and still glowing, was in a nearby flowerbed as he continued in a rant, waving his arms freely while talking into his Bluetooth headset.

Kamran sat in a low chair sipping on his cup of tea, while Sana, developing a sudden craving for a hot *samosa*, stood by the nearby kiosk waiting for the cook to scoop up the next fresh batch of the mouthwatering triangular snacks. Looking from their respective positions, they could sense that something was wrong. Agha Kamal did not return immediately after he ended his phone call; instead, he chose to stay near the car, pacing back and forth for a few minutes, while Kamran and Sana sat near a small hearth, relishing the spiced potato and onion filled *samosas* dipped in mint chutney. The snack tasted even better since they had not had anything to eat since their half consumed breakfast at the Marriott's coffee shop.

"It's terrible," Agha Kamal muttered under his breath as he sat down next to them.

"What happened?" Kamran asked, sensing his grave mood.

"There were terrorist attacks."

Both of them gasped in unison.

"Attacks, you mean more than one? How many? Where . . . ?" Sana asked a series of questions.

"Three . . . in Rawalpindi, Gujranwala and Lahore," Agha Kamal answered solemnly, shaking his head. "At least three hundred dead; they are still searching through the rubble for more. Those despicable dogs waited for the rush hour . . . it is terrible."

"Did anyone claim responsibility?" Sana asked.

"There are a few leads, but nothing conclusive yet; CNN is already blaming Al-Qaeda, as expected. Some unknown government source is pointing fingers at India and RAW, responding to the recent guerilla surge in Kashmir. I'm . . . I'm pretty sure it is neither." He dabbed his generous brow with a monogrammed handkerchief, "I was assigning the team to investigate further before I can start on my editorial."

"I'm also wondering about the timing of these attacks," Kamran, who seemed deep in thought, spoke up, "it just does not make any sense."

"What do you mean?" Sana asked.

"Well . . . ," Kamran searched for the right words, "as soon as any of these events take place, everyone instinctively blames it on Al-Qaeda, the Taliban or anyone of the several active religious organizations. This is something we can thank the Bush, Cheney, Rumsfeld triumvirate for. We blamed Malik Jahangir's murder on them, didn't we? And look where that got *us*. I don't see any religious fanatics in this group?" He smiled and looked at Sana who smiled back sheepishly.

"I understand that these groups are a major concern and have done some heinous things, but they did not have anything against Malik Jahangir. Of all the politicians, he was the only one who wanted to break ties with the West, something that they would agree with. Also, General Hamid has been more accommodating to their demands for Islamic Laws than anyone in the recent past, and he has been able to slow down these attacks. So . . . now that the elections are near and we are not sure what the future holds, wouldn't it make sense for these groups to wait and see what happens? These attacks will only lead to an escalation in military deployment, and further endanger the treaties that have brought relative peace to the northern areas."

"That is also my concern. So much of this whole mess does not add up, and one wonders about the real hands that are pulling the strings backstage," Agha Kamal said, still noticeably shocked by the news.

"It's not just here . . . in Pakistan, I mean," Kamran continued, "look at Iraq, sectarian factions targeting each other in the presence of a common adversary. Suicide attacks and explosions in places . . . sacred places . . . so sacred to all sects that no Muslim, especially a fundamentalist Muslim would dare touch them. It just doesn't make sense."

'I know exactly what you mean," Sana jumped into the conversation, ". . . and these suicide bombings? Where did they come from? They were never a part of our culture. Not even in Palestine before the nineties. They were common in other cultures, the Tamil Tigers had used them as a weapon for years but *us . . . here . . . in Pakistan?* Half of the time they don't even know if it was a suicide bombing. The press labels it; authorities speculate it, Fox and CNN broadcast it all over the world, and then no one cares what really happened . . . ," she paused to take a breath, ". . . all I am saying is that whoever is behind this does not give a hoot about religion and is definitely not seeking any peaceful solutions, not here, not in Iraq or Kashmir and obviously not around Jerusalem."

Darkness had spread its unrestrained wings over these quiet outskirts of the Capital city. Traffic on the Grand Trunk Road flowed smoothly. Shiny new Japanese, German and English luxury cars, belonging to the few and the privileged, rolled with ease amongst the predominant jalopies, the overburdened trucks decorated with portraits loosely resembling past military dictators, and ornately, almost psychedelically decorated buses with the real sons and daughters of Pakistan packed inside, and hanging from every exposed handrail of their aluminum studded exteriors.

No one said much about the bombings or the assassination over the next half an hour or so as they sipped on their teas, dunked their *samosas* in the spicy condiment, and reminisced about the twisted state of affairs the world politics was in. The more they thought about it, the more it became apparent that the gap between reality and conventional wisdom, between what was the truth and what made into the editorials and political dashboards, had grown into a haunting chasm, deep, dark and utterly callous.

CHAPTER 56

PEARL CONTINENTAL HOTEL, RAWALPINDI

Monday 7:15 p.m.

Vincent tossed and turned in his sleep. Images were vivid, almost real. He had found himself in the middle of a desert. His car had broken down and he stood there, unsure about what direction to go . . . he was parched, running through the burning sand dunes, only to find himself back at his origin, again . . . and again. He felt dizzy, suffocated and then he heard them. Children, lots of them, they were laughing at him. Pointing their tiny fingers . . . waving their dirty hands at him. He tried to go to them, but he suddenly got dizzier. Everything began to spin out of control as the sand dunes and rocks merged into one giant vortex; children were gone.

. . . He heard them again. They were scared and thirsty; their fluttering lips, barely hiding missing teeth, were dry and cracked under the blazing sun. He wanted to help them as he ran towards a small pond. He was convinced that it was a mirage, but he did not want to lose hope. The children needed water, and he started digging into the dry sand, but nothing. He dug deeper and deeper, and then suddenly a jet of hot black liquid emerged from under his rapidly moving hands. It was not water. It was oil. He tried to stop the flow, but it came out even stronger, sprouting everywhere around him. Children were covered with it, and it seemed to get thicker and thicker by the second, engulfing their tiny bodies, pinning them to the ground . . . they screamed for help but he could not move. A leaping tentacle of black tarry oil was wrapped around his legs and pulled him into a gaping hole in the ground. He struggled, but in vain . . . "I'm coming . . . just stay there and hang tight. I'll save you," he tried to reassure them, but words got stuck in his throat . . . he felt himself falling into the abyss . . . and then everything went dark.

He woke up, drenched with sweat and lying on the floor, his bed sheet tightly wrapped around him and pressing on his neck.

He sat up straight with cold sweat pouring down his face, blurring his vision. With a Herculean effort, he scrambled to the bathroom, turned on the shower and sat down under the spray of steaming hot water. It took him about ten minutes to gather his senses, and then he wondered what he was doing in the shower with his clothes on.

He dried himself up and walked back into the room. The TV was on. The news was dominated by the details of the terrorist attacks. A reporter was on site at Lahore's renowned Tolinton Market. Her loose hair was flying out from under her *doputta* in a stiff breeze. The scene was littered with paper and blown up bits of fruits and vegetables. Emergency workers scurried back and forth in the background. Ambulance sirens dominated the ambient sounds in a haunting symphony underscored by leaping flames from stacks of dried fruit stalls, and still smoldering remains of an architectural icon that bustled with legendary vibrancy only a few hours ago.

". . . Scene at Tolinton Market is still chaotic, as rescue agencies are frantically going through the rubble in search for survivors. Our sources are projecting the death toll at one hundred and seventy-three, while dozens more are still missing. As you can see volunteers from Edhi Foundation are bringing out another stretcher, carrying a victim. It appears to be . . . a young woman . . . it is a horrible, horrible scene . . . I have never . . . seen . . . anything like this . . . before . . . ," she could not go on.

Vincent turned the TV off and slammed the remote on his bed. His phone was ringing.

It was a number that had become very familiar over the last few weeks. Reluctantly, he picked up the phone. An instantly recognizable voice made him cringe.

"What do you want now?" he asked curtly.

"I see that we are having some problems. I need you to fix them."

"I have done my part. You need to clean your own mess a little bit too. I can't help you with all your problems. I am done, and I need some rest," Vincent replied in a tired, but firm voice.

He heard a deep breath from the other side, and then rapid footsteps pacing back and forth. "Listen to me," the voice was firm but impatient, "you are still under contract. You don't have a choice but to do what you are told to."

"And if I don't?" Vincent asked.

"You don't want to know. I want you to meet me tonight, I'll call and give you the location later . . . and I expect a better attitude."

CHAPTER 57

ARMY HOUSE, RAWALPINDI

Monday 7:30 p.m.

General Hamid was not happy. Remnants of a grueling schedule were evident on his fatigued face in the form of weary eyes and dark circles that had developed under them. Though the deep furrows on his forehead betrayed the tremendous burden on his broad shoulders, he had maintained his erect posture. His head was held high, his prominent chin jutting forward from under his thick moustache. Despite the late hour, he was dressed in his full military regalia. He paced back and forth in the spacious drawing room, while a dozen or so civil and military members of the National Security Council looked on. As was customary with his predecessors, General Hamid Ali had chosen to keep his residence in the Army House, the designated home for the serving Army Chief, rather than moving into the palatial *Aiwan-e-Sadar*, official residence of The President of Pakistan in Islamabad.

"Army House reminds me of my mission and keeps my roots firmly grounded, I'd be lost in that maze called *Aiwan-e-Sadar,* and besides, it's too far from my Army buddies over here." He had responded to a question about the fact that, it was a waste of public funds maintaining the *Aiwan-e-Sadar* when most presidents end up not using it.

In the recent past, the *Aiwan-e-Sadar* was used only for ceremonial proceedings and diplomatic meetings, while the military rulers, namely General Zia-ul-Haq and General Pervez Musharraf had left it empty in favor of Army House for a combined nineteen years. These days, the sixteen-acre contemporary complex perched on a hill overlooking Islamabad was relegated to state banquets and receptions; it even served as a marriage hall for some of the chief executive's favorite political appointees, or their children.

"Do we have any clue about who is behind this?" General Hamid said loudly, his face obscured in a cloud of thick white smoke emanating from his prized Meerschaum pipe."We have more surveillance capability in the tribal areas than ever before, and we still cannot identify a single lead?"

"Sir, we do have a name . . .a small organization." Director General Military Intelligence, Major General Farooq said cautiously.

"That . . . *Paasdaran-e-Jihad*? Do you seriously think that I am an idiot? I want a report on a *real* lead within the next hour, and save these catchy names and references to Jihad, Al-Qaeda and the Taliban for your interview with Fox News; I want the real hands behind this. I want those bastards blown to bits and we'll have to do this our way."

"Sir, I don't think that will be easy. I just talked to General Zaidi. ISI is following some leads but none of their suspects seem likely," General Farooq said.

"Why?" General Hamid had stopped pacing and now looked out a window overlooking a small side lawn transformed into a gorgeous rose garden by the first lady.

"We have analyzed some of the material; the explosive grade that was used is not standard."

"What do you mean . . . not standard?" Interior Secretary, Javed Rehman spoke hesitantly. He was quietly listening from his chair in a dark corner of the room, and wisely so for staying out of General Hamid's direct line of fire, "and how did we get that information anyway? It's hardly been four hours."

"We have our sources. Actually, we received our preliminary report from Faizabad more than an hour ago," Major General Sajjad Baig, a deputy director of Inter-Services Intelligence said loudly, as he entered the room. "I am sorry for being late, sir," he snapped his heels and saluted General Hamid. "I had to stop at HQ to get some preliminary reports."

"At ease, Sajjad, I am glad that you made it, any word from your boss?" General Hamid asked about Director General of ISI who was visiting China at the moment.

"I've briefed him about the incidents, sir. He plans to return tomorrow morning."

"Good," General Hamid appeared relieved, as he looked at Sajjad and smiled. "Now you can explain the explosives finding to Secretary *sahib*. I gather that you heard his question."

General Hamid had handpicked Major General Sajjad Baig to be the Deputy Director of ISI, and it was widely believed that he was being groomed to take over from the soon to be retiring DG. He had met the young and energetic Capt. Sajjad years ago when he had arrived to assume command of his first Infantry Regiment. As a new commanding officer, taking over his first assignment as a Lieutenant Colonel in the northern valley city of Gilgit, Hamid felt nervous as he reached the command center, tucked behind a small garden in the barren foothills of Karakoram Mountains. Capt Sajjad was the first one to greet him with his fresh smile and bright eyes exuding boundless energy, instantly making Colonel Hamid feel better, confident that he was among able men. Later on, since both of them had children close in ages, bringing their wives together like two long lost friends, they had developed a bond that had maintained its intensity through the last two decades. General Hamid Ali, himself a Director General of ISI before becoming the Chief of Army Staff, depended on Major General Sajjad's advice much more than the current DG, a fact that irked a number of his colleagues.

"Well, it is very simple," Sajjad, explained. "You see, we analyzed the explosives used in the Faizabad blast. We have not received samples from Lahore yet, but I am sure that they will match. The explosion was detonated by your run of the mill C-4, most likely left in a bag under the bus."

"*Under* the bus? I thought it was a suicide bombing, at least that's what the media is saying," Sheikh Amir Ali, an ex-senator from Islamabad, and now an interim advisor to the President said, somewhat surprised.

This made a few people around the room chuckle.

Embarrassed, Amir Ali looked around. "What did I say?"

"Well, what they mean to say is that suicide bombers are not really as common as the world believes," Sajjad Baig explained. "It just makes a better news story. Think about it, would you rather read about a crazy psycho blowing things up randomly from the comfort of his hideout, or the notion of a group of passionate zealots who are so committed to their cause that they are not afraid to blow themselves up into a million pieces. The notion of a suicide bomber presents a whole different level of terrorism. You can detect, intercept and diffuse a planted bomb, but to find and stop a human, who is willing to be blown up no matter what, is a security nightmare, and represents terror, uncertainty and helplessness at a psychologically crippling level. Besides, it fits right into the Western world's skewed image of this *uncivilized*, developing culture of ours trying to sabotage their freedom."

"But . . . why?" Sheikh Amir Ali was still not convinced.

"In order to keep the perception of one unified evil entity and a common enemy alive, all one needs is the possibility that it was a suicide bomber, and the involvement of a misguided quasi-religious organization like Al-Qaeda becomes much more plausible."

Sheikh Amir Ali nodded excitedly. "And that . . . gives them a reason to continue their presence in our region. It fits right into our enemies' plans to take over our nuclear capabilities."

"Most likely, and not only that, but it also helps with their foreign policy decisions because people are too afraid of these crazy groups, who are planning an onslaught on their freedom as a means to reach heaven," Sajjad concurred with a smile.

"And receive seventy virgin *hoors*; don't forget about them?" someone said from across the room.

"Who could? I just wonder if there is a way to get them without being blown up," someone else chimed in.

Everyone in the room enjoyed this lighter moment and shared a loud laugh.

General Hamid Ali was not amused. "Enough of this nonsense!" he roared from across the room and everyone, jolted back to reality, slid back into the safety of their seats. Nobody said anything more.

General Hamid walked into the center of the room and gave each of them a long cold stare. "So you really think this is funny? Our religion is being hijacked and made fun of . . . and all you can do is to join the party? We should be proud of being the believers of a faith that teaches us about peace, love and forgiveness, but we have turned it around to be the opposite. We have failed to deserve the torch that was passed on to us fourteen hundred years ago. We are fighting amongst ourselves, killing each other, while our real enemies are standing at the sideline, encouraging us, rooting for us to fail. Why shouldn't they? We are doing *their* job *for* them. I know that we have enemies hiding among us and we must do our very best to identify them. But, blaming others for our own shortcomings is not going to help us. It is about time that we accept the fact that it is our own people; misguided members of our own faith that are behind this. They are the ones who are oppressing our people, usurping the rights of women and closing schools and attacking our brave soldiers and police forces. They want to break our spirit so that they can enforce their skewed thirteenth-century version of Islam on us," General Hamid paused to pace his breathing. An orderly brought him a glass of water that he finished, drinking it all in one long gulp. "It is not the CIA or RAW or the Mossad that is doing this to us. It is *us*! We are doing it to ourselves. Of course, we have enemies. Enemies who are loving this, and maybe even pouring huge amounts of money to encourage this, but that does not take the responsibility away from us. We must follow the money as that is the only way to stop this, but we must avoid misguided blames. That means, no pointing fingers, no conjectures . . . only hard evidence. Our discussions from now on . . . will be positive and focus on what we *can* do to fix it, not the negative talk about external forces that we cannot control. We have to rebuild this nation . . . rectify mistakes of our past, strengthen its foundation and then, only then can we be safe from our enemies," he looked straight into the eyes of General Sajjad Baig who squirmed uneasily in his seat, "Go ahead Sajjad, now you may finish your analysis."

"Okay . . . yes . . . back to my analysis," General Sajjad, caught off guard by the raw passion in General Hamid's words, quickly gathered his thoughts as he regained his composure, taking his time to stand up. "As I was saying, it was C-4, but usually the C-4 we use, and also the kind the Taliban have been using is manufactured with taggants or markers to identify them. It is now well known that ISI was involved in training and supplying ammunition to the Taliban in an attempt to help them unify Afghanistan and bring peace to the region. Unfortunately, the same weapons have been used against us at multiple times. Mostly, our supplies involved US made C-4 that is tagged with dimethyl-dintrobutane or DMDNB. We have also supplied PE4 explosive that is very similar to C-4 but is made by Britain and used by MI-6. Recently, we have also tagged these weapons with RFID or radiofrequency IDs to track their source."

"Why would one use a taggant if it can identify the source?" Saleem Qazi asked, raising his head from a stack of papers on his lap that he had been reviewing, while jotting down quick notes.

"Mostly . . . because they *have* no choice. We like to tag the materials so we know where and how to find them. This way we can track the weapons that were supplied by us. We leave them without a taggant for some specific operations.

"What kind of operations?" someone asked.

"I am not at liberty to talk about that Let's just say that they pertain to such sensitive matters of national security that we cannot discuss them, even in this forum," General Sajjad responded with a smile. "Now to continue with my report . . . ," he rubbed his hands together excitedly, ". . . the intriguing thing is that there were no taggants in the explosive used at Faizabad, and it seems to be closer to PE4 in composition rather than C-4. We have not been able to identify a source and I am not sure we will be able to."

"Could it be ours, I mean our own untagged supply?" General Hamid asked.

"Impossible!" Sajjad replied gravely. "We guard it very well and besides, all our supplies are accounted for, and that is my biggest concern. Someone is smuggling in covert grade explosives into Pakistan, and it is not ISI."

"Who else has access to untagged material?"

"Other than us? Let's see . . . CIA, MI-6, RAW . . . and, of course, Mossad, or any number of such agencies all over, you name it," General Sajjad replied hesitantly, watching General Hamid carefully, expecting a rebuke at any moment.

"Do you think one of them is involved? I mean, can it be India, or Israel, striking while the iron is hot?" the President asked calmly.

Major general Sajjad had always been proud of his poker face but could not hold back a faint smile. "If I have learned one thing from the intelligence community, it is that no matter how much smoke there is the real fire is always somewhere else."

The meeting was over. General Hamid Ali walked over to Inspector General Punjab Saleem Qazi, accompanying him in his walk towards the door.

"I am glad that you made it, Saleem. I know that it must have been hard for you leaving Lahore under the circumstances."

"This is important, sir. What we do here is the means to solve what I reluctantly left behind in Lahore."

"All right, go get some rest. I am sure that tomorrow is not going to be any easier," General Hamid patted him on the back and then, noticing that all eyes were on them, nodded reassuringly before letting Saleem Qazi walk out the door.

The room was empty and the President and General Sajjad were the only people left in it. General Hamid refreshed his pipe and sat down on a baroque divan in a corner.

'Tell me something, Sajjad . . ."

"What's on your mind, sir?"

"Is ISI up to something that I might not be aware of?"

"I don't think so, sir . . . do you have something specific on mind?"

"I just received a call from the Prime Minister of India. He is quite upset about raised insurgent activities in Kashmir. Several soldiers were caught in it, and he is also linking this to a recent suicide bombing in Chennai blamed on Tamil separatists. He thinks ISI may be involved in this. Elections are close and he has to take action. He is escalating military activities on our border as of right now, and knowing the whimsical nature of the voters, I can see where he is coming from. Anything less will be a sign of weakness, and he cannot afford that. I am just asking if there is any factual basis to his claims."

"Sir, I can assure you that we have not initiated anything. There may be a link in Kashmir, but that is purely based on past operations. Do you think RAW was involved in today's events in retaliation?"

"All I am saying is that nothing surprises me anymore. I asked the Prime Minister point blank and, of course, he denied it. We are fully aware that covert operations are never planned on the political level. I just want you to work on this angle. If the Indian press hits international news, CNN, BBC, FOX whatever, I want our best people right there, with our version, ready to answer any questions. We have been passive in the past, victims to a one-sided and rather unflattering portraiture, and we cannot afford for the world to not see our side of the story anymore. It's time we join the game and start playing hardball."

CHAPTER 58

SAFARI VILLAS, RAWALPINDI

Monday 9:00 p.m.

The official Government Guest Houses or Officers Messes, their military counterparts, form a network of fine establishments that serve the few, the powerful and the elite and those who are lucky to have this privileged access, courtesy of their association with an organization that could provide it. In Pakistan, it has been customary to provide these facilities to government officials. These guesthouses are filled with all the luxuries of a home: comfortable rooms, manicured lawns and elaborate kitchens preparing sumptuous meals, mostly free, but if not so, at astonishingly discounted prices, and served through a contingent of servants. A tradition that has lived up to its lore, having it roots in the glory days of the British Raj.

Saleem Qazi always liked his privacy, but even more so recently. He had his eyes closed with his head thrown back in an attempt to shake off the events of a difficult day, as he entered the street leading to his modest villa riding in a standard, chauffeured staff vehicle. It was late on a weeknight and the usually busy street, ringing with sounds of children playing was quiet. Saleem Qazi had sold some of his ancestral property in the native village, investing in a villa in this up and coming neighborhood of Rawalpindi. He liked it because it was at a manageable distance from both Rawalpindi and Islamabad without the traffic and pollution of the city. It was a neighborhood full of affluent young professionals and retired senior government officials, and he looked forward to the day when he would move into his villa for good. For now, he had been using it as his residence during frequent visits to this region, preferring it to the Police Guest House, despite the protocol and luxuries that accompanied the latter.

His was the last villa on a short street, an add-on, where originally an open area was planned; however, the location ensured him the privacy that he liked for himself. He looked at the familiar surroundings and then smiled as he noted the bright green gate of his villa, a distinct feature of his taste that stood out from the monotonous rows of elegant, but cookie-cutter dwellings.

He opened the door halfway before the agile chauffeur took over and then stood beside it with his hands clasped in front. Saleem Qazi handed him his briefcase and noticed a small and hardly visible smear on the white seat covers, ubiquitous to the official cars. The chauffeur followed his gaze and nodded to him, silently committing to cleaning it as soon as he got back. No words were spoken as he led his officer towards the main entrance.

Usually, the chauffeur would wait for the front door to open and then go in with his officer, still holding the briefcase or other belongings until they were securely placed at a designated spot inside the house. Today was, however, different. Saleem Qazi took his keys out of his pocket but noticed that a light in the living room was on. He looked at his watch and smiled. His chauffeur stood still waiting for his superior's next move but Saleem Qazi reached for his briefcase taking it out of the chauffeur's hand, and dismissed him.

"I'll take it from here, Amjad. You may go now."

"I'll take it in, sir," he insisted, fully aware of his duties.

"As I said, it is okay. I'll see you in the morning," Saleem snapped.

Taken aback, the chauffeur obeyed, and took a step back. "What time tomorrow . . . sir?"

"Pick me up at eight."

"Right, sir . . . and *Khuda Hafiz,* sir," the chauffeur said courteously, and turned around to leave. He did not notice that while opening the front door, Inspector General Saleem Qazi had put down the briefcase, and instead of keys, had his right hand firmly gripped around his service issued revolver.

Kamran was walking aimlessly through the aisles of the gas station convenience store. He was not entirely sure if he wanted to buy anything, but he had no choice. Agha Kamal wanted to talk shop with Sana, and he had volunteered to let them be on their own. He finally saw something that he could use; a box of Band-Aids and anti-bacterial ointment for the scrapes and cuts that he hadn't had a chance to think about but which had started to burn, demanding an acknowledgement of their existence.

It was quiet in the store, and he was the only customer. An attendant sat behind the counter and seemed to be dozing off. Kamran continued to look around, finally picking a few items and a pack of mango juice when a wind chime hanging on the door signaled a customer. A policeman walked in and looked around. The store attendant lazily opened his eyes and looked towards the door, waving a halfhearted gesture when he saw a familiar face. The policeman took a seat on a short stool next to the door and opened the newspaper. He did not seem to be interested in the news and skimmed through to the page with movie ads, glancing over the vivid images of romantic Punjabi heroines depicted in provocative dancing poses. Kamran watched him for a few moments, fascinated by his intense scrutiny of the ads before deciding to drink his juice as he browsed over some magazines. The wind chime sounded again, and when he looked towards the door, the policeman was gone.

He turned around towards the magazine rack and saw the latest copy of *Time Magazine* bearing a picture General Hamid Ali.

"The Democratic Dictator: Can he deliver?" the caption said,

Kamran smiled at the oxymoron, and bent down to pick up the magazine when he noticed something right behind him. As he turned around, he bumped into something soft and then noticed a protruding belly barely contained by a tight belt on the service issued khaki trousers. He straightened up and came face to face with two curious eyes staring right at him. It was the policeman, holding the newspaper in his hand with Kamran's picture, in color, on the front page; he had his hand on the holster carrying his gun.

"Don't move . . . and hands up!" the policeman shouted, taking a quick look at the photograph to be sure.

Kamran needed a few moments to catch his breath before his mind started to function again. He looked around slowly. The store was still empty; the store keeper now fully awake, sat curiously behind the counter, watching keenly.

The store was a generic structure with two rows of items, mostly food and snacks. The front row had other everyday items like medicines, shaving aids and some other trinkets and cheap toys. A row of freezers and coolers ran along the back wall. Outside the window, he could see Sana and Agha Kamal wrapping up their conversation as they were heading towards the car. Sana was looking around casually, possibly trying to find out where he was. He looked back at the policeman who did not seem as intimidating as earlier. He seemed to be as uncomfortable and unsure in the situation as he was. His gun was still in the holster with the right hand loosely placed over it. Beads of sweat were beginning to form on his forehead as he took a small, tentative step towards Kamran and then tripped over one of the racks as he stumbled forward, but then regained his balance almost immediately.

The split second impediment was enough for the physically fit and athletic Kamran to lunge forward, squeezing the remaining mango juice into the policeman's eyes, catching him totally off guard. The policeman fell backwards, unable to see for a moment, wiping his face and eyes with his sleeve, he saw Kamran running towards the door which opened with a violent jingling of the wind chime; he was gone.

CHAPTER 59

Monday 10:15 p.m.

Sardar Jalaluddin Khan had just finished saying his *Isha'* Prayer and was sitting on the prayer rug counting prayer beads. Someone knocked at the door. Jalaluddin pulled his *Kalashnikov* rifle, lying on the ground next to him, a little closer before calling out the permission to come in. He was in his private quarters, off limits to all but only a few trusted servants. It was a modest size room with only one window that opened into a secure back yard guarded by high brick walls, topped off by a layer of concrete encrusted with shards of broken glass. The modesty of the room's size did not have any bearing on the extravagance of its décor. The room was painted a darker shade of crimson, lined by brilliant white trimmings that were decorated with gold leaf. Heavy, off white and gold brocaded curtains hung over the solitary window and the room's two entrances.

The cherry furniture that included a canopied bed and sofa set was ornately carved and filled the room leaving little space to move about on the expensive Afghan rug. The garishly baroque décor was in stark contrast to the three sedate impressionist paintings decorating the walls, and it was a reflection of the dichotomies that dominated the life of its inhabitant.

A handsome young man walked in and stood by the door. He was dressed in finely stitched local attire: his head was covered in a turban and he had a woolen black shawl wrapped around his shoulders.

"*Aa-jao, aa-jao*, come-on in, Sohrab Khan," Jalaluddin waved him close. He was a newer addition to his team of servants and had come with strong recommendations. In his relatively short stay, Sohrab had used his efficient nature and friendly personality to make a lot of friends and had managed to enter a small circle of trusted employees, devoted to Sardar Jalaluddin's personal needs.

"*Salamalaikam, Khan baba,* Sultan Khan said that you were tired and could use a little massage."

"*Waalaikum-assalaam* Sohrab Khan, you are a life saver. That is indeed just what I need," he smiled and winked faintly as he answered.

Getting up from the prayer rug, he kissed his prayer beads reverently before placing them on a side table and then very carefully folded the prayer rug placing it on the table next to the beads. Both of them walked over to a low *divan.* Jalaludin sat down making himself comfortable on two oversized gilded pillows, while Sohrab Khan positioned himself behind and started rubbing his shoulders.

Jalaluddin felt very relaxed, his eyes closed as he could literally feel the fatigue escaping his limbs.

"*This kid is good, really good,*" he thought, looking at Sohrab Khan's nubile face.

Sohrab looked at him with his large soft eyes and smiled, making Jalaluddin a bit nervous. Jalaluddin could feel his pulse racing as he watched him intently, and then softly ran his hand behind the young man's knee. Sohrab paused in mid-motion for a split second, but then continued as if nothing had happened.

Jalaluddin cleared his throat, "I want to go hunting tomorrow morning and plan to spend the night at c*hoti haveli,*" he was referring to a small house that he maintained near his hunting and agricultural fields, which he used for his confidential meetings and certain illicit trysts. "Would you like to accompany me?"

"Whatever you desire *Khan baba.*"

"Good. Now go get the car ready, I have to make a stop on the way. You can ride in the jeep and I'll see you later."

Sohrab Khan nodded his head obediently and left the room.

Jalaluddin felt pleased with the arrangement and looked forward to his trip. He had all he needed stocked at the *choti haveli* and did not need to worry about packing a bag. In his line of work, being ready to move at any moment was crucial for survival.

Half an hour later, Sardar Jalaluddin walked out of his home towards his shiny black Mercedes SL550 Roadster parked in the front. Jalaluddin liked to drive his new Mercedes himself, and did not let anyone ride with him. A dutiful Sohrab, well aware of the fact, stood clear of the vehicle alongside other servants and watched him jump into the driver's seat, rev up the engine and drive away, leaving a plume of dust engulfing his loyal household.

As everyone walked away, Sohrab headed towards the stables and looked around to make sure that he was alone. Once assured, he carefully untied his green and black turban pulling out a small black box the size of a matchbox from its folds. A small red LED light blinked in a display showing four small bars signifying a good signal. Sohrab closed his eyes and said a quiet prayer before pressing a small red button next to the display.

A ball of fire formed in the distance and leapt into the sky followed by a loud explosion. Sohrab calmly threw the detonator down and crushed it under his feet, throwing the tiny fragments in a pile of horse manure on his way out.

It was pandemonium, as a shocked congregation of household employees rushed towards the smoldering remains of the Mercedes half a mile from the house. Sohrab screamed for someone to call an ambulance and joined the frantic crowd.

CHAPTER 60

Monday 9:30 p.m.

Sana heard the loud noise made by the wind chime, violently bouncing off the door followed by running footsteps that were rapidly approaching her. She looked towards the elevated store and saw a heavyset, out of shape policeman, running out of its door whistling loudly, and then stopping to catch his breath before shouting at the top of his lungs.

"Stop him! He is a killer."

It didn't take Sana long to put two and two together as she noticed Kamran running full steam towards them.

"We need to go . . . *now!*" Kamran said loud enough for Agha Kamal to hear, who was already in the process of turning the ignition. Sana opened the front door before getting into the rear seat as Kamran came in flying through the open front door. Agha Kamal had his full weight on the accelerator even before Kamran was halfway in. The car lunged forward with a loud but smooth roar of its powerful engine. Screeching tires left a thick cloud of dust behind as Kamran, barely holding on to the dashboard, reached out and pulled the door shut.

They drove in silence, recovering from yet another close call.

"Now what?" an exasperated Agha Kamal was the first one to speak. "I guess now we'll all be in jail together."

"And what a wonderful company that will make," Kamran could not help it and received glaring stares from both Sana and Agha Kamal.

"C'mon, guys, I'm only trying to cheer up the mood."

"Well, it's not working," Sana, snapped.

"Okay . . . okay I get the message," Kamran threw his hands in the air, "now let's figure out what to do."

"There is not much we *can* do," Agha Kamal replied somberly. "There is no one we can trust. That guy who was after you has to be on the lookout; going back home or to the office is out, and if that constable back there has even half the brains to be in police force, there should be an APB out there with our descriptions and unfortunately, my license plate . . . ,"he took a deep breath and sighed, ". . . hmm, I don't even know why I'm doing what I'm doing," he stopped the car on a wider shoulder and dropped his head on the steering wheel. "This will ruin me. What will happen to my family? How could I do this to them? I should have said no. I shouldn't have listened to you . . . I shouldn't have," he kept mumbling.

"You are a good man," Sana spoke.

"What?" Agha Kamal lifted his head and turned around to look at her.

"That's why you are doing it. You are a good, decent human being. You have principles and you live by them. Agha *sahib*, I know and treasure the fact that you care about me, but I believe that in this case, even if it wasn't about me . . . you would have done the same thing."

Sana put her right hand on his shoulder and squeezed it gently. "Our country is full of decent, honest people. Smart, gifted and creative people who are patriotic enough to die for it, but we are still heading in the wrong direction. Sometimes I feel that there is no hope. Why should we struggle when there is no end to this insanity? Then I see people like you and Kamran, and if I am right about him, then Naveed Khan and I feel better. It may be naïve for us to feel that a few of us can make all the difference unless others join our cause, but there is hope; however, I firmly believe that if we stop . . . then . . . all hope is lost," Sana paused briefly, her voice heavy, "I want to keep my one candle lit in the hope that others will see it and bring their own candles . . . until there is no darkness. I know that you believe in the same thing. I know that, because it was your candle that brought me to you. That is why you are here. That is why I am here," tears were running down Sana's face.

Kamran turned around and held her hand, squeezing it tenderly. "There *is* hope."

Agha Kamal lifted his head up. His eyes filled with tears. "Yes there is."

They spent the next few minutes calming down their revved up emotions, holding hands. Sana was the first one to speak.

"So . . . what do we do now?"

"I think . . . ," Kamran sounded hesitant, "looking at our current and rather limited options, there is only one person we could turn to."

"Who?" Both Sana and Agha Kamal spoke together.

"Saleem Qazi."

"Are you sure?" Sana asked.

"I know that he has acted strangely, and I was upset with him but I guess I can understand his side of the story. He's bound by what he is told to do, but deep down, I have always found him to be a decent man and a true patriot. I can't think of anyone else."

Agha Kamal pondered over the irony of going to the Inspector General of the Police for help when the same police wanted them, but he couldn't come up with a better idea. I can pull some strings and try to contact the President, but that is a long shot. I can't trust other journalists, as they will jump all over the story like vultures. I guess . . . and I agree, knowing Saleem Qazi over the years, he might actually be able to help us."

"So we all agree?" Kamran looked at them, holding his cell phone in his hand and received an affirmative nod from both.

"*Bismillahir Rahman ir Rahim* – In the name of Allah, the Beneficent, the Merciful," Kamran said aloud and then dialed the number.

CHAPTER 61

Monday 9:04 p.m.

Saleem Qazi carefully put his briefcase down and took his revolver out of its holster. The street was very quiet, only a distant hum of late evening traffic on the expressway interrupted the silence. Evening had become cooler, as a brisk autumn wind had started to blow across the Pothohar Plateau. The suburban and elevated location of Safari Villas made this breeze very refreshing in the hot summer months, but equally agonizing when winter rolled in. He looked back briefly and saw the driver getting back in the car. He waved at him with an abbreviated hand gesture as he drove away.

A wolf howled in the distance from somewhere past the rapidly developing township that had spearheaded this surreal urban sprawl despite a bad economy. Dogs in the neighborhood took it as their cue to join in the chorus and starting howling in unison.

Saleem took a deep breath, ignored the dogs and opened the door. It opened with a slight creak as he pushed it slowly, cursing the lazy moments of procrastination that had left its hinges devoid of lubrication. There were no other sounds or movement. A short vestibule led into the main living room. It was dark, and it took a few moments for his eyes to adjust to the light. Keeping his eyes focused straight ahead and the revolver pointing forward, he tried to reach the light switch but jumped at a calm but hurried voice emanating from the dark far corner.

"Leave it off."

Saleem Qazi stepped away from the switch and looked towards the source of the voice. A faint light coming in from a solitary street lamp helped him make out a silhouette of the intruder, sitting in a lounge chair, his legs crossed, with no obvious firearms pointed in his direction.

"Why are you here? Who told you about this place?" he asked, sounding more shocked than angry.

"Oh, c'mon, Qazi! You are not that hard to find. If I couldn't even do this, then what good am I in the first place?" The reply was calm, composed.

"What do you want? You are not supposed to make contact until told to. Your instructions were explicit. Don't you realize what kind of trouble we'll be in if someone saw you?"

"Ah! Afraid of the consequences are you?" the stranger seemed to relish the position of power he was in, especially after catching Qazi off guard. "What do you suppose will happen if someone did see me here?"

"Are you threatening me? I have friends; friends in high places. I will survive; you, on the other hand, will be destroyed. Crushed like a helpless fly," Qazi was angry now. He was a meticulous man and liked control, especially inside his own home.

"I wouldn't be so graphic if I were you, Mr. *Inspector General,*" he chewed on the last two words. "I am in a significant position of advantage here, but then of course, I don't need to tell you that,"

"What do you want?" Qazi resigned, realizing his weak position. It was late in the evening and most neighbors were probably getting ready to sleep. The villa next door was empty so there was no chance of anyone noticing or hearing anything, if it got to that.

"May I?" he gestured towards a chair.

"Go ahead, make yourself at home," the reply came with a chuckle that followed a flash of white teeth in the twilight.

Qazi sat on the chair but only halfway on the edge, cautious, and ready to jump at a moment's notice, and he stared hard at the man across the room. Being only a temporary residence, the villa was scantily furnished, and only a makeshift TV table and a small area rug separated the two.

He was able to see better now. Faint light from the yellow streetlight was entering the room through a small ventilator high in the western wall and reflected from the bare white walls of the room. A full-length mirror stood in front of the wall behind the lounge chair and Qazi was able to see that the bedroom door was open, his luggage scattered on the floor. Obviously, the intruder was looking for something, but the fact that he was still there made Qazi think that he did not find it.

The howling outside had stopped suddenly, making the quiet dark night eerily uncomfortable.

Qazi was thinking fast, and knowing the man in front of him, he did not have much time.

"You did not answer my question," Qazi asked in voice that seemed forcibly authoritative, "why are you here?"

White teeth flashed once again. "I want to know why."

Why . . . why what?" Qazi asked, somewhat perplexed.

"Yes . . . why! Why all this? Why am I here? Why are you doing this?"

"Ah!" Qazi smiled for the first time since his arrival. "I knew that you were smarter than just a yes man. I have been waiting for this question for a while now, and I'll tell you exactly why you and I are here."

"Alright, then tell me," the calm, rock-like demeanor that had sent chills through Saleem Qazi's spine was softening now as his confident voice shook a little, excited in anticipation.

"May I?" Qazi asked to stand up and received the permission to do so through a brisk nod of head.

"Come with me, I want to show you something."

His cell phone rang. He picked it up and took the call. As soon as he heard the sound, he held up his finger to his lips, asking the intruder to be quiet and then answered.

"Hello . . . hello, Thank God! Where the heck are you? I've been worried sick."

CHAPTER 62

Monday 9:34 p.m.

Major General Sajjad Baig was satisfied with the day's events. His meeting with the President had gone smoothly, and he was able to control the events with his usual suaveness without raising any eyebrows. Meetings with the National Security Council were always tricky, and it was something that he was still getting used to.

In the past, military decisions were done exclusively by the top brass, without any interference from the political leaders, and this dual system ensured that borders were secure, and in case any threats appeared on the horizon, any offensive or defensive strategy was put in place without the stumbling effects of red tape. ISI's autonomy went beyond it all, and excluding the very few at the very top of the military totem pole, no one had true insight into its activities and operations.

Things had changed in the recent months though. In the past, the two pillars of this parallel system, representing the democratic governments and military, had exerted their own influence from their respective vantage points. Under dire circumstances, however, whenever the civilian system failed and the democratic process broke down, the military, due to its immense clout, widespread respect and mostly superior organization, stepped in to fill the void, and thus at least on paper, saved the country from anarchy. The problem was that whenever that happened, and in Pakistan it did happen quite often, democracy was pushed to the side in favor of the agendas purely based on the whims and aspirations of the new President cum Chief of Army Staff.

In order to avoid these cycles of civilian-military rules and to bring stability to the democratic institutions, General Hamid Ali, in an unprecedented move, had declared the formation of a National Security Council as the first executive order of his presidency.

The structure of NSC involved the sitting president and prime minister, Chief Justice of the Supreme Court, ministers and secretaries of information, interior and foreign affairs and the four provincial Governors and Inspectors General as its permanent civilian members. The president nominated two MNAs (Members of National Assembly) and two Senators. The Chiefs of Staff of Army, Navy and Air force, Chairman of Joint Chiefs of Staff Committee, DG of Military Intelligence, the Director General and a designated deputy director of ISI represented the Armed Forces.

General Sajjad Baig was not a fan of this idea personally but understood the logic behind General Hamid Ali's decision. Considering the turbulent history of Pakistani politics, elimination of the parallel chain of commands and giving the Armed Forces a strong voice in matters of foreign as well as domestic security was the only way to ensure that the next elected government will be able to complete its term.

As much as the idea appealed to general public and was widely hailed as a feather in General Hamid's cap, it created an undercurrent of uneasiness among military circles which thought that this was the beginning of a downward spiral, undermining their authority. None was affected more than Inter-Services Intelligence, and no one in the ISI felt more threatened than Major General Sajjad Baig.

He was sitting in his home office leafing through a stack of intelligence briefings that had been delivered to him. The courier bringing the documents had made sure that he was aware of the red TOP SECRET/URGENT seal stamped across the front of the envelope. It was easy reading and mostly touched on the movements of a fugitive tribal lord, wanted for his association with a recent string of bombing that had rocked a Taliban strong hold in the Swat valley. Something caught his eye.

Memo # 4 – preliminary report

Unauthorized ship involved in Recon activity off the coast of Gawadar. Communication intercepted with a base near Jiwani . . .

Sajjad Baig immediately got up and walked up to a map of the sub-continent that dominated the wall to the left of his desk.

He found Jiwani on the map and then stuck a red pin into it, thinking about whom he had stationed in that region as he continued to read,

. . . Transmission was scrambled but contained large quantity of mathematical data. Analysis is underway. Recent activity of a US company named AmeriGulf in the area. Detailed report will follow.

"Hmm . . ." Sajjad paused for a moment. He did not like the sound of it as he came back to his desk and opened a list of operatives to assign in order to take a closer look at it.

His phone rang.

"Hello?" he asked while still leafing through the report.

"General, how are you? It's Pat O'Neal," a familiar voice replied.

Sajjad Baig was not a big fan of O'Neal but had learned to tolerate him, being very aware of the power he could exert. As if his temper and patronizing tone was not enough, he loved to show that tone even more often with Sajjad, enjoying the fact that he was very uncomfortable with it.

"Are we on a secure line?"

"Yes we are."

"What is going on in your country? Horrible, horrible events happened today! Who do you think is behind it?"

"Not really sure as yet," Sajjad replied briefly. He was fully aware that O'Neal was not being forthright with him and obviously knew a lot more than he pretended to know.

The ISI and CIA had always shared a hot and cold relationship over the decades. Although, strong allies in multiple projects, both veered sharply away on issues that pertained to their respective national security matters. The exchange of information, though free at times, was riddled with cautionary flags leading to vigilant restraint and judicious withholding of information at every turn.

"Do you think these *Passdaraan-e-Jihad* are legit; any other lead on them?"

"Could be anyone; there are too many small groups. Hard to say who is affiliated with whom, but we are working on it."

"What about the assassination? Any leads?" Patrick probed further.

"We are questioning a few people and have narrowed down the list of suspects. I am personally leaning towards a political rather than religious motive. Do *you* have any new information?"

"No, no nothing so far. I think it is purely political. You know how politicians are; one horse out of the race opens up the field for everyone else and . . ."

"By the way," Sajjad interrupted. "We may need a little help unscrambling something we intercepted off the Gawadar coastline."

"What? Gawadar coastline? . . . Very intriguing . . . indeed. What is it about?" Patrick was caught a bit off guard.

"I am not sure yet. You guys up to something over there?"

"No . . . no . . . not at all," Patrick reassured, "and I'll be glad to help."

"We have located the signal in the town of Jiwani, just west of Gawadar. I am waiting for a formal report. I'll let you know if we need any help with the cipher . . . and by the way, what do you know about AmeriGulf?"

"AmeriGulf, hmm . . . well . . . it is a Houston based petroleum company, nothing fancy, your usual run of the mill set up . . . and . . . oh, look at the time! Anyway, I have a meeting; when you have more info, you know where to find me," O'Neal hung up.

Sajjad sat back and closed his eyes. He was convinced that Patrick O'Neal knew exactly what all that was about.

CHAPTER 63

Monday 10:22 p.m.

Agha Kamal stopped his car short of Saleem Qazi's villa and parked in an empty spot on the street. The street was quiet. Faint clouds covered a half moon, making the night even darker. Nobody spoke as each one of them contemplated their own fate in silence. The car's window was open and a brisk cross breeze made Kamran shiver as he stared at his destination. He was not entirely sure that this was the right move, but as he mulled over it repeatedly in his mind, he did not see any other options. Even though he was disappointed in actions taken by Saleem Qazi over the last two days, he had faith in his sincerity to his beliefs. He had known Qazi for a long time and knew well that if there was any hope of ending this nightmare, he was it.

While Kamran had full faith in Saleem Qazi's ability to sort through the facts and recognize reality, he was also aware of his commitment to his job and the fact that he would not back off from arresting them on the spot. He just hoped that he would have enough patience to hear their side of the story before making that call.

The villa appeared dark except for a flickering glow behind the tightly drawn curtains.

"He must be watching TV," Kamran thought to himself as he slowly approached the front door.

Ding Dong . . . , the call bell was loud and echoed through the quiet neighborhood, and startled Sana for a second.

The next few moments were the longest of their lives, as they stood there, staring at each other's anxious faces in the faint light coming from the solitary street lamp, each fidgeting in their own peculiar way. Sana picked her cuticles aimlessly, while Kamran scratched a scar under his right eyebrow, one of various similar mementos from his spirited childhood, with his arms crossed tightly around his chest trying hard not to bite his tongue.

They heard a few faint footsteps and then the door opened with a slight squeak. Saleem Qazi stood there, his face in the shadow, the hazy glow from an incandescent light forming a halo around his head.

"Thank God you are here," he said excitedly, "come inside, it's getting chilly out there," he said, looking quickly up and down the street.

"Did anyone follow you here? Are you alone?" he asked in a bare whisper.

Kamran hesitated before answering the question, thinking about Agha Kamal waiting in the car down the street, and then gave a simple response.

"No."

"Good!" He quickly moved out of the way to let them in.

Once they were in, Saleem Qazi locked the door behind them, and led them into the ground floor bedroom that he had been using as an office.

It was a large room designed to be a bedroom and thus was mostly empty. A large desk dominated the room and was covered with loose papers and official gray files, cluttered upon its faded surface. A table lamp with a stained-glass shade was the only source of light, and it focused on the desk, leaving most of the room in relative darkness. White walls were bare except for a scenic calendar and a family-photograph behind the desk. The floor was mostly uncovered, other than a straw floor mat, making it feel cooler than it was.

"Now tell me everything, start from the beginning," Qazi asked as he walked around his desk to sit down in his leather upholstered swivel office chair. Sana and Kamran sat down on a small couch by the window easing up a bit since they did not feel that Saleem Qazi was in any particular rush to turn them in.

"I am so rude," Qazi said, apologetically. "I am so curious about the details that I have not even asked you for anything to drink . . . tea, coffee . . . ?" he paused, "you must be hungry. When was the last time you ate? I have some frozen food. There are no servants here, but Police Guest House is kind enough to deliver some food when I stay here. I think that I may have some *chicken qorma* and a little *pulao* leftover. I can warm it up for you."

"That sounds really appetizing, Saleem, but we were able to stop and get a snack earlier. Some tea would be nice but you don't have to. We are okay," Kamran declined the offer.

"Oh, it's no trouble at all; I was thinking of making some for myself anyway, I must have some biscuits . . . ."

Sana got up and interrupted him before he could try to get out of his chair. "In that case, just tell me which way is the kitchen and while Kamran briefs you on everything, I'll make us some tea."

"Oh, you don't have to," Saleem Qazi raised his hand. "I am fully capable of making a perfect cup of tea . . . though that is my only virtue in the kitchen, I must say."

"It's no trouble at all Qazi *sahib,* besides, you and Kamran really need to talk," Sana started walking out the door.

"Thank you, you are very kind and I appreciate it; the kitchen is just outside, to your left," Saleem said loudly as Sana walked out of the room.

"Let's get back to where we were," Qazi sat back down.

"You've got to believe me, Saleem," Kamran pleaded. "I had *nothing* to do with it."

Qazi smiled, staring at an empty piece of paper in front of him as he pretended to write on it with his finger.

"I know."

"You do?"

"Yes . . . of course I do."

"Then why is your whole police force still running after me?"

"It's not as simple as it seems, Kamran," Qazi replied calmly. "There are lots of people involved in this. One can't just call back the cavalry without raising questions, and raising questions is something we do not want to do right now. Now tell me . . . *exactly* what happened?"

Kamran told him about his forensic findings, his theory regarding Malik Jahangir's cause of death, and then a brief version of his day running from the likely assassin. He did not get into the attack on Pervaiz, and avoided mentioning their break into the hotel room since he did not want to get Agha Kamal in trouble.

Qazi sat back in his chair as he digested the information. "You can relax now. After a day like that, you need to unwind," he pushed back and reclined in his chair, putting the palms of his hands behind his head. "Who do you think is behind all this? Did Sana come up with something that makes sense of this?" he asked nonchalantly.

"Considering that our likely assassin is a foreigner, there is obviously more to it than just local politics. Sana has been tracking Malik Jahangir and Malik Nisar's movements in the recent past and she thinks that Jahangir's recent flirtations with the Chinese might have ticked off some people, not just locally but also in the western markets."

"Very interesting . . ." Saleem Qazi slowly nodded his head. "She may be on to something. I am looking forward to hearing her thoughts about it over that cup of tea. You two should just thank your lucky stars that he failed to hurt you, especially at Rose and Jasmine Gardens. That place must be deserted in this weather."

The phone rang.

"Hello . . . Shah *Sahib*," Qazi picked it up. "*Waalaikum-assalaam*. How are you? Of course, anything, just send me the papers. Have your assistant bring them to the office in the morning. I should be back in Lahore by the early afternoon."

Kamran, trying to give Qazi the privacy to engage in a private conversation, started to walk towards the kitchen.

"I'll go help Sana," he mouthed to Qazi on his way out.

"Shah *Sahib*, you can reach me anytime you want. Call me on my mobile. Write down the number, it is 0346 . . . 553 . . . 4423"

Kamran was walking into the kitchen when Qazi was giving his mobile phone number, a number that he had dialed many times in the past but this time, somehow it got stuck to his mind.

"0346-553-4423 . . . 0346-553 . . ." he kept repeating the sequence in his mind, there was something more to it.

"What's wrong?" Sana asked, noticing the quizzical look on his face.

"Nothing . . . *0346-533* . . . ."

She smiled, "I've only known you for a day, but I think I have pretty much figured you out. Something is bothering you, but . . . ," She paused. She had also learned that at a moment like this, it was best to leave him alone to sort out the knots in his brain by himself.

Kamran continued to stare at nothing. His mind was racing, something was not right. Something did not add up and then it hit him. Qazi had mentioned Rose and Jasmine Garden. Kamran had talked about Vincent catching up to them but . . . he had not mentioned the location. No one knew . . . just them . . . and Vincent. His eyes widened.

"Wait a minute . . . ," he put his hand in his trouser pocket and fiddled around until he found what he was looking for.

It was the piece of paper from Vincent's hotel room and there it was, clear as crystal.

"These numbers," he whispered to Sana. "It's a mobile phone number.

"It is?" she leaned forward to look at it, "*It is!* How could we not know? It is so obvious, 0346 is the area code, and . . . I wonder whose it is."

"That's the problem," Kamran said in a barely audible voice, "it's his number," he pointed towards the other room.

"What? What are you saying . . . you mean . . . Qazi?" her voice louder than what Kamran was comfortable with.

"Shhhhh . . . ," he gestured to her. "We need to get out of here . . . *right now.*"

Sana looked towards the stove, where the teakettle had started to whistle softly.

"Let's go," she replied without taking her eyes off the faint cloud of steam coming out of the kettle. She dropped the tea bags she was holding, letting them fall on the floor and then turned around.

"I don't think so," a hauntingly familiar voice stopped them in their tracks. The floor seemed to slip away from under their feet as they came face to face with their recurring nightmare blocking the kitchen door.

"Fancy seeing you guys here," Vincent said, wearing a broad smile on his face.

CHAPTER 64

Monday 9:30 p.m.

Mark Zeigler was satisfied with his work. He had transmitted all the data back to Houston and was convinced that his analysis was accurate, and his estimate was as accurate as can be in his field.

Mark had been a nerd all his life and as much success as he has had in petro-geology, the opposite had been true as far as his love life was concerned. The fact that he spent most of his time in a small cubicle, or in front of a computer screen did not help either.

"You've got mail!" his AOL account announced in the familiar cyber tone.

"Oh, Ema! You need to take a break from that laptop," he opened the email. His mother had been extremely reluctant to accept the laptop he had given her for her birthday, but once she had started using it she never stopped. He did not have many friends that communicated via personal emails, so when he got one, he knew exactly who it was from.

"Mark, guess what, next week the Goldsteins are having a bar mitzvah for their grandson. You've got to be back for that. I am sure there will be some nice Jewish girls you could meet. Let me know when you are back so I can RSVP. Love, Ema."

Mark smiled as he sat back and clasped his hands behind his head. Settling down was becoming a viable option for him now. He closed his eyes and pictured himself in a brand new Porsche driving through Rockaway Boulevard, passing by the cool hangout spots from his past.

"Who's the cool dude now?" he said loudly to himself. "I bet the girls will notice me now," a wide grin appeared on his face as he flicked his long black hair back in a sweeping motion, and then closed his eyes, savoring the thought.

The dream was vividly clear. He was driving his brand new red Porsche when he suddenly took a wrong turn and found himself in a dark alley. It started to rain heavily, and he could not see anything. He had no choice to pull over and wait. It was pitch dark, except the bright headlight of a motorcycle heading directly towards him, and then there were two, no, three of them. He was scared. "This can't be good," he thought to himself as he saw three ominously dressed men walking towards him. Leather clad motorcyclists in their long boots reminded him of the three horsemen of the apocalypse. He locked his door but could not drive away. One of the men, wearing dark glasses and sporting a flowing unkempt beard started to bang at his windshield with his fist.

"Open up," the man shouted.

He was scared and started to think about every rare moment he had spent in the synagogue, trying to summon every Hebrew prayer he could, reciting them with his eyes closed, *"Barukh ata Adonai Eloheinu melekh ha-olam, ha-gomel lahayavim tovot sheg'malani kol tov* (Blessed are You, LORD, our God, King of the Universe, Who bestows good things on the unworthy, and has bestowed on me every goodness . . . *Barukh ata Adonai Eloheinu . . . ,"* he kept repeating the prayer.

The banging got louder and constant.

"Open up . . . anybody home?" someone shouted and he opened his eyes slowly, terrified of getting hit with a shard from the windshield glass that was bound to break at any moment.

It took his eyes a few moments to get used to the light, and then he realized that he was not in his car. He was curled up in a ball on the couch in his hotel room.

Bang . . . bang, "open up . . . Mark, are you in there?"

It took a lot of effort, but he managed to get up and walked to the door.

"What the hell is wrong with you man?" a middle aged man dressed in khakis and loose navy blue knit shirt walked in. "I've been knocking forever."

'I don't know," Mark shook his head, still trying to shed the fog. "I must have fallen asleep or something."

"No kidding, hell . . . look at yourself, Mark, did you get beat up by the Incredible Hulk or something?"

"Good to see you too, Joe," Mark replied, somewhat annoyed, "when did you come in?"

"Last night, but I was exhausted; it was a long and bumpy ride here from Karachi. What have you been up to? I've heard that you've scored big and found a big tub of dinosaur lard in the Arabian Sea."

"I'd say it's a bit bigger than that, but whatever you say," Mark took his work very seriously and did not particularly appreciate this simplified and rather demeaning description of the biggest discovery of his life, but he knew better and did not say anymore.

Joe was the liaison assigned to him, and while he was responsible for providing Mark with everything he required, he was also the one Mark reported to, thus leaving him in a catch-22.

Joe sat down on one of the two woven jute stools decorated with a shining green and red ribbon, and pulled a bottle of champagne from an inconspicuous looking plastic bag he was holding.

"Let's celebrate!"

"Oy veh! Are you crazy?" Mark suddenly got up and ran towards the window, and pulled the curtains shut.

"Do you have any idea what would happen if anyone sees us with this bottle? You may get away with something like this in Karachi but *here*, in Baluchistan? These people will hang us in the city square, and *then* they'll really get down to business."

"Hey, don't worry about it man . . . just enjoy," Joe opened the bottle and poured champagne into the two glasses sitting on the nightstand.

"Oh, what the hell . . . let's celebrate. Here's to black gold!" he raised his glass up in the air, and then emptied it in one big mouthful.

A long silence ensued. After drinking four glasses, Mark was feeling relaxed, and then suddenly felt extremely tired. Joe turned the TV on and surfed the few channels that were available in English, his own glass, still full to the brim, sat at the small table next to him.

Joe had nodded off. A slight vibration on his waist woke him up. He pulled the phone off his belt and turned off the alarm. The room was dark except for the flickering glow coming from the TV. He got up, put on a pair of latex gloves from his pocket and emptied his glass in the bathroom sink, washing it thoroughly. He repeated the same ritual with the other glass, now empty and lying sideways on the tan carpet next to Mark who had managed to get to the bed and was now lying halfway on it, his legs still hanging off it and in midair.

Joe walked over to Mark and shook his shoulder gently and then rather forcefully, but he did not budge. He emptied his pockets and pulled out a syringe full of a milky material. After smearing the syringe with Mark's hand, he applied a tourniquet to the upper arm, tapped on the front of Mark's elbow to feel a vein that was surprisingly easy to find, then in one swift motion, pushed the needle through the pale skin and then emptied the contents with a quick push of the plunger. Mark squirmed slightly and then became motionless, his breathing getting visibly shallow with every passing moment. Joe left the syringe in place, awkwardly dangling from the side of Mark's arm. He scattered the contents of a small plastic pouch on and around the bed, placing the pouch still half filled with a white powder in Mark's other hand. After he wiped off his prints from the TV remote and other fixtures in the room and placed the champagne bottle back in the plastic bag, he walked out the door.

CHAPTER 65

Tuesday 12:16 a.m.

The car ride was not the most comfortable. They were huddled in the back seat of Vincent's Corolla. Saleem Qazi took the driver's seat as he was the only one who seemed to know where they were going. Vincent sat in the backseat next to their two captives, holding his Glock at a very uncomfortable distance from Kamran's head, a situation he was painfully familiar with. A chill went down his spine as he realized that this time he might not be so lucky. Vincent, too, was more cautious, learning from the lessons of his previous experience. Their hands were tied with a strong nylon rope and Sana's purse with its belongings, including the perfume spray, was tossed on the front seat, away from their reach.

The car was moving fast on the wide and newly built boulevard passing through this new housing development, fast becoming a benchmark for the rapidly developing string of competing developments now dominating the suburbia surrounding Rawalpindi and Islamabad. Most of it was still undeveloped, but like so many others, the developer had built an impressive network of roads and boulevards, fountains and gardens, even a small zoo to attract customers willing to pay for the heavily priced lots, so far away from the city center.

They passed the cookie cutter houses of Safari Valley, ready to move in, and then through empty plots, already sold and ready to build, moving up a hill where numbered plots suddenly gave way to the beginning of a valley, marking the beginning of the remains of a Pothohar Plateau still untouched by this unbridled urban sprawl. Qazi drove to the end of a cul-de-sac and then continued on to a dirt road. He drove for another minute or so on the barely visible unpaved track and obviously knew exactly where he was heading, until he stopped at an embankment overlooking a sharp drop that seemed to continue forever into bottomless darkness.

Qazi was the first one to get out and then he walked around to the passenger side where a terrified Sana sat with her eyes closed, quietly reciting any prayers and verses of the Quran that came to her mind.

"I guess this is it. End of the road for the two of you," Qazi said with a restrained smile as he pointed his gun straight between her eyes, now wide open and staring right at him. "Now, let's get out and catch some fresh air shall we?"

Agha Kamal knew something was not right and ducked down under the dashboard when he saw them leaving the villa. In the faint light, he could make out four people. Kamran and Sana were in the front, and even in one look, he could read their body language, and it was certainly not a promising sight. Their slumped shoulders and aimless, small indifferent steps told him enough to keep himself from getting out of the car and waving at them. Kamran did not even look at him or gave any hint that he was aware of his presence, reassuring Agha Kamal that he had most likely not mentioned his presence.

The party of four walked towards a car parked on the street across from the villa and paid no attention whatsoever in his direction, confirming his earlier conclusion. He recognized Saleem Qazi who walked past the rest, unlocked the car and took the driver's seat. The fourth person, a tall well-built male, pushed Kamran and Sana towards the back seat. He was holding something in his hand. He tried to make out what it was and then gasped, realizing that it was a gun pointing right at the two of them. Once the two of them were in the car, the tall stranger joined them in the back seat; Saleem Qazi started the car, and with a sudden jerky motion, pulled it onto the road.

It took a minute or so before he regained his composure, contemplating the next move, realizing that he did not have much choice in the matter. Adventure was never his cup of tea: his brushes with the dangers of unexpected occurrences, of shocking developments and of unpredictable scenarios were strictly limited to other characters, going through their thrilling experiences to entertain him as he witnessed them in his imagination from the vantage point of his reading chair. This scenario, however, as unfortunate as it may have seemed to him, was real and he had to do something about it.

In one quick motion he looked towards the end of the street, saw the other car leaving and then make a right turn onto the main road. He turned the ignition, making sure that his headlights were off; he followed them, keeping a generous distance between the two vehicles.

After exiting the compound, they turned left, and then made a U-turn, heading towards the still underdeveloped Phase Eight of the sprawling development. The expansive boulevard was empty and brightly lit, making it difficult for him to stay close, so he lingered back, watching the distant taillights of the Corolla and intently making sure not to lose them in the distance.

He looked at his phone. No signal, they were in the valley.

Frustrated, Agha Kamal slammed his hands on the steering wheel. His face was flushed with anger. Veins were popping on the back of his hands, and his blanched fingers were tightly curled around the leather covering of the steering wheel.

He had been debating about what to do. He was still in shock at what he had witnessed back at the villa. At first he had assumed that Saleem Qazi was arresting them, but then, why not just call the police. Why take them in a car, and why in this direction? Who was that fourth man? Questions tore through his mind like a tornado, going around in endless spirals, twisting around themselves at a horrifying pace and suddenly they disappeared. The world seem to come to a halt around him and the answer to his questions came out suddenly, as clear as the stars in the unpolluted night skies of his childhood. Saleem Qazi was the last person on earth they should have approached. Agha Kamal could not believe it. But it was too late now. Who to call for help? Saleem Qazi was a very popular and well-liked police officer with deep connections. If it came down to his word against theirs, the outcome did not seem very optimistic. He had to reach someone he could trust, and the meager list had suddenly become even shorter.

Through the partially open window, a wet cold wind was whistling. The very thought of the stark reality that stood before his eyes sent a chill through his spine. They were in the middle of nowhere; unless suddenly, there was a solitary dwelling in this wilderness that they were heading to, the intentions of those who had Sana and Kamran captive did not appear to be any less than ominous.

He looked at the phone again, still no bars.

"What is wrong with these people? They've made these roads in the middle of nowhere, can't they put up a new cell tower," Agha

Kamal was getting frustrated; he was realizing that time was running out, fast.

They were going uphill now and the other car had almost reached the top. Looking to buy land in this area, Agha Kamal had driven through this area several times and knew that there was a roundabout nearby, and as they could be heading onto any of the five exits off it, he stepped on the gas as the car roared into a lower gear to tackle the sharp ascent. Instinctively, he looked at the phone again and just like that, voila! Two bars popped up on the screen.

Excited, Agha Kamal grabbed the phone and dialed a number, fumbling with the dimly backlit keypad. A sharp turn just before the roundabout was too sudden, too much.

The car veered off the road onto the unpaved shoulder, jumped off a small dirt mound, lunged forward while partially airborne, then landed sharply into a shallow drainage ditch, rolling over once and then stopped, precariously perched on the edge of the cliff.

CHAPTER 66

Tuesday 12:45 a.m.

Kamran and Sana were on the ground, kneeling, hands tied behind their backs. "Why? I don't understand," Kamran asked. His eyes focused on the service issue, Chief's Special Model-36 revolver pointed squarely at him.

"Why are you doing this? I can understand his reasons," he looked at Vincent, his eyes filled with contempt. "He has no conscience, no soul; he would do anything . . . for money . . . ," Vincent stared hard at him, a poignant look on his face. His face twitched slightly at the remark, but he lowered his eyes quickly and did not say anything.

". . . but you . . . of all people, Saleem, you . . . you were supposed to be the knight in shining armor, beacon of hope in the dark. You were supposed to fight corruption and the disarray that has become the norm in police departments."

Saleem Qazi smiled painfully but remained quiet.

"I believed in you, Saleem. We all did, but . . . but now . . . I don't even know what to say," Kamran's voice cracked a bit.

Saleem Qazi moved forward slowly, and he got down on one knee in front of them, his revolver still pointed at them.

"I liked you Kamran; I still do, and if you can believe me, I did not want you to get in the middle of this. I tried my best to keep you out of it, but you wouldn't listen, and now you have left me with no other choice. You simply know too much. It hurts me to think of the way this will end but the stakes are too high, consequences too severe to give into mundane emotions. "

"What stakes? Who are you working for? Are you working for him?" he pointed at Vincent, but he did not respond and kept staring at the distance right through him.

"Huh!" Saleem Qazi chuckled, "I don't work for him. I don't work for anyone. He is a mere pawn in the grand scheme. I do not take orders from a lowlife hired puppet like him. He doesn't have a clue about anything more than his principle mission . . . ," he spoke in Urdu so Vincent could only guess what was being said, although he could have bet his life that whatever was being said, it involved him.

". . . His fate will not be any different from yours," Qazi added in a cold, detached voice.

"You still haven't answered the question, why?" Sana who had been quiet, overwhelmed by the unexpected turn of events had been mesmerized by the two guns pointed at her finally spoke.

Qazi's face lit up. His bright teeth gleamed through a wide grin in the fading moonlight. "You know, under any other circumstances, I'd be in a hurry to get the job done but, of all the people, you two deserve to know the truth. I do not expect you to agree with me, but I do expect that someone like you can at least appreciate the circumstances, and understand my motives."

Both of them sat up straight. Despite the dropping temperature and increasing wind, they were soaked in sweat. Conversation was able to distract them and kept their mind off the stark reality that faced them. Kamran was not sure where Agha Kamal was. During his car ride, he had tried to take a quick look behind them on sharper turns, but he did not see anyone following them. He could not do more, or he would raise suspicions. As much as he despised Vincent, he admired his uncanny ability to notice even the tiniest irregularities. He just hoped that Agha Kamal saw them getting into the car and had somehow been able to keep up with them. For now, all he could do was to buy time and this was the best way to do it. Saleem Qazi had few weaknesses, however, two personality traits stood out. He was a voracious talker, and he never shied away from expressing his opinions. Kamran planned to exploit them to the limit.

Saleem Qazi did not say anything for a few minutes, but then he walked up to them and asked them to move back and rest against the car. For Kamran and Sana, it was a welcome change as they had started to wonder how long they could last in their current physical positions. Vincent had already found a rock to sit on and was oblivious to the proceedings. Qazi lit a cigar, took a long deep puff and then found another rock to sit on. It was darker now. The moon had disappeared and the distant street lamps were barely making any impression. Distant lights in a nearby village were going off one by one, until only a few remained. A rooster suddenly shattered the silence, most probably confusing a car's headlights for the morning, and then it was quiet again.

"This country is going in the wrong direction," Qazi suddenly spoke up. "Greedy politicians have sold every inch of this sacred land to everyone from the Americans and the British on one end, to the Russians and the Chinese on the other. No one can be trusted. They all have the same agenda; keep their pockets full and their benefactors happy. Look what they did to Thar coal and Reko Diq copper and gold deposits. Everyone got rich except the *people* of Pakistan. No one gives a damn about the country. No one cares about the ideology behind it, the sacrifices that shaped its vision, and the blood of millions that nurtured its roots. My family had everything, wealth, social status, you name it, but they did not have the freedom that every human deserves. In 1947, during the partition from India, when my father packed one suitcase, and then with my mother who was eight months pregnant in tow, left all his possessions behind, crossed the border into Pakistan, he did not care that he did not have a roof to sleep under, he had only one thought. Finally, he belonged, in a society that did not judge him. He was home, in a country where he could practice his religion without constantly looking over his shoulder. He fell to his knees and kissed the earth that would be his home, in life, and then in death. He instilled that passion, that love in me, and made sure that I did not take this country for granted and that I was willing to sacrifice everything, even my life, if needed. That's why I joined the police force, and that's why I am here today," Qazi paused and looked at them expectantly, his tired face flushed with a new found vigor.

"But don't you realize that what has happened will derail any hopes for democracy in the near future? This country needs to be back on track. We need democracy. We need the voice of our people to be heard. We need the army to go back to the barracks," Sana spoke loudly and passionately.

Another big smile appeared on Qazi's face, "Democracy! Surely you can't be serious?"

"I certainly am," Sana replied defiantly. "We have been perpetually kept hostage by power hungry generals and their whims. Finally, we have someone who is willing to give the reigns back to the people. The people of Pakistan deserve that. The institution of democracy and the sanctity of the constitution is the only way for us to march forward and salvage our future."

"You seem to put a lot of faith in democracy," Qazi shook his head, amused by Sana's passionate response. "Modern democracy is not about people. It is about what is best for the reigning super power, for the region and its economy, and for those who run it," he paused to wet his lips and then continued. "Modern democracy does not ensure power to the people. Are you kidding me? Do you really think that politicians who spend millions to win elections are going to put that power in the hands of average men and women? That would be catastrophic for them; total chaos. Democracy does not ensure anything for the people who vote. It just ensures that people, who have their goals locked in for the long term, stay in power. It ensures that these few and chosen people make all the important decisions. They don't give a damn about their so-called fans; the hordes of ill-informed, impulsive and overly emotional masses," he paused again and wiped the gathering beads of sweat off his brow. "Successful democracies are able to achieve this delicate balance between staying the course, while still creating a perfect illusion of power for its people. Is that the kind of democracy you worship, one that cuts out the people, only to ensure that the leaders, the so called public servants, keep their bank balances growing?"

"Don't be so cynical Qazi. There are a lot of good people out there," Kamran argued.

"Really!" Qazi replied in mock amazement, "and where do they meet, Cinderella's Castle, surely not in our parliament? Do you know that Malik Jahangir had already sold the country to the highest bidder? Do you really think that his whole stance for self-sufficiency was genuine? It always amazes me when they win the hearts of our simple people with the hollow rhetoric of being self-sufficient, because we refuse to take money from the West. Doesn't taking it from China instead mean the same? Do you know why he was such a big fan of China?"

"He wanted to decrease American influence on our trade?" Sana offered her opinion.

"That's what you think? He practically begged those *Amriki's* to give him assurances of future contracts, but they have been very careful recently. They don't want to make any wrong moves and alienate the Pakistani people any further. They want our moral support in their plans, so they refused to offer him any kickbacks. That is why he ran to the Chinese. Pakistani people have always loved the Chinese. They consider them our real friends, so the Chinese didn't have any qualms about promising him a fortune for guaranteed contracts when and if he came to power. He had made some shrewd business decisions for himself. You should see his waterfront villa in Nice, and that's just one of them."

"And that is why you had him killed?"

"He was a cancer that was going to spread very fast and destroy our motherland," Qazi replied angrily. "He needed to be cut out."

"No matter what the cost?" Sana was amazed at the conviction in his voice.

"Yes . . . no matter what the cost . . . and I'll do the same to anyone else who threatens it," he was animated now and pacing back and forth, his hands tightly locked behind his back. His face was red with excitement and looked intensely dramatic, even more so in the glow of the car's headlights in the background.

"The people of Pakistan do not deserve the right to choose their own leaders. They have had multiple opportunities to do the right thing, and they have squandered every one of them. They have not learned anything from the past. They follow their emotions and suppress any rational thoughts about who to vote for. We do not vote for a party and its manifesto, or even its ideology. We vote for one person in blind hero worship, falling for the false claims that we are infatuated with; we even vote for its dead leaders who, guess what, are not coming back to lead us. We vote for our clans, *baradris* with no regard for honesty and legitimacy. Our leaders are a bunch of power hungry and arrogant hypocrites who would sell their soul for the right price, and we still keep electing them. When we are done with them, we rejoice when they are ousted because of their corruption, just to elect someone else with the same qualifications, and then when it is their turn to go, we, the great people of Pakistan, in a sheer lapse of sanity, or maybe just a sudden case of profound amnesia, elect the first group again. Don't you see the pattern, the vicious cycle that replaces one crook with another, and you still think that fulfilling this nightmare democracy is the key to our destiny?" Qazi was breathing hard and fast now, and stopped to lean against the car and catch his breath.

"But . . . don't you see?" Kamran spoke up, "that is the beauty of the system. It corrects itself, but only if it is given the opportunity. Our people are simple and emotional. They are crushed under the rigors of a hard life and are easily swayed by false promises, but every time they make a mistake, they learn from it. Unfortunately, the system breaks down too often to maintain any sort of continuity. That is not their fault, maybe it is *our* fault, people like us, the educated, the materially accomplished, but *we* chose not to keep the system going. They just need this process to continue evolving, to shape this flawed system into something very special, and *no one,* including you, has the right to take it away from them."

"You seem to have spent too much time going through your medical books and haven't paid much attention to our history, Kamran," Qazi said in a patronizing tone. "People who were the true architects of this nation came from the Muslim minority areas that are now a part of India. Only they knew what it was like to be a minority and they were voted out by the uncompromising *baradris* in the Muslim majority Pakistan. None of the true leaders stood a chance against the seasoned, professional politicians who had never tasted oppression long enough to understand the true value of freedom . . . ," he was talking fast now," . . . and now, we are ruled by a bunch of self-centered bigots, who have nothing better to do than to please their own vanities. Do you know how many of them are on CIA's payroll? India wants us weak, and Mossad has been more than willing to help them eliminate our nuclear capabilities. The Taliban want to take over and push us into the Middle Age, and our enemies are lined up to pour out cash for it. Why do you think that the Indians are so lovey-dovey with Afghanis? Why do you think they have over a dozen mini-consulates right on the Durand Line? They have no business there, but our politicians never say a word about it. No! I can't trust my homeland to them."

"And you are willing to trust a dictator?" Sana asked. "On the other hand, we don't even have a willing dictator. General Hamid is not even *interested*."

"*Exactly!*" Qazi slapped the side of his head with the palm of his hand. "Don't you see? He doesn't want it. That is exactly why he should get it. He cares for this country and wants the best for it. He just doesn't realize that what he is looking for is right there, staring at him in the mirror."

Qazi finished his speech and sat down on the hood of the car and took a long puff from his half-charred cigar. He looked exhausted.

Kamran saw it as an opportunity. "Don't you realize that by doing this, you are playing right into their hands?" Kamran made a subtle gesture towards Vincent who seemed oblivious to the conversation that was now mostly in Urdu. "Isn't it what you just said?

The CIA, Mossad, RAW; isn't this exactly the kind of chaos they are hoping for? And you are just handing it to them. Give them the well-tested single man rule so they can control one person easily without worrying about anyone else. You too, are selling the future for your own selfish ideology. You may not be after money, but that still does not make you any better than those politicians . . . ."

". . . Because *I am* better than them, and yes . . . I am *not* doing it for the money." Qazi raised his voice and cut him off. "I am doing it for the country. Those *Amriki* people think they know everything, but they have been underestimating us for decades. It is about time that they learn a lesson or two about us. Once I am done with the two of you, it will be his turn," Qazi whispered in Urdu without looking at Vincent, who was still staring at the dark silhouettes of barren hills in the distance.

"And what about Naveed Khan . . . why him?"

"I thought he was better than others, but then I was disappointed. As the elections got closer, he too has been compromised. Look at his demeanor, his statements. He, too, has picked up the political art form, complete with lots of talk and vague promises, but no real substance; there is no conviction in his statements. All the ideals have taken a back seat as he had been busy with meetings at the American Embassy."

"You have to trust someone, sometime IG *sahib*. That is how the system works," Sana added.

"I don't trust the system, and everyone that goes along with it. I have seen too much, and for too long. Believe me, Naveed is a product of the same broken system. He is also popular, people like him, and that in itself is a complication. I cannot let people's emotions derail my plan. He needs to go, one way or another."

"You are insane. You will never get away with this," Kamran said angrily.

"Oh I will . . . and there is nothing you can do about it. You're mere specks of dust in my broader vision" he spat on the ground. "You have wasted enough of my time. Now shut up, and get ready to face your unfortunate demise," he got up and moved swiftly towards them.

"You," he motioned to Vincent, "tie them up well and move them to the edge of this cliff," he walked back towards the car, opened the trunk and pulled out a can full of gasoline. He stood by the car deep in thought before slowly walking towards them.

"I still wish that you had listened to me Kamran, I don't want to do this but I have no choice."

His phone rang. Annoyed by the intrusion, he pulled it out, ready to turn it off when he saw the familiar number flashing on the screen.

"I have to take this; I'll be in the car," he told Vincent, placing the gasoline can and a box of matches next to him, and then spoke in a cold, monotonous voice that sent chills down their spines. "Shoot them, and then burn the evidence."

CHAPTER 67

DEFENSE HOUSING SOCIETY, RAWALPINDI

Tuesday 12:25 a.m.

DIG Tariq Khawaja was unable to sleep. He tried all the usual techniques. A cup of warm milk, a hot bath, even made another futile attempt at finishing Tolstoy's *War and Peace*, but he still laid there, eyes wide open, staring at a stain on the ceiling, the remains of a water leak one year ago. His wife, who woke up from a sound sleep, disturbed by his tossing and turning offered to massage his shoulders, but just when he seemed to relax and his eyes started to get heavy, his phone rang.

He was deeply disturbed by the events of the last three days, and his marathon interrogation session with Naveed Khan had left him physically and mentally drained. Yet, when he finally got home, ready to crash, he could not go to sleep.

Something did not make sense. He had known Naveed Khan for a long time. Before getting transferred to Rawalpindi as DIG Investigations, he was SP (Superintendent of Police) in Lahore. His jurisdiction included GOR-I (Government Officers Residents) keeping him closely involved in the lives of government official as well as elected members and ministers of the Punjab Assembly. On various occasions, he had the opportunity of securing the perimeter of Naveed Khan's residence, which had gained the reputation of being the unofficial think tank for the coalition of opposition parties.

Security concerns, and Naveed Khan's meticulous nature, had given them numerous opportunities to meet face to face, and each one of them had left their meetings with a sense of mutual admiration and respect for the other. Having to interrogate him for Malik

Jahangir's assassination was the last thing he would have expected, and the overwhelming feeling of shock did not get any better after he did.

The other obvious red flag was the uncharacteristic manner in which Inspector General Saleem Qazi had pushed him to go ahead with it, despite the sketchy nature of the evidence provided, which was circumstantial at best, and very risky if one considered the volatile circumstances that surrounded it. He kept thinking about the way Malik Nisar hovered over him, but that was natural, both from the stand point of his cabinet position, as well as the close bond that he had shared with his late cousin.

"Let it go, Tariq," his wife protested, half asleep, "You were gone for twenty-four hours. Didn't you say they'll call Rehan if they need anything?" she referred to one of his colleagues who had volunteered to cover for him.

"I know, I know," just let me see who it is," he replied, somewhat annoyed.

He put his reading glasses on and looked at the caller ID, surprised by the name that appeared on it.

"At this hour," he muttered under his breath as he looked at his watch. Taking a call from a journalist was the last thing he would have done, but this caller was different. He would never compromise on his principles. He would never call him at home, and at this hour, unless it was something critical.

"Who is it?" his wife asked, clearly more awake now.

The phone continued to ring.

"I think I should take this one. It'll only be a minute. Try to go back to sleep. At least one of us will be fresh in the morning, and thank you for the massage," he gently kissed her on the cheek and picked up the phone.

"Hello?"

"Hello . . . Tariq . . . thank God you are home . . . oh no . . . ,"the line went silent.

"Hello . . . hello . . . hello? Agha *Sahib*? Is everything ok?" he heard the screeching sound of tires losing control on wet asphalt, and then there was a loud crash.

"Agha *Sahib*, are you ok? Can you hear me, but there was no reply."

Tariq Khawaja jumped out of the bed and ran towards the closet to get dressed.

He was already in his car when he got the call from police dispatch. Before leaving the house, and after hastily explaining the situation to a now very awake and attentive wife, he had placed a call to the police headquarters in order to locate the origin of the phone call.

Cell phones in ever increasing numbers had created a distinct set of problems for the police force. Until they had arrived, wireless devices without a license were illegal in Pakistan, and thus never a major concern. Now that everyone, from the richest and the most powerful to the middle class all the way down to beggars on the busy sidewalks communicated through cell phones, things were different.

Technology had introduced a whole new dimension to the world of crime. Even the most far flung regions of the country, still devoid of electricity or running water, boasted about the newest cell towers in their midst, connecting them to the modern world.

Finally, with the introduction of GSM systems, police departments had started to catch up, and were able track down the precise location of a phone call.

"What did you find out?" Tariq Khawaja inquired impatiently.

"We were able to narrow it down, sir. The signal is weak, but I think I can give you coordinates within a hundred meters."

"Good, give them to me, and then call for back up. I am heading over there right now."

He looked at the coordinates and entered them on the GPS, and then smiled.

"Bahria Town? This must be my lucky day," he made a quick right turn and headed for the bridge over Sawanh River that directly connected Defense Housing Society with Bahria Town Phase 8.

Agha Kamal felt a sharp piercing pain in the middle of his eyes. He had blacked out, and it took a few minutes before the circumstances of his current state started to come back to him. He tried to lift his head from the steering wheel but it felt like a ball of lead and required all his remaining strength to move it. The windshield had shattered into tiny bits, allowing in a cold and stiff breeze that felt like razor blades on his face scarred by glass fragments. He could feel a warm streak that tracked down from his forehead and then dripped down onto his hand. He wiped his hand across the forehand and noticed a small gash that did not seem big enough to be of any immediate concern, and the bleeding had almost stopped.

A thick cloud of whitish smoke was emerging from under the hood and then slowly ascending like a ghost before dissipating into the milky moonlight, and he took it as a warning to get out of the vehicle.

A sudden gust of wind made the car rock, a sensation that raised an instantaneous alarm in his mind that was clearing up every second. Cautiously, he leaned forward looking into the dark, and then froze in absolute terror. His car was sitting on a sharp rock perched at the edge of a steep drop into the gorge made by Sawanh River. Even the slightest movement from him resulted in a sudden and violent motion, precariously tipping the car forward towards the looming abyss.

With his already outstretched hand, Agha Kamal picked up the cell phone stuck between his seat and the center console and then leaned back, slowly reclining his seat. The car made a creaking sound that almost made him jump, but then it dropped back, its rear wheels softly landing on flat ground. He took a few deep breaths, trying to relax, and feeling his racing heart slowing down a notch; he opened the door in one quick motion and rolled out of the car.

A sudden gust of wind, following this sudden shift in weight made the rear end of the car lift into the air. Pieces of rocks loosened from under it and rolled down the steep drop; then a moment later, with a terrifying crash, the black Mercedes dropped head first to the bottom of the dark gorge.

Agha Kamal did not move; he just lay there, drenched in a profuse sweat, savoring the cold air, looking at the moon slowly dropping towards the horizon. The liberty to enjoy the moment, however, lasted only a few minutes as his thoughts returned to his two friends in peril. He took a deep breath and then, noticing that his call was still in progress, picked it up.

"Hello . . . Tariq? Can you hear me?"

"*Shukr Al-hamdulillah!* Thank you, God!" a relieved Tariq Khawaja responded immediately. "Where are you?"

CHAPTER 68

Tuesday 1:05 a.m.

Kamran and Sana were huddled together at the edge of the cliff. Their hands were still tied with a thin nylon cord that had started to dig deeper into the flesh, creating a sensation that had progressed from merely uncomfortable to notably painful. Vincent had ordered them to move slowly towards the edge and was now standing right above them, fitting a silencer to his gun. He had remained oddly silent throughout the evening, almost detached as if he had no interest in the events that were taking place around him.

Saleem Qazi was still busy with his phone call when suddenly there was a loud crash that seemed to originate from a point just west of them and then echoed from the surrounding hills, almost knocking them from their already precarious position.

"What was that?" a startled Saleem Qazi turned around and spoke in a manner that was closer to being a scream.

And then everything was silent again except the sound of a stiff breeze weaving through the valley. A faint hum of traffic miles away filled the silence with indirect evidence that modern civilization was close by.

Qazi walked to a higher spot on the hill to take a look and then, satisfied with his reconnaissance, continued his conversation. Between the wind and his hushed tone, it was impossible to decipher the conversation so after the initial interest wore off, they stopped making any effort to listen.

"He is going to kill you," Sana suddenly spoke, addressing Vincent directly.

"What . . . did you say something to me?" a surprised Vincent replied.

"Don't you realize . . . ?"

"Realize what?"

"That you are just a pawn in this game."

"What game?"

"The game that these people are playing, global domination, economic manipulation of the poor, or who wants to be the democracy killer, whatever you want to call it," Sana said, sarcastically. "Whoever is running this show is not going to let you live with their secrets."

"You have no idea what you are talking about."

"And you have no idea who are you dealing with," an angry Kamran jumped into the conversation. "People of Pakistan are stronger than that. You can't break their spirits by your arrogant plans. You are underestimating them yet again. Didn't you learn anything from the past? Finally, they have started to recognize their friends and have uncovered their enemies. They have no trust left in the superficial overtures from the west. They can see right through it."

"You know, Sana . . . may I call you Sana?" Vincent asked with a subdued smile. "I don't have a choice either way, do I?"

"Yes, you do!"

Vincent quickly looked back to check on Qazi and then whispered, "I understand your hostility towards me, and I can't change that, but you have to understand this is not just about a few politicians in your country, or even the future of democracy. Your politicians are so much easier to manipulate, and they are so much more willing to be exploited for the right price that if I am running the show, I'd rather go for democracy than put all my eggs in the basket of one dictator. These Army officers are always a little on the crazy side. They *have* to be, in order to get to that level, and it is very hard to predict what they'll do next. What I am trying to say is that even that guy," he pointed at Saleem Qazi with his partially obscure outstretched thumb, "has no clue as to who exactly is pulling his strings."

"So who is . . . pulling the strings?" Kamran asked.

"I don't know. I mean I know some things, but I am pretty sure that the trail is far deeper than that."

"Why do you say that?"

"I have learned a lot of things doing what I do, and I've always followed three basic rules. One, I do not ask questions. Two, I never try to dig deeper than my own footprint. Three, I don't get emotionally involved . . . ," Vincent seemed a bit relaxed now, "and I have broken all three of them," he looked down at his feet and slowly shook his head.

"He's going to kill you once he is done with us."

"I know."

"You do!" Kamran replied, surprised at the calm in Vincent's voice.

"I heard him. Do you think I'd come to a foreign country, for a mission of such proportions, without learning at least *some* local language? I've spent my whole life in New York, eating meals at the neighborhood *Kabab* House, and besides, it doesn't take a genius to figure out a man like your boogey man over there."

Kamran smiled, "You amaze me, Vincent. This morning, you were like an animal, ready to kill us but now . . . now, something has changed. What happened . . . ?"

"What the hell are you doing?" an angry voice boomed from behind them.

Saleem Qazi had returned to find them engaged in a rather casual conversation.

"You incompetent fool," Qazi growled, "all I asked you to do was to finish the job and you . . . ," he stared hard at Vincent and then stopped talking and turned towards Kamran and Sana who were suddenly drawn back into the dreadful reality they were in.

"I didn't want to do it myself, Kamran, I really didn't, but you leave me no choice," His voice became loud, nostrils flared. "You and I are both running out of time."

With one brisk motion, he picked up the gas can, opened its cap and poured the gasoline on both of them. Sana screamed with terror as gasoline soaked her clothes and the pungent fumes started to burn her eyes. She held Kamran's hand tightly and tried to move as far away from Qazi as possible, but tripped on her own feet and fell hard bruising her shoulder, taking Kamran down with her.

Qazi walked up to them, pulled out his revolver and aimed it at Kamran's head, and then leaned in towards him and softly whispered, "I am sorry," as his slightly quivering finger increased its pressure on the trigger.

CHAPTER 69

BAHRIA TOWN

Tuesday 1:28 p.m.

Agha Kamal ignored the stabbing pain that pierced through his right knee and continued to climb a heaping pile of dirt and rock erected to create a cul-de-sac at the end of an elite row of empty but spacious plots.

An amazed Tariq Khawaja, a younger, and theoretically more fit active duty police officer, tried to keep up while stumbling over almost invisible obstacles. They could hear muffled voices beyond the climb, but could not make out any words and then they heard a loud voice.

"What the hell are you doing?"

They froze in their tracks, waiting patiently to make sure they were safe, and then they heard the loud scream. It was just not a scream; it was a cry for help originating out of sheer desperation in the face of unimaginable terror.

Agha Kamal almost fell down the hill but held on to a large rock sticking out of the steep slope. He recognized that scream immediately; it was Sana and he moved on with a new found vigor.

DIG Tariq Khawaja had reached Agha Kamal, not long after his escape from the doomed vehicle, and had found him on the side of the road still stumbling a little, while trying to regain his balance as well as his composure. A shorthand version of recent events gave Tariq some insight into what was going on but he was, as expected, having a hard time accepting Saleem Qazi's role in it.

"There must have been a misunderstanding. I've known the guy for years. There is no one more patriotic than he is."

"That's what I thought, but sometimes, only a thin line separates pragmatic patriotism from jingoism. You'd be surprised to know what is behind the passionate rhetoric and emotional facades of these patriots if you see them from a journalist's eyes," Agha Kamal replied.

Tariq Khawaja, still in shock, overwhelmed by the details, could only nod in silence. They drove on the boulevard slowly looking for any signs of the other vehicle. Their headlights were turned off but visibility was not an issue with ample streets lamps on either side of the deserted street. This in itself was an odd sight in a country where electricity was gold, and power outages for load-shedding were more predictable than the next hot meal.

A large roundabout adorned with a huge fountain was expected, however, five exits going in as many directions presented a dilemma.

"Which way should we go?" Tariq asked.

"My guess is as good as yours."

'Should we wait for the back up to arrive?"

"It will be too late," Agha Kamal, said with a sigh. "Maybe, we . . . are already too late."

They drove around the roundabout, looking for any clues but nothing jumped up to guide them. Finally, Tariq drove up a side street towards higher elevation to get a better view of the valley and then they saw them. Tariq almost disregarded the flickering red lights in the distance as his imagination, but he decided to take a closer look through his binoculars, and then saw the car, parked at the end of a street, its headlights still on. He could not see if there was anyone in it.

They parked the car at the beginning of the street and walked rest of the way; Agha Kamal still hobbling a little bit, rubbing his right knee every now and then.

"Are you okay?" Tariq asked.

"I am fine, must have twisted it or something," he replied without stopping and continued on, until they reached a mound that separated them from their destination. The car was parked at the top of the mound so they decided to climb from the side farthest from it, making sure not to make any noise.

The car was empty. They crawled up to it and, once sure that no one was close, crouched behind it, slowly raising their heads to look beyond. In a bright triangle illuminated by the milky white headlights, the scene was surreal. Two helpless captives, huddled together at the edge of a cliff while a defiant Saleem Qazi, stood erect, towering over them, his gun aimed at Kamran's head.

"Oh no," Agha Kamal slumped down, "we *are* too late!"

Saleem Qazi bit his lower lip and then ran his tongue over his dry lips. He lowered his head as his mind raced through the events of the last two days, his goals that were so near, and yet so far. *"Am I doing the right thing?"* Faces of his family and friends flashed through his mind.*"Am I ready to kill someone I would called a friend under different circumstances?"* Questions kept racing through his mind: was he really helping his country? Were the troubles that plagued Pakistan solvable through the efforts of just one person? He felt a blinding headache in his temples. He felt as if his head was being squeezed in a vice. There was a moment of remorse . . . a twinge of guilt began to gnaw at his insides; he tried to fight it . . . then it was gone. He raised his head again, fire back in his eyes.

"One man alone might not be enough but without it, there will not be any effort at all. Something needs to be done and I'm not letting useless emotions push me off course. I am chosen by Allah to fulfill a destiny," the reassurance brought him peace.

"Allah-u-Akbar" he whispered to himself and raised his hand holding the gun. His right hand shook a little. He steadied it with the other, and pulled the trigger.

CHAPTER 70

Tuesday 1:45 a.m.

Kamran was waiting for a miracle until the last moment. He had always imagined his life as a natural progression of his dreams and ambitions. He had always envisioned himself as an energetic soul, full of vigor and strength. Dying at a young age was not something that he had ever thought of. The history lesson that he had just received from his executioner was right on. These were the questions that baffled him, too. The history of Pakistani politics was riddled with such dilemmas. Even though he was a firm believer in the sanctity of democratic institutions, time and time again, he had been proven wrong by the erroneous choices made by the ill-informed, easily misguided, and often coerced voters. The sixty odd years of Pakistan's existence had witnessed a systematic elimination of its true architects from the halls of government. In the days before TV and the internet, these mostly unknown founding fathers were replaced by land barons and feudal lords, who owed their power and wealth almost exclusively to the generosity of their imperial British masters and who had never experienced oppression or persecution to understand the true meaning of freedom. If only, the father of the nation, Mohammad Ali Jinnah, had lived beyond a year of its existence. He had studied the lasting impact of George Washington's selfless politics on US history, and then a continuation of its spirit through men like John Adams, Thomas Jefferson and Andrew Jackson. A strong foundation indeed, a process that was derailed very early in Pakistani history when its first elected Prime minister, Liaquat Ali Khan, was assassinated on the same very grounds as Malik Jahangir. The history of his motherland and its erratic politics frustrated him, too, but two wrongs did not make a right. He believed that the people of Pakistan needed to learn from their mistakes. The system has the ability to correct itself, but only if it is given a chance. The mistakes of the past could not be erased, but valuable lessons could be learned from them. It was time for the nation to take positive action, and avoid getting caught up in the traps and trepidations that had always been its downfall.

A number of unexpected things could change the course of events. The best-case scenario was also the most realistic, and it involved Agha Kamal, suddenly appearing with a posse of policemen in tow and crashing Saleem Qazi's party. As moments passed by, and the chances of something like that happening became more and more remote, so did the flicker of hope that had kept him strong. He had been calm; he had to be, and he knew that his resolve and unruffled demeanor had kept Sana from breaking down, but now it was over. He heard the last proclamation from Saleem Qazi, and saw him raise his gun; he tightly held Sana close to him, feeling her heartbeat, her trembling body. *"La Illaha il-Allah; Mohammad-ur-Rusool Allah,"* he lowered his head and started to recite the *kalima*. He suddenly felt at ease. A sense of peace and calm overcame him. It was the end, but it was not in vain. He felt confident that only good could come out of this sacrifice. Being here, facing his executioner, and unwavering in his principles, he was at peace. Having Sana right there, beside him felt soothing. He pulled her closer, feeling the comfort of her warm embrace. He felt God watching over him, spreading His radiance on and around them. He looked straight into the hollow barrel of the revolver aimed at him; he was ready.

CHAPTER 71

POTHOHAR PLATEAU

Tuesday 1:45 a.m.

Saleem Qazi pulled the trigger, and his Chief's Special Revolver recoiled after a loud blast.

A small plume of smoke was followed the blazing spark leaping out of the barrel, but Kamran did not feel anything. There was no pain. *"Is that how it is; life coming to an end so suddenly, so unexpectedly, but without any element of physical pain?"* amazed, he looked up, and was stunned to see Vincent moving in at lightning speed, and knocking the revolver out of Saleem's hand, causing the bullet to ricochet off a rock to his left.

It wasn't just Saleem who was shocked. Everyone was stunned for a second. Vincent himself fell hard on his left side as Saleem pushed him violently away. It seemed like an eternity, but it was hardly a moment before both of them became aware of the idle revolver, lying on the ground a few feet away. Saleem sprinted towards it and jumped to take possession, but Vincent was quicker and stronger of the two. Their hands reached the elusive piece of metal together, and then engaged in a heated struggle to gain an advantage.

Agha Kamal ran down the slope, Tariq Khawaja not too far behind. Sana saw them and a broad smile took the place of a countenance writhing in the face of horror. Agha Kamal took out a pocketknife and cut the ropes to set them free. Saleem Qazi saw them coming from the corner of his eye, and in sheer frustration, swung his elbow catching Vincent square in the face. A streak of bright red blood gushed out of his nose, smearing the lower half of his face as he fell backwards; Saleem fell down with him in the process. Everyone around them watched in stunned silence as the battle between the two villains waged on. Saleem Qazi had full possession of the gun, and he pounded Vincent's head and upper body with it. Intense pain was evident from every grimace on Vincent's bloody face. His resistance slowly diminished; he was losing strength.

As Tariq was the first one to recover, he pulled out his own revolver and stepped towards them.

"Drop your weapon and step away . . . sir," he ordered Saleem Qazi.

"What are you doing, Tariq?" Saleem Qazi shouted back. "You have it all wrong. This is the guy who killed Malik Jahangir," he aimed his gun at Vincent, "I have him now. They are his accomplices," he said, pointing at Kamran and Sana. "Don't let them get away. They may be dangerous. Shoot them if they make any moves. This is an order."

Tariq Khawaja took a deep breath, "I am sorry Qazi *sahib*, but . . . you need to do as I say," he said hesitatingly. "I need you to throw your revolver towards me, and slowly move away from this man."

A resigned look appeared on Qazi's face. He got up slowly, and as he turned around he placed his revolver on the ground and then pushed it away with his foot.

"Happy?" he smiled, but with a flat expression, his eyes listless. "But you are making a huge mistake, Tariq. You have to trust me. They . . . ," he pointed to the small group standing behind him, ". . . are the ones who are a real danger to this country."

"Leave that up to me. I'll be the judge of that," Tariq replied with a stern look on his face, his nostrils flared in revulsion.

Vincent moaned loudly as Saleem slowly walked towards Tariq. Sana hurried up to him and tore a piece of her *doputta* and placed it on the bleeding gash on his forehead, while Kaman followed her to assist as for a moment, everyone's attention was diverted in that direction. This was all Saleem needed as he leapt like a cat taking a small pistol out of his jacket pocket and placing it on Tariq Khawaja's temple.

"Okay people, show is over. Make any stupid moves and he dies."

Saleem Qazi wrapped his left arm around Tariq's neck, keeping the barrel of his pistol firmly on his head and walked back slowly, pulling away from the rest of them. Tariq Khawaja had a look of shock on his face as seen so often on those who embrace danger as a way of life, yet never believe that it could be them who might be a victim of it.

"All of you! Hit the ground," Qazi shouted. "Empty your pockets, wallets, key chains, cell phones, everything, and then stay there, face down, arms spread out."

Tariq Khawaja struggled to breathe through his windpipe that was squeezed shut by the tightening grip around his neck. His fair complexioned face was turning into crimson red that had acquired a ghostly hue in the hazy glow of the car's headlights. A pair of bulging eyes still showed a sparkle, underscoring the adamant resolve of a brave warrior.

"It is all over, Saleem," Agha Kamal took a cautious step forward and said softly. "Do not make it any worse. Give up, we can still help you."

"You can't help me, no one can," Saleem replied scornfully. "You have already tried your best to ruin this country, and I will not let you continue to disrespect its ideology."

"The ideals of this country are all that I stand for and I am honored to have an opportunity to uphold them," Agha Kamal replied proudly.

"You, the press and the media are obsessed with profits, readership and viewership. You are more concerned about ratings than the impact of your so-called sensationalism on an illiterate and ill-informed public," Saleem's voice was loud and trembling with emotions. He continued, "you criticize the military for not doing their job, and yet they do; you kill them with a critique that undermines their every effort. If most of the media had been responsible and did not use religious emotions to highlight and exaggerate every civilian casualty, the Taliban would never have generated the countrywide support that they now enjoy. The Army may not have been at its best, but you made the oppressors look like victims, and somehow made every heinous crime they committed appear to be our own fault. In the end, it has been the army that has come through to contain their hegemony. Besides, do you know that a big chunk of money that arms these terrorists, directly or indirectly, involves a large number of our own political leaders?" Saleem Qazi spat on the ground in disgust.

"I agree with you on most of these points, but I don't agree with your methods. Let us go, we can still help you, Saleem."

" . . . No, you cannot help me Agha *Sahib*, you are one of *them*," he took another step backwards and away from them, and then pointed to the ground. "Now back off and lie down on the ground with the rest of them, *right now!*"

Vincent tried to open his eyes and it required some effort. A bolt of blinding headache hit him like a sledgehammer. His eyes were stuck together with the dried blood that was covering his face. Summoning all his power, he pivoted on his left arm and almost chewed his lip off, trying not scream from the intense pain.

"You don't know what you are doing," he said in a bare whisper as he tried to get up.

"Get back on the ground or I'll shoot him, "a somewhat panicked Saleem Qazi reacted to this new development.

"Go ahead; I don't know him anyway," Vincent replied calmly.

"Then I'll shoot them," Saleem waved his revolver and pointed its barrel towards the three of them.

"It doesn't matter," Vincent was suddenly very calm. "I've done this all my life. Believe me, a single life does not mean anything to me, but there *is* something that is more important to me now."

"And what is *that*?" Saleem shot back.

"The People of Pakistan," Vincent replied with a deep conviction that caught everyone off guard.

A surprised look appeared on Sana's face, as she looked at Kamran who was still trying to analyze the statement.

"In one day, I have learned what you have not in decades. People of this country have been exploited, both by its own politicians and power brokers, as well as the foreign powers that use them for their self-interest. While your intentions are admirable," he looked straight at Qazi, "your methods are utterly misguided and come right out of a well-rehearsed and perfected playbook. People who plan to gain from this are hiding behind your patriotism, counting on your emotions to take over your rational desires to make your country great. And believe me, people who will benefit from this are not the poor people of Pakistan, No . . . not by far. It's a game of political gains, territorial controls, and economic forecasts; you are merely a dispensable pawn in it."

"Shut up!" Saleem replied angrily, "Stop . . . right now!"

Vincent continued to inch forwards as if he did not hear anything, "Until this morning, I did not care. All I was interested in was the money, but then I met the two of you," he looked at Kamran and Sana as a tired smile appeared on his face. "You reminded me of the fact that there are still good people in this world, who are willing to put their self-interests behind them, and do what is right. You made a lot of sense . . . ," he looked at Sana, "thank you!"

Sana, still shocked, nodded politely in acknowledgment.

"And then I met the friendly people of this country. Even in the sad, poverty stricken neighborhoods of Islamabad, they showed no sign of bitterness. They did not care what I looked like, or who I was. They were just happy that they had a guest among them. It was a feeling of belonging, being a part of a family that I had not experienced since I was ten," Vincent's voice became heavy as tears started to appear in his eyes. "It was so overwhelming that I could not stand it, and I had to get away . . . and then . . . ," his face stiffened and turned a grayish color, ". . . and then I saw what people like you do to these innocent men, women and children. I saw what happened at that bus terminal in Rawalpindi. I saw ordinary hardworking people blown to bits . . . lose their limbs and their loved ones. I saw mothers clutching at the remains of their dead children. They do not deserve this. They deserve better . . . and that is why you need to be stopped," his voice became heavy as tears started to appear in his eyes. He pulled out his Glock and charged towards Saleem Qazi. Startled by this sudden attack, his grip on Tariq's neck loosened and that was all Tariq needed to pull away and fall on his knees, trying to catch his breath. Saleem ignored him and focused on Vincent, aiming his gun at the lunging body suspended in midair and pulled the trigger. Vincent fell hard on the ground face down just in front of him, a rapidly enlarging circle of bright red blood appearing on his chest just below his left shoulder blade.

For a moment, everyone forgot about everything and stared at the motionless body in front of them. A maniacal snicker preceded a triumphant smile on Saleem Qazi's face.

"It's your turn now. Who wants to be next; any volunteers or do you want me to pick a name?" he bent down and picked up Vincent's Glock.

"And this will be the perfect cover," he laughed and took another step back.

"I can see tomorrow's headlines." Suspects in Malik Jahangir's murder found dead in a gun battle. Deadly assassin killed his accomplices before succumbing to the bravery of IG Saleem Qazi."

"Sirens of approaching police vehicles could be heard in the distance. "Ah, just in time for the coronation," he turned to Tariq Khawaja. "I'll put in a good word for you. You might even get a posthumous medal for this brav . . . ,"he stopped in mid-sentence.

Vincent twitched and then picked up his head. His pupils wide and breath shallow as he turned towards Kamran and Sana.

"I am sorry," the words were barely audible. Then he looked at Qazi. A broad smiled appeared on his face, as with a sudden surge of energy he extended his left hand grabbing his ankle.

"See you in *hell,* Qazi," he said in a loud and clear voice.

Qazi, surprised by the comment, looked down, and then the reality dawned on him. Unknowingly, in the heat of his emotions, he had walked back to the edge of the precipice, his weight, barely held by some loose dirt and rocks. His eyes widened with fear, mouth open in shock and his face turned to an ash grey hue.

"Good bye," Vincent uttered and then sharply pulled the ankle towards him. Saleem Qazi could not contain the loud scream as he flailed his arms in a desperate attempt to gain footing, but the soft dirt crumbled under his weight as he plunged down into the abyss, a loud thud signaling his unwelcoming destination a hundred feet below.

Vincent turned over and whispered, "The concierge."

Kamran leaned towards him.

"Concierge . . . what concierge, where?" Kamran asked hurriedly.

"At the hotel," Vincent could barely whisper now.

"The one at Pearl Continental . . . what about him?"

Vincent nodded his head once, wincing in pain.

"What about the concierge?" Kamran asked again but did not get a reply.

Vincent's eyes, covered with dark blood and barely open, looked straight at the dark skies. It had started to rain. The first few drops fell on his face and washed away some of the blood. A faint smile appeared on his pale lips with much effort, as he heard police sirens, getting louder and just over the hill. He picked up his hand, made the sign of the cross on his chest with his bloodstained finger, and then closed his eyes.

Early the next morning, a weary Kamran walked up to the concierge's desk at Pearl Continental Hotel in Rawalpindi. A Deputy Superintendent of Police and two constables accompanied him. The lobby was quiet other than a few business guests, hurrying through to get to their morning meetings. Most of the shops were still closed.

"*Assalaam-u-alaikum.*"

"*Waalaikum-assalaam,*" a polite concierge replied. "Good morning sir, how may I help you?"

"Did Vincent Portelli, Room 3018 leave something with you?"

"Let me see, sir," he replied, cautiously eyeing the two uniformed officers behind him as he sifted through the cabinet under his desk. "Ah, there is an envelope. Hmm, this is strange," he muttered to himself as he pulled out an 8x11 manila envelope, "it is addressed to . . . whoever comes and asks for it? I guess that will be . . . you?"

Kamran hurriedly extended his hand and took the envelope and turned around to leave but stopped to face the concierge again.

"Thank you very much," he said politely, and then he walked away briskly with the two officers, hurrying behind him, barely keeping pace.

The concierge, a young man in his mid-twenties and still wondering about the envelope, shook his head in disbelief as he watched them walk out the main door; then he went back to work.

CHAPTER 72

CONGRESSIONAL COUNTRY CLUB BETHESDA, MD

Tuesday 4:08 p.m.

Vice President Dominick Spader stood on the seventh tee box at the tips at the Congressional Country Club watching his opponent tee off. The VP was a big time golf fan and often invited his political opponents for a round if they asked for a meeting. It was rumored that although he was never known for wagering money, he did prefer to settle congressional voting deadlocks with something as basic as 'closest to the pin' on the par threes. He was a scratch golfer, and his best came out when stakes were the highest. He was proud of the fact that he had single handedly eliminated more pork projects with his six iron than all the democratic lobbyists combined.

His opponent today was Senator Bob Dempsey (R) from Pennsylvania who wanted thirty-two million dollars to develop an extension to Allegheny State Park that will bear his name and there they were, standing at the legendry 174yard par three.

Senator Dempsey went through his pre-shot routine, wiggled his five iron a few times over his Nike black ball, and then pushed his tee shot into the front right bunker.

Spader smiled broadly as he pulled out his six iron. It was the perfect distance and suited well to his high fade, taking the deep bunkers out of play. He was ready for the set up when he saw Patrick O'Neal walking up to the secret service agent standing behind the tee.

"Pat, what's up? Weren't we meeting tomorrow . . . for lunch?"

"Yes Mr. Vice President, but something came up."

"Everything okay?"

"Yes sir . . . just needed to brief you on some international events."

Dominick Spader did not like the way it sounded.

Patrick wouldn't have come himself if it wasn't urgent, something that could not be said on the cell phone and could not wait until after the round.

With all those thoughts running through his mind, he walked back to the tee and hit a towering shot that did not fade, ending up in the deep left rough, well short of the back right pin on the second tier.

"Damn it," he threw the club down, gouging a huge divot off the edge of the tee box.

"I can almost see that sign with my name on it," Senator Dempsey chuckled.

"We'll see," the VP waved his hand. "You still have ten and thirteen to deal with," he motioned to one of his assistants to continue on his behalf while he talked.

"So, what is it?" he asked Patrick as soon as they were at a safe distance from the group.

"We got exposed in Pakistan."

"How much do they know?"

"They have information to implicate Butch, but I don't think they suspect any of us."

"Are you sure?"

"I am positive. None of those on the ground had any idea about us except the geologist, and we took care of him."

"Hmm, just the way we planned it," Dominick Spader chewed on his words for a moment. "With Butch out of the way, the Republicans will be without their ace. None of the others stand a chance against me."

"Believe me, Mr. Vice President; the Republicans are hurting already . . . they will not rebound from this. Besides, we are monitoring a security situation closely in the Middle East. If our timing is right, we will be able to use it to our advantage. We'll spin it to show the people your true leadership mettle."

"Good, let me know as soon as you have more details."

"I will Mr. Vice president."

"What about the assassin?"

"He was contacted through our people in Donaldson's team; the trail ends there."

". . . and the geological data, did Butch get it yet?"

"AmeriGulf received it yesterday. We have cleaned it up a bit, nothing too exciting there for them. Zeigler's laptop has a crashed hard drive. You know those nasty viruses. What a shame, they crash them all the time," Patrick gave him a slight wink.

Spader smiled, "I guess you have it all under control."

"Yes, Mr. Vice President, we have it under control."

"Do you think that the President will try to look into it?"

"No chance. He has no idea. There is nothing that points in our direction. Besides, he is too busy polishing his own legacy. We'll let him worry about his library; it's your time now. "

"Good. He is a good man. I wouldn't want him involved in any of this anyway. You, on the other hand, can start picking a carpet for DCI's office. I never liked that ghastly décor they have over there right now.

"I am honored that you feel that way, sir." O'Neal tried his best to keep his level of excitement down. "Our friends in Pakistan will not disappoint you."

Dominick Spader smiled and wrapped his arm around Patrick O'Neal's shoulder, "Having friends ruling over Pakistan gives me some room to maneuver. We cannot trust those nukes, or all that oil in the hands of unpredictable politicians. I don't want another Iran scenario giving me nightmares when I am president," he started to walk back to the cart and then stopped, "and also, when the dust settles down over there, set up a meeting with General Baig. I want you to keep an eye on him. You can never fully trust those ISI generals, can you?"

"No sir, you can't. Enjoy your round," Patrick looked up towards the clear skies as he started to walk away. "It's a beautiful day."

CHAPTER 73

BLACK GOLD RANCH, TEXAS

Wednesday 11:30 a.m.

Butch Donaldson was sitting on the dining room table looking at the newspaper. Nothing jumped out of the paper to excite him. There was a small report about his recent campaign rally. Some polls showed him comfortably atop the Republican field. There was a small blurb about a new lead in the assassination of the opposition leader in Pakistan, but no details were available yet. He folded the newspaper, ate the remaining piece of his brunch sausage, and took another sip from his coffee as he stood up to leave.

His cell phone vibrated and started to slide across the mahogany table. He caught it just before it dropped off the edge.

"Hello, hey what's going on?" he opened with a big smile after hearing a familiar voice.

Response from the other side sucked the smile out of his face in a hurry. He slowly lowered his massive body onto his high back chair and leaned backwards; eyes closed and then listened, quietly.

"When?" was all he could say after listening for what seemed like an eternity to him.

" . . . Right now! Okay," the phone slipped out of his hand and fell hard on the marble floor making a loud metallic thud.

He felt like a thunderbolt had hit him. His heart sank to the pit of his stomach, as his faced turned white as a ghost. Sweat started to pour from his forehead; he got up, and then half stumbled across the room. His legs felt like they were going to buckle under him any moment. He barely managed to get to a lounge chair, and fell back on it.

An hour passed, but he just sat there, staring at a blank spot on the wall. Finally, he got up and walked slowly towards the study. The large study had a cathedral ceiling and was lined with bookshelves set in a semicircle around a massive desk. He walked around his desk, rearranged some papers, fixed a crooked picture frame, and then sat down on his plush maroon leather chair. Afternoon sun shone through the tall bay windows behind him bathing him in a flood of golden orange glow. He turned his chair around and looked outside at the rose garden he had worked extremely hard on, feeling the warm rays of the sun on his face, and then closed his eyes.

Two black Chevy Suburbans rolled into the driveway and parked in front of the massive oak doorway. Two agents dressed in black suites emerged, adjusted their earpieces, and then whispered something into their microphones. Their instructions came immediately. They moved their heads in an imperceptible nod and then walked up to the door. They were still contemplating whether to use the doorbell or the large antique knocker when they heard the gunshot.

Butch Donaldson's Presidential campaign and his legendary life story had come to an abrupt and terrible end.

CHAPTER 74

One month later

Malik Nisar was surrounded by members of his party, celebrating a victory in the elections that had all but ensured a parliamentary majority. Malik Nisar had run the perfect campaign. Riding a wave of emotions, downplaying his differences with his late cousin Malik Jahangir, he had rallied his party and the country behind him in the name of revenge and justice, and now he stood tall, in the middle of it all, waiting for his coronation as the next Prime Minister of Pakistan.

The last thirty days had been a whirlwind of political rallies, tall tales of self-pronounced patriotism, followed by capricious promises and secret meetings between the who's who of the political world making back door alliances to ensure their share in power. Naveed Khan took a sabbatical for a few days to do some soul searching before rebounding big. While being behind the wrong side of the law was painful, it was also a humbling experience. The fickle nature of life, especially in public service and politics, had dawned upon him, giving him an insight that was above and beyond his years. Voters had dealt with this rise, fall and rise of a political victim by giving him their passionate support. His party's fifty-five seats, mostly as a result of an enlightened urban movement, were not enough to gather a majority coalition, but had placed him in the driving seat to be the leader of the opposition, a position he coveted more than a high profile cabinet position offered by Malik Nisar in return for his support. Becoming a cabinet member though inviting, would have meant agreeing with the majority party's decisions and hence compromising most of his principle stands, and he was not willing to do that.

General Hamid Ali had announced that he had no intention to pursue an extension of his military service, and would retire at the end of his term in one year. Public response to his selfless commitment to democracy had been overwhelming. Regarded as a hero, he was hailed as a the Savior of Pakistan with his picture plastered or painted on murals around major cities as well as on the backs of trucks and buses throughout the country. He was also honored for his actions that had restored the honor of the Pakistani Military and had restored people's faith in it, and this honor was the one that he cherished the most. He had agreed to be a member of the Security Council for an additional two years on the insistence of its various members in order to help his brainchild grow into a sustainable institution.

All in all, the face of the National Assembly had remained mostly unchanged in the rural scene. Same old characters had won from political strongholds, constituencies passed down from one feudal generation to the next, while the constituents remained powerless in facilitating a change. Despite the military overseeing the process, claims of massive rigging by traditional rivals were made; protestors, marching on the street, destroyed property, but then retreated as quickly as they had emerged when confronted by tear gas and baton charge by the police.

Leaders from all over the world sent congratulatory messages to Malik Nisar, promising cooperation and aid in return for his continual dedication to democracy. There were some of the usual cautionary comments, bordering on a threatening tone regarding Pakistan's nuclear program, as well as its commitment to war on terror and religious extremism.

And, finally, an assembly of probable allies was gathered for an extravagant reception at Rawal Lake, hosted by the US Embassy. After a sumptuous dinner and traditional entertainment, the US Ambassador and British High Commissioner met with the leaders in private for an hour, away from eager microphones and keen eyes of ravenous journalists. As expected, after this vote of confidence, it was only a matter of time before the final press conference by Malik Nisar outlined the composition of his coalition government and as expected, it took place the very next day.

CHAPTER 74

DAMAN-E KOH, ISLAMABAD

Early afternoon

Raja Safdar Hussein admired the breathtaking view from his table next to the large glass window overlooking Islamabad. Even after years of living in this city, he still loved to come here and enjoy the view from this scenic tourist spot built high above Islamabad in the middle of Margalla Hills, and appropriately called *Daman-e-Koh* or literally, Lap of the Mountain. It was just afternoon on a weekday and the place was quiet. Skies were clear and a brighter shade of blue after a rainstorm earlier. Occasional fluffy clouds were scattered around, drifting smoothly in the brisk and chilly November wind. A thick layer of dust from multiple construction projects that had been suspended in the air and then settled on the trees and shrubs had been washed away, giving back the panoramic view of Islamabad, its inherent lush character. He looked at his watch and then sat back, rolling his fingers over the generous moustache in order to bring it into a sharp upturned point.

The manager of the restaurant, well aware of his preferences, had set a private table for him, away from the main dining area. Raja Safdar took another eyeful of the view outside the window and sipped on a steaming cup of cappuccino that the waiter had just brought with a plate of finger chips sprinkled with spices, according to his taste.

"Raja *Sahib*, sorry I am late. These bureaucratic meetings seem to go on and on. No wonder nothing ever gets done in this country," Major General Sajjad Baig dressed in casual civilian clothes, sunglasses and a peaked cap covering his crew cut, walked up to him.

"*Salamalaikum, Gernaile Sahib,* seems like you are beginning to understand the system very well. Take a seat," he offered him the chair across from him.

Sajjad gave him a wry smile, as he pulled the chair back and sat down.

"*Chai,* or coffee?" Raja Safdar offered.

"*Chai* will be fine."

"One *chai*", Safdar hollered across the hall to a waiter, and then he leaned across the table towards Sajjad, "are you pleased with the results, my dear general?"

"I think that we are on the right track. I can't say that I am fully satisfied, but I am hopeful."

"See, this is the problem with you army people, you worry too much, and then overanalyze it. The system works. Once you make the right moves, everything else takes care of itself."

"I know, I know," Sajjad nodded, but the stakes are very high Raja *Sahib*, and time is short. We cannot let this government derail us."

"*Gernaile Sahib* . . . you worry about your end. I've been doing this for a long . . . long time. The coalition is ready, and it has received a vote of confidence from the *Amriki* government. Believe me, I was there. Small differences were no match for the ambassador's statesmanship. Malik Nisar will be hosting a press conference at his house at three, and everything will be final."

"Does he suspect anything?"

"I am sure he does, but I am not worried about that."

"Why?"

"Malik Nisar is a career politician, *Gernaile Sahib*. He understands the meaning of power, and the compromises that he needs to make along the way. Besides, he was not happy with Malik Jahangir's new vision but could not say anything. In a way, it worked out very well for him."

"And, what about you, Raja *Sahib?* What works for you?"

"Oh, the usual stuff, decision making behind the scene, pulling the strings, and watching the hapless politicians dance to my tunes, and, of course, a few big contracts. I don't ask for too much," Safdar replied nonchalantly, "and, also, you have to thank me for convincing General Hamid to stay on the Security Council. I wish he had stayed and delayed the elections, but the more I get to know him, I think that we are better off without him. He's a little too much of an idealist for me. It'll be much easier manipulating the elected politicians."

"I am with you on that," Sajjad replied.

"But, there is one thing that he *will* do without any manipulation."

"And that is?"

"Promote you as the next Director of ISI."

"What about the new Army Chief . . . after General Hamid, how do we convince him?"

"We don't need to; the Pentagon likes General Zaidi, and General Hamid agrees."

"I like General Zaidi, a true professional."

"The Pentagon likes *you*, too."

"I know. I've worked hard to earn that confidence," Sajjad smiled openly for the first time during their conversation. "Who do we have in FATA to replace Jalaluddin?"

"Feroze Khan Salarzai from Bajour Agency has already been contacted."

"I know him well. We have used him in the past."

"Junaid has already visited him, and he is up to the task. He has a vast network that extends deep into Afghanistan. He has been supplying both sides for over a decade, and he has access to both Russian and American weapons."

"Good," Sajjad said, deep in thought, "we just need to watch him closely so he doesn't make any rash moves. Jalaluddin was a big loss for us; but in the end, we all know that it was his big ego that finally caught up to him."

Sajjad Baig slid down a bit in his chair, a relaxed smile appearing on his face; then he lit up a cigarette, "We need to keep our people caught up in this uncertainty. Our military needs the funds, and we don't want to eliminate all the threats. We don't want politicians making friends with the Indians. They have the same issues as us," he suddenly sat up straight and took his sunglasses off, staring directly in Raja Safdar's eyes. "It's *our* funding, and *your* power that needs these issues in FATA and in Kashmir to stay alive. It doesn't matter who they are . . . Al-Qaeda, Taliban or whatever mujahedeen they call themselves, *we* need them . . . as long as they are using ammo."

Safdar burst into a guttural laugh, "You don't have to preach to the choir, General. No one has made more money selling weapons than I. These intellectuals who oppose war have no clue that everything material that surrounds them owes its existence to these conflicts," he paused. "What about the *Amrikis*? How long do you think they'll be interested in us?"

"As long as we keep buying their stuff and as long as the image of Iran can be kept up as a villain. Besides, there is still a lot of oil in this region. I don't think that they are going *anywhere* . . . anytime soon."

"What about you, General, are you happy that they are here?"

General Sajjad Baig thought about it for a few moments as he got up to leave, "We are helping each other with our goals, and so we'll continue our cooperation . . . ," he winked at Safdar as he walked away, " . . . at least for now."

Pakistan Monument

Zero Point, Sunset

Kamran was exhausted. He had not been sleeping well. Every time he tried to close his eyes, the events of the past month raced through his mind like a runaway train. He was trying to make sense of it all but couldn't. He was an optimist, but the outcome of it all had left him more confused than ever. He was pleased to see the youth movement spearheaded by Naveed Khan taking charge in the urban constituencies, but he understood that he would have to struggle against massive odds if he wanted his vision to transform the way things were done in Islamabad.

There were so many questions that remained unanswered. Over the last month, he had tried to piece things together but could not make sense of it all. He was glad that the people responsible for the events were apprehended, but there were names in Vincent's papers that did not fit, names that were not even pursued, as if the authorities were just not interested. He believed that Saleem Qazi was misguided in his patriotism, but he had nothing to do with terrorism directly. The timing of Faizabad and Tolinton Market bombings were timed to distract people. Vincent felt he was in some way responsible for them, but who was behind them? A car bomb killing Sardar Jalaluddin, who was known for his militant ties and was an early suspect in the assassination, and then the mysterious overdose death of an AmeriGulf analyst left too many missing links in the story, but the more he tried to untie the knots the more entangled they became.

He had a pounding headache now. He sat down on a concrete bench on the scenic overlook perched high over Zero Point. A place he had visited more and more in the recent weeks.

He heard footsteps but could not muster up the energy to turn around.

He felt a soft hand on the side of his face and then fingers gently running through his hair. It felt good. He closed his eyes and savored the tender touch, while feeling the refreshing breeze on his face.

"How is Pervaiz?" Sana asked as she sat down beside him, her voice barely a notch above a whisper as she leaned towards him, her lips only inches from his ear.

"*Alhamd-u-lillah*, he's doing very well; I saw him today, he's still weak, but he expects to be back to his usual neurotic self in another two weeks."

"That's great."

They were silent for a minute or so, looking at the view, lost in the deep thoughts going through their heads.

"And how are you?"

"I'm okay. Even better now that you are here," he turned towards her and looked fondly into her eyes.

She blushed and instinctively lowered her eyes. A spontaneous smile appearing on her flushed face.

"What does this all mean?" he said, staring at the distant images of Islamabad's expansive but subdued skyline, washed in the orange glow of the sun, setting behind Margalla Hills. "Nothing changed; the same people are in charge again. Same slogans, same agendas that have plagued us for more than sixty years, and it seems, will continue for many more. When is it going to end? When are *we* as a nation going to realize that our destiny does not follow these time-tested failures? We need new leadership, new blood. Maybe *someday* . . . but I still wonder. Was it all worth it?"

Sana got up and walked around the bench to stand behind him, and gently massaged his shoulders. She was staring down at the heavy traffic passing through the newly renovated Zero Point interchange, the gateway to Islamabad. It was a symbol of change, ushering the nation into the twenty-first century.

"Do you see that Kamran?'

"What?"

"That" She pointed at Zero Point.

"What about it?"

"This is where we are, as a nation . . . at Zero Point. A lot of good things have happened in the last few weeks, and I feel that the worst is over. A new and invigorating movement has taken over the urban centers. We had more voter turnout between the ages of twenty and thirty than ever before. It is only a matter of time before this movement swells into the rest of the country. People want to be educated, they want more schools and very soon *Insha Allah,* we will have them. We *will* be enlightened, but only if we can increase our literacy rate in the rural and tribal areas, and focus on development, and improved quality of life. We can eliminate the relentless exploitation of our simple and hardworking citizens by power hungry politicians and their greedy lobbyists. For the first time in my lifetime, I have faith in our ability to rise against the odds. I can feel the tide changing. If it can happen in Tunisia and Egypt, it can certainly happen here. In the vision of Naveed Khan, and under the guidance of General Hamid, we have finally been able to actually pull it off. We have come back . . . to the beginning. Ready to start at zero point, a fresh start . . . a golden opportunity to redeem ourselves, and we *will* succeed," she affirmed in a strong and confident voice, ". . . so, to answer your question . . . ," her tone softened, ". . . if it was worth it? Yes it was."

He turned around slowly, and stared into her beautiful hazel eyes. His expression brightened and his stiffened lips curled into a gentle smile, as he reached up and tenderly squeezed her soft hand.

"Yes it was."

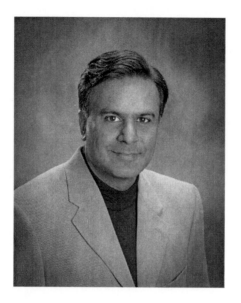

Wasique Mirza has been writing as a hobby all his life. Recently, he has been contributing as a Guest Columnist in the daily *Times-Tribune* of Scranton, PA. He is a physician by profession and lives with his family in Northeast Pennsylvania. Zero Point is his first novel.

CPSIA information can be obtained at www.ICGtesting.com
Printed in the USA
267107BV00001B/4/P